Pemberley RANCH

JACK CALDWELL

sourcebooks
landmark

Published by Sourcebooks Landmark, an imprint of Sourcebooks, Inc.
P.O. Box 4410, Naperville, Illinois 60567-4410
(630) 961-3900
FAX: (630) 961-2168
www.sourcebooks.com

Library of Congress Cataloging-in-Publication Data

Caldwell, Jack.
  Pemberley Ranch / Jack Caldwell.
      p. cm.
  1. Austen, Jane, 1775-1817. Pride and prejudice--Parodies, imitations, etc. 2. Darcy,
Fitzwilliam (Fictitious character)--Fiction. 3. Bennet, Elizabeth (Fictitious character)-
-Fiction. 4. Ranchers--Texas--Fiction. 5. Texas--History--19th century--Fiction. I.
Title.
  PS3603.A4355P46 2010
  813'.6--dc22
                              2010027078

          Printed and bound in the United States of America.
              VP 10 9 8 7 6 5 4 3 2 1

To Barbara,
my life, my love, my muse.

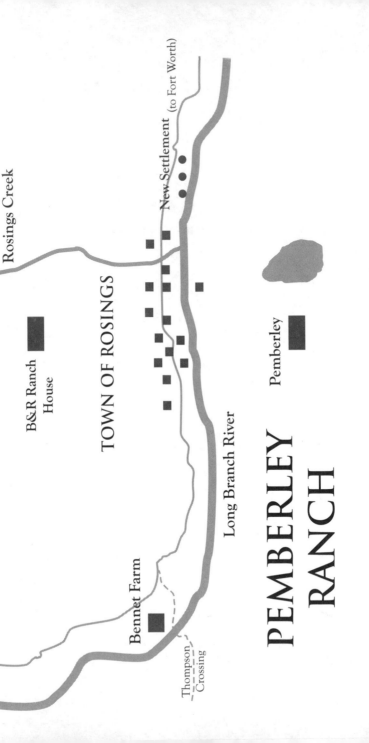

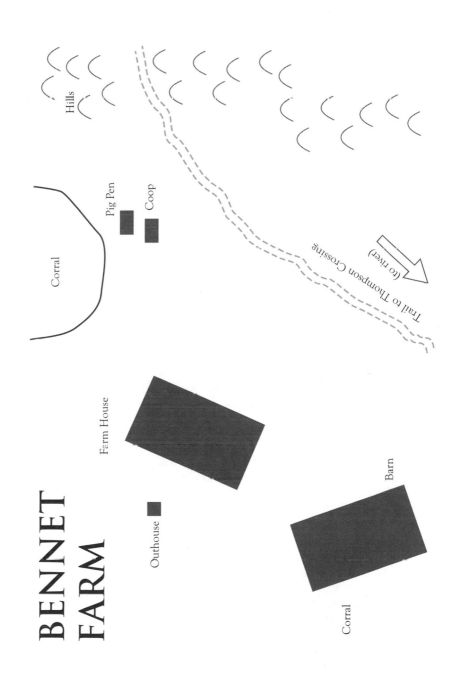

Dramatis Personae

Natives and/or longtime residents of Rosings, Texas:

Catherine "Cate" Burroughs—Owner of the B&R Ranch and
    Rosings Bank; widow of Lewis Burroughs and cousin by
    marriage to Matthew Darcy, William Darcy's father
Anne Burroughs—Only daughter of Catherine Burroughs
William Darcy, Captain, Texas Legion, Confederate States
    Army (CSA)—Owner of Pemberley Ranch and Darcy Bank
Gabrielle "Gaby" Darcy—Only sister to Darcy
José Estrada—Assistant trail boss of Pemberley Ranch
Hill—Farmhand at the Bennet Farm
Deputy Jones
Father Joseph—Rector of the Santa Maria Catholic Mission
    chapel near Rosings
Sheriff Lucas—Longtime sheriff of Rosings; widowed
Charlotte Lucas—Only child of Sheriff Lucas
Judge Alton Phillips

Margaret Reynolds—Cook and housekeeper at Pemberley; former slave.

Deputy Smith

Reverend Henry Tilney—Minister of the Rosings Baptist Church

Sally Younge—Owner and madam of Younge's Saloon, inherited from her late husband

Carl Zimmerman—Owner of Zimmerman's General Store and titular mayor of Rosings

New to Rosings:

Thomas Bennet—Native of Ohio; now owner of former Thompson farm west of Rosings

Fanny Bennet—Wife of Thomas Bennet

Jane Bennet—Eldest Bennet daughter

Elizabeth "Beth" Bennet

Mary Bennet

Kathleen "Kathy" Bennet

Lily Bennet

Dr. Charles Bingley, Medical Corps, CSA—Native of Georgia, now practicing doctor in Rosings

Billy Collins—Native of Georgia, manager of Rosings Bank

Joshua "Kid" Denny, Quantrill's Raiders, CSA—Native of Missouri, gunfighter and foreman of the B&R Ranch

Richard "Fitz" Fitzwilliam, Major, Virginia Cavalry, CSA— Native of Texas, now foreman and trail boss of Pemberley Ranch

Pyke, Corporal, XIII Corps, United States Army, (USA)— Native of Illinois

Thorpe—One of Denny's gang

Washington family—Newly freed slave family from Louisiana, owners of new homestead farm east of Rosings

George Whitehead, Major, XIII Corps, USA—Native of Illinois, now Recorder of Deeds of Long Branch County, appointed by the governor

Others:

Caroline Bingley—Native of Georgia and sister to Bingley, now resident of New Orleans

Capt. John Buford—Member of the U.S. Army Cavalry stationed at Ft. Richardson, Texas

William Tecumseh Sherman, Major General of Volunteers, XV Corps, USA [*]

Ulysses S. Grant, Major General, Army of the Tennessee, USA [*]

Oh, I wish I was in the land of cotton
Old times there are not forgotten
Look away! Look away! Look away! Dixie Land.

In Dixie Land where I was born in
Early on one frosty mornin'
Look away! Look away! Look away! Dixie Land.

Oh, I wish I was in Dixie!
Hooray! Hooray!
In Dixie Land I'll take my stand
To live and die in Dixie
Away, away, away down south in Dixie!

"Dixie" by Daniel Decatur Emmett, 1859

Vicksburg, Mississippi—May 22, 1863

THE DAY WAS SEVERAL hot, stifling hours old when the young, gray-clad captain of infantry once again peeked carefully over the ramparts of his position into the morning sun, telescope in hand. He saw nothing, but he was not deceived. Since the initial assault upon their location three days ago, the enemy had tirelessly moved men and materiel into position for another attack. The sounds of horses and cannon wheels had been constant since before daybreak. The heavily wooded hilly terrain was not only perfect for defense but also for hiding the maneuvers of their attacker.

"Them Yankee boys are gettin' ready to come a'visitin' again, Cap'n?" a voice whispered into his ear.

William Darcy, captain in the Texas Legion, Confederate States Army, turned his bright blue eyes to his sergeant beside him and wiped a dirty hand across his beard-covered chin before answering. "My compliments to the colonel, and report that the enemy is moving forward."

No sooner had the man offered the barest of salutes and moved away from the front lines than the woods opposite exploded with noise. Darcy's screams of warning were unnecessary as men ducked from the incoming cannon fire. Darcy lay at the bottom of the trench like the others, keeping his head as low as possible. On an impulse, the twenty-year-old officer pulled out the pocket watch his father had given him for his birthday two years before.

Ten o'clock exactly.

The cannonballs began to fall behind the lines towards Vicksburg itself. Darcy knew what that was about even before the cries of the enemy reached his ears. He pulled out his sword and stood in a low crouch.

"To the line, boys, to the line! The enemy is upon us! Give 'em hell!"

The bedraggled Texans, in various uniforms of Confederate gray, rushed to the ramparts, muskets in hand, screaming the Rebel Yell that had terrified more than one Union solider since Bull Run. Just in time, too, as the first of the men in blue were mere yards away. Darcy's view of the attackers disappeared behind a cloud of smoke as the muskets fired in a volley. The smoke cleared to show a score of figures in dirty blue scattered on the bare ground before the earthworks, but there were a hundred more advancing. The first line of defenders fell back to reload as the second line took their places.

"Fire at will!" Darcy yelled as he drew his Colt revolver. "Fire at will!"

Time lost all meaning as Darcy fired into the advancing horde again and again. The Texans knew that their position, straddling a rail line, was a key point in the defense of Vicksburg, and they fought desperately against the Union soldiers, who were just as desperate to take it. The din was deafening as gunfire, explosions, and screams blended into an unearthly sound.

Darcy had ducked down to reload his pistol for the third time when he noted that the noise had abated a bit. Creeping up, he saw through the smoke and haze that the Yankees were pulling back in good order. He ordered his men to cease firing and conserve their precious ammunition as he glanced at his watch again.

Ten fifteen.

Darcy and his company had been relieved about midday as fresh troops took up their position in the lunette[1]. They were resting

---

1 A fortification that has two projecting faces and two parallel flanks.

as well as they could, with the occasional cannonball falling throughout the afternoon, when they were approached by a group of officers on horseback. The commander of the legion, Colonel Waul, spoke to them.

"Men, we've got some Yankees that have broken through at the redoubt. They're a stubborn bunch, an' I need some volunteers to help clear the vermin out. Are you with me?"

Darcy looked at his men. "Sir, how many do you need?"

"A score will do, Captain. We muster down the lane here." With that, the party rode off. Darcy rose to his feet and looked around. A good two dozen men volunteered, and soon the detail moved off to the rendezvous point. They joined up with others and the plan was formed. By late afternoon, the force moved into position near the railroad redoubt.

Darcy could see men in blue hiding in the trenches or behind shelter. He knew this assault would be costly.

A shout went up, and the Texans charged. Darcy ran before his men, the Colt in his right hand and a sword in his left. The men to either side fired their muskets on the run and continued the charge, bayonets gleaming in the afternoon light. The enemy returned fire from their positions, but even as men fell around him, Darcy knew it was too little, too late. They were almost upon them. The Union soldiers began to fall back in some disorder. Darcy bared his teeth as he smelled the impending victory…

There was a mighty explosion, and Darcy experienced a feeling of flying before the world crashed into his face.

Will Darcy knew nothing, except that he hurt. Hurt all over. Hurt *bad*.

After a while, he was able to discern something besides the ever-present pain: a low murmuring in the background of his darkness. It took a moment before he realized that it was the sound of men groaning and crying. Darcy opened his eyes to behold a dark, uneven ceiling, lit by the light of lanterns.

He suddenly realized that he could only see out of one eye. In a panic, he raised a hand to his face and tried to sit up. A wave of agony crashed into him, and he could not prevent crying out as he fell back.

Darcy heard voices close by. "Doc—Doc—this one's wakin' up." A moment later a face came into his limited field of vision.

"Captain, how are you feeling?"

Like I'm about to die! his mind screamed. He peered closely at the man. About Darcy's own age, the young man had a broad, flushed face and light-colored hair. It was a face that usually would be happy, he considered. That it wasn't was a cause for concern.

"H… hurt," was all Darcy could manage.

"I should think you do," the unknown man said in a soft Georgia accent with a hint of a smile. The break in the man's serious mien was comforting.

Darcy waved a hand before his face. "E… eye?"

"Rest easy," the man said. "Your eyes are undamaged. You have a serious injury to your forehead, and the bandage must cover one eye. You're in a hospital, Captain, in a cave to protect y'all from the incoming artillery… Don't sit up!" he cried as Darcy moved. "Do you want to lose that leg?"

His patient lay still in fear.

The man grew grim. "Good thing you were insensible when your men brought you in. I had to do a bit of digging to get all the shrapnel out. You've lost quite a bit of blood, Captain. We must keep your leg still and clean, or the gangrene may set in. Do you understand?"

Darcy managed a nod, which only hurt like blazes. He determined he was speaking to a surgeon, as he could now make out the dried blood all over the man's apron.

"Good," the doctor grinned in return. "I must see to my other patients, but I shall stop by later. Rest, sir, and you'll be up and walking again."

As the doctor began to turn, Darcy fought to speak. "Th… thanks. D… Darcy."

The doctor turned in surprise. "I beg your pardon?"

Darcy gestured again. "D… Darcy."

"Ah," the man breathed in realization. "Captain Darcy, is it?"

Darcy nodded.

He smiled. "Charles Bingley, at your service."

Meryton, Ohio—June 20

"Beth! Beth, come back!"

The thirteen-year-old girl disregarded her mother's voice as she ran out the back door. Almost blinded by her tears, she managed to reach the large chestnut tree next to the barn without running into anything. The girl threw herself against the trunk, her body shuddering in sobs.

It was there her older sister found her, kneeling by the tree. Wordlessly, the blond girl gathered her sister into her arms, their hair blowing in the breeze.

"Beth—oh, Beth!" she tried to console the child.

"H… he can't be dead!" Beth Bennet sobbed. "Samuel can't be dead! He can't be, Jane!"

"Beth…" Jane began.

"He promised to come back. You… you heard him. He promised!"

Jane bit her lip as she continued to stroke Beth's curly brown hair, her own tears quietly streaming down her face. She could hear her mother and other sisters wailing in the house, an uproar that began a half-hour before as her father read the words of that hated telegram:

"We regret to inform you that…"

"Beth—oh, Beth!" was all Jane could manage. Her own distress was great. Samuel Bennet, the eldest of the Bennet children and the only son, proud corporal in the Ohio infantry, gone to save the Union as part of the mighty Army of the Potomac, had died of influenza in Maryland. Samuel was beloved by all of his family, but Beth was particularly fond of him. Jane might be Beth's confidante, but Samuel was her hero and could do no wrong. Jane could only hold her sister, allowing her to cry herself out.

Finally, as Beth's sobs subsided, Jane said, "Beth, we must return to the house and see to our parents and sisters. We cannot add to their distress. We must be strong, Beth."

"S… Samuel was always strong, Jane."

"Yes, he was. Now, it is our turn. Our family needs us." She took the girl's face in her hands. "It is what *he* would want."

Beth nodded. Their mother loved her only son almost as fiercely as Beth, and their father doted on him. *They* would be shattered, leaving the three younger sisters little comfort.

Jane got to her feet and helped Beth up. Hand in hand, they

turned to return to the house. As they walked, Jane heard Beth mumble something and asked her about it.

"I said it is *their* fault, Jane," she spat.

"Whose fault?"

"Those damned Rebels!"

"Beth, please!" Jane cried. "Please don't talk like that in front of Mother or Mary! You know how they feel about coarse language."

"Very well, but I'll never forgive those evil slave-owning Rebels—never! It's their fault Samuel went away. Those evil, evil people! I hope God smites them. I hate them! I will hate them for the rest of my life!"

Vicksburg—July 4

Will Darcy sat up in his cot, listening to the cannons going off. He turned to the doctor sitting beside him. "I suppose it's noon, Charles."

Dr. Bingley checked his pocket watch. "Yes, it is. Precise, aren't they, these Yankees?"

Darcy sighed, flexing his body. His recovery from the wounds he suffered in May had been hampered by a persistent fever. He had only grown strong enough in the last week to go to the chamber pot unaided. He desperately wanted to return to his command, but now it was too late. Confederate Lt. General John C. Pemberton had surrendered Vicksburg to Union Major General Ulysses S. Grant after a forty-two-day siege, which brought suffering and starvation to troops and civilians alike inside the ramparts. Pemberton had no choice—he had tons of ammunition, but virtually no food. They could hold out no longer.

"We've already furled banners and stacked arms; we were to do that before the Yankees took possession of the city," Bingley observed. "I'm told we're to get parole." He patted the captain on the arm. "We get to go home, Will."

"Maybe." In the last month, Bingley spent all of his free time with Darcy, playing cards or telling stories, and they had developed a deep friendship.

Before Bingley could ask his morose companion his meaning, there was a noise at the entrance of the cave. "I'd best see to that," he excused himself. Darcy watched him walk off to the exit of the ward when the doctor was pushed back by three blue-clad soldiers.

"Here, what's this?" Bingley cried. "This is a hospital!"

"That's for us to see, Johnny Reb," drawled a private.

"We're to secure this place and take prisoner any stragglers," said another.

Bingley grew angry. "These are all wounded or ill men. Be quick about your business and leave."

The third man waved a pistol. "The only one leaving, mister, is you."

"I'm a doctor and these are my patients. I won't leave!" The soldiers ignored him and began searching the belongings of the patients. "What are you doing?"

"Searching for contraband," said what appeared to be the leader of the band as he fingered a pocketknife. He put the object into his pocket and picked up a book.

One of his fellows laughed. "'Contraband!' Oh, good one, Pyke!"

"Since when is a man's Bible contraband?" Bingley cried. He moved to confront the man Pyke. "Put that back!"

Suddenly, Pyke drew a knife. "Resistin' the surrender,

mister?" he growled dangerously. "You don't want ta be doin' that—no, sir."

During the whole time, Darcy had lain quietly, pretending to be asleep, all the while slowly reaching beneath his cot. As Pyke gestured at Bingley with his knife to the enjoyment of his fellows, Darcy whipped out his saber and threw himself at their tormenters. Sweeping backhanded, he struck one on the head with the pommel, stunning the man, before grasping Pyke with his left arm about his throat, threatening him with the sword and using him as a shield against the last soldier.

Darcy stared at the third man with a cold, deadly look. "You will *not* threaten the doctor while I live."

"Don't do anything!" cried Pyke. "He'll kill me!"

"No, he won't," came a voice from the entrance to the ward. "Drop that sword, Johnny Reb." Darcy turned, forcing Pyke between him and the new threat. He saw a dark-haired man in a blue captain's uniform holding a pistol on him from his left hand.

"I am Captain Darcy," Darcy said in his best command voice. "Are you in charge of this rabble?"

"I am, Captain. My name is Whitehead. Release that man, or I shall be forced to shoot you."

"Your men, Captain, were stealing from sick and wounded men and were about to attack a doctor. This is strictly against the rules of war. Tell *them* to stand down."

Captain Whitehead's mouth twisted into an amused grin under his pencil-thin moustache. "Were they? Very well." Whitehead barked out an order and the two Yankee soldiers backed away, holstering their pistols. "Good enough, Captain?"

Darcy hesitated a moment, then slowly withdrew his strong left arm from Pyke's throat. Pushing the frightened corporal away, Darcy reversed his sword and offered the pommel to Whitehead. "My sword, sir. I am yours to command."

Whitehead holstered his pistol and took the weapon. "A fine saber, Captain. Where on earth did you get it?"

"It's Spanish, sir—fine Toledo steel. It's been in my family for four generations."

"Hmm." Whitehead inspected the workmanship with ill-disguised envy. "You would hate to lose it, I am sure. Well, have no fears, Captain." Whitehead glanced at his men standing behind Darcy and nodded. Bingley saw the men move to his friend and cried a warning, but it was too late. A moment later, Darcy lay sprawled insensible on the cave floor. Bingley tried to help, but a soldier seized him, pinning his arms behind his back.

Whitehead walked over to the prone man and laughed. "Yes, Captain, I would not concern yourself over your sword. You'll have no need for it where you're going." He turned to his remaining men. "Take this man prisoner—hold!" As the two lifted Darcy from the ground, Whitehead rifled through the unconscious man's pockets.

"You bastard!" cried Bingley as he struggled in the soldier's grip. "You're no better than a common thief!"

"Now, now, Doctor," Whitehead remarked as he withdrew Darcy's pocket watch, "there's nothing *common* about me at all. Besides," he turned to Bingley, "you're a Rebel and a traitor. You're fortunate that I don't shoot you out of hand where you stand."

"You won't get away with this," Bingley vowed.

"Oh, I think I will. *You* are nothing. I'd keep quiet if you value your parole."

Bingley threw a rather strong curse at Whitehead, and the officer lost all good humor.

"Very well, Doctor. Take him away, boys."

July 5

Major General Ulysses S. Grant, commander of the victorious Army of the Tennessee, sighed as he enjoyed an after-supper cigar and whiskey in his tent with his friend and subordinate, William Tecumseh Sherman, Major General of Volunteers and commander of his XV Corps.

Sherman puffed his cigar. "I told you, Grant, that if you stayed in the army, some happy accident might restore you to favor and your true place. Well, when news of this victory reaches Washington, you'll be the toast of the nation."

"Perhaps, perhaps. You did give me good counsel, though."

"Hah!" Sherman gulped down a bit of his drink. "You stood by me when they all thought I was crazy before Shiloh, and I stood by you when they all said you were a drunkard!"

Grant eyed him. "I was not a drunkard."

Before Sherman could respond to that, an aide came in with a message for Grant. The weary-looking bearded man scanned the two-page dispatch while Sherman refilled his glass. He looked up as a curse escaped Grant's lips. "Trouble?"

The general tossed the notes upon his field desk. "Yes! Some fool is demanding that a Rebel doctor and one of his patients be arrested for insubordination, assault, and violation of the surrender."

"So?"

"Well, there is also an affidavit from the doctor stating that Union soldiers were stealing from the patients, and he demands I take action against them!"

Sherman sat back. "It happens, no matter how many orders we issue or men we arrest. If it gets too bad, we put a few in the stockade. Is there something else?"

"The officer involved is a George Whitehead, attached to XIII Corps. Made captain because his father is the postmaster back in Illinois and active in the Republican Party. I've had complaints before about this fellow, but McClemand always stood by him."

"You think Whitehead is guilty?"

"I've no reason to trust the man."

Sherman grunted. Both the Union and Confederate armies were filled with political officers—men who received their rank not because of military training or experience in battle but because of their civilian connections. They were usually incompetent troublemakers for their professional brethren, but they had friends in high places, and it was detrimental to one's career to oppose these men without being very careful. The former XIII Corps commander, Major General John A. McClemand, had been just such a man, and it had taken Grant months to orchestrate his removal.

Grant pinched the bridge of his nose with two fingers. "I finally got rid of McClemand, and now I must divest myself of *another* political officer. Damnation! I've a war to fight!"

"That was good work, shipping out that vainglorious fool," Sherman said as he took a sip of his whiskey. "Why not do the same with this bastard? Kill two birds with one stone."

"Eh? What's that?"

"Whitehead. Have him escort his precious prisoners to prison camp with a letter requesting transfer. Let him be someone else's problem. Meanwhile, you don't have to try both Whitehead and those Rebels."

Grant sat back. "Sherman, I knew there was a reason I let you drink my whiskey."

Jackson, Mississippi—1865

It was the end of the line, and Darcy and Bingley climbed off the train in the early evening with scores of other veterans of the late war. All about the Jackson station was damage and disarray, evidence of the five-year cataclysm from which the country was now trying to recover. The two needed a place for the night but were not surprised to learn from the station master that all the available rooms were taken. Once again, they had to face a night on the cold, hard earth, and they began their search for a spot, relatively safe from thieves, when they came upon a campfire.

"Hello!" Bingley cried to the lone figure next to the flame. "May we share your fire for a while?"

The man looked up from under the broad brim of his hat, which sported a silver hat band. He wore the uniform of a major of Rebel cavalry, a Sharpe carbine rifle close to his hand. The light from the fire was reflected in his dark eyes. "Come on in, Georgia, you and your companion, an' set a spell."

Bingley and Darcy sat on the opposite side of the fire, and the doctor continued to speak. "Thank you kindly, sir. But how did you know I'm from Georgia?"

The stranger chuckled. "I've an ear for accents. Am I right?"

Bingley confirmed he was, introduced himself and Darcy, and named a small town in Georgia as his hometown.

"My name's Fitzwilliam," said the major. "What brings you this far west, Dr. Bingley?"

Bingley stared at the flames. "There wasn't much left for me back at my family's plantation, Netherfield."

"I take it your place was visited by Sherman and his horde?" Bingley confirmed that his family home had fallen victim to Sherman's March to the Sea. "And you, Mr. Darcy, where do you hail from?"

"Rosings—a little town west of Fort Worth."

Fitzwilliam grinned. "Always a pleasure to meet a fellow Texican. I'm from Nacogdoches, myself."

Darcy narrowed his eyes. "Nacogdoches? You're wearing the uniform of the Virginia Cavalry, sir."

"You've a sharp eye, Mr. Darcy. No, I didn't steal these clothes, though I did help myself to this here carbine from a Yankee trooper who had no further use for it. Help yourself to some coffee, an' I'll tell you my tale."

The two helped themselves to the pot. The steaming black concoction had more acorns and leaves in it than coffee, but at least it was hot.

"I was orphaned at a young age an' was raised by relations on a cotton farm near Nacogdoches. My uncle had some connections in the army from the Mexican War, so I got a commission to attend the Virginia Military Institute. I was there when the war broke out an' followed Stonewall Jackson to take on the foe. Ridin' suited me better than walkin', so I hooked up with Jeb Stuart. Rode with him from Manassas to Gettysburg to Yellow

Tavern." He lifted his mug. "Here's to you, ole Jeb, may you rest in peace."

Darcy and Bingley had a bit of food and offered to share it with Fitzwilliam. As they ate, they told stories of their war experiences. Fitzwilliam did most of the talking, as Darcy and Bingley were particularly quiet about their time as prisoners of war.

Finally, Fitzwilliam asked, "So, what are your plans, Dr. Bingley?"

Bingley swallowed a spoonful of beans. "Call me Charles, Fitz. Goin' west with Will, here. He tells me there's need for a doctor in Rosings, so I'm goin' to give it a try. What about you? Headin' back to Nacogdoches?"

"Nah. Never did take to farming, to the grief of my uncle. I got an itch to ride the range, punchin' cattle an' such. I'm headin' west—goin' to sign on with a cattle ranch."

Darcy eyed him. "Ever rode cattle, Fitz?"

"Not yet," he grinned. "You offering me a job, Darcy?"

"That's up to my daddy, but you can come along."

"Thank you kindly, Mr. Darcy."

Darcy grinned for the first time. "Good that you know your place, Fitz. Pour me some more of that black stuff you're passing off as coffee."

"Hell with that," Fitz returned as he pulled a small bottle from a saddlebag and tossed it to Darcy. "Take a snort o' this."

"Holding out on us, Fitz?" asked Darcy as he took a swig. A moment later he coughed down the rotgut whiskey, to Fitz's and Bingley's laughter.

"Had to have a reason to celebrate. I've a feeling we're goin' to have interestin' times, Darcy."

Meryton—1868

After church on Sunday, Thomas Bennet looked on his family as they ate the midday dinner: Jane, at twenty, his surviving eldest and in the full bloom of her beauty; Elizabeth, his darling Beth, eighteen and as free-spirited as ever; Mary, almost seventeen and as serious as Beth was playful; Kathy, thirteen and on the cusp of womanhood; and Lily, the baby, a very pretty and precocious twelve and her mother's delight. For a moment the memory of his only son, Samuel—five years in a grave in Maryland—flashed before his mind. Samuel was a hole in his soul that would never heal.

His eyes fell upon his cohort for the past quarter-century, his wife, Fanny. He loved her dearly, but he was not blind to her shortcomings. Never an intelligent or introspective person, she had been a gay and kind companion during the majority of their life together, but Fanny had changed since the loss of Samuel. She was now prone to fits of anxiety and, therefore, less of a guiding light to the three youngest than she had been to Samuel, Jane, and Beth in their youth. The children had been given free rein to indulge in their more unfortunate tendencies: Mary was unsociable, Kathy was as emotional as her mother, and Lily was terribly spoiled. Bennet was loath to admit that he bore some responsibility for this sad state of affairs; he had found young children uninteresting and had given his attention only to his eldest.

Samuel, oh Samuel! he thought again. The loss of his heir would cost his family more than they knew.

Bennet cleared his throat. "My dears, I have an announcement to make." The Bennet women turned their attention to him. Bennet inwardly grimaced in anticipation of the uproar to come. "For quite a while we've lived in comfort. Working the land with my brothers has adequately provided for us for these many years."

"Adequately provided?" cried his wife. "It's all right for you to say so, Thomas, if you believe having five unmarried daughters with no dowry to speak of 'adequate,' or even enough money to have but one store-bought dress each, but I don't believe it is so!"

"Indeed, my dear. And now with the return of my nephews from the war and their growing families… Forgive me, Fanny."

Mrs. Bennet wiped the tear from her eye. "Please, Thomas, say no more about that, or I will think of our poor, lost Samuel again." She could say no more as she wept, and Kathy joined in. Jane and Beth consoled the others, Mary sighed in disapproval, and Lily looked bored.

Bennet held his tongue until his wife was tolerably composed. "My dear, now that our nephews are having families of their own, the Bennet Farm will not produce enough for all of us. Therefore, I have spoken to my brothers, and they have agreed to buy me out."

"Buy us out! But, Thomas, what shall we do?"

Jane spoke up. "Are you buying another farm, Father?"

"Yes, I am—a place of our very own."

"Will we have to leave home?" Kathy gasped.

"Yes, we will—"

Fanny cut him off. "Oh, who cares about this old house; we inherited it from Grandmother Bennet! A house of our own! How delightful! Is it near the river, dear? I hope it is near the river."

Bennet glanced down at his plate. "It *is* near a river, Fanny."

Beth frowned. "But, Father, how much did our uncles pay?

Land near the river is so very dear. They surely couldn't pay that much."

"They paid enough, Beth. We will have a new farm near a river, but it will not be here."

"Not here!" Mrs. Bennet looked at her daughters. "But where? Is it nearby?"

"No, dear."

That got Mary's attention. "We will have to change churches?"

"I am afraid so, child."

"I know!" Mrs. Bennet claimed. "You always knew I favored the next county. So lovely, and I have family there…"

"Pooh! I don't care for them!" cried Lily. "Last time we visited, the boys pulled my hair!"

"That was three years ago," said Jane gently. "Surely they will be kinder now."

Bennet raised his voice. "Please, enough of this! We are not moving to the next county." The women all stared at him. "I have found a wonderful place where we can grow vegetables and corn almost year-round and still have room for cattle."

"Year-round! Thomas, you tease me. One cannot grow vegetables in Ohio in winter!"

"One can in Rosings."

"Rosings! I never heard of such a place. Where in Ohio is this paradise?"

Bennet took a breath. "It is not in Ohio; it is in Texas."

Bennet was surprised. The room was quiet much longer than he anticipated. But the explosion that followed was all he expected.

"Texas!" Beth cried again for the countless time. "How can Father make us all go to Texas?"

Jane sighed as she brushed Beth's hair, their nightly routine before bed. "He's doing the best he can. The farm he described is large enough to take care of all our needs. We'll have farmhands to help. It sounds delightful."

Beth was not appeased. "If Samuel were here, he would talk Father out of this!"

"Beth, if Samuel were here, we might be buying out our uncles. But he is not. We must try to persevere. Father needs our support, not our censure."

Beth bit her lip as she recalled her mother's unkind exclamations at table. "You're right. Father is trying to care for us. But… oh, Jane! Texas! I can't believe it. I hate it!"

"It is very far away from here—that's true."

"It's not Texas that I'm talking about, but the Texans! I haven't forgotten that they turned their backs on the Union and most disgracefully took up arms against us, all to preserve their vile practice of slavery!"

"Beth, we are taught to forgive. Perhaps they have seen the wickedness of their ways and have repented."

"Perhaps," Beth said, but to herself, she thought, *You may forgive them, Jane, for you are good. But I will never forget that if not for them, Samuel would still be alive. I will never forgive them. Never.*

Chapter 1

Rosings, Texas—September, 1870

A LONE FIGURE SAT astride a tall, black Arabian under a single oak tree atop a ridge. It was a hot day, and in the early afternoon sun, the shade was welcomed by horse and rider alike, standing as still as a statue. He was a tall man in a white shirt with dark trousers and black boots, his unbuttoned vest flapping in the slight breeze, a tan, wide-brimmed, ten-gallon hat pulled low over his brow. Before him stretched a sea of prairie, dotted with hundreds of cattle, lowing and grazing. They were not alone; a handful of wranglers carefully moved their cowponies around the vast herd, keeping an eye out for trouble. The movement of the horses disturbed the man's mount, and he reached down to gently stroke its neck.

"Whoa there, Caesar, rest easy," William Darcy cooed. "We'll just stay here under the shade for now. Enjoy the cool." The stallion nodded his head in apparent agreement and bent to take a few nibbles of grass. The man's attention returned to the scene before him, his bright blue eyes taking in every detail.

A flash of moving white caught his attention. He turned away from his perusal of the herd and twisted in the saddle. There! Across the ridge of hills was a rider, moving fast. Darcy narrowed his eyes in concentration. The horse was a brown-and-white paint, and none of his riders had such a horse. A stranger—on his land! Caesar began to prance in place, feeling his master's tension through the reins.

The rider seemed to be alone, and while Darcy had left his gun belt and Colt revolver at the house, he did have a rifle holstered to his saddle. "What say we go check that out, boy?" The horse agreed, and they loped down the hill.

Darcy moved at an angle to the stranger, holding Caesar back until necessary. The intruder was at a full gallop, flying across the crest. Darcy lost sight of the paint as he reached the valley between the hills, and he allowed Caesar his head. The stallion dug in and moved quickly up the rise, and Darcy saw with confidence that he was in the proper position to cut off the paint. Caesar spotted his quarry and headed toward the other horse, waiting for direction from his master.

As they grew closer, Darcy could see that the rider and paint moved in perfect harmony. The horse was rather small, but so was the rider. A *boy?* Darcy thought, before noticing the wild, curly hair flying on either side of the rider's hat. As Darcy pulled to a halt, blocking the paint's progress, a shock of realization coursed through him. *That's no boy—that's a girl! A girl in men's clothing!*

He pulled his hand away from his rifle, and unarmed, raised his palm in an unmistakable sign. "Hold on, miss!"

The surprised girl came to a halt a few feet away, dust swirling in the breeze. She had on a red-and-white gingham shirt and dungarees, boots firmly in the stirrups. She wore a wide-brimmed floppy hat, shading her face, but even at that distance, he could see her blazing eyes.

"What do you want?"

Her voice was lower than Darcy expected from so short a person—she could not be more than five feet two inches—but it was not unpleasant to his ears, though it was Northern and unfriendly. Darcy was not used to answering demands from anyone in the last four years, and he wasn't going to change for some strange female.

"Who are you?" he demanded. "This is private property. Who gave you leave to ride across Pemberley?"

"Private?" It was clear he surprised her. "All this? I thought this was open range."

"Not hardly. Everything this side of the Long Branch belongs to Pemberley Ranch." He considered her. "You're not from around here, are you?"

The girl raised her chin. "We are now. Our place is across the river. My father owns the farm there."

Darcy relaxed a bit. "The old Thompson place?" She answered with a nod. "You're one of Tom Bennet's daughters? I was told he had a herd of them." Almost immediately he recognized how his choice of words could be considered an insult, but it was too late.

The girl's voice was ice cold. "Tom Bennet is indeed my father, sir, and I thank you for your kind observations about my family. Now, if you'll pardon me." She pulled her reins to return from whence she came, only to be halted by Darcy's words.

"I'll escort you back to the ford, miss, if you don't mind."

She looked over her shoulder at him. "I *do* mind. You've

made it clear that I'm not welcomed here, and I can see myself home. Good day." To her increased irritation, Darcy fell in beside her. "I see there was no cause for me to voice my preference!"

"The ground is uneven here, and as it's unfamiliar to you, you might meet with misfortune."

"So—I cannot ride my horse, is that what you mean?"

Darcy snapped back, "I truly don't wish to offend, miss, but you're being mighty stubborn! Your pony might fall into some gopher hole and break his leg and have to be put down. Now, I call that a tall price to pay for your pride!"

The girl said nothing, she only lowered her head. But Darcy could see the color rise on her cheek as she bit her lip. The two rode in silence for some time along the ridgeline before turning right and making their way down to the river. The trees grew more plentiful and thick next to the riverbank. Darcy tried to come up with some conversation, but the girl's studied avoidance of his glance stilled his tongue. After a few more minutes, they reached a shallow ford across the Long Branch.

"Well, here we are—Thompson Crossing. Your daddy's farm's on the other side. I reckon this is how you crossed over?"

The girl's sarcastic side reasserted itself. "It is. Thank you so much for assuring I didn't cause Turner any injury. I am forever grateful!"

Darcy blinked. "Turner? Your horse's name is Turner?"

A grin stole across her face. "It is, sir."

"Strange. Most girls name their ponies Star or Brownie or Buster."

Her grin turned into a mocking smile. "But I'm not like most girls, as I'm sure you've discovered." With that, she spurred the paint across the ford, splashing water everywhere, leaving a bemused Darcy behind. He shook his head before turning Caesar back toward the Pemberley ranch house. It was only then he realized that he had neglected to introduce himself.

No harm done, he thought. *It's not likely we'll meet up again.*

The girl in the wide-brimmed hat had just dismounted next to the barn when she heard her mother's call.

"Beth Bennet—there you are! Come inside and change this instant! There's company for dinner!"

"Yes, Mother." She led Turner into his stall and removed his saddle. Hill, the farmhand, assured her he would see to the paint, so Beth hurried to the house and into the bedroom she shared with two of her sisters.

"Beth, you're late," said Mary unnecessarily as she was putting her own hair up.

"I'll help you," said Jane as Beth tugged off her shirt.

In a few moments, Beth had changed from farm tomboy to countrified young lady. By then, Kathy had joined them, brushing her hair as Jane helped button up the younger girl's dress.

"Hurry!" cried Lily. "George is just arriving!"

"Lily!" scolded Mary. "That's Mr. Whitehead! You should have more respect for your elders!"

"Oh, pooh! He's like family. He gave me leave to call him George, didn't he, Kathy?"

"Oh, yes," Kathy responded with a dreamy look in her eye. "Isn't he the handsomest man?"

"I don't know," Beth said as she glanced at Jane. "What say you, Jane?"

Jane gave a smile. "He's very handsome, to be sure."

Kathy laughed. "But not the *most* handsome, is he? Not like a certain doctor in town?" Giggles erupted as Jane blushed.

The door opened, and Mrs. Bennet stuck her head in. "Girls! Come along! Mr. Whitehead is here. Ah, Beth, you're almost ready. Hurry, hurry!"

"I'll help her, Mother," Jane assured her. "The others can greet our guest." With that, Lily and Kathy almost ran out of the room, Mary following at a more sedate pace.

Jane helped Beth finish her hair. "There, beautiful as usual!"

Beth laughed. "Oh, Jane, you are too good! The only way I can be called beautiful is if you're not in the room."

"That's ridiculous. You are very pretty, and one day a young man will fall on his knees, assuring you of your loveliness when he asks for your hand, just mark my words."

Beth laughed. "Is that what Charles did, dearest?" She laughed again as Jane blushed for a second time, but the laughter died a moment later. "Why did he refuse our invitation to dinner tonight?"

Jane pretended to arrange the brushes on the table. "Charles said he had pressing business, and he would dine with us tomorrow."

"Jane, you know he stays away just because George is our guest for dinner! Why is he so stubborn? Surely he must accept our friends if he is to marry you. George is a brave and honorable man. To hold the fact that he fought for the Union against him is very unseemly, I'm sorry to say. Why, haven't we forgiven him for being a Rebel?"

Jane glanced at Beth, her mouth a firm line. "I will not question my fiancé, sister. I shall be loyal to Charles."

Slightly abashed, Beth took Jane's hands into her own. "As shall I, I promise! He is to be my brother, and I will love him as such. I just worry over the influence of others on him."

"You mean his friends, the Darcys?"

"Yes! You've heard what George has said about them—unrepentant Rebels, unfriendly to anyone not in the intimate circle."

"I've heard that Mr. Darcy has taken the loyalty oath."

"Oh, Jane! What comes out his mouth is not what's in his heart, I can assure you. He has only taken the oath, I can believe, to be allowed to vote again. But he hasn't changed one whit. Why, none of us has ever met him or his sister—even you haven't, and you are to marry his best friend. And just today, one of his ranch hands warned me off his property."

"Oh, I'm sorry to hear that. He wasn't unpleasant, I hope."

"Very!" Beth claimed, trying not to recall that the rude man on the Arabian was also undeniably fine looking. At Jane's alarmed look, she quickly added, "But he was polite, all the same. I'm unharmed."

She rose and they moved towards the door. "Beth," said her sister in a worried tone, "I'm sorry you will have to stand with Mr. Darcy at my wedding, but Charles has no family here, and the man is his friend."

"Don't fear, Jane. For your happiness, I would do anything, even suffer Mr. Darcy. And I truly adore your Charles. Now, shall we go to dinner?"

George Whitehead patted his mouth with his napkin. "Mrs. Bennet, may I say once again what a marvelous table you set. A better dinner I have not had these four years since I left Illinois."

Fanny Bennet giggled like a schoolgirl. "Oh, Mr. Whitehead, how you go on! Would you care for more of the beef? Pass him the plate, Kathy. Kathy—I'm speaking to you!"

Kathy Bennet stirred from her admiration for their dashing guest. "I'm sorry, Mother, what did you say?" Lily unsuccessfully hid a snigger, which earned a glare from her sister.

"The meat, the meat! Pass the plate to Mr. Whitehead!"

"Umm, dear, perhaps Kathy should wait until George has finished his portion?" suggested Mr. Bennet.

"Yes," replied Whitehead smoothly, "but I shall certainly take seconds."

Beth nearly rolled her eyes at their guest's embroidered gallantry. As much as she liked George Whitehead, he could lay on the compliments a bit too thickly for her taste. But as he meant to compliment her mother, his bit of foolishness was forgiven at once. And the man was devilishly handsome with his dark hair, elegantly styled vandyke, and impeccably tailored clothes. Yes, a person with whom it was very difficult to be exasperated.

As Mr. Bennet preferred to listen rather than lead the conversation about table, it fell to Whitehead to steer the discussion. "Miss Jane, I am sure you are looking forward to next month's nuptials."

"I am, George, thank you." Beth had hoped she would bring up the antipathy between Charles and George, but she was disappointed.

"My best wishes for your felicity. And you, Miss Beth—still enjoy riding all over creation on Thomas?"

Beth hid a smirk. Not only had George failed to understand the hidden joke of her horse's name—most people did—he had forgotten it completely. "Turner, sir. Yes, I was just riding this afternoon, in fact, and I was most rudely treated by our neighbor."

That caught Bennet's attention. "What happened, my dear?"

Whitehead was most solicitous. "I hope you were not mistreated by a B&R employee, Miss Beth."

"Oh, no, it was a rider from Pemberley! I had not realized that they owned all of the land across the river. While enjoying my ride, I was intercepted, warned off the land, and escorted off. Why, you'd think I was a cattle rustler by the way I was treated."

"Were you mistreated, Beth?" her father demanded. "I won't stand for it! Did anyone threaten you?"

Beth realized she had overstated the case and tried to put the company at ease. "Father, I misspoke. I was indeed informed that I was trespassing, but I must admit that I suffered no hurt to my person, only my feelings. I was not mistreated, either by words or actions. Besides receiving a scolding, I have no complaints, save that I must remain on this side of the river."

"How rude!" cried Mrs. Bennet in maternal solidarity. "To treat any child of mine so! Tom, you should have a talk with Mr. Darcy about the character of his men."

Whitehead shook his head. "I'm not certain that would have any effect, Mrs. Bennet. Recall that I know the Darcys well, and they do not take kindly to others telling them how to run their business. I, myself, after having extended the hand of friendship to that family, have also been, as Miss Beth so elegantly put it, 'warned off' Pemberley. Who was the man who accosted you, Miss Beth?"

"Accosted is a bit strong, George. As I said, my ride was interrupted by a Pemberley rider, but he didn't offer his name."

"I'll wager I can guess the man. Ruddy-faced man on a brown quarter horse? Wearing a black hat with a silver hatband?"

Beth shook her head. "No, he was tall with a tan hat. Dark hair and clean shaven, like you, and his horse was black."

Whitehead stared at her. "His eyes—did you note the color of his eyes?"

Beth licked her lips. She had left that part out, for they were the most intense eyes she had ever beheld, but she would not be reticent. "Blue—bright blue."

Whitehead let out a bark of laughter. "Why, Miss Beth, you've met the man himself! That was William Darcy, esteemed owner of Pemberley Ranch, Darcy Bank, and half of Long Branch County! Do you not feel fortunate at such a meeting?"

Beth could not help stealing a glance at Jane. Sure enough, her sister was red in the face with mortification. For the sake of *her* feelings, Beth labored to defuse the situation. "I'm always happy to meet new people, George, but I can't vouch for others. As he said, it's his land, and I shall respect that." *No matter how little I respect him!*

"Well said, my dear," injected her father, "we should always respect other people's property."

George did not take the hint to change the subject. "It's not surprising that you didn't know who he was, for he is a rather peculiar fellow. He's practically a hermit, and he keeps his sister close to Pemberley with him. Had you never seen him in town?"

"No, none of us have," Beth replied.

Mary decided to have her share of the conversation. "We certainly have not seen them in church on Sunday, unlike other respectable members of the community."

How like Mary to note that! Beth considered. But it was true. The Darcys did not attend services at the church in town, while Catherine Burroughs and her daughter, Anne, made a very notable procession every Sunday to their reserved pew in the front. Sheriff Lucas, Doctor Bingley, and George

Whitehead were all members in good standing of Reverend Henry Tilney's congregation.

"Well," Whitehead grinned, "we are commanded to be faithful, yet we are all poor sinners. But what can you expect from a man who has taken up arms against his country?" Beth winced a little at the latest disparagement of Darcy, knowing how it would give Jane pain, as the same could be said of Charles.

Finally, Mr. Bennet roused himself to take control of his dinner table. "Any news from town, George? We've been very busy here with harvest time upon us."

"Yes, a new family has just moved in east of town in the new settlement—the Washingtons, a former slave family from Louisiana, looking for a better life out here."

Bennet frowned. "East of town, George? You mean that land near the river?"

"That's the place."

Bennet pursed his lips. "It's a bit low there, don't you think? Wouldn't you say that land's prone to flooding?"

Whitehead stared at Bennet for a moment, his face made of stone. He blinked and a shy grin grew across his face. "Well, I'm no expert about that, Tom. I'm only the recorder of deeds. Mrs. Burroughs sells the land. But I've been here four years, and I've never seen any flooding in the new settlements."

Bennet shrugged his shoulders as he sipped his coffee. "If you say so, George."

"Well," cried Mrs. Bennet, "if everyone's finished—no seconds, Mr. Whitehead? Are you sure? Well then, girls, help me clear the table for dessert. Blackberry cobbler!"

William and Gabrielle Darcy walked the small man in the black cassock to his carriage. "I'm pleased you could join us for dinner, Father."

Father Joseph smiled as he spoke in a heavy Spanish accent. "No, my son, it is I who should thank you, your sister, and most particularly your cook, Mrs. Reynolds!"

"Oh, Father," said Gaby, "you're welcome anytime." She curtsied as he took first her hand and then her brother's, before making the Sign of the Cross over them in blessing.

"May Our Father bless you and all here." The priest climbed into his carriage.

"Go with God, Padre!" Will shouted as the brother and sister waved in farewell.

"That there's a good man, even if he does wear a dress," drawled Richard Fitzwilliam, leaning on a column next to the steps leading down from the veranda.

"Maybe you should come to Mass with us sometimes, Fitz," said Gaby. "It'll do you good."

Fitz laughed. "Me? All that kneelin' an' bowin' an' such? Thank you kindly, Miss Gaby, but that ain't for me."

Gaby shook her head in fond resignation as she continued into the house. Will and Fitz sat down in two rocking chairs on the veranda and lit cigars. "Heard 'bout the latest homesteaders come to town?" Fitz began. "Former slaves bought some o' that bottomland from your cousin, like the rest o' them."

Darcy closed his eyes for a moment. "Damn!"

"Yeah," Fitz took a puff, "don't know how folks 'round here will cotton to a family of former slaves movin' in."

Darcy glanced at his friend and ranch foreman. "You've got a point, Fitz, but that's not what I meant. You're not from around here. There's a reason that land's lay fallow 'til now. It's low and prone to flooding. I remember back in '55 when the Long Branch came up from its banks after a heavy storm. It's been dry ever since, but that won't last. We get one big rain, those people in the new settlement will have three to four feet of water in their homes."

"Your cousin, Mrs. Burroughs, must know that. Why's she sellin'?"

"Oldest reason in the world—money. Whitehead and that fancy-pants bank manager of hers, Collins, talked Cate into it."

"You could talk her out of it."

Darcy stared out onto his land, his features set. "Nope. That isn't my concern anymore. I learned my lesson in the war, Fitz. I worry only about my family, my people, and Pemberley. Everything else can see to itself."

The two finished their cigars in silence.

"Ah, here you are, Beth," said her father as he walked into his study.

"Yes, I was reading and keeping Samuel company." Beth was in an armchair near the bookcase, an oil lamp on the side table, and the precious lone photograph of Samuel that had been taken before his departure with the rest of the Ohio troops lovingly hung on the adjoining wall. Bennet walked up to it, sighing.

"You know, I think Samuel would have liked Texas," he observed before turning to her. "You've certainly changed your mind about the place."

Beth put down her book. "Texas is a lovely place." She then smiled impishly. "If only it wasn't full of Texans!"

Bennet laughed. "Now, that's not quite true. You've made great friends with Miss Charlotte Lucas, the sheriff's daughter. Reverend Tilney's a good man." He paused. "You're not holding the war against Doc Bingley, are you?"

Beth bit her lip. "No. How can I? He makes Jane so happy—"

"Don't you like him for himself?"

Beth colored. "I do. It's just…" she glanced at Samuel's portrait, "I feel as if I'm betraying Samuel's memory."

Bennet laid a hand on her shoulder. "Beth, you've got to try to forget about the war."

"I try, but I'm afraid if I do, I'll forget Samuel."

Bennet just shook his head. "Well, I'm going to bed, my dear. Don't stay up too late." He kissed the top of her head and left. Beth watched him go and then turned her eyes to the photograph.

Softly to herself, she repeated her vow. "I'll not forget you, Samuel. No matter what the others do, I'll stay true, just watch. I'll never forget you." With that she extinguished the light and left the room for bed.

Chapter 2

October, 1870

"I HEREBY PRONOUNCE YOU man and wife. What God hath joined, let no man tear asunder." The Reverend Henry Tilney then raised his hands to the congregation. "Friends, let me present to you Dr. and Mrs. Charles Bingley."

To general applause, the happy couple walked down the aisle, Bingley in his best blue suit and Jane in a store-bought dress ordered direct from St. Louis. Behind them was a slightly less joyous couple: maid of honor Beth Bennet and best man William Darcy.

The newlyweds, their family, and friends proceeded by foot to the only place in Rosings large enough for a reception, Younge's Saloon. Sally Younge, proprietor and madam of the place, promised that her "working girls" would be gone from the premises for the duration of the festivities, to the relief of the Bennets and the despair of some of the male townsfolk.

True to her word to her sister, Beth had said not a single disparaging word to her escort, although she dearly wished to. She was uncomfortable, and not just because of the words spoken to her a month ago by the man now walking beside her. They still stung, and Beth was loath to either forgive or forget. But what made matters worse was how downright handsome the man was. Darcy was impeccable in his suit, not a hair was out of place—and his smell! A subtle yet wondrous aroma filled her nostrils whenever he stood near, a far finer smell than the *eau de cologne* favored by George Whitehead. Beth tried valiantly not to look into his face, for a man with his blue eyes was far too dangerous.

Darcy, too, was in turmoil. To his dismay he realized the tomboy to whom he had been so short was the Bennet girl he was obligated to stand with at Charles's wedding. She was quite simply the fairest girl he had ever seen. True, Jane Bennet—now Mrs. Bingley—was as lovely as Charles had claimed, but Darcy's eye would not leave the woman beside him. All the Bennet girls were pretty in their own right, but Darcy was enchanted by the fire in Beth Bennet's eyes. A man could get lost there, he knew, and he vowed not to allow himself to be tempted.

The party soon reached their destination, and the place was quickly filled, for in as small a town as Rosings, one could not have a wedding and not invite the entire population. The piano player took his seat, and Charles and Jane waltzed for the first time as a married couple. Darcy and Beth watched, in admiration on his part and apprehension on hers, for the last duty of their joint office was to dance the second dance.

Darcy decided to make conversation. "Your sister looks very happy, Miss Beth."

Beth resolutely stared at the couple dancing. "Yes. When we moved here, I'm sure we had no thought that Jane would meet so agreeable a person as Dr. Bingley."

"She's very fortunate. Charles is a good man."

Beth was glad at his statement, for the implied suggestion that Jane was a husband hunter gave her a reason to let loose her animosity towards Darcy. "Indeed? I'm glad you think so. I know my family feels the same. However, knowing Jane as I do, it is my decided opinion that Charles is getting the best of the bargain. There's no one so good as my sister."

Before Darcy could respond, the music ended, and he was occupied applauding the couple. He then reached out for Beth's hand, and the two of them joined the Bingleys and the Bennets for a dance. Another waltz began, and Darcy took Beth's left hand in his right, placed his left on her waist, and whispered, "Just follow my lead, Miss Bennet, if you're unsure of the steps."

Beth was forced to bite her tongue, for it would not do to make a scene at Jane's wedding, no matter how insufferable this tall, handsome, pompous ass could be. Not trusting herself, she refused to talk to him during the whole of the dance. She glanced at him occasionally, and for the first time noticed a faint scar on his forehead. Darcy took her silence as evidence of her nervousness and did not press her for conversation. The assembled watched two people perform the figures of the waltz flawlessly, as if they were a machine.

Not too soon for either, the dance ended, and Beth would have made her escape after the requisite bow had not her partner refused to release her hand. He instead deposited it upon his arm, and she was forced to suffer his escort back to her parents.

Darcy bowed slightly to the Bennets. "Mr. Bennet, Mrs. Bennet, my congratulations again on your daughter's marriage." The Bennets civilly thanked him for his courtesy. Darcy straightened up and made a gesture at a couple nearby. "May I present my sister to you? This is Miss Gabrielle Darcy, and this is the foreman of Pemberley Ranch, Mr. Richard Fitzwilliam. Gabrielle, Fitz, this is Mr. and Mrs. Bennet and their daughter, Miss Beth Bennet."

Miss Darcy, a black-haired girl dressed in the latest fashion, shyly greeted them. "I'm happy to meet you. I've met Miss Jane, now Mrs. Bingley, last week, and I'm glad to make the acquaintance of her family."

She was tall for her age and had a well-formed figure. She owned the same olive skin tone as her brother, but her eyes were of the deepest black. She had a faint exotic air about her, in spite of the awkwardness common in a girl too old to be a child and too young to be an adult. Beth pitied her, as she well recognized the condition. It had bedeviled both her and Mary, and Kathy was suffering it even now. Only Jane and Lily, the beauties of the Bennet girls, seemed to escape the gawkiness that most women experienced.

"As am I," Fitz added with a grin. "Always happy to meet two such lovely ladies!" A slim man in his late twenties of middling height, Richard Fitzwilliam had a ruddy complexion and fair hair. His suit was not nearly as fine as his employer's, but his greeting was all that it should be in sincerity and friendliness. Beth could not but like him at once.

Mrs. Bennet giggled at his flattery, and her husband was amused. "Is that so, sir? Shall I need to call you out in defense of my wife's honor?"

"Oh, Mr. Bennet—how you go on!" cried his wife. "Pleased to meet you, Mr. Fitzwilliam. And you, too, Miss Darcy. What a lovely girl you are and such a fine figure to go with such a pretty dress! I am sure you got that in St. Louis. My brother, you see, owns a shop in St. Louis, and the dresses—oh my! Nothing but the best from Gardiner's—but I'm sure you know about that. How old are you, my dear?"

Beth was mortified at her mother's monologue, and her embarrassment grew at Darcy's dark look. Miss Darcy took a half-step back in response to the outburst but answered, "Sixteen, ma'am."

"Sixteen! My, my—you're of an age with my Lily! You must meet her and my other daughters! Here's Mary, but where's Lily and Kathy? Oh, Tom, do you see them?"

"Umm, perhaps another time, Mrs. Bennet," Darcy coldly said as he took Gaby's elbow. He quickly made their farewells and strode off, his sister's arm still grasped in his hand. Fitz watched in some confusion, quickly bowed, and followed. Mrs. Bennet, still a bit overwhelmed by the attention, was insensitive to their abrupt departure, but the action fueled Beth's displeasure with Darcy. Her father was more sanguine.

"So, that is our neighbor. Tall sort of fellow, isn't he?"

"All the better to look down his nose at others," added his daughter spitefully, in a low voice.

He gave her an unreadable look. "Do you think so? Hmm."

Beth had no opportunity to ask his meaning, as she was happily met by her friend, Charlotte Lucas.

Darcy made his escape from the ridiculous Mrs. Bennet, but he was at a loss to know what to do. Deciding to forward the acquaintance between Gaby and the new Mrs. Bingley, the pair found themselves in the newlyweds' company, Fitz having deserted his employer to wet his whistle at the bar. He correctly surmised that the exceedingly kind Jane would bring Gaby out of her shyness. It was just a moment's work to have the two talking together like old friends.

"I want to thank you again, Will, for everything you've done," Charles said earnestly.

Darcy blanched, his eyes darting about. He took Bingley by the arm and moved to an unoccupied wall. "Say nothing of it, Charles. Consider it a wedding present."

"Ha! More like a present to my father-in-law! He doesn't know that he's only payin' a fraction of what this soirée is costing, thanks to you. From what Younge's charging, there's no way he could've afforded it."

"Will you keep your voice down?" Darcy said irritably.

"Why? Jane knows." At Darcy's horrified expression, he added, "She's agreed to keep it a secret. But why? Why don't you want Mr. Bennet to know of your generosity?"

Darcy stared out into the crowd, his hands stiffly behind his back. "To tell him would be boasting, Charles, and I can't abide a braggart. When a man does a kindness, it should be for kindness' sake alone. I couldn't allow Sally to take advantage of the man, but he doesn't need to know about it. Expecting gratitude for a gift is… unseemly."

Bingley sighed at his friend's intransigence. The man's moral code was a bit over-the-top at times. "Like your cousin, Catherine Burroughs?"

Darcy's grim demeanor cracked a bit as his lips twitched. "Exactly."

"Where is she, anyway?"

"You didn't really expect her here?" Darcy was amused. "The wedding of a doctor to a farmer's daughter? She'd sooner go to a rodeo. And she keeps Anne away, too. A shame—she has few friends, and it would do her good to know somebody like your wife."

"You've been very good to Jane."

"We enjoyed her company at Pemberley last week. She's kind and charming. Gaby likes her very well."

Bingley smiled. "Her sisters are fine girls, too." He was surprised Darcy lost his smile. "Will, you don't disapprove of them, do you?"

Darcy grunted. "Charles, I can say nothing against Mrs. Bingley, but the rest of her family? You're not blind, man. Look at them! The two youngest are incorrigible flirts, the middle one is a bluestocking if ever I've seen one, and the mother is impossible. Why, you should have heard the impudent questions she put to Gaby, all within a minute of meeting her! I barely held my composure."

"I'm sure you did," Bingley laughed. "They're very nice people, Will; they're just a bit... boisterous. There's not a mean bone in their bodies. Once you get to know 'em, you'll see."

"And why should I do that?"

Charles frowned. "They're my family now, Will. You'll be in their company in the future if you're goin' to be in mine. I won't throw off my wife's family."

Darcy had the good manners to look abashed. "You're right, Charles. I'm sorry. I shouldn't have said that."

"I know Miz Bennet can talk a blue streak, but she don't mean anything by it. It's just her way. 'Sides, you can't say anything bad about Mr. Bennet, or Beth."

"She's a bit of a tomboy, isn't she?"

Bingley shrugged. "She grew up on a farm, Will. What did you expect?" He elbowed his friend with a grin. "She sure cleaned up nice, though. Almost as pretty as my Jane."

Darcy's eyes narrowed. Yes, Beth Bennet looked very pretty in a proper lady's dress. But he couldn't get out of his mind the way her dungarees showed her backside to advantage in the saddle…

Bingley's low voice cut in. "Uhh, Will, don't look now, but Whitehead's talking to Gaby."

Darcy's eyes flew to his sister. Halfway across the room, George Whitehead had engaged Jane Bingley and Gaby Darcy in conversation. Jane was as polite as ever, but Gaby wore a slightly panicked expression.

"*God dammit!*" growled Darcy under his breath.

Bingley was grim. "I didn't want to invite that son-of-a-bitch, but he's a friend of Mr. Bennet's. I couldn't say no without causin' a ruckus, and then I'd have to explain—"

"I understand, Charles. Nothing you could do. You'd think that no-good dog would stay away from her, after the last time."

Bingley glanced at Darcy. "You're not goin' to cause trouble, are you? Whitehead's pretty popular 'round here."

"Then folks need to make better friends." Darcy took a breath and slowly and resolutely walked over to his sister, Bingley trailing behind. His stare would have burned a hole into George Whitehead's face. His target was aware of the scrutiny, the sardonic look he returned an obvious challenge. Fists clenched, Darcy stopped a couple of feet away.

"Good afternoon, Darcy," said Whitehead with seeming affability. "I see you managed to tear yourself away from your ranch and grace us with your presence. We've greatly missed you and your sister, who I can say is lovelier than ever. Wonderful day for a wedding, wouldn't you say?"

Stone-faced, Darcy gestured at his sister, who quickly came to his side. "Mrs. Bingley, I beg your pardon." He then turned his attention to the smirking man before him. In a low, calm voice, he said, "Whitehead, I told you to stay away from my family."

Whitehead indicated the room. "But this is not Pemberley Ranch, this is Rosings. Your power doesn't extend here. I'm appointed by Governor Davis, and last I heard, you are not he. I have legal authority in this county."

"As recorder of deeds—a clerk—as long as General Reynolds's puppet remains in office, which won't be forever, from what I've heard. We've been readmitted to the Union, and all of us Texans now have the right to vote, as you'll find out in a couple of years. Your army won't be able to steal the election then. I'll tell you one last time, Whitehead—stay away from my family. This is my final warning."

"That sounds like a threat, Darcy."

"A promise, Whitehead. Mrs. Bingley, again forgive me. C'mon, Gaby—we're leaving." Darcy took his sister lightly by the arm and turned away.

"I can have you arrested for threatening me," Whitehead claimed, causing Darcy to look sideways at him.

"You can try. You come on by Pemberley, and you'll learn my boys will be waiting for you. You and your hired killers." He gestured at the bar with his head before walking to the door, the crowd parting before him.

It may have been a Baptist wedding, but the bar was still open, and Fitz was enjoying a beer when he noted his boss across the room staring at someone. Instantly coming alert, he saw George Whitehead talking to Gaby Darcy. Fitz turned around, leaning his back against the bar, watching the action as Darcy walked over to his enemy. He noted a movement by a man down a ways from him.

From the corner of his eye he saw it was Kid Denny, a gunfighter supposedly working at the B&R Ranch, but Fitz knew better. The man was so intently watching the confrontation he didn't notice at first Fitz moving towards him.

"Afternoon, Denny." Fitz stopped next to him.

"Whatta ya want, Fitzwilliam?" the gunman demanded.

"Just bein' neighborly. Nice day for a weddin', ain't it?"

"Get lost." Denny turned back to the quiet confrontation, his hand slipping off the bar towards his gun belt.

In a deceptively friendly tone, Fitz said, "I wouldn't do that, if'n I was you."

Denny half turned back, his eyes quickly taking stock of Fitzwilliam. "Yeah? Big talk, mister, seein' as you ain't wearin' your gun."

Fitz chuckled. "Yeah, well, packin' a gun seemed a rather unnecessary embellishment for a weddin', at least for honest folks."

"You better shut up, Fitzwilliam," Denny snarled, "or I'll shut ya up fur good."

Fitz shook his head. "Tsk, tsk—ain't no cause for being unsociable, Denny. Is there, José?"

"No, *señor*," came a voice from Denny's blind side. "We is all friends here, today."

Denny whipped his head to see a large man grinning just behind him.

"You know José Estrada, don't you, Denny?" Fitz smiled as he leaned on the bar. "No? He's my Number Two at Pemberley. José, this here's Kid Denny, ranch boss from the B&R. He considers himself to be some kinda gunfighter, which is why he's got the lack o' manners to bring a six-shooter into a weddin' reception. Now, José here don't need no gun, as he can pull your arm clear off without tryin'. Can't you, José?"

José showed his teeth. "*Sí*, I can do that, Fitz, *no problema*. But I can shoot, too, you bet."

Fitz's eyes never left Denny's face. "Peter, you find that shotgun behind the bar?"

"Oh, yeah, boss," came another voice. Denny didn't need to turn around to see that another Pemberley rider was behind him.

Denny gritted his teeth. "You think you're pretty smart, don't ya?"

"I have my moments." Fitz waved Sheriff Lucas over. "Sheriff, it seems Denny here's weighted down by a big, heavy gun. It's spoilin' his drinkin', ain't it, Denny? Now, that don't seem right, does it?"

Lucas looked at both men. "That's enough of that, Fitz." He held out his hand. "Denny, the sign outside clearly said 'No Guns.' Hand it over, an' you can pick it up at the jail later."

Denny hesitated before handing over his Colt. Lucas grunted, slipping the pistol into his waistband. "I don't want any trouble from any of you, got it? Be on your way."

"Mr. Darcy's leaving right now, Lucas, an' we'll be followin' him," Fitz assured the sheriff.

"This ain't over, Fitzwilliam," Denny spat.

"See you 'round, Denny," Fitz said coldly. The three Pemberley riders backed out of the saloon after Darcy and his sister.

Whitehead had noticed the end of the confrontation between Denny and Fitzwilliam as Darcy and his party walked away.

"Well, Mrs. Bingley, I must apologize for Mr. Darcy's rudeness—"

An angry Bingley held up his hand. "Stop. Don't—say—a—word, Whitehead. I won't hear anything against Darcy. I didn't invite you—you're only here as a favor to my father-in-law."

Whitehead tilted his head. "That's mighty unfriendly, Doctor."

Bingley knew Jane was upset, and he hated that he was spoiling the reception. "Look, I don't want any trouble. I stand by what I said when you moved to town. You go your way, an' I'll go mine. You get sick, an' I'll treat you like anybody else. Other than that, I've got nothing to say to you." He saw that Jane's sisters were walking their way, and he didn't want to prolong the conversation, especially in their presence. "Now, if you'll excuse me, I want to dance with my bride." With that the two took to the floor, Bingley whispering in Jane's ear he would explain later. Just as they started to dance, an angry Beth with a curious Kathy and Lily joined Whitehead.

"George, I couldn't help noticing that you and Mr. Darcy had cross words," Beth observed.

A corner of Whitehead's lip twitched. "Yes, you could say that."

Kathy looked towards the door. "Imagine! Causing a scene at Jane's wedding! What a disagreeable person! I hope Jane wasn't too upset."

"I'm sure she's not, Miss Kathy. Your new brother-in-law has caught her attention." Sure enough, Jane was beaming at her groom as they moved to the music.

"I thought there was going to be a fight!" cried Lily. "You could take him, couldn't you, George?"

"Lily!" admonished Beth.

"Far be it from me to start such unpleasantness," Whitehead

assured them. "I was just congratulating your sister when Mr. Darcy dragged Miss Darcy away." He shook his head. "Some people won't let bygones be bygones. It's a shame. But what can you expect from someone with Darcy's... erm, background?"

Kathy's eyes flew open. "Background? Whatever do you mean, George?"

Whitehead leaned close. "Didn't you know? Darcy's not... quite... *white*, you see. It seems his grandfather took up with a squaw, so he's at least one-quarter Indian."

Shocked, Beth remembered both Darcys: olive complexion, jet hair, and high cheekbones.

"My goodness! Mr. Darcy is a half-breed!" laughed Lily.

Whitehead grinned. "So it would seem. People around here only tolerate the Darcys because of their wealth. Money, you see, does buy respectability. But, enough about that! Would you care to dance, Miss Lily?"

Beth watched as Whitehead escorted Lily to the floor, feeling a confusing mixture of shock, amusement, and a tiny bit of shame.

Chapter 3

January, 1871

IN THE WEEKS THAT followed, the Bennets saw very little of their neighbors. Winter had come to Rosings, and while it did not have the bitter cold and heavy snows familiar in Ohio, the ever-present wind brought its own miseries. No matter the weather, there were chickens to feed, pigs to slop, and cows to milk, and with Jane's marriage, one less person to share the chores. Beth's favorite job, as it always had been, was in the barn, caring for the horses. She would brush the animals and see to their water and feed before helping her father and Hill care for the cattle.

On the coldest days, the family was thankful that the long-departed Mr. Thompson had built his house so that the pump for the well was inside. Nothing could be done about the outhouse, of course, but at least when the infrequent snowstorms came, the snow was never very deep.

Their diet was mostly dried beans, peas, and whatever salted meat was still available. Vegetables were a distant memory, but there was always fresh milk, eggs, cheese, and bread. Hill shared his meals with his employers before returning to his warm room in the barn. Mr. Bennet had prepared well, and cords of wood were close by to feed the life-sustaining fire in the hearth.

Still, Sunday was Sunday, and only the most extreme of weather could keep the Bennets from church. Of all the daughters, Mary and Beth were most keen on going. Mary, while always a pious child, seemed to have another incentive for attendance: Pastor Tilney was young, handsome, and unmarried. Beth's interest was of a secular nature as well—the family always stopped by the Bingleys' for Sunday dinner, and Beth was in the presence of her beloved sister once again. Mrs. Bennet had her own reason to see her eldest—the first grandbaby was on the way, expected in August.

Christmas came and went, as did the New Year. Day piled upon day, with the only variance from the monotony of the chores being the condition of the weather. No one would visit, and Beth was assured of seeing no one outside her family, except on Sundays and the odd shopping trip to Rosings.

The year of Our Lord 1871 was only two weeks old when something unusual happened. Beth returned from the barn after spending time with her horse, Turner, to the surprise of finding house guests. The weather had moderated a bit, but not enough for friends to come calling. This had to be business, and it was. Her father was behind the closed door of his study with George Whitehead and another man. Neither her mother nor her sisters knew what it was about, so Beth had to be content with a cup of tea to warm her chilled body while she waited.

Before long, the door opened, and Mr. Bennet brought his companions to the table. "My dears, let me introduce my banker, Mr. Billy Collins, manager of the Rosings Bank."

Mr. Collins bowed. "It is indeed a pleasure to meet your fine family, my good sir." He was a short man with mutton-chop sideburns, balding, though only in his thirties, dressed in a blue suit, a thin bow-tie at his throat. As Bennet introduced his daughters, Collins eyed each one closely, paying them compliments in a rather oily manner. He dismissed Beth almost immediately and set his gaze most markedly upon Kathy. Beth was happy she was still in her dirty work-clothes.

"Mr. Collins, how nice to meet you," said Mrs. Bennet. "And you too, my dear Mr. Whitehead—it's always a pleasure to see you. What brings you out here in such frightful weather?"

"Can it not be your lovely family, Mrs. Bennet?" Whitehead smiled.

"A-hem," Bennet cleared his throat. "Mr. Whitehead and Mr. Collins came to see me on a matter of business, my dear."

"Oh, how tedious—but I do appreciate your attentions to us, Mr. Whitehead. Is your business completed?"

"Indeed, Mrs. Bennet, to everyone's satisfaction."

Beth raised an eyebrow. "May we be apprised of the nature of your business?"

Whitehead and Collins both looked at the girl, Collins fairly gaping, while Bennet choked back a chuckle. The banker recovered his wits to stammer, "It was gentlemen's business, Miss Bennet—nothing to worry yourself over."

Beth's eyes flashed dangerously, and Bennet thought it was a good time to intervene. "Yes, yes, well… enough of that. Can I offer you gentlemen a drink?"

"Oh, and dinner! Please say you'll stay for dinner," cried his wife.

Whitehead shook his head. "Alas, we have a prior engagement. Perhaps we can impose upon you at another time?"

Mrs. Bennet was disappointed, and her attempts to disguise her feelings were halfhearted. "Oh, very well, if it can't be helped. I'll hold you to your promise, sir. Both you and Mr. Collins. You will have dinner with us."

"Of course," Whitehead said as he bowed.

"I shall count the hours," Collins added, whose comment almost caused more than one Bennet daughter to lose her composure. The men slipped on their long jackets and left soon afterwards. The family then sat for dinner. Beth longed to know what the men had discussed for so long in private, and she had every expectation that her father would tell her. But Mr. Bennet refused to answer any of Beth's questions until dinner was done, when they retreated to his study.

"As you know, George Whitehead has been a valuable friend since we moved to Rosings. Thanks to him, we were able to secure our mortgage with Rosings Bank at a more favorable rate than Darcy Bank offered. He has now offered even more help. It seems he has contacts with people in Fort Worth who have access to more modern farming implements—new plows and tools, better seeds, a few more bulls. I must say, the improvements could be substantial. Our yields could be significant—perhaps a fivefold increase, according to what George tells me. That should be enough to buy a new store-bought dress or two for you girls without us worrying over the cost," he added with a smile.

"Father, I certainly don't need such finery—and the cost! How can we afford the improvements?"

"That's why Mr. Collins was here. A refinancing of the mortgage will provide the capital." He reached over and took Beth's hand in his. "And you certainly will buy a new dress,

Beth—I insist upon it. It is my dream to provide my wife and children a better life. That's why I moved all of you to Rosings. Now, Jane is settled with a fine husband, and I have the chance of making all our lives better. All will be well—trust me."

Plans for the spring were made in other places besides the Bennet farm. In the ornate blue and gold sitting room of the B&R ranch house, the owner held court.

A tall, middle-aged woman, Catherine Matlock had once been considered very handsome, if not downright pretty, in her native New York. Her father was rich and her dowry was substantial. But her older sister was prettier than she, and monopolized the available beaus. And Catherine's decided opinions and her tendency to share them with everyone had severely limited her choices as to a companion of her future life.

So, when her cousin from Texas, Lewis Burroughs, came to visit one summer and expressed a desire to have her as his wife, Catherine had little reason to refuse him. The idea of being a queen in a small pond, rather than a minnow in the ocean that was New York society, was undeniably attractive. Lewis was not repulsive—he was handsome enough, did not smoke, and he was moderate in his other vices. So with little trepidation, Catherine Matlock became Cate Burroughs and relocated herself to Rosings Ranch in Rosings, Texas.

She soon found she had a knack for organization and a keener business mind than her husband. In all but name, she ran the ranch. At her urging, Lewis changed the name of the ranch to B&R, for "Burroughs and Rosings." As for the other duties of marriage, she engaged in them enough to bear a daughter named

Anne. Her doting father made Anne his and Cate's heir, and her mother, her obligation done, saw no reason to undergo the process of childbirth again.

How Lewis felt about her decision would never be known, for he was dead before Anne's fourth birthday. The official inquest said he was set upon by a band of Comanche while riding his land, but few in Rosings gave much credence to the commission. To this day, whispered speculation of what drove Lewis to self-murder would occasionally be overheard in town.

"Then it is settled," declared Catherine Burroughs, widow of Lewis Burroughs and owner of B&R Ranch and Rosings Bank. "Your men, William, will drive B&R cattle along with your Pemberley herd to Abilene at the same price per head as last year."

Darcy appraised his elder cousin critically. No sign of the attractive New York debutante remained. Instead, Catherine was a thin, weather-beaten, middle-aged woman, her silver hair swept back and done up on the top of her head. Her dress was a rich silk burgundy, but her face was as hard and lined as a fence post. She sat on the divan like a princess. Anne sat next to her, on the edge, seemingly ready to dash out of the room at a moment's notice.

"Yes," Darcy agreed, "as long as your herd's assembled and ready on the appointed date. Fitzwilliam here leaves no later than the last week in April, right behind the trail breakers."

The matron turned to Fitzwilliam, standing hat in hand next to Darcy's chair. "So early… why so early? You never left before the middle of May before."

"Miz Burroughs, we ain't the only outfit that's tryin' to sell our beef. Will and I figure that the early bird gets the worm, as they say, and we'll steal a march on the others by gettin' to Abilene first. Get a better price, I'm thinkin'."

"The weather will be wet." Mrs. Burroughs's expression showed she didn't enjoy discussing business with *employees*—they were to be told what to do, not question their betters.

"That's true, ma'am, but the grass'll be green, an' there'll be plenty o' water. As long as the herd don't get spooked by lightnin', we ought to be fine."

"Fitz knows what he's doing, Cate," Darcy assured her.

"Very well," Mrs. Burroughs ended the discussion.

Darcy had another subject to bring up, but it involved family. "Fitz, would you excuse us?" The Pemberley foreman picked up his hat and was escorted out of the room by Bartholomew, the Burroughs' longtime butler.

Once the door closed, Darcy turned to the two ladies seated before him. "Cate, I want to talk to you about George Whitehead."

"Again? That subject is closed, William."

"You don't know what kind of man he is."

She waved her hand in dismissal. "I know you two had some unpleasantness during the war, but that is all in the past. He has proven to be a worthwhile advisor, and I have the money in the bank to prove it. He has connections with the government in Austin, and that is worth its weight in gold in times like these."

"He talked you into selling that bottomland to those settlers. You know what's going to happen to them if we get a flood."

"It's been years since we had any problems. Besides, that land was useless—it was doing me no good. Why shouldn't I make a profit?"

"Money—is that all you care about?"

"What else is there? Where did this foolishness come from?"

Darcy glanced at Anne, who had been sitting quietly throughout the discussions. They both knew his arguments were useless with her mother. Plain, sweet Anne had, unfortunately, inherited most of her looks from her father. Sick for much of her childhood, she still bore the scars from her scare with the measles.

"Cate, I urge you to cut all ties with Whitehead. He can't be trusted. Look, he brought in that Denny character and his entire gang. They're running your ranch! I think you're making a big mistake…" He stopped, surprised at his cousin's reaction. "What do you find so funny?"

"You," Mrs. Burroughs chuckled. "You think I don't know about Denny and his so-called cowboys? My men keep a close eye on them, don't worry. When I have no more use for them, I'll run them off." She then leaned towards Darcy. "As for Whitehead, he's been far more useful than you can possibly imagine. Take my word for it. When everything is said and done, you'll see."

Darcy narrowed his eyes. "What are you up to?"

Mrs. Burroughs wore a very sly expression. "Never you mind." She looked at her daughter. "You know, I wouldn't need Whitehead's help if you would just do your duty and marry Anne."

"Mother!" "Cate!" The two cried together.

"I do not understand why you two are so opposed to marriage! You're second cousins—surely there's nothing unseemly about that! Besides, you would finally reunite Pemberley with the B&R."

Anne hid her face in her hands. "Mother, please."

Darcy gave Anne a sympathetic look before addressing his cousin by marriage. "Do we have to go through this again? I've told you—I love Anne like a sister, but I want no closer relation-ship with her, and she feels the same."

"But the land! You would control all of Long Branch County!"

"Great-Grandfather Darcy split up the land for a reason—Pemberley for Grandfather George and Rosings for Great-Aunt Elizabeth—and I've no desire to undo what he did."

"That has nothing to do with anything. That is not a reason to defy my wishes."

"And Anne's wishes? What about them?"

"Anne will do as she's told," Catherine demanded.

With a sob, Anne fled from the room. Darcy watched her go before rising to his feet, fury painted in broad strokes across his face.

"Why do you do that?" he demanded. "Why do you diminish her at every turn? She's your daughter, madam!"

"How dare you speak to me that way? Indeed, she's my daughter, and you've nothing to say about how things are done in my house! Until you marry Anne, she lives here, follows my rules, and you can keep your opinions to yourself!"

Darcy sat down, working to control his temper. He had no desire to wed Anne, but he did wish to broaden her rather limited horizons. He had to be at his convincing best. "Please pardon my outburst, Cate. You're right—this is your house. Whatever our disagreements may be, I'd like it if Anne kept a close relationship with Gaby."

"Her name is Gabrielle, William. I despise pet names."

Darcy seethed. "Be that as it may, I'd like my sister and Anne to spend more time together."

Catherine nodded. "That is a suitable activity."

Her smile was not lost on Darcy. *She's thinking, no doubt, that any closer attachment between Anne and Gaby can do nothing but further her goal of a union of Pemberley and the B&R. Poor, deluded fool! How could my cousin have married such a woman?*

"Thank you. Perhaps they can see each other after church some Sunday soon, if the weather moderates?"

February

The weather stayed cold and windy for most of January. It wasn't until the second week of February that the temperature rose. So it was that the Bennet women walked from the church that Sunday in a relatively balmy forty-five degrees towards the Bingley household. They would have accompanied Jane and Charles after services, but Mary delayed their departure, speaking at length to Reverend Tilney about the musical selections. Mrs. Bennet and the others were impatient to leave—Mr. Bennet having already ridden home to see to chores—but Beth saw what her mother did not, thankfully for Mary.

She sidled up to her sister during their short journey. "The reverend was *very* accommodating today, wasn't he?" she teased.

It was not the air that caused her sister to blush. "I… I don't know what you mean," Mary stammered.

"Don't worry," her sister whispered in her ear. "I won't let Mother know."

Mary pretended ignorance. "Know what?"

Beth gave Mary a condescending look. "Mary, you can't fool me. I know you like… *someone.*" If anything, Mary blushed brighter. With amusement, Beth added, "And I think he might like you, too."

"Yeah," Kathy agreed, who had been listening in.

Mary began coughing, which turned Mrs. Bennet's attention from her discussion with Lily over the dresses favored by the other members of the congregation. She fussed over her middle daughter, claiming that she had certainly caught a cold, while Beth and Kathy shared a giggle.

"What's so funny?" Lily demanded.

"Nothing," Beth managed before giggling again.

Lily pouted. "No one tells me anything."

"That's because you're the baby, and you don't understand such things," Kathy opined.

"I do too!" the youngest Bennet cried.

"What is this?" Mrs. Bennet turned from Mary. "What are you arguing about?"

Kathy crossed her arms. "Lily is being nosy again."

Lily was indignant. "Am not! You're keeping secrets from me again. It's not fair!"

"Now, Lily…" Beth tried to placate her, but was interrupted.

"It isn't. But just you wait. One day, I'll have a secret to keep from all of you. The biggest secret in the world! And I won't tell any of you a thing!"

Mrs. Bennet hushed her daughter. "Stop it, all of you! Do you have no compassion for my nerves?"

"Oh! You always take her side!" cried Kathy.

In this manner the five women continued to their destination, earning not a few curious stares from the townspeople they passed along the way, only ceasing the complaining once Mrs. Bennet reached the Bingleys' small porch. The door was opened within moments of her knock by Dr. Bingley, as if his mother-in-law's action was anticipated.

The Bennet ladies entered the small sitting room, used

during the day as a waiting room for patients, only to find it was already occupied. Beth, for one, was so stunned by the identities of the visitors she cried out.

"Mr. Darcy?"

Indeed, the owner of Pemberley Ranch was standing by the settee, a cup of coffee perilously balanced in one large hand, next to two fashionably dressed women. Beth recognized them as Miss Gaby Darcy and Miss Anne Burroughs. Jane was in a chair next to them, obviously in the middle of an interrupted conversation, and all wore expressions of astonishment at Beth's outburst.

Charles stepped forward. "I believe y'all know Mr. Darcy, Miss Darcy, and Miss Burroughs. We were pleasantly surprised when they dropped by right after we got home."

The Bennet ladies confirmed that they had met the Darcys but said they were not acquainted with Miss Burroughs, though they had often seen her in church. The introductions were made, Miss Burroughs lingering with Beth and Mary, while Jane and Gaby entertained the others. Beth could see Lily and Kathy openly staring at the Darcys as if they were creatures on display. For the first time, she regretted George Whitehead apprising them of the Darcys' colorful background.

"I understand from your sister that you play, Miss Beth, and that you and your sisters sing very well," Anne managed to say, keeping her eyes lowered.

Beth laughed. "Not very well—my sister is obviously having fun at my expense." She noticed Mary's hurt look and quickly added, "But Mary here is the musician of the family." *Now that Jane has left us—and a poor substitute she is,* she added to herself.

Mary puffed up, pleased at the compliment. "I would love to hear you play, Miss Burroughs."

"Me?" the girl squeaked. "Oh, no, Miss Mary, I don't play!" Anne's face turned from white to red, and the other two ladies were mortified.

It was Darcy who came to her rescue. "It's true Anne doesn't play, but my sister does, and the two of them have sung some very pretty duets in their time." If anything, the compliment seemed to embarrass Anne even more.

The four of them stood about in an awkward silence, none knowing what to say next. Beth could not stop glancing at Darcy's dark good looks. Finally, Darcy broke the impasse.

"It seems we've intruded on a family get-together, Charles. We'll take our leave."

Despite Mrs. Bennet's halfhearted protests, and Jane's sincere ones, the three outsiders made their goodbyes and moved towards the door. Just as Charles was opening it, Darcy turned to Beth.

"Ah, Miss Beth, I almost forgot the message I wanted to give you the next time we met."

"Oh?" Beth's eyebrow rose, expecting a renewal of her banishment from Pemberley.

"I've let my riders know that you have permission to ride across Pemberley if you take a fancy to cross the Long Branch again."

The unexpected civility shocked the girl. "Oh! I… I thank you, Mr. Darcy. That's kind of you."

He shrugged. "You won't be a bother to anyone, so it's quite all right. I've described your horse to my men, so they'll keep an eye out for you, to make sure you don't get into any trouble." A strange expression lit his face. "I'm sure your horse—Turner, isn't it? Turner is itching to run all over creation after the winter we've had."

The condescension in the first part of his reply destroyed whatever pleasure she felt at his kindness, but the second part puzzled her. Why would *he* care about her horse? "Yes, you're right," she said. "Turner is nothing if not spirited."

Darcy almost grinned, as if he knew a secret. "Yes, I would suppose so—a paint named Turner."

Beth had a sinking feeling in her stomach. "What?"

"Turner. Named after J.M.W. Turner[2], the British landscape artist, right?"

Beth's jaw dropped as Lily laughed. "Ha, ha, ha! Someone finally got your silly joke, Beth! You should see your face!"

An amused Darcy escorted his charges out the door with a parting shot. "Interesting name. A rather controversial choice for a young lady, given that he died in his mistress's house, wouldn't you say?" Without waiting for a response, he was out the door.

Beth stared at the closed door while Mrs. Bennet demanded who Beth knew that was keeping mistresses, and Kathy and Lily giggled in each other's arms. Jane walked over and put her arm around her sister.

"Have you finally met your match, Beth? Mr. Darcy's very clever."

"Insufferable, you mean!" Beth proclaimed. She turned to the room, determined to think of his tall form no more.

---

2 Joseph Mallord William Turner (23 April 1775–19 December 1851) was an English Romantic landscape painter, watercolorist, and printmaker, whose style can be said to have laid the foundation for Impressionism. Although Turner was considered a controversial figure in his day, he is now regarded as the artist who elevated landscape painting to an eminence rivaling history painting.

Chapter 4

March

THE SHORT PERIOD BETWEEN winter and summer in Central
Texas—called "spring" in many parts of the country—finally
arrived in Rosings, encouraging its denizens to leave their
houses for reasons other than chores and church. Wednesday
was the traditional shopping day for the Bennets, both in
Meryton and Rosings. Fanny Bennet was never one to pass
up the opportunity to see and be seen, gossip and be gos-
siped about, and inquire in intimate detail about any new
item available for sale in any shop without the least intention of purchasing any of them. Since she was never a great
reader, it was her favorite diversion besides visiting with her
married daughter.

Mrs. Bennet may have wished for all the finery in the world,
but she was as tight as any good farm wife. Her mother had
been a spendthrift, and after living hand-to-mouth until her
marriage, Fanny Gardiner swore *she* would never have to worry
for money again, and she made sure of that when considering
a potential husband. Tom Bennet had proved to be not only a

caring companion but also a dutiful provider, and she trusted him utterly with their finances. She managed to live within her allowance, praying that Tom's promises of a better life would come true someday.

However, this Wednesday was different, as it was left to Beth and Mary to shop for the week's provisions. Mrs. Bennet had come down with a cold and taken to her bed at her son-in-law's instruction. The presence of Kathy and Lily was required to wash the clothes and wait upon their mother. Beth and Mary took the wagon to the Bingleys' to collect their sister before continuing into town.

Beth had to admit to herself that things in Texas weren't as bad as she'd feared. It was a beautiful place. The summers could be unbearably hot, but after a lifetime of Ohio winters, she could manage with a little sweating if that meant she didn't have to walk through knee-high snowdrifts. The wide, open plains enchanted her. She never dreamed the sky could be so wide or the land so vast. She loved to point Turner in whatever direction beckoned and just run wild.

As for adjusting to the locals, that took longer. The populace was far more diverse than Beth had ever experienced. She had never before met a slave, much less someone from Mexico. It was both exhilarating and frightening. She found the townspeople to be closed and suspicious—not open and friendly to her as in Meryton. Only Reverend Tilney was unreserved from the beginning. The Bennets' association with George Whitehead seemed to garner only deference, not amity. But once Beth had made friends with Charlotte Lucas, the town opened up a bit more for her. Beth sometimes felt that by befriending the sheriff's daughter, she had passed some test, and the strange, nagging feeling of unsettledness whenever she met with the townsfolk faded.

Beth and Mary were soon at the Bingleys, and once Jane had climbed onboard, Mary suggested that they go by the rectory. "Perhaps Reverend Tilney needs our assistance," she mentioned with what she thought was a straight face. Beth nearly laughed out loud.

Jane was all that was sweet and good, but she was not as quick as Beth. "Assistance? With what? Is something wrong? Is he unwell?"

Mary blushed. "No, no! I... I just thought as he has no sister or... wife, that he may need our help in, well, umm... shopping for provisions... or something." Beth could no longer contain her mirth, causing a mortified Mary to stutter a disavowal of her sug-gestion. Jane caught on and, reaching out to take the red-faced girl's hand in hers, declared Mary's intention to be a noble one and that the three of them should proceed at once to the church.

It turned out that the preacher was not otherwise occupied and was very grateful for the Bennets' offer to help him restock his larder. As the church was in the center of town, the wagon was left there, and the small party strolled to Zimmerman's General Store.

Carl Zimmerman was the son of German immigrants whose family had moved to Rosings when he was a child. He inherited the family store before the war after traveling back east to meet, marry, and bring back Helga, his wife by arranged marriage. As gregarious as he was short, the popular storekeeper had served as the mayor of Rosings for almost ten years. It was mainly a ceremonious position; his only power had been the Mayor's Court, and that had been taken away by the occupation government. All judicial authority in Texas was now wielded by appointees, who were invariably loyal to the governor. In Long Branch County, Texas native Judge Alton Phillips was still in office only because of an advantageous switching of his political affiliation to the Republican Party.

So, except for the speech given each year on the Second of March—Texas Independence Day, the date the Republic of Texas declared its break from Santa Anna's Mexico—Mayor Zimmerman was essentially a shopkeeper.

The ladies and gentleman entered the store only to have their ears assaulted by strong words uttered loudly. All attention was called to the long counter that bisected the room where the slight storeowner was berating a black woman wearing a light-colored dress with a blue apron, a wide-brimmed straw hat on her head.

"Now, I told you not to come in by the front door!" Zimmerman's face was flushed with anger as he shook a finger in the woman's face. "If you want something, come by the back door. The back door!" he emphasized by pointing with that finger.

"I'm sorry. I won't do it again," the woman mumbled.

"I tell you and I tell you, but you won't listen! You understand English, eh? Understand this, Mrs. Washington—front door for whites only!"

Beth was aghast and mortified at the woman's treatment. Allowing her eyes to escape the distressing scene, she noted a couple in a corner of the store by the front window. She was startled to see it was Mr. and Miss Darcy, both wearing disgusted expressions.

"But," the woman addressed as Mrs. Washington stuttered, "I seen Mrs. Gomez come in here—"

"Are you back-talking me, woman?" Zimmerman demanded. "Go to the back door! If you don't like that, maybe I don't sell you anything, eh?"

"No, no! I need my order... got money. I... I'll go—around back, okay?"

Just then, Tilney stepped forward. "Here, that's enough of that!" He walked up to the pair.

Zimmerman looked up. "Eh? Reverend Tilney, what do you want?"

He ignored the shopkeeper and addressed the woman. "Mrs. Washington, how do you do?"

"Fine, Reverend Tilney, just fine."

Zimmerman broke in. "I was just telling her that she has to go 'round back, Reverend."

Mary could stand for no more. "And why is that?"

Before Zimmerman could respond to her, Tilney broke in. "Miss Mary! We must remember this is Mr. Zimmerman's store, and as such, he makes the rules." He threw a glare at the shop owner before turning to Mrs. Washington. "May I escort you around to the back, madam?"

The humiliated woman waved him off. "Oh, no, Reverend Tilney, I can find my own way. Don't bother yourself."

Tilney smiled. "Very well. I'll be expecting you at church this Sunday. We haven't seen y'all there yet."

Mrs. Washington smiled. "Thank you kindly for the invite, but I don't want to intrude."

"All are welcomed in God's house."

She thought for a moment. "Then we'll be there. Thank you again." With as much dignity as she could muster, she walked out of the store.

Zimmerman was troubled. "Preacher, you're inviting slaves to services?"

Tilney turned to him. "Are you questioning the way I run the church?"

"I *am* on the board committee," Zimmerman's brows dipped.

Just then, Darcy approached the men. "Excuse me, but I was wondering if my order was ready?" Darcy wore a completely blank expression, as if the confrontation had not occurred.

Zimmerman was all that was amiable to Rosings's most affluent customer. "Yes, sir, Mr. Darcy. Just step this way." Zimmerman scampered behind the counter and walked quickly to the far end. Darcy turned to follow, begging the others' pardon once more.

"Well," said Beth under her breath, "he's certainly the lord and master 'round here!"

Tilney cocked one eyebrow. "He was here before us, Miss Beth. We can wait our turn."

Mary was about to have her share of the conversation, but she was caught by the intense look on Mr. Zimmerman's face as Darcy spoke to him. The tone was far too low for her to hear, but the effect was instantaneous. The shopkeeper almost ran to the back door, his face, if anything, redder than before.

"My mistake," Darcy drawled to his sister, "apparently, we have a customer before us."

The altercation had put all of them off their proposed shopping expedition. Beth and the others gathered on the front porch, taking in the town for several minutes. The front door opened, and Miss Darcy walked out followed by her brother, his arms filled with packages.

"Gaby, you wait here while I put these in the wagon," Darcy advised. Tilney and Jane immediately walked over to keep her company while her brother finished his task, the Bennet sisters following in their wake.

"How do you do today, Miss Gaby?" Jane said. The girl exchanged greetings with everyone before discussing the weather until Darcy rejoined them.

Mary was waiting for this opportunity. "Miss Darcy! I was talking to Reverend Tilney earlier and expressed the desire to improve the church choir."

"That sounds like a very noble undertaking, Miss Mary," the girl said.

"Perhaps you would be interested in joining us?"

Gaby Darcy blushed. "Oh! Oh, I… I'm sorry, but I can't. I'm not a member of the church."

"Uhh, Mary—" Tilney began, but the girl overrode him.

"Well, that's easily taken care of. If your brother is too busy to bring you to services, perhaps I can speak to my father. It would be no trouble for us to take you."

"Mary!" Tilney hissed. Darcy began to frown.

Mary continued as if Tilney said nothing and turned to the rancher. "But you should go, Mr. Darcy! You need to be in church. All the money in the world won't do you a bit of good in the afterlife if you ignore God's words. Remember, the Good Book says, 'It is easier for a camel to go through the eye of a needle than for a rich man to enter into the kingdom of heaven.'"

Beth noticed Miss Gaby blanch, as Darcy's face grew very red. *Heavens, the man is furious!* However, when Darcy spoke, it was with deceptive calmness.

"Thank you for the warning, Miss Bennet. Rest assured that both my sister and I take Our Savior's words very seriously and do well to remember them in church every Sunday. Come along, Gaby." The Darcys walked away towards their carriage.

"Church?" Mary looked at Tilney, who held his hand over his eyes. "But… but they don't—"

Jane took Mary by the arm. "That's enough. You don't know what you're saying. The Darcys attend church every Sunday."

Even Beth was bewildered. "Where?"

Tilney lowered his hand. "At the mission across the river. The Darcys are Catholic."

Now it was Beth's turn to go pale, for just then the Darcy carriage rolled by, Darcy stone-faced while an unhappy Miss Darcy held a handkerchief in her lap.

Mary grasped Tilney by the arm and cried, "Catholics! Oh, my! Reverend Goldring back in Meryton said that Catholics weren't really Christians and that it's our duty to save their souls."

The pair in the carriage started—Mary's voice had carried over the sound of the wheels—and the preacher lost his temper.

"Miss Mary, that's foolish talk!" Mary bit back a sob as Tilney fought to control his annoyance and wait until the Darcys were out of earshot. "Miss Mary, religious study is a wonderful thing. It's been my honor and pleasure to read and ponder the words given to us by Our Maker. But, before you quote scripture again, I would suggest you consider this passage: 'Let he who is without sin cast the first stone.'"

If Tilney intended his statement to be a gentle correction, the result was not as he planned. Mary's face screwed up, and she threw herself bawling into Jane's arms. The good reverend looked helplessly at Jane and Beth.

It was Jane who came to the rescue. "I believe we all could use a bit of tea, don't you think? Shall we repair back to the house?"

Tilney seized upon the proposal. "Excellent idea, Mrs. Bingley. But may I suggest that the parsonage is closer? I would be happy to have *all* of you as my guests." He gave Mary a most particular glance.

It served. Drying her eyes, Mary nodded and the party walked back to the church.

Darcy was working in his study the following evening when there was a knock on the door. Looking up, he saw the butler, Reynaldo, standing at the threshold.

"Begging your pardon, *señor.* Reverend Tilney is here to see you."

Blinking back his surprise, Darcy bade him to bring in the minister. A moment later, Henry Tilney stood in front of the desk, hat in hand.

"Mr. Darcy, I've come to apologize for what happened yesterday."

Darcy stood and turned to Reynaldo. "Where is Miss Darcy?"

"I saw her going towards the parlor, *señor,* to practice her music."

He turned to Tilney. "Reverend, I thank you for coming. As my sister was involved in yesterday's incident, I think she should be part of this conversation, don't you?" Darcy couched his demand as a suggestion, but Tilney wasn't deceived.

"I agree. I'd be happy to speak to Miss Darcy."

Darcy nodded, and the three went directly to the parlor. Gaby was looking through some music sheets when the group entered the room.

"Gaby," her brother said with the gentleness he reserved for her, "Mr. Tilney wants to talk to us."

Brother and sister assembled on a couch, dismissed Reynaldo, and waited for Tilney to begin. Resolutely refusing a chair, he stood before them, hands behind his back, and expressed his regret for the mortification the two had undoubtedly suffered.

"I can't speak for what the Bennets' minister back in Ohio preached," he continued, "but if he was anything like my predecessor in Rosings, I must tell you I don't agree with it. I don't hold with the mistrust and hostility that some in my denomination have expressed about Catholics. The Bennets speak out of ignorance. It is unintentional but still hurtful. Miss Mary in particular means well, but it was wrong of her to say what she did. If I can, I mean to heal the division between our churches. I have briefly explained this to the Bennet ladies and plan to visit with them again to discuss this subject soon."

Darcy stood and extended his hand. "Well said, Reverend. Thank you very much." Gaby nodded, too embarrassed to say a word, but her expression was less strained than when they had walked in.

Tilney took his hand with a smile. "We're all on a path to God, and we both pray to Our Lord and Savior, Jesus Christ. That's good enough for me, Mr. Darcy."

"I'd be pleased if you would call me Will and my sister, Gaby."

"Then I'll do that. My name's Henry."

"Have you met Father Joseph, Henry?" Gaby asked. Told he had not yet had the pleasure, she turned to her brother. "Can we plan a dinner when we can invite both?"

Assured that was a capital idea, Darcy asked Tinley to stay for supper. It took some begging from Gaby, but the preacher soon relented, and the girl took to the piano to entertain the gentlemen before the meal. Darcy was always happy to abandon his paperwork for the joy of hearing his sister perform, and he and Tilney took their seats to listen to the impromptu concert. Gaby started with a short, light piece that delighted her audience before starting a slower, more moody composition.

Tilney leaned over to Darcy. "She's very good."

"Thank you. My father was lucky enough to hire Mrs. Annesley to be Gaby's tutor and companion several years ago. She and Gaby spend several hours a day practicing."

"I can tell. Her time is well spent." Tilney listened for a moment. "I'm sorry I never got to meet your father. I hear he was a good man, well-respected by everyone."

Sadness overcame Darcy's features, causing the minister to regret bringing up the subject. "Yes, he died only a little while after you came to town."

"I was new and had no way of making his acquaintance, as he was sick at the time."

"Yes." Darcy sat quietly, trying not to think about those terrible days gone by, allowing the conversation to wilt in the face of Gaby's music before changing the subject. "How well do you know the Bennets?"

Tilney was glad to put the gloomy subject behind them. "As well as any of my congregation. Very faithful attendees for services. Friendly enough and not too overbearing in their manners. Unusual for Yankees."

Darcy grinned, knowing he was referring to Whitehead. "Yes."

"I find Mr. Bennet well-read for a farmer. Mrs. Bennet is very… loquacious, but very kind as well. Mary Bennet is surprisingly well versed in theology for a woman. Of course, I know many ladies who know their scripture backwards and forwards, but Mary has read some other religious texts, too. I'd say she's done more in that sphere than I did before entering seminary. Extraordinary girl…" He trailed off, looking into the air.

Darcy raised an eyebrow at Tilney. "Reading isn't always understanding, Henry."

Tilney colored. "I can't disagree with you. Further study on her part would not be a bad thing—not just learning the passages but the meaning behind them, too. We must all be on our guard lest we fall into cant." He smiled. "Lily Bennet is young and lively, and her youth must be her excuse for her more exuberant antics. Kathy Bennet reminds me a little of Mrs. Bingley—in her looks, I mean. In spirit she's more like her sister, Beth."

"Really?" Darcy turned his head towards Gaby. "I've met them both but saw no similarity."

"True, Kathy is not the great lover of the outdoors that her sister is, but both have taken after their father in wit and intelligence—Beth more so. Very well read, Beth's both clever and a sharp judge of character. Don't let that smile fool you. Beth Bennet doesn't suffer fools gladly."

"You make her sound judgmental."

"I wouldn't say that. She's very kind to everyone, especially the less fortunate. She'd rather laugh at a fool than berate them unless a friend is hurt. Then, she's very quick to their defense. She's very loyal to family and friends, like all her sisters."

"You know," Tilney said thoughtfully, "the reason for the unfortunate incident today was Mary's desire to improve our church choir. All the Bennet girls sing; Mrs. Bingley and Mary play, and they hoped to enlist your sister and cousin. But I have another idea. Would you like to hear it?"

"By all means."

"Instead of a church choir, what about a ladies musical appreciation society? Would your relations be interested in that?"

Darcy sat back as he thought, letting Gaby's music flow over him. He had wanted both Gaby and Anne to make more acquaintances in town, but he hadn't thought of bringing them *there*; he was more of a mind to have their interactions under his watchful eye at Pemberley.

Tilney seemed to anticipate Darcy's concerns. "I think my church would be an excellent place for the ladies to gather. We have a fine piano, and the caretaker and I are always around. They'll be well looked after."

Especially Miss Mary, Darcy thought. He had not missed Tilney's expression when he spoke of her. So, town was safe, as long as the meetings of this society were held at the Rosings Baptist Church. The Darcys were secure enough in their faith not to have any issues over entering another denomination's building—as long as it wasn't during services.

The question remained whether the Bennets were proper acquaintances for Anne and Gaby. They were Yankees, true, but not as obnoxious as others they had met. Jane Bingley proved to be kind; indeed, she was unquestionably a superior person, but what of the rest of them? Tilney pledged to talk to them about Miss Mary's unfortunate statement, but would the girls be kind to Darcy's relations? Was the apparent shallowness of Lily adequately compensated by the seeming depth of Beth? Darcy could see her deep, remarkable eyes, penetrating and expressive. There was something *there*—he knew not what, except he was drawn to find out.

As Gaby finished the sonata, Darcy turned to Tilney. "I'll think about it, Henry."

"Oh, there's some news from town," Tilney added. "I just heard that the Parkers, one of the families that bought land in the new settlement, are leaving the county."

"What? My cousin only started selling that land two years ago. Why are they leaving?"

"Rosings Bank foreclosed on them."

Darcy sat back, an unreadable expression on his face. "Cate was always hard-nosed when it came to business, but this seems a bit rash. Foreclosed, you say?" Darcy shook his head. "It happens. Never liked that land—I guess it was only a matter of time. Where are the Parkers headed?"

"Farther west—New Mexico, I hear."

Just then, Mrs. Reynolds came to the door. "Mr. Will, Miss Gaby, sir, supper's on."

The trio began to follow the cook to the dining room when the sight of the black woman recalled something else to Tilney's mind. "By the way, Will, yesterday at the store—can you tell me what you said to Zimmerman? He looked like you were about to set the dogs upon him."

Darcy tried to wear an unconcerned expression. "Oh, that. I just told the old coot that if he continued to treat cash-paying customers with disrespect, perhaps there was room in town for another general store."

Henry Tilney was not the only person making an evening visit. Responding to a knock on the door, Charlotte Lucas opened it to see a man with a black hat in one hand.

"Evenin', Miss Lucas."

"Good evening, Mr. Fitzwilliam." The air had cooled since

sundown, and Charlotte pulled her wrap about her shoulders. "What can I do for you? The sheriff's still at the jail."

Fitz ran a hand nervously through his hair. "Yeah, well... I ain't come to see the sheriff, miss. I come to talk to you."

Charlotte's eyes grew wide. "Me? Whatever for?"

Fitz looked out into the growing dusk, gathering his thoughts, the light from the oil-lamp sidelights framing the door, glistening on his hatband. "Well, you see, I'm leavin' on a cattle drive to Kansas in about a month. Drivin' Mr. Darcy's and Miz Burroughs's cattle to market. I ought to be gone for a few months."

Charlotte stepped onto the porch. "Yes, I heard that y'all were leaving early."

Fitz nodded. "Well... it's become a bit of a tradition for me to buy somethin' for Miss Darcy after I get to Abilene. Nothin' big, you understand, just a trinket or two for remembrance." He smiled as he fidgeted with his hat. "She's like another little sister to me, and it pleases her no end."

"That's very nice."

Fitz studied his boots. "Yeah, well... I was thinkin'... maybe I could... uh..."

Charlotte tilted her head, not sure what he was talking about. "Yes?"

He peeked shyly at her. "Bring back somethin' for you."

Her jaw dropped. "Me?" she whispered.

In the limited light, Fitz's expression was hardly visible, but the stammer in his voice gave away his lack of composure. "Uh, yeah. There ain't much pretty things 'round here for a lady. I've been thinkin', and seeing as you got no brothers to buy you stuff like that at the end of a drive, I thought that maybe... I could."

Charlotte Lucas was the only daughter of a widowed sheriff. That alone put off most would-be suitors. On top of the situation at home, Charlotte was a woman who would be considered handsome by only her most charitable acquaintances and plain by the world in general. She had never had an admirer, much less a sweetheart, and at twenty-five, she expected nothing more than being the town spinster, taking care of her father in his dotage.

She wasn't blind or uninterested in the male sex. Occasionally, Charlotte would allow herself to dream of a life with a kind and handsome man with children at her feet, if only she looked more like Jane or Beth. If asked, of the men in town, she liked Richard Fitzwilliam. The good-looking cowboy always had a kind word for her since he came to town. He had been one of the fixtures in her dreams. But dreams never came true for the likes of Charlotte Lucas.

Therefore, it was no wonder that Fitz's astonishing words sent a shock through her. She grew hot and cold at the same time. Unconsciously, she pulled her wrap more tightly about her. "What kind of... pretty things?"

Fitz looked everywhere but at her. "Oh, I don't know. Things you can't get 'round here, I suppose. Umm... a piece of lace or a figurine. Maybe some o' that fancy perfume that smells of flowers." He looked up. "Decent things—I wouldn't buy you anything not decent. That wouldn't be right."

Charlotte bit her lip. "No, of course not."

The corner of his lip turned up. "Have to be pretty, though."

Her mouth was dry. "Why?"

"Pretty girls need pretty things."

Silence hung between them. "You think I'm pretty?"

Fitz's eyes grew dark as he licked his lips. Time seemed to

stand still as she awaited his response. He took a half step closer, his smile growing a bit.

Another voice called out from the darkness. "Charlotte, who are you talking to? Oh—Fitzwilliam. What can I do for you?"

The two jumped away from each other as Sheriff Lucas reached the porch, Charlotte unable to hide her flushed expression. The sheriff, scowling, eyed his daughter closely.

"Get yourself inside, girl."

"Paw, we weren't doing anything," Charlotte protested. "Fitz was just visiting."

"I said, get inside," Lucas growled. "We'll talk later."

Embarrassed, Charlotte nodded at Fitz. "Good night," she managed before fleeing inside. Sheriff Lucas then turned to the cowhand.

"Unless you've got business with me, you best be goin'," Lucas said coldly.

Fitz straightened up in indignation. "Sheriff, we weren't doin' anything wrong. I just came by to call on Miss Charlotte, respectful like."

"Yeah, when I wasn't at home."

"That wasn't my intention. I'd be glad to come by anytime you like. I wouldn't do anything to hurt Miss Charlotte's reputation."

Lucas got between Fitz and his door, his hands on his hips. "What are your intentions?"

Fitz flushed. "I'm an honorable man; you know that."

Lucas was resolute. "I know you're a hired hand at Pemberley."

"Surely, you've got nothin' against Darcy?" Lucas just stared at him and realization hit the ranch foreman. "Oh, it's me. What's the matter, Lucas, don't think I'm worthy o' courtin' your daughter?"

Lucas stared him right in the eye. "Charlotte's my only kin—she's all I got. She deserves everything good in the world. She deserves a man who can provide for her better than me, you understand?"

"So, I ain't good enough?" Fitz spit out between gritted teeth.

"No, you ain't."

Fitz flinched, but he never broke eye contact with Lucas. "Well, you made your sentiments clear."

Lucas nodded. "Nothin' personal, Fitz. I gotta do what's best."

Fitz didn't respond until he replaced his hat and climbed aboard Jeb Stuart. He then turned to the sheriff. "I've said my piece, an' I've taken account o' your opinion. Only one thing remains."

"And what's that?" Lucas demanded.

"Hearin' Miss Charlotte's opinion o' the matter. That's the only one that counts in my book. Be seein' you." Fitz pulled Jeb Stuart's head about and set off at a trot towards the Long Branch Bridge and Pemberley.

"You're wastin' your time, Fitzwilliam!" Lucas shook his fist as he walked into the street. "Mine is the word she'll listen to. Don't come around here! You hear me?" He stood in the middle of the road in the dark, continuing to yell at the retreating figure.

Any passerby would question whether the man was trying to convince the rider or himself.

Chapter 5

April

EARLY ON A BRIGHT, sunny spring morning, Will Darcy walked up to a tall, brown horse and reached up to shake the rider's hand.

"Take care, Fitz! See you in June!" Gaby called out from the veranda.

Fitz tipped his hat to Miss Darcy, his silver band flashing in the sun. He put the spur to Jeb Stuart, crying, "All right—let's move 'em out!"

The Pemberley riders began to shout, swinging their coiled lariats about their heads as they rode around the vast herd of cattle. Hundreds of longhorns moved ponderously to the north-northwest, a huge cloud of dust rising in their wake. The drovers dashed about watching for stragglers; the cook in the chuck wagon and the wrangler with the *remuda*, or spare horses, brought up the rear. The mass moved at a steady pace towards the river. It wasn't long before the head of the drive reached Thompson Crossing.

By then, Darcy on Caesar had overtaken the herd, and he

and Fitz splashed across the river to Bennet Farm. They rode up to the farmhouse's porch, where a group of people awaited them.

"Mornin', ladies, Mr. Bennet." Darcy tipped his hat. "Are your cattle ready?"

"Yep, they're waiting in the corral," Bennet replied as he walked towards it, Hill standing by the gate. "Twenty-five head. You won't lose them, will you, Mr. Fitzwilliam?"

"I'll do my best to get 'em all to Abilene, Mr. Bennet," Fitz said with a grin.

"You'll get paid the same for what gets there just like the rest of us, Mr. Bennet—less the per head fee—just like we agreed. We won't cheat you." Darcy's face was far more relaxed than his words. He had not taken offense at Bennet's comment; he was just reciting their deal.

Bennet looked up at Darcy. "If I thought you would, Mr. Darcy, I wouldn't have your people drive my cattle."

Darcy nodded, pleased that they understood each other. "Wait until we get the rest of the herd across the river before you open the gate. My boys will take it from there." Fitz rode back to the crossing while Darcy looked towards the northeast. "Fitz will take them across the B&R, pick up their cattle and some extra hands, then cross Rosings Creek. Ought to make ten miles today and hook up with the Chisholm Trail by tomorrow."

The men watched the enormous herd pass south of the homestead after crossing the Long Branch. Hill waited until a couple of riders approached before opening the corral gate. The cowpokes expertly guided their charges towards the mass of walking beef.

Bennet was impressed. "Smartly done, Mr. Darcy."

Darcy wore an easy smile. "Thank you; they're good men. You wouldn't think this is Fitz's sixth drive, would you? He's a natural—that's why he's my foreman."

"You don't go with them?"

Darcy's look darkened. "No, not since—" he caught himself. "I don't do that anymore."

Bennet nodded. "I understand—someone's got to look out for your place."

Darcy just grunted and turned Caesar around. His eye naturally fell on the porch and the lovely brown-haired girl in dungarees. She stood next to her mother, arms crossed over her chest, unintentionally pushing her breasts out and filling her shirt. Darcy caught himself staring at her chest and turned away, missing the suspicious glare on the girl's face. She did not see the admiration in Darcy's face, but her father did.

Mrs. Bennet was oblivious. "Will you stay for breakfast, Mr. Darcy?"

Darcy forced himself into impassivity. "Thank you kindly, Miz Bennet, but my sister's waiting for me, and I'd best be getting back."

"Another time, then?"

Darcy, not trusting his voice, simply nodded at the woman before taking his leave of Mr. Bennet, who watched him ride off with a thoughtful expression.

The light from the oil lamps filled George Whitehead's office with a yellow glow. Whitehead was trying to get some paperwork done at his desk, but it was hard to concentrate while Denny paced in the middle of the room. Sally Younge, sitting on a couch across the room, shrugged her shoulders at Pyke, who was leaning against the far wall.

"Denny," Whitehead sighed, "will you stop that confounded walking back and forth and sit down? It's distracting."

"I just don't git it, Whitehead," Denny grumbled while he continued to move about the room like a caged animal. "Why don't we just move in an' get rid o' Darcy now?"

"Have patience. We'll take care of Mr. Darcy when the time's right."

"But Fitzwilliam an' half the Pemberley hands are gone to Kansas. He ain't got nobody there! We can take 'em easy—just ride up, an'…" He whipped out his Colt and pantomimed shooting it. "Everything's over."

Whitehead sighed and put down his pen. "And then what? Assuming we got past the *other* half of Darcy's men—you don't think he's undefended, do you? But let's say for argument's sake we were successful in storming Pemberley. What do you think would happen then? Governor Davis might be an Abolitionist Republican, but he can't ignore the murder of Long Branch County's most prominent citizen. He'd have the U.S. Cavalry or his new State Police on us in no time. And then where would we be? How can we hold on to Pemberley or the B&R with soldiers poking in to everything?" Whitehead laughed. "'Everything's over'? Yes, by God, everything *would* be over—for *us*!"

"Then what am I supposed to do?"

"Do what you've been doing, Denny! For God's sake, haven't you paid attention to anything I've said in the past three months? Everything is coming to fruition—better than we originally hoped!" He stood up, crossed over to the table near Pyke, and poured four drinks. He carried two and handed one to

Sally, while Pyke helped himself. "Your men are well positioned at the B&R. Burroughs doesn't even realize she's lost control of her own ranch." He handed a drink to Denny. "We already have half the county in our hands. Once this latest deal goes through, we'll control the rest—including Pemberley—without firing a shot!"

Denny took a big swallow of his whiskey. "Controllin' ain't ownin', Whitehead."

"True." Whitehead returned for his own glass. "But once we have everything in place—and all the money—then, well… if Will Darcy fell afoul of some desperados some evening, it will be up to *Sheriff Denny* to look into it, the man appointed by *Mayor Whitehead*. Understand?"

Denny threw back the rest of his drink. "Yeah, yeah, I've heard it all before. Big talk. But when? When is this all gonna happen? I'm tired o' waitin'!"

"Soon. By the end of this year, as long as you do as you're told."

"An' them settlers? They ain't all leavin' yet."

"They will when the foreclosures start in earnest. But we can't move too quickly, or we'll invite an investigation. Just trust me, Denny."

The gunman wiped his mouth with the back of his hand, a cold light in his eyes. "I've been trustin' you. But my boys are gettin' restless. You better come through, an' soon."

"I will."

"If'n you've been playin' me—"

"Now, that would be incredibly stupid on my part, wouldn't it? I need you, Denny—you're my partner." Whitehead grinned. "Why don't you go over to the saloon and get a drink? It's on me."

Denny hesitated, then nodded, and left the room. Whitehead exhaled the breath he had been holding and returned to his desk.

"He's dangerous, you know," Sally said as she got up from the couch.

"She's right, boss," added Pyke unnecessarily.

"Really? That's fucking observant of you two." Whitehead took a drink. "Pyke, go keep an eye on him."

Pyke quickly scrambled out of the room as Sally crossed behind Whitehead, running her hands through his hair. "I mean it. There's no tellin' when he's gonna turn on you, George. Where did you find him, anyway?"

Whitehead allowed Sally's ministrations to soothe his rage. "I met Denny in a barroom in Fort Worth, where I went to lick my wounds after Darcy ran me off Pemberley. Can you believe my bad luck? There was nothing for me back in Illinois, with my father dying during the war, and I had to go to this godforsaken place to make my fortune. I worked my ass off to get a political appointment from the Texas governor, and he sends me to the hometown of one of my prisoners from the war. I didn't realize he was the same Darcy till he came riding up as I was paying court to Miss Gabrielle after her father died. Damn, she was ripe for a seduction! Another week or so, and there would have been nothing Darcy could have done about it but call me brother.

"I knew I needed a new plan to get what I want, and I needed men to back me up. Don't get me wrong, my dear," he smiled. "My investment in your establishment has been profitable, but I have bigger plans than being the owner of a whorehouse.

"Denny and his boys seemed a good candidate, and a couple of drinks later he agreed to throw in with me. It didn't take much to get Mrs. Burroughs to agree to use him on the B&R."

"Was that the same time you met that Elton fella?"

"No, that was later. Hah, Fort Worth's been pretty good to me."

Sally frowned. "I don't trust Denny. Why don't you get rid of him?"

Whitehead shook his head, interrupting Sally's massage. "I can't; I need him for now—him and his gang. That's my army against Darcy. But don't worry. Kid Denny's days are numbered. He just doesn't know it yet." He took another drink. "He needs to get his mind off things. Go send him a girl—a young one, I think. He likes the young ones."

Sally dropped her hands. "George, no. Don't ask me that. He's an animal—he hurts the girls."

"Did I ask your opinion?" Whitehead abruptly stood up and grabbed one of her arms. "Don't forget, my dear, who is the senior in our partnership. If I hadn't come along and bailed you out when I first got to Rosings, you would have lost the saloon and been forced to trade your wares on the street." He sneered as he ran his free hand over her cheek. "And such lovely wares they are."

Sally was desperate to stay on Whitehead's good side. She drew close, pressing herself against him hungrily. She put her lips to his ear. "Don't be mad, sugar... Let's go to bed. I'll give you a good time, you'll see."

He laughed. "Still trying to set your brand on me? Don't fool yourself in believing that I'll choose you over Miss Darcy or Miss Burroughs. I haven't given up on that part of the plan. True, they lack your... expertise," he said as he groped her, "but thousands of acres of land makes up for much. I'll get one of them once this is all over, one way or the other—it doesn't matter which one."

"I know that, sugar, but you won't forget your Sally." She tried to kiss him, but he pushed her away instead.

"Do as I said—go get a girl for Denny." He sat down and continued, "I suppose it ought to be Camille. She should be able to handle him."

Sally nodded, relieved that he had suggested the one whore in her stable who seemed to enjoy the rougher types, rather than one of the more delicate girls. She turned to leave.

"And bring back a bottle with you—the good stuff. Not that rotgut shit you serve the cowpokes."

She turned, but Whitehead was already back to his ledgers. "Sure, George, sure. Nothin' but the best for you."

George Whitehead didn't answer as he continued to work.

May

Summer came on fast in Central Texas. It was the middle of May, and the temperature was already reaching the ninety-degree mark. It made riding the range hot work for man and beast, as Darcy was experiencing.

Caesar walked along the ridgeline, head hanging low, as a sweaty Darcy watched his cattle. With half the workforce riding north along the Chisholm Trail with the herd heading for market, Pemberley needed every hand it had to do the everyday chores. So it was that Darcy fell back into his old job of supervising the herd as he had done before and after the war, before his father's passing. The work was long and hot, but Darcy paid it no mind—it was what he was born to do. Besides, it gave a man the time to think.

Darcy's thoughts, as much as he tried to steer them elsewhere, kept coming back to the mystery that was Beth Bennet. She was a mystery to him, at least.

It was midday, and the sun beat unmercifully upon Caesar, so Darcy moved towards the river, intending to wash his face in the cool water. He found himself a bit upriver of Thompson Crossing, which brought Beth back into his thoughts. He worked his way south along the trees and brush that lined the riverbank, making his way to the ford.

He would later have no idea why he stopped well short of his goal. He would recall no particular sight or sound, just a feeling. He looked around, but only saw dense bushes near a large oak, its branches hanging low. Darcy dismounted, tying Caesar's reins to a branch, and began to make his way through the brush. He could make out the faint sounds of splashing, so he half-crouched, removing his hat in the shade and cover. A couple of feet from the bank, he sat back on his heels and carefully peered through the undergrowth.

It was a vision right out of his most intense dreams. A brown haired nymph was playing in the water just off the opposite bank. She was swimming in what best could be described as a small cove shielded on three sides by trees hanging right over the water. Darcy realized that he was in the one perfect spot to observe her; a few feet to the left or right and the leaves from the overhanging limbs would conceal the cove completely. It took him a moment to realize that the nymph was Beth Bennet.

The next thing Darcy knew he was sitting down in his little spot, an audience of one for the erotic show. He couldn't see all that much, as Beth's head was the only portion of her body above the water, her long hair trailing behind. But even ignoring the bundle lying carefully on the opposite bank, the river was clear enough for him to know, with an electric charge racing through his body, that the lovely lady was without a stitch of clothes on.

Decency, honor, a lifetime of training—all fled in an instant. Darcy could not tear his eyes from what he now realized was his one desire. Trembling, he breathed as slowly as he could, so as not to reveal himself. Darcy existed in a world of agony and ecstasy; he knew he should turn away, but could not. He wanted to jump in the river, swim over to her, and take her—love her— again and again. Instead, he sat as still as he could, sweat dripping down his face, his jeans becoming as tight as his breathing.

Beth dropped beneath the surface. At this, Darcy became alarmed, but before he could move a muscle, she came up again, only to lie back and float in the lazy current. Darcy froze; her breasts were exposed, their perky perfection kissed by the dappled sunlight through the canopy. Time stood still, all sound ceased, as Darcy was frozen by the siren song of desire, a real-life Calypso unknowingly taunting Odysseus. Lust and passion roared through his veins, and he felt he was going to explode.

By the time Beth dipped underwater again, Darcy found himself on one knee, beginning to move to the riverbank. He stopped himself and pulled back, just as she rose again, this time for good. She moved to the shallows and stood up, her back to him, water cascading from her shoulders and hair, running down her pale form, caressing her lovely buttocks, before dripping back into the river. Mesmerized, he watched her reach for a towel and had a glimpse of her dark treasure as she dried herself. Then she was gone—a bush hid her from view as she dressed herself.

Darcy sat back, panting as if he had run a great distance,

feeling both great discomfort and intense guilt. He knew that spying on the girl was wrong, terribly wrong. And he shook from the realization that he had been mere moments from revealing himself, to her almost certain horror and his assured everlasting shame. And yet his traitorous body cared not a bit—it only craved release between her soft, warm thighs.

Darcy took a long, trembling breath and slowly made his way back to Caesar. The horse seemed to give him a curious look as he loosened the reins. He walked the horse in the hot sun like a pilgrim seeking penance until they reached Thompson Crossing. There he drew Caesar to the river and allowed him to drink while he splashed water on his face and neck. Darcy's mind was in utter confusion, except for one thought. He would certainly need to go to confession this week before Mass.

Beth quickly dressed in the private little glen she and her sisters used for their forbidden swims. Charlotte had introduced the Bennet sisters to this watering hole the first summer they arrived, and Beth and the others enjoyed it immensely, even though their father was uneasy about it, and their mother had strictly prohibited such unladylike activities. The girls paid no mind—the place was secret, hidden from view, and it was too blasted hot in the summer not to go swimming.

She was making her way back to the house when she heard a horse whinny. Turning towards the ford, she strained to see a tall man riding away from the crossing on a black horse. A chill ran through her, glad that the swimming hole was so well hidden. She would have been mortified to death had anyone come upon her like that!

Mary was fidgeting on the seat of the family wagon as Beth, next to her, handled the reins. Her sister had to hide her smile—Mary claimed her excitement was over the first meeting of the Rosings Musical Society, but Beth was sure her sister's nerves were more unsettled by the expectation of the attendance of their host, Reverend Tilney. The wagon rolled easily down the road into town, giving Kathy and Lily, in the bed of the wagon, little reason to complain. That they did anyway was in keeping with their characters.

All the Bennet girls were going to the outing. Mary, of course, was one of the organizers of the society, and Beth owned a lovely singing voice. Kathy and Lily, on the other hand, were not known for their musical prowess, preferring to listen and dance rather than perform. Still, given the choice of putting on a nice dress and going into town or staying at home to churn butter, the two youngest Bennets claimed to be the greatest music lovers in Texas.

The girls arrived early, even after stopping by the Bingleys' to pick up Jane. Beth and Lily moved to secure the horses while the others went into the church, Mary almost running. They were happy to receive assistance from a couple of friendly passersby.

"Well, Miss Beth, Miss Lily," smiled George Whitehead as he took the reins and affixed them to the hitching post while Billy Collins stood nearby, "I suppose you're excited about the new musical society I hear is being formed."

"Lord, yes—anything to get out of chores!" Lily laughed.

Collins smiled. "And you, Miss Beth, is your interest in the group as practical as your sister's?"

Beth smiled. "Not so very practical, Mr. Collins. I do love music, and the chores will be awaiting us when we return."

Lily stuck out her tongue. "Oh, pooh, you're such a spoil-sport, Beth! George, are you staying to listen? Say you will. We need an audience. You, too, Mr. Collins! Beth, help me convince them."

Whitehead laughed. "I wish I could, Miss Lily, but we do have work to do."

Lily stamped her foot in a halfhearted pout, but her attention was caught by a wagon moving slowly down the street, a woman driving the team of oxen, while a man walked beside it. "Oh, look at that! Is that the new homesteaders moving in?"

Collins colored and started to cough. Whitehead turned back to the two girls. "No, moving out, I'm afraid." He lowered his voice. "Those farmers lost their place."

Lily put a hand over her mouth. Beth asked, "What happened?"

Collins waited until the wagon was past. "The usual thing, miss. People move in, borrow more than they can afford, get overextended, can't meet the payments." He shrugged.

"Foreclosure," Lily whispered. "Oh, how dreadful!"

Beth realized Collins wouldn't meet her eye. "Was it Rosings Bank that foreclosed on them?"

Whitehead jumped in. "Rosings did hold the paper—Collins and I were just discussing it. He told me that he and Mrs. Burroughs did everything they could to extend more credit, but," he smiled, "it wasn't enough."

"Enough? But it's the bank! You've got all the money in town!" Lily claimed.

"Not all the money—there's Darcy Bank," Collins pointed out.

"Yes," Whitehead agreed, "and if Darcy Bank had helped

those poor people out, Rosings may not have been forced to call in the loan."

"How greedy can they be? Mr. Darcy is a mean man!" Lily cried.

Collins simpered. "Not everyone is as concerned about the community as Mrs. Burroughs and Rosings Bank. But there's only so much we can do. A shame, really."

Whitehead glanced down the street and then turned back quickly. "We'd best be going. We've got a meeting in a few minutes."

Collins looked at his pocket watch and blanched. "Goodness! We're late. Mrs. Burroughs will be displeased. Good day, ladies."

The man began to scamper down the sidewalk, leaving Whitehead to make their proper farewells to the Bennets. Lily laughed about Collins's antics as the two ladies joined the others inside, Beth happy to see that Charlotte was already there. It was only a moment later that the front door opened and three other people walked in.

"Mr. and Miss Darcy, Miss Burroughs, welcome!" Tilney strode up the aisle to take Darcy's hand. Beth schooled her face to hide her surprise. She knew they were invited, but she never expected that they would actually attend. By their sudden arrival, she wondered if George had seen them approach and had gone to avoid the unpleasant rancher.

Darcy greeted only Jane with more than the barest civility. Beth had the strangest feeling he was avoiding looking her in the face, but was staring at her back as she talked to Miss Darcy and Miss Burroughs. She did her best to ignore the man and focus her attention on the two girls.

Both were quiet, polite, and reserved, but that was almost the only similarity between the two. Anne Burroughs was a short, pale, plain girl in her mid-twenties. Her brown hair was pulled up in a tight bun on her head, making her appear even more severe than Mary. Gaby Darcy was a sweet girl, just seventeen, tall and well developed. Her black hair, worn down, set off her dusky complexion. Her dark eyes shone with a restrained exuberance.

The only other similarity was that both girls had an intense desire to become acquainted with Beth. Their object could only wonder at it.

"I'm very glad to meet you, Miss Beth," Anne was able to manage.

"Oh, yes! We've heard so much about you! Haven't we, Anne?" Gaby cried.

Beth was confused. "I can't imagine where—"

The rest of her comment was interrupted as Mary and Jane called the group to order. The two had decided between themselves to organize the society, Mary realizing that Jane was far better suited to the task than she. The ladies all took their seats and began discussing the purpose of the society and how often they should all meet. It was quickly decided that it should be a monthly gathering, weather permitting, and that in future they would have themes to the meetings, such as the works of a certain composer or a type of music.

For this first meeting, Jane suggested everyone play or perform their favorite piece, either alone or with others. Henry Tilney, standing to the side of the group, showed the ladies over to the piano and pump organ and then, with a bow, walked to the back of the church. Beth was surprised that he wasn't alone—Will Darcy was also seated in a back pew, his arms crossed over his chest. Beth assumed the man had left after greeting everyone with so little enthusiasm. To her discomfort, he seemed to be staring at her again.

Of course, she realized, glancing at Miss Darcy sitting next to her. *He can't trust his sister out of his sight for a moment! Poor girl, to have such an unpleasant brother!*

Mary opened the performance with a hymn. Beth hid a wince. Once again, Mary was trying too hard to achieve a stateliness to her performance, while damaging the musicality of the piece.

"She's very… solemn," whispered Gaby in her ear.

Beth giggled. "Oh, yes—very solemn, indeed."

Gaby blushed. "Forgive me, Miss Bennet, I meant no harm."

Beth reached over and took Gaby's hand. "No offense taken. And you must call me Beth if we're to be friends."

Gaby's relieved smile almost broke Beth's heart. "Call me Gaby, please, Beth. And Anne—you'll call her Anne, won't you? We're so glad to make new friends."

It had been a long time since Darcy had as much enjoyment as he did sitting on a hard church pew in the back of a Baptist church. Each of the ladies who could play an instrument took a turn, first performing by themselves then accompanying those who only sang. Mary Bennet was adequate, although Tilney seemed to enjoy her singing well enough. Darcy hid an amused grin. Jane Bingley was no surprise—he had heard her often at dinners he had attended to know of her talent. He had a bit of concern as Gaby took to the instrument to play "Joyful, Joyful We Adore Thee," but after an early falter, she rallied and played flawlessly, gaining confidence as she went on. Darcy restrained himself from joining the others jumping to their feet in delight after she finished.

He was spellbound as Beth Bennet sang "Amazing Grace" as Jane played. Hers was not a classically trained voice, but the feelings she produced were authentic and moving. His admiration of her talents and thankfulness for the kindness she showed to Gaby and Anne only fueled his desire for her. The sound of her voice seemed to dance across his skin. Oh, to have those full lips sing his name as she took her pleasure! Darcy shifted in his seat.

"Will, are you all right?" Tilney asked him. Mortified, Darcy assured him he was well.

They were startled as the doors crashed open. "Jane! Jane!" Doc Bingley cried as he ran up the aisle, waving a slip of paper in his hand. Alarmed, the two men ran after him, the concert coming to an abrupt halt.

"What is it, Charles?" Jane instinctively covered her pregnant midsection.

"She's coming today! I just got this from the telegraph office." Charles shoved the paper into his wife's hands. It only took her a moment to read the message. She paled.

"But... but she wasn't coming until June! You read her letter." The two talked as if all the others had disappeared. They had not—they all stood around in various stages of alarm. They knew *something* was amiss, but it was a mystery as to what it was exactly.

"I know, but she's on today's stage. She'll be here at any time!"

"But I'm not ready!" Jane cried in a panic. "Her room's not ready. How can she do this to me?"

"I'm sorry, but what can I do?"

Darcy stepped in. "Forgive me, but what the devil are you two talking about?"

"Caroline! Caroline's coming! Today!" Charles said.

Darcy's eyebrows rose. "Caroline? Who's Caroline?"

"My sister, Caroline, from New Orleans. I'm sure I mentioned her."

Beth gasped. "But you said she wasn't coming until June. That's at least two weeks away."

Tilney broke in. "Uhh, folks, if Doc Bingley's sister is on today's stage, I suggest we get to the hotel. It's due any time now."

Charles was wide-eyed. "I know! That's why I'm here. Jane, can you come?"

"My house!" Jane cried.

"It's all right," Beth assured her. "We'll see to everything, won't we?" She turned to her sisters, who quickly agreed. Charlotte, Gaby, and Anne excused themselves, but Jane would not hear of it, insisting that they remain to enjoy themselves.

"Jane," Darcy said in a firm yet gentle voice, "why don't we adjourn to the hotel and take our leisure? My cousin, sister, and I would be glad to keep you and Charles company."

"Oh, thank you, Will! Beth! Beth, you come, too. Please!"

The group broke up into two parties. Mary, Kathy, and Lily went to the Bingley house to prepare it for the guest, while the others walked over to the hotel. Charlotte joined them, but Tilney excused himself. An hour later, a now-composed Jane and Charles Bingley, with their friends and relations, met the stagecoach as it pulled up. A gloved hand waved from the window.

"Charles! Oh, Charles! How wonderful to see you!" called a high female voice from within.

Charles stepped up and helped a blonde woman descend from the coach. Her traveling dress was dusty, and the feathers on her hat drooped into her face.

"Oh, you must be Jane!" Without ceremony, the woman drew Jane into her arms. She gave her a quick kiss and released her, turning to Charles.

"My God, Charles, what god-forsaken place have you dragged me to?"

Caroline Bingley had arrived.

Chapter 6

June

IT DIDN'T TAKE LONG for Beth to come to the decided opinion that Caroline Bingley was the most unpleasant woman in the world.

With Caroline's early arrival in Rosings, Beth naturally wondered if the plan for her to move in with the Bingleys in June to help out until after the baby was born was still necessary. Jane assured her that it was, so Beth moved into the lone guest room in the Bingley house as scheduled, sharing it with Charles's sister. Beth truly intended to get along with Caroline, and she tried mightily—for a week.

It wasn't because Caroline was outright mean, Beth would later admit to herself. She would have to be noticed first by the blasted woman to be directly insulted. Caroline typically ignored her existence and refused to talk to her unless absolutely necessary. She was treated more like a servant than a relative.

Beth's job was to do everything that Jane normally would, so her sister could take her rest in preparation for the baby. The work of washing, cleaning, and cooking wasn't difficult—Beth had done it her entire life. But instead of doing it for three people, she was doing it for four. Caroline, by hook or crook, refused to lift a finger to help. Bingley's sister either didn't know how to cook, had to keep Jane company instead, or developed a headache when chores had to be done.

Caroline had plenty of opinions, though, and spent most of her time expressing them. It was terrible that Bingley couldn't afford a servant, she had said. It wasn't like the old days back at Netherfield. The town was so small, and she wondered how Charles and Jane could tolerate it. No theater, no music. It was simply barbaric! She couldn't abide the simple farmers and dirty ranch hands. There were too many "others" in town—by that, she meant Mexican people. But she reserved her greatest ire for the "carpetbaggers" and "scallywags," like George Whitehead and Billy Collins.

"Imagine a son of Georgia working with that slimy Yankee!" she declared one day when she and Beth had met the two on the street after a shopping trip to Zimmerman's. "But, I suppose he was the son of a shopkeeper or something. Class always tells, Miss Beth."

Beth gritted her teeth but kept an indifferent expression. "Mr. Whitehead is a very respectable man. He was appointed by the governor himself."

Caroline dismissed Elizabeth's comment with, "Another scallywag in the pocket of those vile carpetbaggers."

Beth tried to be polite. "Perhaps, but Governor Davis was elected by the people of Texas."

Caroline smiled patronizingly. "After the Yankee soldiers purged the voting rolls! Charles told me all about it. Oh, Miss Beth, you have no idea what we've had to put up with down here." She paused. "Y'all are from Ohio, I understand?"

"Yes, we are."

Caroline's nose seemed to rise. "That explains things. You have a lot to learn, Miss Beth, bless your heart."

It didn't take long for Beth to realize that Caroline used "bless your heart" as a means of taking the sting out of her most pointed insults.

Passing a ranch hand on the street: "He probably hasn't had a bath this year, bless his heart."

After meeting Charlotte: "Not every girl can be born pretty, bless her heart."

Beth's clothing: "I suppose livin' on a farm you have to make your own dresses, bless your heart."

When Caroline wasn't holding court over the shortcomings in Rosings, she reflected on life at Netherfield, where the Bingleys grew up, or waxed elegant over New Orleans, where she was currently living with her sister and brother-in-law, the Hursts. The music, the food, the society—everything was superior in the Queen City of the South. She talked endlessly of the fine parties and balls she had attended, particularly about an event called "Mardi Gras."

"A *bal masque*," she explained, "only attended by the cream of society. Oh, Charles, if only you lived in New Orleans! With Mr. Hurst's connections, I'm sure that you and dear Jane would soon be in the highest circles." She then turned to Beth. "And I'm sure we could do *something* for you, too, dear."

The only resident of Rosings who seemed worthy of Caroline's notice was Will Darcy. He brought his sister to dinner one night, and Beth was amused at how Caroline practically threw herself at the man. It was obvious that the woman's interest was purely monetary, for she spent the entirety of the dinner asking Darcy about Pemberley Ranch, ignoring Gaby altogether. Beth swore she could see dollar signs in Caroline's eyes.

For his part, Darcy treated the woman with the same disdain he held for everyone. Beth almost laughed when the rancher grew so desperate for other conversation that he actually tried to talk to her. Beth's eyes danced in mischief each time she spoke with Darcy, knowing that her actions would infuriate Caroline. Beth knew that if looks could kill, she would be dead. It never occurred to her to pay attention to Darcy's expression.

At least the two women could share a room without incident. There were two beds—fortunately—and as Beth tended to retire and rise early and Caroline was of the opposite inclination, one was always asleep when the other was not.

Beth could not talk of Caroline's behavior to either Charles or Jane. Beth did not want to trouble her tenderhearted sister in her delicate condition. And Charles was oblivious. "Oh, that's just Caroline," he would say. "It's just her way. She's had a hard time. You shouldn't take it to heart." The man was useless.

Charlotte was her only confidante, and Beth told her the story of her strained relationship with Caroline on the way home from church that Sunday.

"Beth, I'm so sorry. I had no idea that a sister of Doc Bingley could be so unpleasant."

"It is a surprise. I keep waiting for Charles to say something to her, but he never does. He keeps saying she's had a hard life and I have to forgive her. I don't know how much more I can take."

"How does she treat Jane?"

Beth thought. "Well, she's never really mean to *her*. Caroline's got plenty to say against everybody else in town, including my family, but it's like she exempts Jane from criticism because she's Charles's wife. But she's lazy and demanding and no help at all!"

Charlotte grinned and slipped into a Southern drawl. "'We Southern belles are so delicate, we get the vapors if we do anything more than breathe, I declare.'"

Beth laughed. "She has her nose so high in the air she needs a guide to help her walk down the street, *bless her heart!*"

The girls laughed all the way home.

George Whitehead followed Pyke down the upstairs hall of Younge's Saloon, towards room number five. He had received a letter earlier in the day from a Mr. Carson requesting a private business meeting. The pair paused before the door.

"You searched this fellow?" Whitehead asked Pyke. His henchman assured him that Carson's person and luggage had been inspected and no weapons had been found. Whitehead touched his own gun belt and indicated that Pyke should knock on the door.

"Come in," called a male voice.

"Stay close by," Whitehead told Pyke as he turned the knob. Pyke nodded and stepped away to the head of the stairs.

Whitehead slowly walked into the bedroom. The room was bare—only a bed and dresser joined a small table with a couple of chairs. Whitehead's quick glance took in a battered suitcase at the foot of the bed and a hat on one of the series of hooks on the wall opposite—but no inhabitant.

As alarm bells went off in Whitehead's head, a voice softly said, "Close the door quiet like, or I'll plug you right now."

Moving slowly and deliberately, Whitehead stepped far enough in to close the door. Hands outstretched away from his body, he turned back towards the door. Standing beside it, in a spot where he could be hidden from the outside, was a man holding a pistol.

"If you're holding me up, you're bound for disappointment," Whitehead said with a trace of bravado. "My wallet's in my office."

"Shut up. Move over to the other side of the room. Don't talk."

Whitehead became nervous. The man's voice was deadly calm, indicating this was a planned ambush. He handled the gun with practiced ease. Whitehead knew he had to be very careful, or he would not leave this room alive. Hands up, he did as he was bid, placing the table between himself and the man called Carson.

"All right, now unfasten that gun belt—one hand only."

Whitehead's eyes never left his assailant as he slowly unbuckled the belt with his right hand. The holstered gun slipped to the carpeted floor. Whitehead stared hard at the man opposite. There was something familiar about him.

"I suppose you have a reason for all this, Mr. Carson—if that's your real name."

"Oh, I have a reason, all right. You're George Whitehead, right?"

"I am."

"The name Churchill mean anything to you?"

Whitehead's blood ran cold—a ghost from his past had come visiting. He knew that yelling for Pyke would do no good. By the time Pyke could open that door, Whitehead would be dead.

"Yes," Whitehead said. "James Churchill and I served in the war together."

"I know. He told me all about it. I'm his brother, Frank."

Whitehead said nothing, his mind racing.

"Where's the money, Whitehead?"

Whitehead's first thought was to deny everything, an impulse he dismissed immediately. Lying would do no good. He had to stall, though—he had to find out how much James had told Frank.

"Here."

"I've come to get Jimmy's share."

"It's not that easy."

Churchill raised his gun. "*This* says it's easy. Half of twenty-five thousand—that's twelve thousand five hundred. I want it."

"And then you'll kill me?"

"Get me the money, and we'll see. Don't and you're dead."

"No, you'll shoot me as soon as you get the cash. And I don't blame you."

Churchill gritted his teeth. "You killed my brother."

"No, I didn't. He saved my life."

"Don't you lie! You killed Jimmy and took all the money! The law came to the house during the war saying Jimmy took that money an' was hiding out. But I knew that was a lie! Jimmy would never just leave and not get word back to his family. When months went by, we knew he was dead." A feral look came into his eyes. "I knew what really happened, because Jimmy wrote to me—told me what you two had planned. Stealin' a U.S. Army payroll. So I knew it was you that did away with him."

Whitehead shook his head sadly. "That's not what happened. Things didn't work out like we thought. There was an extra guard, and he got the drop on me." Whitehead grunted. "A bit like you did tonight. I thought it was all over for me when Jimmy jumped the man. Before I could pull my gun out, there were a couple of shots, and they were both dead. There was nothing I could do. I got the strongbox and Jimmy out of there and hightailed it."

"I knew it. I knew Jimmy was dead. What did you do with him?"

"Buried him."

"Where?"

"I really can't tell you—in a farmer's field, but it was in the middle of the night. Doubt I could find it again. I hid the money in my footlocker—right in plain sight." Whitehead looked at Churchill. "Look, Jimmy didn't tell me about you—all he talked about was his sister."

Churchill nodded. "Jimmy and Jenny were close, that's true. What does this have to do with the money? You spent it all?"

"Not spent it—invested it." Whitehead waved his hand. "Some of it's right here—I'm a partner in this saloon. And there's other stuff, too, like land and buildings. That's what Jimmy and I talked about—getting rich off our investments."

Churchill grimaced. "How much you got in cash?"

"Maybe five thousand, but most of it is in the bank. I got some in my safe in the office, but it's only two or three hundred. The bank doesn't open until morning."

Churchill cursed. "That's not too good for you, Whitehead."

"Frank, right? Frank, call me George. Look, I didn't cheat your brother. We were always going to be partners. Split it right down the middle. But things worked out different. Half of what we got belongs to him, but I can't turn it into cash. You understand? Look, I'll be as fair as I can. I can get you four thousand in the morning and we'll call it fair."

"Four? You said you had five!" He raised the gun again.

"Frank, I've got to have some cash on hand. You know, for expenses."

"You said you had some cash in your safe. Five thousand, Whitehead."

Whitehead sighed. "All right, all right, five thousand. Mind if I sit down?"

Churchill agreed and both took a seat at the small table, across from each other.

"You know," Whitehead said conversationally, "it's been a long time. Seven years. How come you're just looking me up now?"

"I couldn't leave home until recently, 'cause my folks needed me. Now that they passed on, I began to look for you."

"And your sister?"

"She ran off with a traveling salesman four years back. Last I heard, she was in Detroit."

"Hmm."

"What's that mean?"

"You're a smart man, Frank. It's not like I was hiding, but still, you found me. That shows a sharp mind. I can use a sharp mind. What did you plan to do with Jimmy's share?"

"I don't know. Didn't think that far."

Whitehead leaned across the table, lowering his voice. "You know, I got some people working for me that... well, they ain't got one brain between them. I've got to do all the thinking and planning, and it's wearing on me. This guy Denny I have riding for me? I think he's loco, and I have to get rid of him. I was just thinking the other day how things would be if Jimmy was here. We'd be a lot further along, I'll tell you that. You think of settling down?"

Churchill blinked. "What—here?"

"Sure. Jimmy was always supposed to be my partner. You're smart—you could take his place. I need somebody I can count on. How 'bout it?"

"You asking me to throw in with you?"

"It would be worth a lot more than half of twenty-five in a couple of years. I've got plans."

"What kind of plans?"

Whitehead grinned. "Oh, no. You want to know, you got to come in. But think about it. Would I be hanging around this pissant place if I wasn't going to be rich?"

Churchill licked his lips. "I don't know. Can I trust you?"

Whitehead laughed. "Hell, can I trust *you*? You're the one with the gun!"

Churchill placed the pistol on the table, just under his right hand. "I got to think about this. You're going to just give me half of everything you've got going?"

"Frank, Frank, I ain't stupid. What I've built up already is worth more than the original stake. At twelve and a half, your part would be something like… one third. Junior partner, but still my partner.

"But the sky's the limit. You can have any woman you want in this saloon. People jump when you talk. And in a couple of years, we'll have this whole county. That's better than sleeping in a bedroll outside with the snakes and Indians, right?" Whitehead's eyes gleamed.

"Yeah, it is."

"Look, why don't you sleep on it, all right? Come see me in the morning, and we'll get the papers drawn up. Or if you'd rather pass, we'll go down to the bank for your money."

"Yeah, and I just let you walk out of here—to bring back

your men for me. That ain't going to happen." Churchill put his hand on the gun.

Whitehead wore a hurt expression. "Aww, Frank. I wouldn't do that. Tell you what—you come with me. Stay in my house. No one's going to touch you—you've got my word on it." He stood up, extending his right hand.

Without thinking, Churchill automatically lifted his right hand off the pistol and took Whitehead's hand. Whitehead's eyes never left his as they shook. Suddenly, Whitehead's grip tightened and his left hand came up, holding Churchill's gun. Before Churchill could scream, Whitehead fired into his chest. The man fell backwards onto the floor, and Whitehead walked around the table, gun extended. Churchill tried to talk, the pain just starting to register, but the last sound he would hear was Whitehead's low snarl.

"You should've paid closer attention, Frank. Nobody ever expects a left-handed man."

Whitehead shot him again as Pyke forced the locked door, gun in hand. "Boss! What happened?"

George whirled on him, anger clearly written on his face. "I thought you searched him!"

"I did, boss, I did! He must've sneaked it in somehow."

Whitehead jammed the still smoking barrel in Pyke's throat. "If I thought for one moment you tried to cross me—"

Sally Younge ran in. "George, don't! It's not his fault!" Whitehead turned. "That man had a package delivered a few minutes before you got here."

Whitehead released Pyke. "I'm sorry, boss, I'm sorry—"

Whitehead cut his henchman off. "Shut up. We got to clean this up."

Younge patted Whitehead on the arm. "I'll go settle the

patrons. Tell 'em some drunken cowboy was plinking holes in the ceiling. They'll believe it—it's happened before." She dashed out, closing the door behind her.

Whitehead looked down at Churchill's body. "Wait until later," he told Pyke, "then wrap him up in the carpet and get him out of town. Get rid of the body. Bury him somewhere on the B&R. Don't throw him in the river. I don't want him found. You hear me, Pyke? No one finds him. Don't mess *this* up."

Pyke assured him it would be done as instructed. Whitehead took one last look at the body.

"Yeah, Frank, you were Jimmy's brother, all right. Just as stupid." He tossed the pistol onto the body and walked out of the room.

Beth couldn't escape Caroline. For a woman who didn't enjoy her company, she always seemed to be around. She invited herself to the Musical Society and immediately took over the meeting. Beth's resentment of the woman was such that she couldn't give any credence to her perfectly fine performance of Mozart.

When Caroline wasn't bragging about the music teachers she once had, she was trying to ingratiate herself with Will Darcy. Darcy, as was his custom, had accompanied his sister and cousin to the meeting, and Caroline took advantage of it, talking to him at every opportunity.

"Look at that," Charlotte whispered to Beth. "Doesn't the woman have any pride at all? She's almost shoving her bosom into Mr. Darcy's face. For all the good it's doing her—Mr. Darcy's clearly uncomfortable."

"Mr. Darcy's always uncomfortable," Beth returned spitefully. She couldn't understand her resentment. She should have laughed at Caroline's exhibition and Darcy's embarrassment, but she could not. Instead, she was angry. Angry at Caroline for the way she was acting, and angry at Darcy for not doing… something. Beth wasn't sure exactly what it was Darcy was supposed to do, but he should have been doing it. Her strange thoughts only added to her confusion and aggravation.

"Poor Caroline!"

Beth turned to her friend. "Poor Caroline? Why should you feel sorry for her? She's a selfish witch who thinks she's better than us."

Charlotte smiled slightly. "You sound a little jealous."

Beth gaped. "Jealous?"

Charlotte put her hand on her arm. "Shush! They'll hear you."

In a much lower voice, Beth said, "I'm certainly not jealous of Caroline Bingley."

Charlotte still wore that slight smile. "Well, she's certainly jealous of you."

"Whatever for?"

Charlotte just shook her head and looked pointedly at Will Darcy. It took a moment for Beth to catch on. It was then she did laugh.

"Will Darcy? You think she's jealous over Will Darcy? Then she has no eyes in her head! He and I agree on one thing—we can't stand one another."

Her friend gave her a look of pity. "Oh, Beth, Caroline sees better than you think. Better than you, apparently."

"I assure you, I don't like Mr. Darcy."

"But Mr. Darcy likes you, I think."

"Impossible. That man hates everyone, me in particular.

Why, he only stares at me to find fault. No, Charlotte, you're very wrong about Mr. Darcy."

Charlotte tried to respond, but she stopped when Anne Burroughs approached.

The lady smiled nervously. "You're both going to get an invitation to Mother's Fourth of July party at the ranch, but I wanted to personally encourage you to come. You… you will, won't you?" Anne only relaxed when both Beth and Charlotte assured her of their attendance. "Oh, that's wonderful! Beth, may I ask you something?" She paused as her color rose. Beth waited patiently for her friend to speak and gave the girl her most encouraging smile.

"Will you come and stay for a few days before the party?" Anne asked in a rush.

Beth clearly was taken aback, and Anne's face crumpled, fearing a rejection. Beth took her hands and said, "I would be delighted, but I have to help Jane—"

Anne cut her off. "I've already asked Jane, and she said she could spare you for a few days. Please come. I've never had anyone over to the house before, except for my cousins. I mean, I love my cousins, but it's not the same."

Beth glanced at Jane, who was smiling at her from across the room. Beth shrugged her shoulders and returned her attention to Anne.

"Very well, I'll ask my father when I visit home tomorrow. If he says yes—"

Anne laughed in girlish joy, a sound Beth had never before heard from the shy and serious heiress. "Oh, he will, he will! Thank you, Beth. Oh, Will, Beth is coming to the ranch to visit with me! Isn't it fine?"

Beth whirled around to find Will Darcy standing behind her. She felt herself flush—from embarrassment, she reasoned.

"I think that's a grand idea, Cousin," he said gravely, his blue eyes brighter than before. "Thank you for your kindness, Miss Bennet."

"Wait," cried Caroline. "Who's going to help me with Jane?"

By then, Mrs. Bingley had arrived and had taken her sister-in-law in hand, assuring her that they would get along splendidly. Beth fell into a conversation with Anne, Charlotte, and Gaby about the party, but she could feel Will Darcy's eyes upon her as he stood enigmatically against the wall.

"Hush, boy, let's be quiet now," Darcy whispered in Caesar's ear as they crept along the riverbank. The horse responded, as his rider knew he would, and made almost no sound as he walked upriver, close by the bushes.

They reached the familiar tree, and within moments, Caesar was grazing while his master stole closer to the riverbank. He found the spot and settled down in anticipation of his quarry. He didn't have long to wait. Only minutes passed before a lovely female figure made her way down the opposite bank and began undressing.

Darcy had tried and tried to resist the siren song of watching Beth Bennet bathe, and it had turned into a losing battle. His mouth was dry as he beheld paradise across the Long Branch. Gloriously nude, the girl slipped under the water, moving slowly in the cool shade.

Darcy's shirt, wet with sweat, clung to his body. His jeans felt too tight, for reasons unrelated to the blistering June heat.

The water, the woman, was just too inviting. He could not wait any longer.

As quietly as he could, he slipped off his boots. Setting them by his hat, he took off his shirt. His pants were next and moments later, naked as Adam, Darcy waited behind the bushes until Beth turned her attention to the far riverbank. He slipped into the water unnoticed by the girl but then froze. What to do now? He couldn't just swim over there without warning, could he? That would frighten Beth, and frightening her was the last thing Darcy wished to do.

"Miss Beth," he called out softly.

The girl cried out and ducked as low in the water as she could and still breathe. Quickly, she turned around. "Mr. Darcy?"

"Miss Beth, don't be afraid, it's just me."

"What are you doing here!? Go away!"

"Shush, quiet. I don't want to raise any ruckus."

"But I'm not decent!"

Darcy smiled. "Well, neither am I. I figure that makes us even."

Darcy swore she hid a smile at that. "How did you know about this place? Have you been spying on me?"

Darcy had the grace to look embarrassed. "No, really. The first time—the only other time—was an accident. Really."

Rather than looking offended, the girl just treaded water, her hair fanning out behind her. "But you came back."

"I couldn't help myself."

She frowned. "You wanted to see an undressed girl."

"No! I wanted to see an undressed *you*. You're the prettiest girl I've ever seen."

"You're just saying that."

"No, it's true, I swear. Can I come closer? I don't want my voice to carry."

She seemed to think about that. "All right, but not too close." Darcy swam across the river until he was a couple of feet away. "That's close enough," Beth decided.

Indeed, it was close enough. Darcy could make out her pale form under the surface of the water. He looked up to see with a shock that Beth was carefully looking back at *his* body.

"Do you swim a lot?" she asked.

"Yes, but not in the river. We've got a big lake on Pemberley. I've been swimming there since I was a boy."

"Is it warmer than the river?"

"Yeah. Are you chilled?"

She nodded.

"It is cold. Maybe if I got closer, we could keep each other warm."

She seemed undecided, and a crease formed between her eyebrows. "That sounds indecent."

Darcy flushed. "Sorry."

Beth smiled slightly. "I didn't say no. I said it sounded indecent. Can I trust you?"

"Yeah."

She nodded and turned her back. Darcy slowly swam to within a foot of her, resolutely keeping his eyes fixed on the back of her head.

"Is that better?" he asked. The water was shallow enough for him to touch bottom—in fact, he had to squat to keep his torso underwater.

"A little." Beth looked over her shoulder and bit her lip.

"I've seen that look before. You stare at me all the time. The society meetings and at Jane's. You do it a lot."

Darcy licked his lips. "I can't help it."

She turned away. "You like looking at me?"

"Yeah." Darcy's voice cracked.

"So do I," Beth said softly.

Darcy couldn't believe his ears. "What?"

She turned slowly to him, her arms crossed to shield her breasts underwater. "I like that you look at me. I like the way you look at me. Nobody's ever looked at me like that before."

"That's because no one else loves you the way I do," Darcy blurted out.

Beth's eyes grew wide. "You *love* me?"

Darcy couldn't say anything; he just nodded.

Beth stared at him, eyes boring into him, looking for the truth.

Darcy glanced away from her scrutiny. "I'm sorry—I just thought there shouldn't be any secrets between us, given, well," he shrugged, "our present situation."

Beth giggled a bit and then sobered. "Look at me," she commanded. "Look into my eyes. I can see people's feelings in their eyes."

Darcy could do nothing but obey. For long moments he allowed himself to get lost in her gaze. Finally, Beth gasped.

"You *do* love me," she declared.

Without thinking, he reached for her under the water. His fingers gently caressed the soft skin of her upper arms and shoulders. Instead of recoiling, she sighed and fell into his embrace, her hands the only thing between them. Slowly, with the utmost care, Darcy lowered his lips to her slightly open mouth. The kiss began gently, like the wings of a butterfly, until Beth moaned and returned the kiss. Before Darcy knew it, their arms were about each other, her soft, warm body firmly against his. A fire was ignited—hands and lips were everywhere—promises and declarations were demanded and made. When Darcy felt Beth's leg curl around his, he reacted instinctively. He reached down, carried her in his arms, and strode to the soft riverbank.

As he laid her down, Beth looked up in fear. "Oh, please, don't dishonor me!"

Darcy's earnest gaze took in her scared eyes, inflamed lips, and erect nipples. "I can't dishonor you, my love. I can only love you. You're to be my wife—I promise you that here, before God and nature. We'll never be parted from this day forward." With that, he kissed her deep and long, a kiss she returned full force.

Beth's knees parted and Darcy settled between them. He paused in his attentions to her breasts to guide himself into her. She arched her back in desire, and he slipped inside, her legs coming up and around the back of his. There was a resistance, and Darcy tried to hold back, but he was undone by the exquisite sensations. Beth cried out.

"I'm sorry, love, I'm sorry," Darcy said over and over again into her shoulder.

"No... It's all right... I'm fine... Don't stop."

Never one to turn down a lady, Darcy did as he was bid, moving slowly, then faster and faster until they both reached their release. Beth gasped as Darcy cried out her name. Spent, he collapsed upon his lover, and she, for her part, slowly ran her hands up and down his flanks.

"I... I never dreamed," she said in wonder.

"Beth, oh, Beth, I love you so—"

"What the hell is this?"

Beth screamed as Darcy tried to roll off her. There, standing in the opening of the small clearing by the river, was a furious Tom Bennet, shotgun in hand.

Beth, in tears, tried to cover herself with her hands, scrambling towards the bushes. Darcy knew he was in enormous trouble and raised his hands over his head, desperately trying to think of something to say that wouldn't make the situation worse.

"Mr. Bennet, I know this looks bad, but—"

"Shut up, you cur!" Without another word, the angry farmer raised his shotgun to his shoulder. All Darcy could see were two enormous black holes.

"Father! Nooo!"

There was an explosion, and Darcy's world went black.

Chapter 7

WILL DARCY AWOKE FROM the nightmare with sweat running down his face. His dream was so real and disturbing that he was both aroused and frightened. He rose to sit on the edge of his bed, his feet on the floor and his face in his hands as he tried to calm his wildly beating heart.

Darcy needed no soothsayer to tell him what his dream meant. His desire for Beth Bennet had become overwhelming. He needed to do something about it—either forget about her, put her aside, or…

Or what?

The lessons drilled into him by his mother and the priests would not let him even consider taking Elizabeth Bennet as a mistress. His conscience would allow only two alternatives.

He would make Beth his wife or he would give her up.

July 2

A wagon from the B&R picked up Beth at her sister's house. As the flatbed wagon was filled with supplies, Beth sat on the seat next to the ranch hand driving the wagon, a man named Wilkerson. The cowpoke drove through the center of the little town, turned north at the main crossroads, and headed out of town.

It was a warm day, and the wagon creaked as it rolled over the uneven road alongside Rosings Creek, the original namesake of the ranch. The ride forced Beth to bump into the cowboy, eliciting an apology from the girl.

"No harm done, little lady," the man leered. "You can bump inta me anytime you like."

Beth could think of nothing to say in response that wouldn't insult the man, so she slid as far away from him on the bench as possible. Her actions caused the driver to laugh.

"Afraid o' gettin' your pretty dress dirty? That's no cause to be unfriendly, missy."

"I'll thank you to remember I'm a guest of your employer, Mrs. Burroughs," Beth said coldly.

The man scowled and turned his attention back to the team pulling the wagon. Beth's thoughts turned to her luggage. She packed every dress she owned, thinking that Anne's mother would never approve of Beth's normal working clothes. Yet she felt that none of her frocks was good enough for the party a few days hence. She was afraid she was going to look like a country bumpkin.

That feeling only increased after her first view of the B&R main house. It was two stories and built in the Greek Revival style favored by many of the plantation houses in the South. Large pillars framed the front of the white mansion, and the windows sported dark green shutters. Behind the house, Beth could see men laboring to erect a huge tent—for the festivities, she surmised.

Beth had seen illustrations of such houses, but there was something wrong with this one. As she grew closer, she realized what it was that bothered her about the B&R house. What was meant to be impressive seemed pretentious. A house that would look beautiful framed by sleepy live oaks next to a lazy river was completely out of place in the middle of the plains of Texas.

The wagon pulled in front of the house where three men awaited her. A short, white-haired man helped her down from the wagon.

"Good afternoon, Miss Bennet. My name is Bartholomew, and I'm the butler here. Shall we go in? These men will bring your belongings to your room. Mrs. Burroughs and Miss Anne await you in the sitting room."

The main door opened to a long, wide hall. Beth followed Bartholomew past a few doors before stopping. He softly knocked on one.

"Enter," came a voice from the other side. Bartholomew opened the door and indicated that Beth should walk through. The room was in blue with gold furnishings in the French style. Gauzy curtains covered the windows, framed by heavy gold drapes. An intricately designed, ornate rug covered most of the floor. Facing the door from the other side of the room was Mrs. Catherine Burroughs, sitting in a rather large chair, a severe expression on her thin face. The lady wore a white blouse over a full dark skirt. Anne sat next to her on a small settee with a nervous smile. Beth wondered for an instant if Queen Victoria's sitting room in Buckingham Palace could be any more flamboyant. She made a small curtsey; it was the right decision.

"Ah, Miss Bennet, please come closer," Mrs. Burroughs said pleasantly, satisfied with the girl's discretion. "Sit down, sit down. Anne, make some room for her. Tea? Do you wish for tea, Miss Bennet?"

"Umm—" Beth was not quite seated yet.

"Of course, you do. Bartholomew!" The little man appeared as if by magic. "Bring tea with scones and apricot preserves."

"Yes, ma'am." He left as quickly as he entered.

"Well, Miss Bennet, we are happy you are able to stay with us. Anne has spoken very highly of you. I understand you are from the North?"

Beth had never heard anyone dominate a conversation like Mrs. Burroughs. Her mother appeared downright quiet in comparison. And the woman's language! Where did she learn to talk that way? Beth glanced about—did she take a wrong turn and end up in England?

"Come, come—speak up! Where is your family from?"

Beth found her tongue. "We're from Ohio, Mrs. Burroughs." She was surprised at the response.

"Ah, the country. I am a Matlock. I was born in New York City, you know. I was raised and went to school there. Yes, school—a fine finishing school for young ladies. I highly recommend it. Anne, of course, could not take advantage of such a place herself, living as we do in Texas. Oh, I could have sent her back East, I suppose, to my family, but it would have been terrible to lose the company of my only daughter. Do you have siblings, Miss Bennet?"

"Yes, ma'am. I have four sisters."

"What? No brothers?"

Beth bit her lip. "My brother died in the war."

"My sympathies, Miss Bennet. Many families have suffered grievous loss. Ah, the tea is here."

While Mrs. Burroughs saw to the tea, Anne reached over and took Beth's hand. "I didn't know about your brother. I'm so sorry." Anne's genuine sorrow made up for her mother's false concern. After the tea was poured and tasted, it was time to renew the interrogation.

"I understand your eldest sister is married?"

"Yes, ma'am, to Dr. Bingley. They would be attending the party, if she was not so close to her time."

"Yes, I noticed her condition in church. It is best that she remain at home for the babe's sake. Tea, not coffee, is the best thing to soothe her stomach if need be. And mint. Tea with mint, I always say. It helped me immensely with Anne. You must tell your sister, Miss Bennet."

"I will, ma'am."

"I noticed the rest of your sisters in church. What a burden they must be on your family. Your father bought the old Thompson Farm, yes? Good land there. A pity about the family—died of yellow fever many years ago. Didn't you know? Oh, well. I understand your father is rather friendly with George Whitehead."

"He is a friend of the family."

"Yes. A clever man, for a clerk. He does some work for me. You see, I do not hold any grudges over the late unpleasantness. We must all look forward under the new order. This land has been in the family for over three generations, and I have every intention of passing it along to my dear Anne, intact and improved, when the time comes, of course. I hope your father has his affairs in order. Who is to inherit, may I ask?"

Beth was taken aback. "Mrs. Burroughs, I hardly know. My father is in good health, and the topic hasn't come up in conversation over our dinner table."

"It should. One should always be prepared for the unexpected. I only ask to see if your father is forward enough in his thinking to make one or more of his daughters his heir. I cannot abide the primitive practice of descent along the male line. The Burroughses never did."

An incredulous Beth glanced over at Anne, but her friend was not puzzled over her mother's behavior. She only looked resigned. Beth decided to try to change the subject.

"I understand you're related to the Darcy family," she said.

"Yes. Old George Darcy was Anne's great-grandfather. At his death, he divided his land along the Long Branch River. This side, originally called Rosings, went to his only daughter, Elizabeth Darcy Burroughs. The other side, Pemberley, was George Washington Darcy's, her brother. There were two other brothers, Harry and Richard Darcy, but they moved west to California where their descendants reside today. I have no idea why Mr. Darcy broke up his ranch into two parts. It makes very little sense to me."

Beth thought about what she knew. George Whitehead told her GW Darcy had been involved with an Indian woman. Did his father punish him by giving away half the land to his sister? Why only half—why not disinherit him altogether? It was not a question she could ask Mrs. Burroughs.

"My husband, Lewis, was the heir of Rosings. We changed the name to B&R shortly after our marriage. We also built this house."

"It is very beautiful, ma'am."

"Thank you. We wanted a house worthy of the land and our position. I believe we accomplished it. Now, tell me of this musical society of yours. My daughter attends along with her cousin, Gabrielle Darcy. Who are the other members?"

"My sisters and Charlotte Lucas."

"The sheriff's daughter. A good sort of girl. A pity she's so plain. Do you all play?"

"My sisters, Mary and Jane Bingley, do, as does Miss Darcy." Beth almost said Gaby and was glad she caught herself. Something told her that Mrs. Burroughs would not be happy to learn that she was on a first-name basis with the lady's cousin. "Miss Darcy is the best, I think."

"Oh!" Anne piped in for the first time. "But Jane—Mrs. Bingley, I mean—plays very well, too, Mother."

Mrs. Burroughs gave her daughter a cold look. "I am sure she is competent, but need I remind you that Gabrielle has studied for many years under her own tutor? I believe Miss Bennet has the right of it—Gabrielle is the most accomplished." She turned to Beth, and in a tone that would brook no opposition, asked, "Is that not so, Miss Bennet?"

Beth was mortified at the way Anne was treated. "You... you are right, ma'am." She took a sip of the now-cool tea to soothe her nerves. While she did so, it occurred to Beth that she needed to get out of the old dragon's presence before she lost her temper and said something she would regret.

She set the cup down. "Mrs. Burroughs, I beg that you excuse me. I wish to clean up and rest after my journey here. Perhaps later Anne might show me around."

"Of course, Miss Bennet, I certainly understand. I will have Bartholomew show you to your room."

"Mother, I would be happy to help Miss Beth. And there is something particular I want to show her. May I, please?"

"I would like that very much, if that is all right with you," Beth added.

Mrs. Burroughs seemed pleased that Beth had deferred to her. "I am very glad that you have become a friend to my daughter, Miss Bennet. It shall be as you wish." The grand lady stood up, dismissing the other two. "Dinner is at six."

"I hope Mother didn't offend you," a worried Anne asked as the two ladies walked to her room.

"Not at all," Beth lied. The woman had deeply offended her, but she would keep it to herself rather than distress poor Anne. Beth was afraid the shy thing would break down at any time. "What is it you want to show me?"

Anne opened the door. "In here." Beth followed her friend into a well-appointed bedroom to see a four-poster bed covered in ball dresses. Anne bit her lip as Beth gawked.

"I want you to take your pick," Anne said. "For the party. I'd like you to pick a dress for the party, if you want."

Beth wandered over to the bed, her fingers touching the soft fabric, her eyes delighting in the rainbow of colors. She knew none of her own dresses were as fine. Lace, silk, taffeta… she shook her head. "Anne, I don't know how I can accept…"

"You don't have to, you know. But I thought you may want to try one on. I've got so many, I… I thought it would be fun."

Beth turned to Anne. "We're not exactly the same size, you know."

Anne blushed. "I know you're… more endowed than I am."

It was Beth's turn to blush. "But one of our maids is an excellent seamstress, and I just know she can make any alterations we need." She looked down. "Please, Beth, I don't have a sister to share these things with me. I'd really like it. Would you please?"

Beth's last resistance to the gesture broke down. "Very well. But I can't promise any will look as good on me as they undoubtedly look on you."

A broad smile broke out on Anne's face. "Let's find out! I'll call for Bertha now."

An hour later, Beth looked at her reflection in the full-length mirror as she modeled a dress of pink silk and lace. "That is very nice," Bertha the maid observed.

"I don't know," mumbled Anne.

"Anne," cried Beth, "this is the sixth dress I've tried on. They're all beautiful! I'd be happy with any of them."

"But they're not right! Are they, Bertha?"

"Do you have something else in mind, Miss Anne?" the maid asked.

"Don't you think Beth would look best in a darker color?"

Bertha nodded. "Yes… but all these dresses are in light shades."

A gleam was in Anne's eye. "Wait right here." She turned and reached into a closet while Bertha helped Beth out of the pink dress. When Beth turned, Anne was holding a blue dress. "Try this one, Beth."

Beth admired the dress. It was dark blue silk with silver embroidery. It was the most beautiful dress Beth had ever seen.

"Oh, no, Anne, I couldn't!"

The heiress would not take no for an answer. A few minutes

later, Beth was twirling before the mirror, Anne clapping in delight. "Oh, it's perfect! It's perfect! Just like he—like I said it would be!"

Beth did not pay close attention to Anne's words, for she was mesmerized by the dress. The dark shade set off her pale complexion while complementing her hair. It felt like a dream, and it moved as if it were alive. She felt like a princess.

Bertha watched with a critical eye. "If I let out the bodice…" She pulled at the top. "Yes, that will do. Lovely!"

"I don't know what to say," Beth said.

Anne walked over to take her hands. "I have plenty of dresses, and that one looks so well on you. Can we have it ready before the party, Bertha?"

"Oh, yes, miss. If I start right now, it will be done tonight."

Beth tried to resist one last time. "Are you sure it's no trouble?" Assured it was not, Beth had no other argument. "All right, then."

Anne laughed and danced about the room.

July 3

Early the next morning, Anne rode her thoroughbred along Rosings Creek towards Rosings. About halfway there, she made her expected rendezvous with a tall, dark-haired man.

"Hello, Anne," called out Will Darcy. "And how's Princess today?"

Anne reached down to pat her beloved horse's neck. "She's fine, Will. And how are you? Looking forward to tomorrow's party?"

Darcy sighed. "What's gotten into your mother, anyway?

Having a Fourth of July party, for heaven's sake! The only reason folks will turn up is for the free vittles and beer."

"Is that why you're coming?" Anne said with a small smile.

"You know why," Darcy responded. "Well?"

"You were right. The blue dress looks beautiful on her."

"Does she suspect?"

"No. Will, are you sure about surprising her?"

Will nodded. "I know what I'm doing."

"I don't know. Are you certain that she likes you? I mean, I think she does, but I can't tell if she likes you in, well, *that* way."

Will grinned at his innocent little cousin. "Anne, Anne, Anne. Just look at the way she talks to me. She's always teasing—it's obvious she's flirting with me. Time I gave her back a little of her own. It'll work out, just watch." At her doubtful expression, he leaned over his saddle horn. "Aren't I always right?"

Anne grinned slightly. "I suppose you are." As the smile slid off her face, Darcy grew concerned.

"Annie, is everything all right? You've been awful quiet lately."

Anne wouldn't meet her cousin's eye. "I don't know what you're talking about, Will."

"How are things at home? Cate's not mistreating you, is she?"

"Mother's the same as she always is. I'm fine, really."

"Annie, look at me." The girl raised her face. "You can talk to me. You can trust me, you know that."

"I do," she said quietly.

"We've got a place for you at Pemberley if you want it."

Anne's eyes flew open wide. "No! I'm... I'm fine. Everything's fine." She glanced at the rising sun. "I'd better get back to the house. I promised to go riding with Beth, and I better get back, or she'll think I left without her. Bertha's been keeping her busy, but she can't do that much longer, or Beth'll think something's wrong. See you tomorrow, Will."

Anne turned Princess's head around and headed back to the house. Darcy watched her go for a few moments, still uneasy over his cousin's demeanor. Finally, he could remain no longer, or he chanced discovery by Miss Bennet.

"C'mon, Caesar, let's get back to the barn, huh?" He put spurs to horse, and the great, black beast shot forward, racing over the plains. Will exulted in the ride, his mind moving from concern over his cousin to anticipation about the entrance of another lady—a very pretty, curly-haired lady in blue.

Chapter 8

July 4

"AH, WILLIAM, GABRIELLE," WELCOMED Mrs. Burroughs from the foyer after Bartholomew opened the front door. "Good morning. You're prompt—very good. Gabrielle, you look lovely today."

Darcy hardly heard his cousin's monologue, for he was too busy scanning the people already assembled in the B&R ranch house for a woman in a blue dress. Mrs. Burroughs noticed his preoccupation and thought she knew the reason.

"William, Anne is still upstairs. She will be coming down... Why, here she is now."

Darcy's head jerked around, his gaze steady upon the two ladies descending the staircase. Anne appeared quite pretty in her attractive pink and white dress, and Gaby was delighted for her. But Darcy dismissed his cousin with a nod of the head, his attention captured by the vision behind her.

Darcy was aware that the domineering Cate stood beside him, and he schooled his features to appear as disinterested as possible. Yet, his eyes were locked on Miss Bennet, splendid in a blue and silver gown, her hair up and away from her face. The lady must have felt his stare, for her eyes locked on his and opened wide.

She knows! Darcy thought. His initial impulse was to damn propriety and approach her, but with Cate in attendance, that would never do. He knew he had a part to play in front of his cousin. He would have to wait to enjoy the pleasure of Miss Bennet's undivided attention.

He stepped forward and correctly took Anne's hand. "Good morning, Cousin. You look very well today. And, you too, Miss Bennet," he said as he turned to her.

"Th… thank you, sir."

Cate began speaking again, drawing Darcy's notice, so he did not see the confused look in Beth's eyes.

"Come," the grand lady commanded, "the opening ceremony is about to begin. Darcy, escort your cousin. Gabrielle, attend me."

Darcy walked out of the house, Anne's arm in his, feeling very satisfied. Had he been able to study Beth Bennet longer, he would not have been so pleased with himself.

It was high noon when a deep voice in his best Army dress blues called out, "Hats off!"

The men assembled removed their hats as an honor guard of U.S. Cavalry soldiers raised the flag of the United States on a temporary flagpole. The thirty-seven stars and thirteen stripes floated in the light breeze as it rose, accompanied by a rolling cadence. Beth, standing with the Burroughs and George Whitehead, looked on with pride, her hand over her heart, smiling in the sun. Her eye caught a motion, and to her disgust, she observed Will Darcy staring a hole in the ground, his friend, Richard Fitzwilliam, next to him doing the same. Gaby Darcy looked on impassively, occasionally glancing at her brother.

Beth recalled that George Whitehead once described Darcy as an "unrepentant Rebel." *Yes, he certainly is!* There was a sense of disappointment in her musings. She was taken aback by his attentions earlier. The blasted man looked stunning in a dark blue suit, a black tie at his throat. And there was something unusual in his bright blue eyes for a moment, before it was extinguished. For one brief moment, her heart had been in her throat. Beth shook her head, angry that she kept thinking about the annoying man. *I will ignore him for the rest of the day*, she promised herself.

Once the flag reached the pinnacle, George stepped forward and began reciting from the Declaration of Independence:

> "We hold these truths to be self-evident, that all men are created equal, that they are endowed by their Creator with certain unalienable Rights, that among these are Life, Liberty, and the pursuit of Happiness. That to secure these rights, Governments are instituted among Men, deriving their just powers from the consent of the governed. That whenever any Form of Government becomes destructive of these ends, it is the Right of the People to alter or to abolish it, and to institute new Government, laying its foundation on such principles and organizing its powers in such form, as to them shall seem most likely to effect their Safety and Happiness. Prudence, indeed, will dictate that Governments

long established should not be changed for light and transient causes; and accordingly all experience hath shewn, that mankind are more disposed to suffer, while evils are sufferable, than to right themselves by abolishing the forms to which they are accustomed. But when a long train of abuses and usurpations, pursuing invariably the same Object evinces a design to reduce them under absolute Despotism, it is their right, it is their duty, to throw off such Government, and to provide new Guards for their future security."

Beth noticed that several of those assembled, Darcy being one, rolled their eyes or shuffled their feet during Whitehead's recital. Whitehead then jumped ahead to the last section of the Declaration:

"We, therefore, the Representatives of the United States of America, in General Congress, Assembled, appealing to the Supreme Judge of the world for the rectitude of our intentions, do, in the Name, and by Authority of the good People of these Colonies, solemnly publish and declare, That these United Colonies are, and of Right ought to be Free and Independent States; that they are Absolved from all Allegiance to the British Crown, and that all political connection between them and the State of Great Britain, is and ought to be totally dissolved; and that as Free and Independent States, they have full Power to levy War, conclude Peace, contract

Alliances, establish Commerce, and to do all other Acts and Things which Independent States may of right do. And for the support of this Declaration, with a firm reliance on the protection of divine Providence, we mutually pledge to each other our Lives, our Fortunes, and our sacred Honor."

A restrained cheer went up, men donned their hats again, and the party commenced, as the band struck up "Hail Columbia" followed by "The Star Spangled Banner." Gaby approached Beth, who had decided not to shun the girl because of her unpleasant brother. Beth, Anne, and Gaby spent a few minutes in pleasant conversation when the master of ceremonies, Mr. Zimmerman, called out for everyone to form up for the first dance.

George approached the group, and for a moment, Beth thought he was going to request a dance from her, but instead he claimed Anne's hand. Beth could not decide if she was relieved or envious when she heard a low voice beside her.

"Miss Bennet, you do look lovely today." She turned to behold Will Darcy. "Forgive me, but I promised this dance to Gaby. May I request another one?" His bright blue eyes discombobulated her.

"I… I…"

"The third one!" hissed Gaby with a twinkle in her eye.

Beth was puzzled. "The third dance?"

Darcy took it as agreement. "The third dance it is—thank you, Miss Beth. Gaby, shall we?"

Consternation gripped the girl, for she had violated her vow of ignoring Will Darcy within fifteen minutes of the start of the dance. "Hateful man!" she hissed to herself.

"Pardon me?" asked Billy Collins, who had at that moment appeared at her side.

"Oh! Mr. Collins, what can I do for you?" she said automatically. By the time her brain caught up with her mouth it was too late, and Beth took her place for the Grand March with Mr. Collins. The only good thing about it was she finished the dance without injury to her toes.

Another gentleman claimed the second dance, a Virginia reel, which was a favorite of Beth's. Her joy increased as she saw that Reverend Tilney was still dancing with Mary, and that neither looked to be in any hurry to find other partners. Beth was giggling about the state of Mary's affairs with Charlotte Lucas when they were approached by Darcy and Fitzwilliam.

"Our dance, I believe, Miss Beth." His voice held an edge of humor in it, which Beth could not account for, but she could not refuse or turn to Charlotte for assistance. Her friend was already heading to the floor on Fitz's arm, unmindful of the glare from Sheriff Lucas. Beth sighed and offered her hand to Darcy. It was only as they took their places that she realized the depths of Gaby's treachery.

"The Viennese Waltz," Zimmerman called out.

Beth blushed as Darcy took her hand. "I believe I know the steps, Mr. Darcy," she said.

Darcy grinned, an unsettling sight to Beth. "I don't doubt it. I remember our last dance very well."

The music started, and they began to move with the others. Beth tried not to notice, but her body tingled at his touch. She could sense the strength of Darcy's arms and the warmth of his body as he held her, smelled his cologne as they swirled around the dance floor, and was mesmerized by his good looks as their eyes met.

His masculinity flooded her senses. She felt beautiful, as though she were floating in the sky, the music and the man utterly intoxicating her. Feeling lightheaded, she closed her eyes, part of her wishing it were over, another part hoping the dance would never end.

"Miss Beth?"

The spell broken, she looked up into Darcy's face.

"The dance is done," he said. "Are you all right?"

"Um… I feel a little faint. Perhaps I need to sit down."

"Of course. Just this way." With the utmost gentleness, Darcy guided Beth to a chair. After she was seated, he offered to bring her something to drink.

"Oh, no. Rest is all I need. I feel better already."

"It is a bit warm. You shouldn't overdo."

Beth couldn't decide if he was being polite or overbearing. She settled on the former. "It is a little warm. I'll keep that in mind."

Darcy smiled. "I'll just keep you company until your next dance partner arrives."

"That would be me," said a voice behind him. "Thank you for taking care of Miss Beth."

Darcy lost all expression at the sound of Whitehead's voice. He turned slowly. "Miss Bennet is tired. She may wish to rest for a while, Whitehead."

"Oh, no!" the lady cried. "I'm fine. George, give me your hand." As Whitehead did so, Beth could've almost sworn that Darcy flinched. "Thank you for your kindness, Mr. Darcy."

"Think nothing of it," Darcy replied in a bored tone. "Enjoy your dance." Before Beth's confused eyes, Darcy turned on his heel and walked away.

"My good friend, Darcy," George smirked, "charming as ever." The two began dancing, but Beth was still thinking over

Darcy's abrupt change of countenance. Did it have something to do with George Whitehead?

"What disturbs you, Miss Beth?" George asked.

She looked up at him and blurted out, "Why did you come here?"

"I beg your pardon?"

Beth blinked. "To Rosings, I mean. My family moved here for land and a new start. Why did you come to Texas?"

"Ah. Well, I suppose it was to do good. Help those who had been put down all their lives. Right the injustice that was perpetrated here."

"Help the former slaves?"

"Yes, you could say that."

"But, there don't seem to be any slaves around here—except for the Washingtons, and they moved here recently."

"Well, when one is a public servant, one goes where one is assigned. But what makes you think there haven't been slaves around here?"

"I haven't seen any. You mean there are, or were? Did the Darcys own slaves?"

George sighed. "Most rich people in the South owned hundreds of slaves."

"But what happened to them?"

"I don't know. Ran off when they heard of Emancipation, I suppose. Would you want to live near your former owners?"

Beth had to admit she wouldn't. She finished the dance, her mind in turmoil until George walked her back to her chair, Lily occupying the one next to it.

"Perhaps you *are* a bit tired," George said. "May I get you something?"

"Beth, are you unwell?" asked her sister.

"No, no, I'm fine," she protested.

"All right, then," said Lily. "George, you promised me a dance!"

"Yes, I did. Please excuse us."

Beth did not watch them walk away. She had too much on her mind.

Darcy was furious watching Beth dance with Whitehead. The only reason he didn't explode was the expression on Beth's face. It was apparent she wasn't enjoying herself. *Perhaps*, he thought, *she sees Whitehead for the snake he is.* He knew he would have to explain to her why he feigned disinterest in her. It wouldn't be good for Whitehead to suspect that Darcy had feelings for Beth until it was too late for him to do anything about it.

"Hey, Will, come over here an' meet my newest friend."

Darcy turned, his lips curling into a smile. "That will be a first, as you don't have any friends." He saw Fitz leaning against the makeshift bar with an Army officer, both with beers in their hands.

Fitz grinned. "This here's Captain John Buford of the United States Cavalry, stationed at Fort Richardson. He's here to protect our bacon from the savage natives that infest these here parts."

Darcy extended his hand. "William Darcy."

The officer, tall and dark, shook his hand with a firm grip. "Pleased to meet you, Mr. Darcy. I've heard a lot about you."

Fitz laughed. "Nothin' good, I assume."

Buford smiled. "Like I'll get the straight story out of you."

Darcy leaned on the bar, signaling for a beer. "You sound like you know each other."

"Yes and no," Fitz said. "Buford here was a blue-belly colonel chasin' my ass all over the Shenandoah Valley during the late unpleasantness."

"And a slippery man you were, Major." Buford turned to Darcy. "I rode with Custer."

"You stayed in the army," Darcy observed.

"It's my profession. I resumed my permanent rank after the war." He looked Darcy right in the eye. "And you, sir?"

"Texas Legion, Vicksburg. I've seen the elephant.[3]"

Buford nodded. "Thought so. I've got a few ex-Confederates in my company. Good men. Ex-officers, although they're enlisted now. Regulations," he shrugged.

"And you're at Fort Richardson. Not with Custer and the Seventh Cavalry," Darcy observed.

Buford lost a bit of his good cheer. "No, I'm no longer with Colonel Custer. I find my current assignment much more to my liking." What was left unsaid hung over the room.

Fitz tried to change the subject. "Such as raising flags at parties?"

Buford smiled again. "One of my more pleasant duties, I assure you. My colonel assigned me to a detail to do the honors." He looked around. "Although I'll probably catch the devil from my wife, Deborah, when I get back. She dearly loves a dance."

"She's at post with you?"

"Yes, and expecting another addition to our family in about a month. It'll be our third, but you worry every time."

"I expect so." Darcy took a sip. "How are things otherwise?"

A knowing look crept into Buford's eyes. "It's quiet down here, but up along the Red River, it's another story."

---

3 "I've seen the elephant" was a term used by Civil War soldiers in letters and diaries to describe the experiences of undergoing battle during wartime.

"I thought I heard something along those lines. Tell me, is the army planning anything soon?"

Buford looked away, considering. "Are you planning on driving any cattle north?"

"Fitz here just got back from Kansas, delivering a herd."

"Good, good. Let me say this—it's a wise decision you made, going early. Very wise."

Darcy and Fitzwilliam nodded, getting the message. The army was planning a major operation against the tribes. Just then, Caroline Bingley walked up.

"There you are, Mr. Darcy. I do believe it's time for our dance... oh." She noticed the army officer.

Darcy did the honors. "Miss Caroline Bingley, this is Captain John Buford." Buford bowed slightly, but to the gentlemen's surprise, Miss Bingley turned away from him without a word, delivering the cut direct. Darcy did not know the root cause of the woman's behavior and decided the best way to quell any further incident was to offer the lady his arm for the dance, and they moved away. Fitz was mortified.

"Sorry about that, Buford."

The officer took a swig of his beer. "Am I supposed to know her? Have I done something to warrant that?"

"Umm... she's from Georgia."

"Ohhh... I see. I understand now. The March to the Sea?"

"Yeah."

Buford cursed. "Damn that war."

Anne finally escaped the smothering attentions of George Whitehead and went to look for her friend, Beth. Anne wished her mother would believe her when she told her about Whitehead, but she would only dismiss her. *"Nonsense,"* she would say. *"Mr. Whitehead knows his place. He would not look so high as you—he knows better. Enjoy the attention, and who knows— maybe it will finally make Darcy jealous."*

Anne saw Beth standing off to one corner of the tent away from the dance floor, looking in the other direction. Anne walked over to her, catching her attention, but before she could say anything over the low rumble of the crowd, a loud voice was heard.

"I must say I'm amused by what the rustics here about call a ball, Mr. Darcy."

Both girls saw Caroline Bingley standing close to Will Darcy a few feet away. As they were both behind the pair, they were unnoticed. Anne saw Beth trying to restrain a giggle, holding one finger across her lips. They could clearly overhear the conversation.

"It's true we don't have the facilities found in the city, Miss Bingley, but we're able to manage," Darcy said dryly.

"And the dresses! Certainly not up to St. Charles Avenue standards, bless their hearts. Except Miss Darcy, of course. No one can disparage *her.*"

"Of course not."

Beth threatened to laugh out loud, and Anne had to admit she was amused as well by the pretentious debutant.

Caroline sighed dramatically. "But—oh! Poor Charles! What a waste!"

"I beg your pardon?" Darcy said.

"What Charles could be, given the proper situation! I assume he's a very good doctor."

"I believe so."

"Then he must be. I know several physicians in New Orleans, and all are of the highest circles. There's great demand not just for their talents but for their society as well. They're accepted everywhere. By the houses they live in, they're all rich, or will soon be so.

"But here, in the middle of nowhere! There's no chance for advancement or fortune, I declare. Only caring for farmers and cowboys—and their animals, I suppose. What kind of life is that for Charles, who grew up at Netherfield? He isn't what he should be."

Beth lost all mirth and listened intently.

"And what should he be?" Caroline's companion asked.

"He should be a prestigious physician in a great city like New Orleans, his name on everyone's lips, not wasting his life here in the wilderness."

Darcy drew a breath. "He could leave if he wanted to."

"Don't think I haven't dropped a few hints, but no—he'll never leave. It's the fault of that wife of his."

"Mrs. Bingley?"

"Yes, She'll never leave her family. She's trapped him here. He shouldn't have married her. Don't you agree?"

Darcy was silent for a terrible moment. Anne could see Beth's anger grow.

Darcy began to speak. "I can't deny that Charles has certainly limited his opportunities by moving to Rosings. He'll never be rich here, and by marrying Jane Bennet, he'll never leave. In my opinion, Jane would never be happy away from her family, and I think Charles knows that. So, I suppose you're right, Miss Bingley—by his marriage, Charles has forever doomed himself to be poor."

Beth turned white, spun on her heel, and left the tent. Anne, aghast at what she had overheard, waited a moment and then followed her friend.

Beth quietly left the ballroom tent for the house porch to seek relief from the sweltering heat and to settle her own jumbled emotions. She fanned herself as she stewed. It was bad enough that Will Darcy disrespected the flag that her beloved Samuel died defending, learning that he disapproved of Jane was more than she could stand. How, she thought, could a sweet girl like Gaby have such a detestable brother? How could Anne or Charles or Fitz stand to be in his company?

And yet, she could not erase from her treacherous mind the image of Darcy, tall and dark and enormously handsome, approaching her for their dance. How intoxicating it felt to be in his arms! Never had Beth experienced such a reaction from just being in a man's presence. Could Charlotte be right? Could she be attracted to him? She couldn't be, it was impossible… and yet—

"Miss Beth?"

Beth closed her eyes in anger. The very last man she wished to speak to had somehow found her—was now standing behind her, invading her privacy. It took all the control she had not to turn on the cousin of her hostess and lash out at him. Instead, she resolutely stared out at the rolling countryside, one hand on the porch railing, not favoring Mr. Darcy with so much as an acknowledgment of his presence. She hoped her slight rudeness would put the man off.

She was disappointed. Darcy moved to her side, just far

enough away to meet propriety. He, too, gazed at the expanse of the range. "I don't blame you for seeking the quiet of the veranda. It's very close inside," he said softy. He half-turned his face to her. "Would you care for a lemonade? A glass of wine, perhaps? You must be parched."

Beth could not help but turn to him. "Thank you, no. I require nothing but solitude."

"You and I are alike, then," he said with the ghost of a smile, which raised Beth's ire. How dare he compare himself to her!

"You look very lovely tonight."

That got Beth's attention. Her head whipped around of its own accord to behold Darcy looking at her in that familiar, intense, unexplainable manner. One corner of his mouth still twisted up.

"Yes, blue is your color. I'm glad Anne took my suggestion. That dress favors you very well."

"What?" she cried. "You... you spoke to Anne about my choice of dress?"

"Yes. I'm very glad I did. You look quite beautiful, Beth. Much better than in dungarees. You were born to wear that dress. I'm glad I bought it." He took a step forward, almost touching her. Beth could not move, so surprised was she at his statements.

His half-smile faded as he seemed to struggle with himself. Finally, he blurted out, "It won't do. It won't do anymore. I must tell you that I have quite lost my heart to you. I can't go on, can't see myself without you." He suddenly took her hands, his thumbs running over the calluses on her fingers. "So rough," he said sadly, looking at them. "Living on a farm, doing chores." He raised his eyes to hers. "No more. Let me take you from all that. Let me take care of you. Come with me—you'll never have to work again. Whatever you want, you'll have. Dresses, books, music—anything." He lifted her hand to his lips. "I'll give you everything if you'll only say you'll be mine—"

"*No!*" Beth's astonished mind had finally regained control of her voice. She yanked her hands from Darcy's grasp. "How dare you! Are you insane? How dare you touch me!"

Darcy colored and took a half-step back. "I'm… I'm sorry. I only meant—"

"I know what you meant, and I won't be one of your conquests!" She reached back, ready to slap him, only to stop at his confused expression.

"Conquests? What are you talking about?"

"Are you playing me for a fool? I won't be your mistress!"

Darcy gaped. "Is that what you thought I was talking about? Beth, I'm asking you to marry me!"

Beth's hand dropped. "Marry you?"

"Yes! I love you! How could you think I would ask something dishonorable of you? What kind of man do you think I am?"

Darcy's question seemed to break the dam of resentment Beth was holding against the man. "I know *exactly* what kind of man you are, Will Darcy. You say you'll give me anything if I go with you. Am I for sale? Do you think you can buy me like one of your slaves?"

"No—I didn't mean—I've never—I've never had slaves."

"Don't lie to me! George told me all about the slaves you've bought. Just like all of you Southerners—you've all owned slaves. How can you live with yourself?"

Darcy drew his mouth into a thin line. "You think that, do you? And what about Charles? Do you feel the same about him?"

"You dare bring up Charles? I heard what you said about him

and Jane to Caroline. About how he could have done better had he not come to Rosings—that his marriage to Jane must always doom him to be poor. And you call him your friend! And Jane, who has always defended you—what has she done to earn such scorn?"

Darcy's face went white. "If you overheard that, didn't you hear the rest of the conversation?"

Beth ranted on, heedless of his rejoinder. "You sit in your big house, unwilling to take any notice of anything that's going on. People are losing their homes, and your bank does nothing! You make sure no one unsuitable even touches one inch of your precious Pemberley. But, oh, if your sister shows the least interest in doing something that may broaden her horizons, like going to town and meeting other people, well, then, you shadow her like a mother hen! Making sure we're all worthy of her acquaintance. Insulting fine, upstanding people like George Whitehead. You're as proud and unpleasant as Mrs. Burroughs and with less reason. She's old and set in her ways. What's your excuse, except you think you're better than the rest of us?"

Beth could almost hear Darcy grind his teeth as his face turned red. "If you believe George Whitehead to be a fine, upstanding person, then you're a fool, Miss Bennet. Whitehead's the biggest piece of scum in the county."

"George Whitehead is a war hero! And what are you? A traitor to the country of your birth! My brother went to fight to save the union, not break it apart. He fought to end slavery, not defend it. And he died doing it. You killed him—you and any who took up arms against the United States. If it weren't for people like you, Samuel would still be alive! Marry you? I hate you!"

Darcy recoiled as if struck. He said nothing; he only stared at her wide-eyed, as the music from the ball filled the silence. Beth, tears running down her face, refused to break eye contact with him. After a moment, the man seemed to deflate.

"I see. It seems I was under the impression you enjoyed my company. I now see I was wrong. Please excuse me for bothering you." He gave her a quick nod. "I'll leave you now, as my presence is understandably unwanted. My... my best wishes to you and your family." His voice almost broke at his final words, and he walked swiftly away down the veranda. Beth did not move until he turned the corner of the house and she could flee to the sanity of her guest room upstairs, hoping her passage would go unnoticed.

In that, she failed, for out of the shadows at the other end of the veranda stepped a distraught Anne Burroughs.

Chapter 9

As much as she tossed and turned, Beth could find no rest. She sat up in her bed, staring at the richly appointed walls of the guest bedroom that had been given over for her use. A single candle flickered uncertainly in its holder on the bedstead, its pitiful light adding to the gloomy atmosphere suffered by the room's only occupant.

Beth could not comprehend her agitation. True, Darcy's totally unexpected proposal had unnerved her, but that was hours past. She could not understand why, once her righteous indignation over the arrogant man's presumption had burned out, it was replaced by numbness. She tried to remember George's words and fought to keep Samuel's portrait in her mind, but she was failing miserably.

All she could hear was Darcy's passionate declaration: "*I love you!*" All she could see was the flash of intense pain in his face before it returned to its habitual expressionless demeanor as he voiced his surprising and unexpectedly cordial farewell. Beth could do nothing—not sleep, not answer Anne's earlier knock on the door—while she wrestled with *whatever* was consuming her.

Will Darcy loved her. It was impossible, she kept telling herself. He didn't know her, had hardly spoken with her. He was everything she disliked, and she should have been as distasteful to him as he was to her. Yet, he had declared his love—almost shouted it, in fact. George had been wrong. Darcy wanted to marry her, despite her lowly beginning. A rich Southern rancher wanted a Yankee farmer's daughter. It was absurd.

Beth was mortified to learn that she had been wrong, so very wrong, about his constant staring. His look was the same one she had seen in one of her dreams, as a wet Will Darcy emerged from the river, his shirt plastered to his skin, his hand outreached for her… *No!! Stop it! Stop thinking of him!!*

Her frustration grew as her overactive imagination betrayed her again. She needed a distraction. Beth looked about the room, searching for something to read, but there was nothing. The place was as impersonal as a museum. Besides her few personal items on the dressing table, the only other thing in the place that took away from the stark perfection of the expensive décor was the blue dress, carefully draped on a chair.

Beth sat in bed, contemplating the dress. It was the prettiest thing she had ever worn, and Darcy had ruined it for her. As much as she would have liked to believe otherwise, she knew his claim of choosing it for her was not an idle boast. Darcy would not dare lie, knowing how friendly Beth was with Anne, who would know the truth. She could never think of the dress or the way she looked in it without recalling his soft words, and that would never do. And the remark he made suggesting that Anne dress her in that color— it was as if he already owned her and could dress her as he liked.

Beth stood and put on a dressing gown over her cotton nightdress. Without a clock, she had no idea of the time, but the silence of the house told her that everyone must be abed. She could chance going down to the library for a book. Reading always helped her sleep.

In a matter of minutes, Beth was proven correct; the house was as still as a tomb. She made her way down the stairs without incident, pausing only when she saw light streaming from the library. Courage almost failing her, she nearly turned back in defeat before her need overcame her caution, and she forced herself to pause at the threshold, listening for noises within. Hearing nothing, she crept inside.

A candle burned on the mantle, her view of the fireplace blocked by a sofa before it. Soundlessly, Beth moved between the shelves of books at the other end of the room. She had put down her candle and picked up a random volume to peruse, when she was startled by a sound of a hiccup.

All senses on full alert, Beth quickly replaced the book and scanned the room. Nothing. Just as she told herself that she had been hearing things, a low sound nearly made her shriek.

Moaning? Heavens! Someone's in here—on the sofa! I have to get out of here!

Beth removed the fist she had jammed into her mouth and took two steps towards the door before pausing, trying to decide if she needed her candle. It was her undoing, for the library door flew open, and Anne entered with a determined stride, carrying something in her hands.

"Here is a mug of hot coffee, Cousin," she said, her eyes moving between the cup and the sofa. "Perhaps after you sober up a little, you can explain what you did to upset Beth so much."

"Upset Beth?" came an unsteady, yet familiar deep voice. "Whaddabout me?"

Darcy! Beth's mind screamed.

"What *about* you?" Anne scolded him as she held out the mug. Slowly, the back of Darcy's head emerged from the couch as he took the coffee.

"In case you didn't notice, you eavesdroppin' li'l busybody, *I'm* the one rejected 'round here, not her."

"Drink up," she demanded. "I refuse to reason with an intoxicated man…" Anne's voice trailed off as she realized they weren't alone in the room. Her eyes flared as Beth began to creep out, one finger on her lips.

Darcy stood abruptly. "I ain't intoxicated—I'm drunk!" To Beth's horror, he turned his face enough to catch a glimpse of her out of the corner of his eye. He swung his arm up, pointing in her direction, and bellowed, "An' *she's* the reason why!"

Darcy's accusation raised Beth's ire, overcoming her embarrassment. "*I'm* the reason? How do you figure that? You're the one surprising innocent ladies with unwelcomed proposals!"

"Will you two lower your voices?" Anne begged in a whisper. "You'll wake the whole house."

"Right," Darcy said as he staggered around the sofa, "can't interrupt Cate's beauty sleep." There was the clink of boot against glass, and an empty whiskey bottle rolled across the carpet.

"I see you're a drunkard on top of everything else, Mr. Darcy," Beth declared icily.

"You see *nothin'*," Darcy shot back. "I've never been drunk afore in my whole life. But if there's a woman alive that'll drive a man to drink, *you're it.*"

Beth drew back, affronted. With as much dignity as she

could muster in a nightgown, she straightened her shoulders and threw her head back. "I don't have to stand here and listen to this. Good night, sir!" She turned, but her progress was halted by his voice.

"Yeah, run. Run like th' coward you are. Run away from th' truth."

She turned to look over her shoulder. "How dare you!"

"'How dare you!'" he mimicked with a crooked grin. "Whassamatta, scared o' me? You sure weren't scared earlier." He turned to a mortified Anne. "'Sides, we got Annie here to chaperone. I think your virtue's safe." His expression darkened. "But it won't be if you keep hangin' 'round Whitehead, let me tell you that."

"Will! Your language!" Anne implored.

"No, Annie. She's gonna hear me out." He turned to Beth. "I let you have your say earlier. You gonna be a man about it an' let me have mine? Uhh, I mean woman… uhh. Oh, hell—you gonna hear me out?"

Anger and curiosity battled within Beth. Curiosity won. "Very well, as long as you refrain from using crude language."

"There ain't no other kind to describe Whitehead, but all right." He gestured for her to be seated. Beth chose the sofa, and Anne joined her. Will ran a hand through his already disheveled hair and peered blearily at the two of them. "Y'all want a drink?"

Beth raised her eyebrows. "No, thank you." Anne simply shook her head.

"Well, I'm gettin' one." Darcy walked over to the sideboard.

"Don't you think you've had enough?" Beth's voice dripped with sarcasm.

Darcy snorted as he poured a brandy. "Nope—not if I gotta

talk about that lyin', no-good son of a… snake-in-th'-grass." He returned to stand between the couch and the fireplace. "Now, let me remember what it was you said." He scratched his head, a gesture that seemed very out of place in Beth's perception of the man. It looked… endearing.

"First, about that there dress. Why did you get so upset about it?"

Beth gasped. "Because you bought it for me! You had no right to do that."

"Beth, he didn't," Anne said quietly.

Darcy frowned. "Annie's right—I didn't buy that for you; I bought it for her over a year ago. Remember, Annie? My last trip to Fort Worth?" Darcy grinned. "Huh! Good thing Cate never found out, 'cause otherwise I'd never hear the end of it. Anyhow, I just told Annie I figured that dress would be real pretty on you, is all."

Beth felt both relieved and disappointed, but she chose to put those thoughts aside. "Don't you see? It implied that you had a claim on me. I was mortified!"

"Didn't mean no harm by it."

"You still shouldn't have done it."

Darcy waved off her objection. "I was just tryin' to do somethin' nice for you. Didn't mean to hurt your feelings. I'm sorry I did, an' that's all I'm gonna say 'bout that.

"Next thing. You said you heard me talk poorly o' Charles an' Jane. Somethin' 'bout that he could have done better if he didn't move here."

"That's right. I overheard your conversation with Caroline Bingley."

He frowned. "What is it with the women 'round here,

sneakin' about, eavesdroppin' on private conversations?" Both Beth and Anne blushed at that. "Annie here is always over-hearin' things. Quiet as an Injun, she is. Huh an' they call *me* a half-breed." Beth was amazed at his statement—she never dreamed he could make light of his heritage.

He turned back to Beth. "If you heard all that, did you hear what else I said? Charles is one fine doctor. That man saved my life. In a big city, he could write his own ticket, be as rich as Midas! But he don't want that. He came here 'cause he wanted to go to a place that needed him, and lucky man that he is, he found him somethin' better than all the gold in th' world. You know what that is?"

Beth bit her lip. "Jane?"

"That's right. Charles would rather be poor an' married to Jane than be rich and lonely in New Orleans, or wherever. An' if I was in his shoes, I'd choose the same. That's what I told that… woman." Darcy nodded as he took a drink.

"What else? Slaves—that's right, you said I owned slaves. Who th' hell told you that? Whitehead?"

Beth blinked. "Yes, but… but you can't deny that. Everybody knows white people owned slaves in the South."

"Well, well, think you know everythin', don't you? Well, you're wrong, Miss Beth. Annie, did Cate ever own slaves?"

Anne looked at Beth. "No, we've never had slaves."

Darcy paced before an astonished Beth. "Miss Beth, do you know what it's like ridin' the herd? A man's gotta be self-relic… self-relie… gotta be able to look out for himself without some-body else keepin' a close eye on him. Gotta be able to protect himself, his fellows, an' the herd from coyotes an' rustlers. How can you give a slave a gun? No, ma'am, you can't. I ain't sayin' there's never been slaves on ranches, but there sure ain't been any in these parts. There ain't no slaves on Pemberley an' never have been. One more lie from Mr. Whitehead."

Darcy grew more agitated while Beth digested his words. They flew in the face of everything she had believed. Everyone up North believed that most, if not all, Southerners owned slaves. It was in the papers. Reverend Goldring preached against it. And yet, she could not refute Darcy's words. They made too much sense. And Anne backed him up.

Beth colored as she thought of George. He had been here longer; he must have known the truth. Yet, he had purposely misled her—or rather, allowed her to continue to hold to her misconceptions. Why? She had come to the conclusion months ago that George stretched the truth at times—it was part of his charm. But this was an out-and-out lie. Why would he do it? And what else had he lied about?

"Whitehead… Whitehead," Darcy was mumbling. He stopped suddenly and turned to Beth. "Are you in love with him?"

"No!" The denial flew from Beth's mouth before she could think.

He peered closely at her. "You sure?"

Beth's mind began to work again, and she grew irritated at his questioning. "Mr. Darcy, while my personal life is none of your concern, I shall repeat myself. I am not in love with George. He is a friend to my family—that is all."

"George Whitehead is nobody's friend. He's a carpetbaggin' piece o' scum. I remember you callin' him a war hero. Ha! A jailer is what he was." Darcy pointed at his chest. "My jailer!"

"What?"

"Captain George Whitehead was second in command o' th'

Camp Campbell prison camp in Missouri, where Charles an' me were taken after Vicksburg. Now, ole George may have been the assistant commander, but since his colonel spent the better part of every day tryin' to get inside of a bottle, George had a free hand runnin' th' place. For a year we enjoyed his hospitality, us and a thousand other prisoners." His face grew soft. "At least there were a thousand when we started out. By th' time Charles an' me were transferred to Camp Douglas in Illinois th' next summer, three hundred of us were in th' ground."

Beth was shocked. "Three hundred men died? But... but the papers all said that Confederate prisoners were treated well." She looked at Anne, who also sat with an astonished look on her face.

"You... you never told us, Will," was all she said.

"It ain't somethin' a man likes to remember, Annie. God help me, I wish I could forget."

"What happened?" Beth asked.

"Three things—mismanagement, malnourishment, an' mistreatment. Ha, didn't think I could get all that out." Darcy looked perversely proud of his alliteration. "Camp Campbell wasn't supposed to be a prison—it was a way station. But the real prisons weren't ready. So there we stayed, as more an' more men came. A thousand souls on a few acres. Sickness an' starvation took more of the victims."

"*Starvation?*" Beth cried. "But what of the food the War Department sent?"

"Oh, it came, what little they actually sent. We were right by the railroad siding, an' we saw the Yankee soldiers unloadin' the freight cars. Funny thing, though—not all of it got into the kitchens. Charles was workin' in the camp hospital at the time, an' he made friends with some o' the guards. He found out from them that a lot of the food for the prisoners was sold to the townspeople."

"By who?"

Darcy gave her a look. "Who do you think?" Darcy took another drink as Beth digested the implication. "We couldn't complain about it without bein' labeled malcontents and bein' charged with insurrection. But we complained anyway, for all the good it did. George liked that word—insurrection. Most of us were accused of it at least once. He also liked the whip." An unreadable expression came over Darcy before he turned to the fireplace. "Flogging was a weekly occurrence."

Beth was having a hard time handling what she was hearing. How could a handsome and charming man like George Whitehead be the ruthless and dishonest monster Darcy was describing? It couldn't be true, could it?

Darcy continued in an unemotional voice. "By the time they shipped us out, there were three hundred graves in the Confederate cemetery. Some o' the townspeople didn't want individual headstones—said it was ugly an' we didn't deserve it anyway—but decency won out. An' as for Captain George Whitehead, he got a promotion to major.

"Camp Douglas[4] in Chicago wasn't any better. We were crammed in with twelve thousand others in a place designed for half that many. Eighty acres o' hell. They wouldn't let Charles serve in the hospital. We never knew how many died—four to

---

4 Camp Douglas POW camp was real and has been referred to as the "Andersonville of the North," Andersonville being the infamous Confederate POW camp whose commandant was executed by the U.S. Government for war crimes. It is difficult to know how many men died at Camp Douglas, as many records were hidden or destroyed by the camp officials. Camp Campbell is fictitious.

six thousand, Charles thinks, most in unmarked graves or tossed into Lake Michigan. An' unlike Andersonville, nobody was punished for it."

Darcy bowed his head before turning back to the ladies, both shaken by what they had heard. "All that kept me alive was wantin' to get back home and see my daddy an' my sister again. In the summer of '65, I finally got back to Rosings, only to find my daddy sick. You remember, don't you, Annie? I had to take over runnin' Pemberley. For two years, Daddy and me ran the ranch together, me from a horse an' him from his sickbed. By then, th' Yankee carpetbaggers were movin' in, but we paid them no mind. There was a ranch to run.

"Fitz an' I took a herd up to Kansas in '68. By the time I got back, Daddy had been in his grave for three weeks. And sittin' on the front porch o' Pemberley, pretty as you please, was good ole George Whitehead, late of Illinois an' newly appointed Recorder of Deeds for Long Branch County, and Judge Alton Phillips, who had kept his job by kissin' the asses o' the occupation government in Austin. Whitehead was tryin' to get himself named executor of my daddy's estate an' he was payin' court to my grievin' sister, while she was still wearin' her mournin' clothes."

Beth's jaw dropped. "Paying court to Gaby? But... but she's not of age now!"

Darcy's face screwed up in fury. "That's right—and she wasn't yet fifteen years old at the time."

Beth thought she was going to be sick.

"Only reason I didn't shoot that bastard and his scalawag friend right then an' there was that Fitz stopped me. Convinced me that bein' hung for killin' those two would not help Gaby at all. But I told them—told them both—that if I ever saw either of them on Pemberley land again, I'd kill them.

"I told Cate what had happened, an' you know what she said? Told me to forget it. That times had changed, an' we had to change with them. There was a new game in Austin, an' if we were going to get ahead, we'd have to play along." He drank down the last of his brandy.

"So, I'm sure you can understand why I don't give a good goddamn what happens in Rosings, Miss Bennet. I went to war to serve my town an' my state—defend my new country—an' when I came back an' needed help, where were the good people of Rosings? I ask you—where were they? Hidin' under their beds! The hell with 'em!" He staggered back over to the sideboard for a refill.

Beth turned to Anne. "Is it true?"

Anne nodded. "We all heard about it. We were afraid Whitehead was going to call in the army and occupy the town. We were all scared for the longest time. But when nothing happened and Whitehead started charming everybody, the town... forgot."

Darcy turned from the sideboard and raised his refilled glass to the ladies. "And so I hope I've been exonerated of bad behavior towards the Honorable George Whitehead. Here's to you, you son-of-a-bitch." Darcy tossed down half the glass. "And you're now free to hate me, Miss Beth, on my own merits and not on other people's opinions."

"I... I..." Beth composed herself. "I really don't know what to think right now, Mr. Darcy."

Darcy just stared at her. "I'm sorry about your brother. I lost a lot of friends in that damned war, but I didn't lose a brother. I'm really sorry for your loss."

Beth bowed her head. "Thank you."

"You gotta understand war," Darcy went on. "When you're on th' battlefield, nothin' matters except survivin' and watchin' out for your fellows. The other side, well, it's like they're not people, you see. They're not human. You've got to kill them, 'cause they're tryin' to kill you. If a man stops to think about what he's doing, about what war really is, you… you just can't do it. You hesitate. An' if you hesitate, you die, or the man next to you dies. You can't allow yourself to think."

Darcy took another drink. "If your brother was here today, I'd shake his hand an' call him friend, 'cause he would know what I'm talking about. Just like that Buford fella I met today. Country, cause, flag—it don't mean anything when th' shootin' starts. Only keepin' alive. He'd know; he'd understand. I'm sorry, Beth. I'd give anything if he could be here today. Anything." To Beth's dismay, tears freely ran down Darcy's proud face. "I'd trade places with him, if it would make you happy—"

Just then, Darcy lost his footing and, with a crash, fell to the floor. The two ladies jumped up and ran to his side to find the young rancher insensible on the floor, blood seeping from one side of his scalp. Beth was alarmed and stood to get help when they were joined by a white-haired man in a black jacket.

"Bartholomew!" cried Anne. "Where did you come from?"

"I was just outside the door, miss," the butler said as he examined Darcy.

"Were you there the whole time?" Beth asked.

His eyes flicked over to her. "For much of it. It's my job to look after you, Miss Anne," he explained.

"Are you following me?" Anne demanded angrily.

"Of course not," he said smoothly. "I just happen to be in your general vicinity as often as possible." He glanced at her. "Mrs. Burroughs knows nothing of this."

Anne stared at him, confused.

"I think Mr. Darcy struck his head as he fell," the butler determined. "The damage is less than it seems. Head wounds do bleed freely. He needs to rest. I don't envy his head when he wakes in the morning." He slid his hands under Darcy's arms and tried to lift him. Beth immediately moved to help.

"Miss Bennet, please! It is unseemly!" Bartholomew complained.

"Mr. Bartholomew, it's obvious you need assistance, and I am no helpless female. I will help you get Mr. Darcy upstairs." Beth's words inspired Anne to do the same, and despite the butler's protests, they worked together to maneuver the barely conscious man up the stairs and into a guest bedroom just across the hall from Beth. They were fortunate that Darcy could still make his legs work, for he was too tall and heavy even for the three of them. A towel was placed against his head to stem the bleeding before they allowed him to fall upon the bed.

"That won't last," Bartholomew said as he observed the towel turning red with blood. "I will fetch new cloths straight away." With that he left the room.

Beth stared at the man sprawled across the bed, trying to come to terms with her feelings. She was mortified to learn that most of what she held against him was based on her own ingrained prejudgment and other people's lies. Just who was William Darcy?

"I'd give anything if he could be here today," Darcy had said. *"Anything. I'd trade places with him, if it would make you happy."*

Will Darcy would die for me?

Anne moved over to Darcy's towel-covered head. "Beth, help me."

"What? What are you doing?"

"If we don't get his shirt off, he'll get blood on it."

Beth hesitated a moment, frozen by the impropriety of the suggestion, before her innate sense of the absurd promoted itself. *Beth Bennet, you're already in a gentleman's bedroom after spending a half-hour talking to him late at night in your nightgown. It can hardly get any more improper than it already is. At least Anne is here with me.*

With a shrug, she reached over to assist. They turned Darcy over, careful not to dislodge the towel, and unfastened the buttons. For the first time, Beth saw the bare chest of a man unrelated to her. And a fine, broad one it was. Unconsciously, she licked her lips.

Beth glanced up to see Anne grinning at her. "What?"

She laughed. "Nothing. Oh, we can't get this off. We'll have to turn him over again." Once again on his stomach, the ladies were able to remove the shirt completely. They weren't prepared for the sight before them. Beth gasped and Anne let out a sharp scream.

Bartholomew dashed into the room, arms filled with cloths and towels. "What is it? What is the matter—Oh, my God!" He stood stock-still at the foot of the bed.

Anne's eyes filled with tears. "What happened to William? Who did this?"

Beth could not answer; her attention was fixed on Darcy's back—a back completely covered in angry, white scars.

Chapter 10

July 5

WHEN BETH CAME DOWN for breakfast the next morning, she was not surprised to learn that Dr. Bingley had been sent for. She didn't need to ask who Charles was there to see. Indeed, she was hard-pressed to get the man out of her head.

Anne glanced sheepishly at Beth, but with her mother in attendance, she refrained from speaking. It wasn't until Mrs. Burroughs retired to her study to work on ranch matters that Anne moved to the seat next to Beth.

"Beth, about the dress, I'm so sorry. It was Will's idea to surprise you—"

Beth cut her off. "Please, the less said about yesterday, the better."

Anne, chastised, stared at her plate. "I hope you're still my friend."

Beth sighed. "I am. But friends don't deceive each other." Beth instantly regretted her words as Anne's eyes filled with tears. But before she could console her, Charles came into the room.

"Well, he'll live, but I can't say he'll enjoy it." His jovial manner dissipated with one look at Anne's unhappy face. "Forgive me, I shouldn't be joking," he said, misunderstanding Anne's concern. "Will'll be fine. He just needs a day o' rest. He'll be fit as a fiddle come tomorrow morning."

Anne smiled her thanks to Dr. Bingley, and Beth realized she was relieved, too. Anne offered Charles some breakfast, and he sat down.

"Thank you, Miss Anne," Charles said. "Beth? We'll leave right afterwards, if you're ready."

Beth waited until Charles's surrey was well out of earshot of the ranch house before she turned to her brother-in-law.

"Charles, I've recently learned some disturbing things about the war."

"Is that so?" A puzzled Charles turned to her. "What brings this up?"

Beth had no answer but the truth. "Will Darcy and I were… talking yesterday, and it just came up."

"Talking about the war? At a party?" Charles was flabbergasted.

Beth turned away to hide the flush on her face. "All right— we had an argument. He said George Whitehead ran one of the prisons you and Mr. Darcy were in. Is that true?"

"Yeah. Will doesn't usually talk about those days."

"Nobody does!" Beth cried. "It's like it's a great big secret!"

"Beth, war is a thing a man wants to forget."

"Have you talked about it to Jane?"

Charles ignored the impertinence of her question. "A little. Where's all this leading?"

"Last night, when Mr. Darcy got… himself injured, Miss

Burroughs and I helped Mr. Bartholomew get him to his room. In the course of caring for him we… we saw his back." Charles's eyes grew wide. "Charles, where did those scars come from? Was Mr. Darcy whipped in prison?"

It took a moment for an astonished Dr. Bingley to say, "That's not my story to tell."

"Then he was. Charles, you can tell me. Mr. Darcy himself told us stories about horrible mistreatment in the camps, so you wouldn't be telling me something I haven't heard. He said George liked to have people whipped. Was it George who had Mr. Darcy whipped?"

Charles stared straight ahead. "Yes," he admitted in a low voice.

"Why?"

"Because of me."

"*You?*"

"Beth, this ain't easy for me to talk about." He took a breath. "Will and I were at Vicksburg, but instead of being paroled after the surrender like the others, we were arrested by Whitehead on false charges."

"What were the charges?"

"Resistin' the surrender, but that wasn't the real reason. We knew too much. You see, we saw Whitehead and his men stealin' from my patients. I complained, but instead of punishing Whitehead, his commanders placed him in charge of bringing us to prison." Charles went on to talk of their trip to Camp Campbell in Missouri—how the transfer point-turned-prison was totally insufficient for the purpose intended, and how Captain Whitehead essentially became the commander of the place.

"The sanitary conditions were awful," Charles continued.

"The latrine wasn't suitable for even a third of the men we had there. I was workin' in the camp hospital—there was a shortage of Yankee doctors—so I went to the Yankee colonel to get permission to have a new latrine dug. The drunkard turned me down flat—said his engineers told him what we had would be more than adequate. Beth, he was wrong. That thing was dysentery waitin' to happen.

"Food was always scarce, so Whitehead had the idea of us makin' a vegetable garden for the guards. Each day, a team of men would be issued hoes and tools to work the ground. I saw my opportunity and went to Will with my idea. If the men spent an extra ten minutes a day at the end of their shift diggin' a new latrine, we'd have it done in less than a week. Will told me to go ahead, as long as the guards knew what we were doin'. I didn't have any trouble with them, 'cause I had pulled a tooth for the head of the detail, and he took a likin' to me.

"Everything was goin' along fine until, in an unexpected fit of sobriety, the colonel decided to hold an inspection. He took one look at the nearly-finished latrine and started yellin', accusing us of diggin' an escape tunnel. Guns were being pointed every which-way, so I stepped up and told him what it was. I was immediately taken in hand and dragged to a court of inquiry.

"There I was, standin' afore the colonel with a nervous Whitehead at his side. Now, you see, it was ole George's idea to have us prisoners make a garden an' put tools in our hands, so he was ultimately responsible. I figure he was there to make sure *I* took the blame, not him. So Whitehead said nothing when his commanding officer accused me of organizing a mass escape, until the colonel started talking about havin' me shot. I guess that was too much even for Whitehead—that, or else he was afraid of an investigation from higher authorities. That's when he suggested that shootin' a doctor would be bad for morale and flogging would be enough of a punishment.

"Just before sentence was read, there was a disruption at the tent entrance. I turned around to see Will walking in like he was a commanding general, surrounded by two guards. He was yelling that this hearing was illegal, a violation of the Articles of War. The colonel got mad, I can tell you, and demanded an explanation. Will said that they couldn't punish a man following a lawful order, and that he, as commanding officer of the Confederate prisoners, had ordered me to build that latrine.

"I was shocked to see him, Beth, and not just because of his words, which was stretchin' the truth a bit. That he was allowed anywhere near the tent was amazing. But I noted that one of his guards was the same sergeant whose tooth I pulled, so I guess he was repayin' the favor by bringin' Darcy to the hearing so that he could object.

"The colonel was spittin' mad—screaming that he ought to shoot us both. Whitehead put a hand on his shoulder to quiet him down. He said, 'Colonel, the captain is correct—we can't punish a man for following a legal order.' He then turned to Will, and Beth, I swear the man actually smiled as he said, 'But we can punish an officer who encouraged insurrection against the lawful authority. Since Captain Darcy issued the order, let *him* be punished.'"

Beth's hands flew to her mouth. "Oh, Charles!"

"Beth, I tried to stop it—I objected at the top o' my lungs—but Darcy rode me down. Ordered me to be silent and obey. Whitehead had the guards take Will out immediately and execute the sentence." He passed a hand over his face. "I wasn't at the flogging, but since they didn't revoke my hospital privileges, I was there when they brought him in afterwards. I'll never forget that sight for as long as I live. They almost beat him to death—I feared for his life for nearly a week."

Charles paused in his recount. "When Will was able to talk, I asked the damn fool why he did it. He told me, 'Charles, I'm expendable—you're not.'" He looked at Beth, his chin trembling. "And that's Will Darcy for you."

Beth blinked as her tears flowed freely.

Bingley pulled himself together. "As Will got better, we got the word that there had been a surprise inspection from the War Department and that the camp had received a commendation for the new latrine. It seemed Whitehead didn't have the time to have it filled in, but it worked out to his advantage. He took credit for it, from what the guards told me. Helped lead to his promotion."

It took awhile for Beth to compose herself. "Does Jane know this?"

"Not the details, but enough to know that Whitehead's not the man he seems."

"But why not tell her everything? Why not tell the whole town? They need to know how ruthless George is."

"Beth, it's not that easy. For one thing, it's not just my story; it's Will's, too. Just by tellin' you, I'm going against Will's wishes." He sighed. "You see, there's a code out here—what's in the past stays in the past. A lot of folks came out west to escape the past, so people in these parts aren't ones to bring it up. A man's judged by what he is and not by what he was.

"For another, Whitehead's close to the government in Austin, and he can make a lot of trouble for any that get in his way. He's got Mrs. Burroughs on his side and a private army in Kid Denny and his gang. A lot of people just want to put the war in the past, and Whitehead's made friends here—your daddy, for instance.

"Darcy just wants to let it go. He's afraid if he starts up something, people will get hurt, and there's no guarantee that if we drive Whitehead out of town, the army or the government wouldn't come in and make things worse."

By now, the surrey had reached the outskirts of the town, passing the cemetery on the hill. "Beth, I reckon we just let things go on as they have. Sooner or later, this occupation by the army will be over, Whitehead will show his true stripes, the town will turn on him, and that will be the end of him. 'Til then, we'll just keep our heads down and look out for our own, just like Will says."

"But what about Father?"

Charles nodded. "I'll talk to him again—make certain he's not gettin' in over his head in his dealings with Whitehead."

"Again? You've talked to him before?"

"Yeah."

Beth wasn't sure that was enough, but she kept her concern to herself.

Darcy didn't return to Pemberley until the next day. Everyone was concerned over his absence, Gaby most of all, and she asked for an explanation. Darcy declined to answer fully, mumbling something about an "indisposition," and he immediately claimed a desire to see to the paperwork awaiting him in his study.

Once he locked the door and seated himself behind his desk, Darcy simply stared out the widow, ignoring the papers on his desk. Ever since he woke up the day before with a pounding head and sickly belly, he had been obsessed in reviewing what had happened—how things had gone so wrong and how he could have misjudged things so badly.

He raised one hand to his forehead. He still suffered from a headache brought on by his excessive drinking and his injury. He had no recollection of how he had hurt himself. He had awakened with a bandage wrapped around his head and a chamber pot close by, which he used to empty the contents of his stomach. It had been a full day since Charles had tended to him, and he still refused to rest. Darcy well remembered everything prior to falling down, and it was those memories that haunted him. He accepted his pain as penance for his arrogant behavior.

It had taken all of the day and most of the night before Darcy allowed himself to see past his pain, both physical and emotional, and accept the truth. Beth Bennet hated him, and he had no one to blame but himself.

The study door opened. "Will," Gaby stated without pre-amble, "I'm going for a ride, and you're going with me."

"No, I'm not."

"Yes, you are. I'm getting Buckskin and Caesar saddled right now." Without another word, she left the room.

A few minutes later, Darcy was astride his black steed with his sister next to him on her palomino, riding towards Pemberley Lake. Darcy had to admit the hot sun felt good against his face and the movement of his horse settled his emotions, if not his head. He wondered when his sister had grown so wise.

The two stopped at a shady willow overlooking the lake, and they dismounted. Brother and sister took their ease sitting at the base of the tree as the horses drank from the water.

Darcy was thankful for the quiet; it allowed him to set his thoughts in order. The water before him reminded Darcy of Beth's clandestine swim, and he finally came to the realization that he had confused his lust for Beth Bennet with love. It was the only reason he could think of that would so blind him to the truth.

Heck, even Anne saw that Beth wasn't in love with me. But did I listen? Naw—I had to go my own way and make a damned fool of myself. No wonder she thought I was making some kind of improper request of her. In a way, I was. The only reason I wanted to marry her was to get her in my bed. And now, thanks to my drunken performance, there's no way she'll ever give me the time of day again.

"Will, is something wrong?" asked Gaby.

Darcy looked at the water for a while, thinking. *Damn, I probably ruined Gaby's friendship with Beth. Anne's, too. What the hell was I thinking with that dress? That's just it, I wasn't thinking. I was treating her as if she was mine already. And all I accomplished was to drive her off and hurt Gaby and Anne.*

A woman as fine as Beth Bennet deserves to be wooed, courted. Not just ridden down and lassoed like I was roping a calf—tossed, tied down, and branded. I haven't the faintest idea how to earn the good opinion of a proper lady. I am the biggest idiot in Long Branch County.

"Will?"

Darcy sighed. "Gaby, I've made a mistake—a very, very big mistake—and I don't know how I can ever make things right." He tossed a twig towards the water's edge.

Gaby looked at Will in surprise. It never occurred to her that her perfect brother could ever err. "What happened?"

"Hurt somebody I thought I loved."

Gaby thought for a moment. "Beth?" she gasped. "What did you do?"

"I'm embarrassed to talk about it. Let's just say that after what I did, she'd be the last person on earth to go get help if I was drowning in the lake there."

"That's hard to believe with George Whitehead in town."

"He's part of the problem."

"What do you mean? Oh, you don't think Beth's in love with *him*, do you? Because if you do, I can assure you she's not."

"No, she told me she wasn't." Will, to his shame, remembered almost everything from the late-night discussion in the Burroughses' library, except how he managed to earn a knot on his head. Before Anne told him what had happened, he half-figured that Beth had taken an empty whiskey bottle to him. "But he's been telling stories." He turned to Gaby. "How do you know she doesn't love Whitehead?"

"A woman can tell these things." She played with the grass beside her. "Will, when I... when Whitehead tried to... court me, I suppose... you made me talk about it. I didn't want to, but you said it would make me feel better. And it did. Will, I think you need to talk to me now."

"And it'll make me feel better?"

"I don't know. It worked for me. At least you'll know you won't be alone."

Darcy thought about that for a minute. "Well, I can't feel worse." And so he told Gaby *almost* everything. Seventeen-year-old girls didn't need to know about spying on naked people swimming, after all.

The Bingley household took their ease in the front parlor after supper. Charles read from a week-old newspaper, while Jane mended one of his shirts. Beth attempted to concentrate on a book of poetry, trying to keep her thoughts away from the mystery of Will Darcy, but Caroline defeated her by holding forth on the Burroughses' ball.

"It was certainly not up to Netherfield standards," she told her brother. "The food, in particular, was the usual primitive cooking so prevalent in these parts. 'Barbeque,' I believe it's called. Do you remember the last party we held at Netherfield?" She turned to her sister-in-law, a faraway look in her eye. "Jane, the food was so elegantly presented and was as delicious as it looked."

"I'm sure it was, Caroline," Jane replied, never taking her eyes off her task, in a tone of voice that told Beth her sister had heard these tales before. Charles kept his face in the paper.

Caroline was insensitive to it. "And the dresses! Yes, they spanned the colors of the rainbow, I'm sure. Silk and taffeta and all good things. A far cry from what I saw here." She turned to Beth, interrupting her reminiscing, a slight frown creasing her brow. "Your dress, however, was very fine, Miss Beth. May I ask where you got it?"

Mention of the blue dress brought Darcy—and his reaction to it—to Beth's mind, and she hoped she didn't blush as she told a small lie. "It belonged to Anne Burroughs, and she was kind enough to insist I wear it. It was very pretty."

Caroline seemed relieved at the intelligence. "I see. It did favor you, though—much better than it would have done for Miss Burroughs."

"Caroline! That is not very kind," Jane mildly scolded her.

"Oh, Jane, you know it's true," Caroline cried. "I hope she's been blessed with a substantial dowry, because she'll never attract a suitor with her looks, bless her heart."

"Anne has been my friend. She's been very kind to me," Beth said pointedly, irate at the slight to her friend.

"I say nothing about her personality," Caroline protested, "but you must admit that there is a lack of beauty in Rosings. Why, if it weren't for the Darcys and our family, well… the dance would have been a challenge to behold, I'm afraid. Nothing like our Georgia peaches, eh, Charles?"

Charles lowered his paper. "I believe you're being a little hard on Rosings, Caroline."

His sister went on smugly as if he had said nothing. "The dresses did nothing to improve the ambiance, what little it could accomplish. I declare, I've never seen so much gingham and calico in my life."

Beth seethed, as she remembered how proud Mary had been of her beautiful blue calico dress. She had had enough of Caroline's snide remarks and superior ways. In her sweetest, most insincere voice, Beth observed, "Georgia sounds lovely, Miss Caroline. With your descriptions of what a paradise it is, I'm surprised you don't return to Netherfield."

The reaction to her comment was electric. Caroline paled, and even Bingley blanched. Jane sat up, the darning forgotten, and cried, "Beth, please! You don't understand—"

"I understand that Georgia is apparently heaven on earth," Beth went on heedlessly, in her annoyance dismissing the warning in her sister's voice. "I'm astonished that Miss Caroline left home, the way she carries on about it."

Charles put down his paper. "Beth!"

Beth was surprised to receive an uncharacteristic reprimand from her placid brother-in-law. The man was plainly mortified. With a nagging feeling that she had once again spoken without thinking, Beth's eyes returned to Caroline. It was as if a mask had slipped from the woman's face; her complexion had gone from white to red, her eyes wide. Her usual careless expression was replaced by one of pure anger and pure torment.

"*I have no home!*" Caroline cried. "My home is gone—destroyed by your precious Yankees!"

Beth's eyebrows rose at the ridiculous accusation. "Are you saying that Union soldiers did something to Netherfield?"

"Did something? Oh, yes! They burned it to the ground is all—right before my eyes!"

Beth's jaw dropped. "*What?* But… why?"

"Ask General Sherman!"

"Sherman?" Beth thought about what the papers had said about Sherman in Georgia. "I remember reading about the March to the Sea, freeing the slaves—"

"And destroying everything in his path!" Caroline was livid as she relived the event. "A damned host of fifty thousand Federals marched three hundred miles from Atlanta to Savannah, burning a swath sixty miles wide! They stole food, grain, livestock—anything they could carry. And what they couldn't take, they burned." She lifted her eyes from Beth and stared into the distance, as if she could see something far away, both precious and lost forever. "Farms, plantations, towns—just for spite. Sherman boasted he would make Georgia howl, and we did howl—in anguish!"

Beth was dizzy as her preconceived notions took yet another blow. First Will Darcy, then Charles, and now Miss Bingley.

She shook her head to clear her thoughts. "But… but the papers said… the slaves. Sherman was freeing the slaves and attacking the means of war. Railroads, arms factories—"

"Lies! I was there!"

Caroline had leapt to her feet, her eyes so wide the white around the irises could be seen. Charles, too, had risen from his chair and attempted to soothe his sister.

"Caroline, please, calm yourself—"

"No!" the woman shouted, pointing at Beth. "I will not be silenced! She needs to know just what her damnable country-men did!"

Her outburst had silenced the house—everyone was trans-fixed. Caroline paused, breathing in and out in a shuddering manner, before pacing about the room like a cornered animal, her hand jerkily accenting the words that spit out of her mouth.

"When the hordes came, all our slaves ran away to join them. All but my maid, Maybel. She alone stood by me as they ransacked my home. What those god-forsaken blue bellies couldn't take, they destroyed. For a time, we were terrified that one or more of those *animals* might try and take *me*!

"But, no—they didn't so much as touch a hair on my head. Instead they ripped my heart from my breast! We watched those *monsters* turn our beautiful Netherfield into *ashes*. Everything I owned was burned. *Everything*. All I had left was literally the clothes on my back!" By now, tears were running down her hard features.

A stunned Beth turned to Charles, who nodded, verifying his sister's account. Beth's insides roiled in mortification at her earlier thoughtless words. "I… I'm sorry. I didn't know."

"Sorry… sorry. Is that all you Yankees have to say—that you're *sorry*?" Caroline continued to rage. "After the war, the carpetbaggers and their scallywag friends stole what was left of Netherfield when we couldn't pay the taxes!" She stopped her pacing and turned to Beth. "You tell me you're sorry? Prove it! Give me back my home! Give me back Netherfield! *Then*, I'll accept your apology." Her tearful eyes gleamed with malice. "Until then, allow me to hate y'all as much as I can."

"Caroline, that's enough!" Charles thundered. "Beth, please excuse me. I need to talk to my sister."

A weeping Beth made her way into her borrowed bedroom, her pregnant sister close behind. Once she closed the door, Jane joined Beth on her bed, taking her hands.

"Are you all right, Beth?"

Beth shook her head. "I'm... I'm shocked. I can hardly believe what she said. But Charles's face... oh Jane!" She held her face in her hands. "Is *everything* I know about the war wrong?"

Jane rubbed her sister's back. "Beth, do you remember how scared we were back in '63 when we heard of Morgan's Raid[5]? How the Rebels were riding along the Ohio River, stealing from folks? We were afraid they would show up at our door any minute. Father always said not to put too much stock into what the papers wrote. People are people, and you can't expect Northern troops to act any differently than the Southerners."

Beth looked at Jane and saw only concern, not surprise or censure. "Did you know about this?"

"Yes. Charles told me what happened to his family's home some time ago."

---

5 Morgan's Raid, or The Calico Raid, June 11–July 26, 1863, was a highly publicized 1,000-mile incursion by 2,400 Confederate cavalry into the Northern states of Indiana and Ohio during the Civil War and was one of the northernmost military actions involving the Confederate States Army.

"Why didn't you tell us?"

"Charles and I decided not to. What good would it have done to tell you that our Union soldiers took everything away from the Bingleys? It would have only made things uncomfortable for everyone. Charles has made his peace with the war. Mother and Father have more than accepted Charles; they love him as a son. What's in the past is in the past. We both want to make a new start here in Texas."

"You still should have told us, but I understand your reasons. Poor Caroline." Beth made a sound between a sob and a nervous laugh. "I never thought I would ever say that. Oh, my God, what that poor girl has gone through."

"I know, but I don't excuse what Caroline said. She's a very bitter woman." Jane sighed. "I'm not blind. I know she doesn't like me, and she's disappointed that Charles married me. I know she wants him to move to New Orleans. But the war has deeply damaged her. She's been forced to live with the Hursts, far away from a home she loved. It's driven out most of her tender feelings, leaving only pain and anger and false pride to hide behind. Do you know that as pretty as she is, she has no beaux in New Orleans? It's because it's written on her face that she can't love anymore."

"If you believe she dislikes you, why do you put up with her?"

"Because she's my sister." Jane stroked Beth's hair. "If you came down sick, I would nurse you, you know that. Caroline's sick, but in a different way. She's sick in her heart, and we're trying to help. Perhaps one day, Caroline will allow herself to love again."

"You're a better person than I am, Jane," Beth said in awe.

Jane smiled. "No, I'm not. You're special in your own way."

They sat quietly for a moment. "Has Charles told you any-thing else about the war?"

"Some. What are you asking?"

"Has he told you about George Whitehead?"

"He told me Whitehead did some wicked things in the war, if that's what you mean."

Jane's use of George's last name told Beth that her sister was deeply angered by the man. "I've heard some things, too. I think we should tell Father."

Jane glanced away. "Charles has tried to warn Father, but..." she shook her head, "he dismissed him. He thanked Charles for his concern but said that things were different now." She turned to Beth, confusion written over her face. "I don't understand."

Neither did Beth, but before she could say so, the bedroom door opened to reveal a grim Charles with Caroline behind him. Miss Bingley once again wore an expression of supreme indifference.

"Beth, Caroline would like to say something to you." He gestured for his sister to proceed.

A stone-faced Caroline stared at a point above Beth's head. "I hope you will pardon my strong words earlier, Miss Bennet. If, by my honest account of the misfortunes that have befallen my family, you've taken offense, I am sorry."

Charles was not happy about the halfhearted apology. "Caroline..."

Beth stood up, intending to end this disagreement. She was not fooled into thinking Caroline was in any way sincere. Her use of "Miss Bennet" rather than the more familiar "Miss Beth" was ample evidence of that. But that was neither here nor there. Caroline deserved her pity and forbearance, and she intended to make amends as best she could.

"Thank you, Miss Bingley. May I say how sorry I am about the hardships you have been forced to endure? I thank you for telling me, and I hope there are better days ahead."

Caroline's eyes flicked to hers, and Beth was shaken by the resentment she beheld there. For the first time in her life, Beth was truly hated by another person—not for *who* she was, but for *what* she was. She realized that Caroline Bingley would never forgive or forget; she would nurse this hatred for the rest of her days. It was a disconcerting experience for Beth, especially as in essence she had sworn to do the same.

Still, Caroline extended her hand, which Beth took gingerly. "Thank you. I trust we will get along just fine in the weeks we have left together." Her smile was devoid of any warmth.

"I… I believe we shall." Beth was shaken again. Never before had any apology she offered been so effectively dismissed. Matters were hopeless.

Caroline sighed. "It's your usual time to retire, I believe."

"It is. Good night, Miss Bingley."

The lady nodded again and swept out of the room, Charles following in her wake, still unhappy. Jane kissed Beth good night and left for her own room.

Beth shook her head sadly as she prepared for bed. It was going to be a long month.

Darcy and Gaby stood outside the Baptist church until they finally spied their quarry. Gaby gave her brother's hand a squeeze before waving at the two ladies approaching.

"Miss Caroline! I'm so glad you came today. There's something I'd like to get your advice on."

Miss Bingley, who heretofore had simply been walking to the meeting of the Musical Society with Miss Bennet and had been concentrating on following Charles's unexpectedly harsh command to be polite to the woman, looked up in surprise. "Of course, Miss Darcy. How may I help you?"

Gaby threaded her arm through Caroline's. "I, uhh, wanted to discuss my musical selection with you. I need your help to pick the right piece. Your taste is so fine; I know you can choose the proper one."

Caroline looked between Darcy and the girl. Her desire to spend time with the handsome rancher was overcome by the combination of the appeal to her vanity and the opportunity to prove useful to Darcy's sister, thereby impressing the man. "Certainly, Miss Darcy."

Gaby practically dragged her into the church. "My music is inside." Caroline looked back helplessly as the doors closed behind her.

Darcy's thoughts changed from the reward Gaby was sure to demand for this piece of theater—perhaps a new saddle for her horse, Buckskin—to the half-confused, half-amused lady before him. Just as she began to follow the others, Darcy stopped her.

"Miss Bennet, may I have a moment of your time?"

Beth turned to him warily, an unfamiliar expression on her face. "Yes?"

Darcy removed his hat and steeled himself. "I'm sorry for the unease our meeting must give you. I'm very aware that my presence is a trial to you. But I've been waiting for an opportunity to apologize for my reprehensible behavior during our last meeting. I'm heartily ashamed of myself, and I offer no excuse. I don't ask for your forgiveness—indeed, I don't deserve it. This charade," he waved his hand, "wouldn't be necessary and I'd never presume to disturb you again if not for the sake of my sister and cousin. I beg you—do not end your friendship with *them* because of *me*."

He watched with anxious eyes as Beth stood before him, blinking. She seemed astonished, but Darcy would not trust his observations. Too many times in their acquaintance had his instincts been very wrong about this girl.

"Mr. Darcy, I... I thank you. I would never throw off Miss Darcy or Miss Burroughs, even though *we've* had our... disagreements."

"Then, may I tell them that you still welcome their company?"

"Oh, yes, indeed! I'm... I'm only surprised."

"Surprised about what?"

She glanced away. "Surprised that you still think me a suitable companion for your sister and cousin, given my mistaken opinions about you."

"Miss Bennet, I can think of few people I would entrust my sister to, other than you." Beth blushed, and Darcy cursed himself for being too forward.

"I'll accept your apology only if you'll accept mine. I've been blind and ignorant about many things, especially about you—"

"Misled, I would say!"

Beth allowed a small smile. "Perhaps, but I thought myself to be a good judge of character. I now know I'm not. Thank you for teaching me that lesson. I shouldn't have said the things I did."

"I don't think you need to apologize to me, but I'll accept it, if that means you'll remain friends with Gaby and Anne."

She nodded. "You mentioned a charade. Do you mean that Miss Gaby wasn't as interested in Miss Bingley's company as she appeared?"

"No." An embarrassed Darcy allowed himself a smile. "I figured you might be coming to the meeting together, and I had to find a way of speaking to you privately. This," he gestured as before, "was Gaby's idea."

Beth giggled a bit, and then looked around. "Is Anne here? I didn't see her with you."

The rancher grew serious. "No. She was unsure of her reception. She's afraid you wouldn't want her company anymore."

He saw Beth become distressed. "Oh, no! That's not true. Please tell her she's still my friend."

"I will."

Beth looked down. "I hope Miss Darcy still thinks kindly of me, as little as I deserve it."

"She likes you very much."

"As I do her." She sighed. "I wish I could be friends with her brother."

At that, Darcy's heart sank even lower than it had been.

Beth continued, "But how can I, when it's apparent I don't even know him? I've been very foolish."

For the first time since the party, Darcy dared to hope. Carefully he said, "Perhaps you could get to know him. Start over."

She glanced up at him. "Will he be willing to give me that chance?"

"He seems to be a nice enough fellow. I'm sure he will, if it was welcome."

Beth blushed again. "Thank you," she whispered. Darcy nodded and the two stood in awkward silence for a moment.

"Excuse me," Beth said. "I must be going inside. The meeting's about to start."

Darcy put his hat back on. "And I have a meeting as well—at the bank. Good day, Miss Bennet."

"You, too, Mr. Darcy."

He watched Beth enter the church before turning and crossing the street to the Darcy Bank in a better frame of mind than he had expected a half-hour before. He waved at the teller, Mr. Rushworth, in his cage before knocking on the manager's door.

"Bertram, got a few minutes?"

Edmund Bertram got up from his desk. "Certainly, Mr. Darcy. Have a seat. Can I get you some coffee?" Two mugs were quickly prepared, and Bertram returned to his desk, facing his employer. "What brings you to town, sir? It's been a long time."

"Too long, Bertram. I've been away too long." Darcy took a sip as Bertram raised an eyebrow. "I want you to tell me everything that's been going on around town."

"Everything? That's going to take some time."

"I have the time, if you do."

"Then I'd better tell Rushworth to put on another pot. We'll be here awhile."

Chapter 11

August

THE NEW MONTH SAW the end of Jane's confinement, and Beth and Caroline were able to put aside their mutual loathing long enough to help Mrs. Bennet and Charles bring Susan Jane Bingley into the world. Beth thought the little girl was the prettiest thing she had ever seen. Caroline's only comment was, "Susan—Susanna—was my mother's name. That'll do." Beth wasn't sure if she saw a gleam in Caroline's eye, so swiftly did the other woman excuse herself to rest.

Jane recovered quickly from her ordeal, so only two weeks later, Charles helped his sister to board the stagecoach back to Louisiana. Caroline made one last attempt to convince Charles to move to New Orleans before taking her leave of Jane. The party waved as the stage left town, Beth feeling guilty relief that the woman was out of Jane's life.

Beth, too, found her help was no longer needed and returned the next day to the farm. She was content to fall back into the routine of chores and was happy in the familiarity of her family. She was pleased to see that Kathy continued to mature and take more responsibility around the house, but Lily was still Lily—young and lazy.

The only other change was with her father; he seemed to spend more time than usual closed up in his study. When he was with the family, mostly at table, his face carried lines never seen before. There was a slight air of worry about the man, but when Beth asked him about it, he dismissed her concerns with a smile.

Mrs. Bennet mentioned something about the harvest not being what it should, but she was confident that, if this year was tight, next year should be better. Other than that, she appeared to have changed little. Beth shook her head. For all her mother's emotional outbursts, she was a farmer's wife through and through. Fanny Bennet was a levelheaded, dependable sort of person, except when it came to her daughters' futures. Knowing a good marriage was the difference between plenty and poverty, happiness and hunger, she worried incessantly over the lack of eligible men in Rosings. When it came to the farm, however, she was as stoic as her husband. It was a farmer's lot to be held hostage by the whims of markets and weather. The phrase *Things will be better next year*" sustained the Bennet clan through the worst of times in the past, and Beth knew it would serve as a source of steadiness for her family in the future.

A few days later, Beth, riding her beloved Turner, found herself at Thompson Crossing. The horse started to move forward, but Beth held him back. Normally she would not have hesitated to cross the ford and allow Turner free rein across the vastness of Pemberley, but after her argument with Darcy at the B&R, she had second thoughts.

Yes, Darcy had forgiven her—he made that clear in town—but Beth still felt uneasy. Her terrible accusations, mostly built on lies and willful miscomprehensions, were unworthy of clemency. Beth felt a need to punish herself for hurting such a man as Will Darcy.

Looking at the situation dispassionately, Beth could finally see that there was little to complain about when it came to the owner of Pemberley Ranch. He was kind to his kinfolk and respectful of others. True, he was a reserved person and hard for strangers to approach, but the man's ironclad sense of justice and generous, forgiving nature more than made up for it.

Beth could now understand the incident in Zimmerman's store months ago. Darcy had somehow expressed in a few words and a quiet look his displeasure at how poor Mrs. Washington had been treated. That was why Mr. Zimmerman rushed to the back door to see to the woman's order. Beth had to shake her head. How many other rich men would wait in line behind anyone, especially a former slave?

Stupidly, Beth had not considered the enormous compliment Darcy had paid her by allowing an affectionate acquaintance to blossom between herself and his relations, particularly after Mary's overheard outburst about Catholics. Beth knew in her heart *she* wouldn't be so forgiving over such an insult to her faith. She was glad that Henry Tilney had set her family straight about the matter, but Beth hardly thought about the matter anymore. She shouldn't have forgotten, she berated herself, because that belittled the gesture made by Will and Gaby, reaching their hands out in friendship.

Beth had ignored all that. She had allowed herself to hate someone without knowing who he was. George's falsehoods found fertile ground to grow in Beth's mind because she had spent years cultivating it. She, alone in her family, held on to anger over the war. She was the only one not to put it truly behind her.

She now knew the reason she wouldn't let go of the war—she was afraid she would dishonor the memory of Samuel. Her initial anger at his death was understandable, but she had perpetuated her anguish by embellishing the facts. Samuel wasn't killed by the Rebels; he died of influenza while in camp. An honest person would have to admit that it could have happened anywhere at any time. Didn't a cholera epidemic sweep through Ohio in '49, the year before she was born? Her parents told her the family was lucky to have been untouched by it.

Fair was fair, and Beth had not been fair to Will Darcy or the South. Truly, the person she had been angry with was, in fact, Samuel himself. She never wanted her brother to enlist in the first place, but, caught up in the patriotic fervor engulfing the community, Samuel couldn't wait to don the blue of the Republic, march off to defend the Union, and put paid to those foolish Rebels. Beth felt abandoned as her beloved brother and playmate joined the army and left home. Her only consolation was that the war would be short. Surely those silly Southerners would come to their senses and beg for mercy at first sight of the mighty Union Army. Only after Bull Run and Shiloh did both sides realize they were in a struggle to the death.

For almost two years, Beth waited in fearful anticipation for news of her brother. Perversely, she held on tightly to his promise to return, a promise no man could be certain to keep. Providence would either take Samuel or return him. When the hated telegram came, Beth wanted to lash out at someone, but it couldn't be Samuel, and it couldn't be God. It could only be the Confederates.

By the time she reached Texas, she thought she put the war behind her. After all, she had made friends here. But her confrontations with Darcy and Caroline, and the explanations afterwards, made her reexamine her thinking.

What she found made her uncomfortable. She realized she had *allowed* herself to befriend Charlotte, Gaby, and Anne, not because of their innate goodness, but because it flattered her own vanity. Beth permitted herself to be friendly to Southerners to prove to the world that she was open-minded, tolerant, and forgiving. Though she enjoyed her friends' company, did she really respect them? Did she ever listen to their views without a critical ear? Did she ever give credence to their opinions? Charlotte told her about Darcy, and Anne tried to apologize, but Beth had dismissed them. In her estimation, Beth knew she was superior to them, not because of wealth, position, or education, but by the simple accident of where she was born.

Northerners were better than Southerners; it had been her belief for most of her life. The word of a Northerner must be taken over that of a Southerner. That was why she listened to Whitehead. Darcy challenged her, so she dismissed him. She felt free to heap all of her pain, grief, and disappointment onto a fine man who had suffered and lost more than she had.

No, Beth told herself. She wasn't better than Southerners. She certainly wasn't better than the man on whom she had heaped all her pain and disappointment over Samuel's death. William Darcy, rather than being a wicked representation of all that was wrong with Texas, was the best man she had ever known. Instead of being thankful for his friendship, grateful for his understanding and patience, and appreciative for his regard, she had been mean, thoughtless, and hypercritical.

Beth fought back her tears. *What a fool I was! How cruel and judgmental I was. I, who prided myself on my ability to read character and congratulated myself on being kind to those less fortunate, have been nothing but mean and critical. I believed everything George said because his stories confirmed my prejudices. Had I been in love, I couldn't have been more wretchedly blind.*

Pride has been my weakness. George didn't seduce my heart but my vanity. His stories allowed me to remain comfortably ignorant and allowed me to look down on my neighbors. Even Miss Bingley, for all her haughtiness, deserves more compassion from me than censure. How would I behave had her misfortunes fallen upon me?

And Will Darcy. Why am I so distressed over him? I couldn't be falling in love with him—it's impossible. Yet, when I think how I wronged him, my heart is filled with a terrible sorrow. I don't know why, but the very idea that he's alive and might think poorly of me is unbearable!

I know he said he's forgiven me—in fact, he apologized for his own behavior—yet, I can hardly credit it. For him to be so kind to me after I cruelly abused him is astonishing. I'm blessed I have the chance of being his friend and the chance to change for the better.

Poor Caroline. Her hates and disappointments are destroying her. Oh! But for the Grace of God that could be me! Thank you, God, for my family and friends, for You have surely saved me from a pitiful existence. The lesson taught me is hard, but I will be grateful for it the rest of my life.

"Howdy, ma'am!"

Beth looked up to see a cowboy in chaps waving on the Pemberley side of the river. He stood next to his horse, which was taking a drink. The ranch hand seemed to be about her age—or even younger; there was certainly a boyish enthusiasm about him.

"Afternoon," she returned tolerably, the distance allowing Beth to compose herself.

"Are you Miss Bennet?" he asked to her surprise.

"I am," she answered warily. "How do you know my name?"

The young man grinned and pointed at Turner. "Your horse, ma'am. We was told to be on the lookout for a paint with a girl in… umm… dungarees. I reckon you're her."

Disappointment overcame Beth. Obviously, Darcy had rescinded his open invitation to ride his range. Not that she could fault him. Though she did not intend to take advantage of Darcy's former goodness, she was crushed to learn of his changed feelings.

"Ain't cha comin' over?" the cowboy asked.

"Pardon me?"

"Just wonderin' if you was of a mind to ride today."

"I… umm… don't know."

"'Cause if'n you was, I was gonna tell you that the herd was about two miles that-a-way," he pointed northwest, "an' you may wanna avoid that, 'cause of all the dust."

"Oh! Thank you for letting me know."

"That's okay, ma'am. Mr. Darcy told us to keep an eye out for you. Why, just this morning he said to… umm… 'offer you every courtesy.'" He grinned, pleased at his memory.

Beth tried to hide her joy. "He said that?"

"Yep, that's just what he said. Sure as I'm standing here."

Beth smiled, reassured that Darcy really was the man she was coming to believe he was. "I think I will ride today. C'mon,

Turner." The horse happily crossed the shallow ford. "Thank you, Mr. ...?"

"Aw shucks, ma'am, I ain't no mister. Name's Ethan. Me an' my brother, Peter, are drovers for Mr. Darcy. Been ridin' for him near onto three years now." He mounted his steed. "That's a fine-lookin' horse you got there."

"Thank you, again."

"But, I gotta ask, what kinda name is 'Turner'?"

Beth laughed. "Ask Mr. Darcy next time you see him."

Ethan tipped his hat. "I will. You be careful. You need somethin', we're right over that there ridge."

Beth waved as the young cowpoke rode off. She then leaned over and whispered into Turner's ear, "Ready to kick up some dust?"

The paint shook its head and took off at the slightest urging. Within moments Beth was flying across the ridgeline, her hair trailing behind her, horse and rider in perfect harmony, reveling in the summer sun.

Tom Bennet rubbed his forehead as his favorite daughter left his study. He knew she was angry, but he could do nothing about it.

Beth had tried to warn him off George Whitehead. She calmly told him wild tales about false imprisonment and the torture of captives, of lies and chicanery. Once she finished, she asked if he was going to continue to have dealings with Whitehead and was flabbergasted when told that he would.

"How can you?" she had demanded. "Don't you believe me?"

"Yes, dear. I believe you."

"Then, why? Is Whitehead holding something over you?"

"No. I'll tell you the same thing I told Charles. War is a terrible thing, and I won't judge a man by his actions under fire. George has been a valuable counselor, and I'll deal or not deal with him on that basis. The past is in the past, my dear. Let the war go."

"But, Father—"

"Enough, Beth."

At that, she had stormed out of his small study, leaving an aggrieved and disappointed parent behind.

Bennet stood up and looked at the portrait of his son. How much Samuel resembled his late grandfather, he thought. *My son, my dear son. How I miss you. How I miss your grandfather, too.*

Tom Bennet worshiped the very ground his father walked; he considered him a man without fault until the night—the first he had shared drinking with his father and uncles—when they talked of the "old times." What he learned shook him.

Bennet knew his father fought in the War of 1812. What he didn't know was that he was with General Zebulon Pike during the failed invasion of Canada of that year. For the first time, his beloved father talked about the looting and other atrocities committed by U.S. troops during their weeklong occupation of York, the capital of Upper Canada later known as Toronto, culminating in the burning of the government buildings.

"And that was the worst thing we ever did," he remembered his father saying, *"because two years later, the Brits used it as their excuse for burning Washington D.C. Never forget, son 'For they sow the wind, and they shall reap the whirlwind.'"*

Later, his uncles would talk of the Indian Wars and his cousins of the Mexican War. All talked of friends reduced by battle, fear, and anger to do unspeakable things. His beloved uncles killed Indians indiscriminately during attacks on hostile camps. It was impossible to distinguish between the belligerent and the innocent during the heat and smoke of battle, he was told.

It was then Tom Bennet had his epiphany—that good men can do bad things during war and should not be held to account for their actions. Wasn't his father the best man he had ever known? Yet he looted a helpless city. His uncles were church elders. His cousins would walk miles in the snow to help a neighbor. Should he shun them for what they felt they had to do while wearing a uniform?

Yes, Bennet believed the stories told to him by Charles and Beth. War was awful enough for such things to occur. Besides, he was a born cynic. He took the propaganda in the newspapers with a grain of salt. He knew the South wasn't the only side to commit atrocities. He knew of men—good men—who had been thrown in prison and had their *habeas corpus* rights suspended simply because, as anti-war Democrats, they had spoken out against the policies of the Lincoln administration. Bennet supported the war, but he wasn't blind to the hypocrisy of violating the Constitution in order to save it. Bennet was friends with the sheriff who arrested these men and the judge who sentenced them to prison, but he knew they were wrong. History taught him that war was so evil it could corrupt whole governments, and here was proof of it. But Bennet never held anything against either side.

If Tom Bennet could forgive his relations and his neighbors, he had to do the same for George Whitehead and Will Darcy. It was only fair. It was why he could so quickly put the war behind him. It was why he could happily accept Charles Bingley into his family. Why couldn't Beth see that?

Bennet rubbed his neck. He was happy that Beth finally seemed to put aside her dislike of all things Southern, but this new loathing for Whitehead was troubling. It seemed to him that his daughter had to dislike someone. If so, it was a character flaw he was incapable of fixing. *Well,* he considered, *if ignoring her behavior worked before, maybe the best thing to do now is be patient until this new obsession passes.*

Tom Bennet was determined to stand by his own unique principles. Until Whitehead, Darcy, or anyone else proved a threat to what he had built, he would act as he saw best for the future of his family.

Beth attended the next meeting of the Musical Society with far less trepidation than the month before. She was eager to go, for she wanted to see Gaby and Anne and prove to herself that she could love them for who they were, not in spite of where they came from. In the back of her mind, she admitted to herself that she'd be disappointed if Will Darcy didn't take up his old habit of observing the gathering from the back pew. She no longer feared Darcy's ill opinion of her, although memories of their confrontation still invaded her dreams.

Beth and Mary drove into town in the wagon a bit early at Mary's insistence. To their surprise, the Darcy coach was already there. Darcy and his relations were talking with Reverend Tilney outside the church doors. Tilney gestured at the approaching wagon, and Darcy turned to stare at Beth. For a moment, the two were in a silent battle, neither willing to take their eyes off the other, but Beth was the first to surrender. She busied herself climbing off the wagon as Darcy and Tilney secured the horses.

Therefore, she didn't see the rancher approach until he was almost on top of her.

"Miss Beth," Darcy touched his hat, "Miss Mary. Good afternoon. I hope y'all are doing well."

Mary returned the greeting before turning her attention to Henry, who was more than happy to escort her into the building. Beth could not help but smile at the pair's obvious affection.

Will, too, was grinning. "Am I to offer someone congratulations?"

"No, Mr. Darcy—except to my sister, Jane."

"Of course, and I would hold myself lax in not expressing my happiness at the Bingleys' joyful event, had Gaby and I not already paid them a call last week. But allow me to tell you that we hold the opinion that Miss Susan is one right pretty girl, and we wish Jane and Charles all the best."

Darcy's compliments to Susan could not but please Beth, and she favored the man with a dazzling smile. "I thank you, sir, on behalf of my family."

Darcy swallowed and his face became serious. "Miss Beth, before you go in, I have a request from my sister. She's wanted to show you Pemberley for some time. Would you be available to be her guest this weekend?"

Beth could not hide her surprise at the invitation, and Darcy grew uneasy. "I… I thank you, but…" Beth managed, "but are you sure? I mean," her face flushed, "I don't want to cause anyone unease."

Darcy grew grim. "I understand. Please don't worry yourself over that. I have plenty of work to do. You would hardly know I was there—"

"You misunderstand!" Beth cried. "I was concerned on

your behalf, not mine! I would never drive you out of your own house."

Darcy stared at her, his face more unreadable than ever. He seemed to mull his response. "Miss Bennet," he said slowly, "*both* my sister and I would be happy to have you as our guest at Pemberley. Will you come?"

The anxious look in his face delighted Beth. Her relief that the man didn't hate her made her bold. "Very well, sir. I will ask my father—on one condition."

"And that is?"

"My name to my friends is Beth."

Darcy blinked, and a slow smile grew on his face. "Beth, will you come to Pemberley?"

"Yes, Will."

Beth had had no idea that Will's eyes sparkled when he smiled. "With your father's permission, I'll send a carriage to your farm Friday afternoon. Will that suit you?"

"That would be very nice, but I don't need a carriage. I can come on my own."

"Nevertheless, one will be sent, so don't bother arguing," he teased before he offered his arm. "May I escort you in before I take my leave of you?"

"Oh! But aren't you staying to listen?"

"Wouldn't like anything better, Beth," his voice seemed to caress the letters of her name, "but I have business in town to see to. It's my loss, I assure you."

"We'll be sorry to lose our audience, but I understand. Thank you for the invitation, Will." She felt slightly giddy, enjoying using his Christian name. Beth took her leave of him and entered the church, where she was immediately besieged by an excited Gaby, demanding to know if Beth was to visit Pemberley. Beth was able to assure her that was her intention, and the next ninety minutes flew by in a happy manner.

Angry voices were being raised at the B&R a few nights later.

"Mr. Whitehead," said Catherine Burroughs in a manner that would brook no opposition, "I want to know what is being done to secure the last of the deeds in the new settlements."

Whitehead carefully set down his coffee cup, knowing Collins's worried eyes were upon him. "We have that all under control, Mrs. Burroughs. All but a couple are already in our possession. We've moved slowly so as not to invite suspicion. It should only be a matter of time before we have the rest of that land."

"Who is left?"

Collins spoke up. "The McDaniels and the Washingtons."

"Will there be any trouble?"

"Umm," Collins pulled at his shirt collar, "the McDaniels have run up a few debts in town, so we can foreclose on them at any time. As for the Washingtons… umm… they present a bit of difficulty."

"Why?"

"They put down more money when they bought their homestead, and they haven't been behind in their mortgage payment, not even once. We'll be hard-pressed to justify an expulsion."

Denny, leaning against a wall, smoked a hand-rolled cigarette. "I'll take care o' them. Just leave things to me." Whitehead and Pyke exchanged looks.

Judge Phillips blanched. "No violence! You said there'd be no violence!"

"And there won't be, Alton, if everyone's reasonable," Whitehead said smoothly.

"I want my land back." Mrs. Burroughs's voice was ice cold. "Spare me the details, but do whatever needs to be done."

Denny's sneer faded, and he stood up straight. "What's that?" One hand on his pistol, he moved towards the door and threw it open. There in the doorway was Bartholomew holding a tray. "What th' hell do ya think you're doin', partner?" Denny snarled as he jammed his pistol barrel into the surprised butler's stomach.

The man looked down at the gun, and then raised his eyes to his employers. "I was about to knock, ma'am, to see if you desired more coffee. Apparently, I've disturbed something."

Whitehead put a hand on Denny's shoulder. "Put that gun away." He smiled at the butler. "Sorry, friend, but Denny here gets jumpy sometimes. Goes with the territory."

Denny holstered his Colt. "Yeah, jumpy. Don't like fellas sneakin' 'round. Makes me itchy."

"I will strive to remember that, Mr. Denny," Bartholomew dryly replied.

Mrs. Burroughs cried out, "Bartholomew! We are having a business meeting. You are excused for the evening."

"Very good, ma'am." With that, he closed the door.

"You think he heard anything?" asked Phillips.

"Bartholomew?" Cate laughed. "He's been in my employ for years. He knows what to see and not see, hear and not hear. My employees know how to behave," she added, giving Denny a withering look.

Denny snorted. "He better learn to make more noise, if'n he don't wanna git hurt."

"Let us continue with the meeting," Mrs. Burroughs

requested. The gathering went on, this time at a lower volume. Had anyone bothered to look out the door, they would have seen Bartholomew watch a female figure in white quickly ascend the stairs and go into a bedroom.

The butler sighed. "They almost caught you this time, my dear," he said to himself. He turned and walked to the kitchen.

Chapter 12

It felt strange to sit in a beautiful landau carriage, Beth considered, as the contraption made its way through town and across the Long Branch Bridge towards Pemberley. The wood was black and shined to a luster so fine she could see her reflection in it. The leather of the seats was a soft dark brown, so comfortable that she felt she could have slept in the carriage as it rolled along the rough dirt road. She felt like a princess from one of the stories in her father's library. Of course, Beth was far too excited to sleep, and she kept her eyes firmly fixed forward as she rolled along. Clouds were moving in from the southwest, signaling that rain was coming.

The only building to distract her attention from catching sight of the ranch house was a small stone church near the river. The building and a small rectory were surrounded by a low adobe wall. A small cemetery was behind it. Ethan had been assigned to drive Beth to Pemberley and he pointed at the structure with his buggy whip.

"That there's the Catholic Church—Santa Maria, they calls it."

Beth nodded. Her conscience twinged at the remembrance of Mary's unfeeling words months ago. Her thoughts moved once again to the owner of the spread before her, marveling at the man's forbearance. It seemed Beth and her family had done nothing but insult the Darcy family, and yet they still wished to continue their acquaintance. More than that—Gaby was a good friend and Will... Will had wanted to marry her at one time.

Beth sighed. Her feelings had been at war for the last week. One moment she was telling herself it was foolish to believe Will Darcy still desired her hand. Her cruel and ignorant words must have killed any tender feeling he might have owned for her at one time. He was only trying to be her friend for his sister's sake, she thought. The next moment she was sure Will loved her—loved her so much that he had forgiven her.

This visit had been his idea. He seemed to want her near him, to want to change her mind. In her most romantic fantasies, Will would surprise her with a huge ball at Pemberley, and the entire town was there—her family, friends, and neighbors. Even the Burroughses and Whitehead attended. Will would claim all of her dances, and they would waltz for hours and hours, she in that exquisite blue dress. At the end of the ball, after he ordered soldiers who had magically appeared to arrest Whitehead, Will would look deeply into her eyes and ask her to marry him. And she... would wake up.

Beth, having never been in love before, found it difficult to describe her feelings for Darcy. She liked him, she admired him, and she trusted him. Her heart beat faster when she was near him. She felt strange urgings when his eyes fell upon her person. She wanted to run and hide, yet touch him, all at the same time. Was she mad, or was she in love? If he did ask her again, would she accept him?

She didn't know. She hoped that this weekend would help with her struggles. If not, she would have to be satisfied with visiting her friend and her handsome, intriguing, infuriating brother.

The landau crossed over a crest of a hill, and the sight that lay below caused Beth to gasp. Along the road about a quarter-mile away was a large, low house. Done in the Spanish style, terra cotta tiles covered a roof supported by numerous white columns, lining a full porch, surrounding the entirety of the house. Dormer windows broke up the hip roof, white plaster surrounding the glass. Several large trees framed the building, a flower garden was in the front, and a row of cedars to the west of the house swayed in the breeze.

Beth pulled her eyes away from the house to gaze at the rest of the ranch. Barns and stables were set some distance from the main house, and a large, long building with windows was close by the barn. Beth expected it was the bunkhouse for the unmarried hands. Men worked in a corral next to the barn, and smoke rose from what Beth took to be a smithy. Smaller single houses dotted the area. Cattle were everywhere, and in the distance, she could see the sunlight dancing on the surface of a small lake.

"Oh my goodness," Beth could not help herself from saying.

Ethan turned to her with a grin. "It's somethin', ain't it? Prettiest house I've ever seen."

Beth could only agree, and her admiration for the house grew as she neared it. *And Will wanted me to be mistress of all this? Is he crazy?*

Gaby was almost hopping in her excitement as she waited next to Will on the porch for Beth to descend from the carriage. She promptly threw herself into Beth's arms once she was on the ground. Will's welcome was far more restrained, but Beth did not doubt his sincerity although he seemed a bit nervous all the same. Ethan carried Beth's carpetbag from the landau as Gaby and Will escorted their guest inside.

The house was cooler than Beth had expected for the middle of the summer, and she said so. With a smile, Will explained that between the high ceilings and large windows, Pemberley was designed to take advantage of any stray breeze that might come along. Beth looked up at the large wooden beams high above her head, the brown of the wood contrasting nicely against the whitewashed plaster walls. The furnishings were a mixture of large, dark, heavy Spanish and lighter Chippendale pieces. The carpets over the wooden floors were lovely, and Beth was astonished to learn that they had come all the way from India. The wealth all this represented made Beth uneasy, but Gaby soon lightened her mood.

On the way to what the Darcys called the music room, they came across a line of family portraits. Will stopped at the first one. It was a dark-haired lady with rather square features, dressed in a white gown, a small cross at her throat. The expression at first seemed severe, but Beth caught a mischievous gleam in the eye of the subject.

"Mary Grace Darcy, my grandmother and matriarch of the family," Will named her with pride, half-turning to Beth.

"She looks so regal," Beth judged.

Will smiled. "She should—she was a princess of the Cherokee Nation. Her birth name, loosely translated, was Running Water. Her family—and most of her village—were wiped out by Comanche raiders when she was little, and she ended up in a convent. The nuns gave her the name Mary Grace, had her baptized Catholic, and taught her English and Spanish. When she grew up, the Mother Superior didn't know what to do with her. It was one thing to raise an orphan Indian; it was a whole other thing to bring her into the order. As it turned out, Grandmother was a pious woman, but that didn't mean she wanted to be a nun, and when George Washington Darcy rode by one day from boarding school and fell in love with her at first sight, she was happy to marry him and go to Pemberley. Great-Grandmother Agatha wasn't too thrilled at the news, and it didn't get any better when Mary Grace converted Grandfather to Catholicism. Still, they learned to get along, and Grandmother told me that they became friends before Great-Grandmother Agatha passed. It was Grandmother Mary Grace who saw to the improvement to the mission."

"Did you see it on the way here?" Gaby asked. Beth said that she had and asked Gaby if she remembered Mary Grace. "No," Gaby said sadly. "She died before I was born. I barely even remember my mother."

"My father, Matthew Darcy, was the eldest, along with my Uncle John and Aunts Anne and Mary," Will continued. "Anne and Mary married and moved away. John died of the typhus when he was still in his teens. My daddy was sent to school in Austin, and that's where he met this lady." He pointed at another portrait, this one of a strikingly beautiful black-haired lady. She was obviously Spanish.

"Consuela Helena Diaz Pérez was from a very prominent Spanish family that emigrated from Seville many years ago. Her father fought alongside Sam Houston at the Battle of San Jacinto for Texas's independence." Will laughed. "If you thought Mary Grace and Agatha didn't get along, Momma and Grandmother were like oil and water. Daddy and Grandfather spent a lot of time getting between them, keeping the peace." He looked at her portrait fondly. "Some of it was Momma coming from a prominent family, while Grandmother was an orphaned Indian. But mostly it was a battle as to who was going to run the family. Two strong-willed women, neither of a mind to back down. Things changed, I was told, after Grandfather died. Momma's authority was now undisputed, so she surprised everyone when she insisted that Grandmother remain in the main house instead of a small place that had been built for her. They had their arguments—I was witness to a few—but Daddy always said that the two of them seemed to enjoy their disagreements. I suppose he was right, because when Grandmother took sick, Momma wouldn't leave her side, and when she finally passed, Momma cried for three days straight. You never really know how people feel until something like that happens."

"I was named for Grandmother, you see," Gaby said. "Gabrielle Maria. And then Momma died a few years later. It was just Daddy, Will, and me after that."

Beth said nothing, overwhelmed by the stories she had heard. Deep inside, her anger at George Whitehead for his snide asides disparaging the Darcys' heritage was renewed, as well as self-loathing at her own prejudices, which allowed her to accept his cruel statements. Not only were Will and Gaby not embarrassed at their mixed background—one-half Spanish-Mexican and one-quarter Indian—they were proud of it. Beth was ashamed. Hadn't she been slightly guilty of the same fault she had accused Southerners of—that is, considering a human somehow less a person based on their heritage? She had never enslaved anyone, that was true, but the similarity hit just too close to home for comfort.

Will seemed to sense her discomfort and suggested that Gaby show her to her room to freshen up for dinner. Beth gratefully agreed, and the two girls went up to a second-floor guest bedroom, Beth feeling Will's eyes follow her as she climbed the stairs.

The storm that had been threatening all afternoon finally broke during dinner, but the rain did nothing to dampen the spirits of those inside Pemberley's dining room. Will performed his duties as host without flaw, as far as Beth was concerned, and during the times that the conversation began to drag, Richard Fitzwilliam, who had joined the family and Mrs. Annesley at table, could be counted on to inject his own sardonic observations, delighting those assembled.

Beth had never enjoyed a dinner so much. The slow-cooked barbecued beef was delicious, served with roasted corn, beans, and a couple of items Beth had never eaten before—sweet potatoes, and a soft, flat bread called *tortillas*. Will explained that tortillas were a favorite of his mother's, and Mrs. Reynolds, the cook, learned to make them to please her.

Beth could tell that Darcy was pleased with *her*, or, at least, with what she was wearing. Beth, her mother, and her sisters had worked for hours on the pretty yellow dress. She liked it almost as much as the blue gown she wore at the B&R. At first, Beth was alarmed at the bare shoulders, but when she came down the stairs and heard Darcy's quiet gasp, she had to admit to being very pleased with herself.

The party retired to the music room after dinner, and Mrs. Reynolds visited with them at Will's request before Gaby started her concert. The black woman accepted with a smile the praise heaped upon her for the dinner. "Thank you kindly," she said. "It's always a pleasure to cook for guests, although we don't get to do it much—not like when Mrs. Darcy was alive, bless her soul."

"You've been with the Darcys for a long time, I take it," said Beth.

"Oh, yes, ever since Mr. Matthew came to get me over twenty years ago."

Beth blinked at the woman's choice of words and even more so as Gaby demanded happily, "Tell Beth the story! Tell her the story! It's so romantic!"

"Now, let's not bore the young lady with old tales like that," Mrs. Reynolds demurred, but Will smiled and stood up.

"We've had lots of riders on Pemberley. Men of all colors and creeds. We've only asked one thing of them: Give us a full day's work for a full day's pay. Treat us fair, and we'll treat you fair. When I was young, we had a freedman by the name of Isaiah Reynolds working for us. He was as good a man with a cow pony as we've ever had, Daddy told me, and he earned the respect of the other hands. Well, most of 'em. Anyhow, one day he came up to Daddy and said, 'I'm gonna have to quit you, Mr. Darcy.' Daddy asked Isaiah if he was unhappy, and he said, 'No, sir, you've treated me fair. But, I want to find a woman an' get married, an' there ain't nobody 'round here for me.'

"Daddy asked him, 'If you leave, where are you going to go?' Isaiah didn't really know. He thought about New Orleans, because of all the freedmen there, or maybe he'd go west and meet up with a Mexican girl, or an Indian. He was scared of going east, not sure if the locals would believe that he wasn't an escaped slave.

"So, Daddy asked Isaiah to wait a month before he made a firm decision. A few weeks later, Daddy came back from a trip east with a young former slave girl in the wagon."

"Was that you?" Beth asked a smiling Mrs. Reynolds.

"Yes, indeed. I was a slave on a farm near Shreveport and the master was fixin' to sell me 'cause he had too many slaves as it was. Mr. Darcy knew him and wrote, askin' if there were any young female slaves for sale. When Mr. Darcy came by the house, the master looked at him funny." She snorted. "I believe he thought Mr. Darcy was buying me for his own use. I was scared, too, but Mr. Darcy talked to me. He said, 'Margaret,'—that's my name, Margaret—'Margaret, I need some help. I've got a good, hard-working freedman working for me, but he wants to leave me because he wants to go looking for a wife. He's a free man and a good man, and I think he'd make a fine husband. I'd be willing to buy you off of your master if you would be willing to meet Isaiah and consider marrying him.' I said, 'Whoa, Mr. Darcy—you want me to marry a man I haven't met?'

"He said, 'No, I want you to meet him and give him a chance to convince you to marry him. If you marry a free man, you'll be free.' I told him, 'Yes sir, I know that. But what if I meet him, an' I don't want to marry him?' He told me I'd be free anyway—he'd give me my freedom, and there would be a job for me, payin' money, at Pemberley.

"I tell you, Miss Bennet, I just broke down and cried right there. That good man was gonna buy me an' set me free, an' all I had to do was to ride back to Pemberley with him. I only asked if Isaiah was a good Christian man, an' he said he was, an' that was good enough for me. Mr. Darcy brought me, I said goodbye to my momma, an' got in the wagon with him. A few days later, we got to Pemberley, an' I met Mrs. Darcy, an' a better lady I've never met. I could cook, so she had me set up in the kitchen.

"Mr. Darcy was ready to give me my papers that would make me a free woman, but I said, 'I haven't met Mr. Reynolds, yet. A deal's a deal.' So, Mr. Darcy calls for Mr. Reynolds, and he come in, not knowing what was going on." Mrs. Reynolds laughed. "He was so surprised to see me, and he was even more surprised when Mr. Darcy told him what he had done. He then left us two alone in the library to talk things over.

"And we talked. Isaiah was indeed a fine, good-looking man and as kind as he was good. We came to an agreement in short order, and Mr. and Mrs. Darcy couldn't have been happier when we told them.

"The only problem was that the Baptist minister in town— that was before Mr. Tilney got here—wouldn't marry no former slaves in the church. We was willing to have it someplace else, but that weren't good enough for Mrs. Darcy. No, ma'am! She heard about that, an' she took us right down to the mission church, askin' the priest to marry us. He agreed, as long as we would join the church.

"So I became Mrs. Reynolds and Catholic on the same day, an' that was the best day of my life."

Beth was enchanted. "What a wonderful story!"

Mrs. Reynolds smiled. "Isaiah was a good man, and we were happy the five years we were married." Her smile disappeared. "Then, he left on a cattle drive before the war, and he never came home. He was killed by rustlers tryin' to steal the herd." She turned her head to look out the window. "He's buried out there, somewhere, under a shady tree, the other riders told me. That's good—Isaiah always liked the shade, you see." She sighed. "Five years, but I've no regrets. I know he's waitin' for me upstairs, along with the angels."

She wiped a tear from her face with her apron, while Beth and Gaby used their handkerchiefs. "Well, if'n you would excuse me, I've got to clean up in the kitchen. Good night, all."

Darcy watched her go. "They never had children, but you'd hardly know it from her. She helped raise me, and she was like a mother to Gaby after Momma passed. Daddy always said buying Mrs. Reynolds's freedom was the best purchase he had ever made." He coughed, and to Beth it suspiciously sounded like he was covering up a sob.

"Gaby, I think you said you'd play for us?" Fitz broke in.

Gaby collected herself and moved to the piano.

An hour and a half later, Gaby announced a desire to retire, and she and Mrs. Annesley made their excuses. For her part, Beth was restless. She should be tired, she knew, but the revelations of the past few hours would not allow her to rest. The gentlemen showed no inclination to go to bed, so Darcy, Fitz, and Beth walked out to the veranda and, as the storm had abated, watched the now gentle rainfall. Beth sipped a sherry as the men shared brandy and cigars.

"You're awful quiet, Miss Beth," Fitz observed. "You're sure you're not tired?"

"No, not at all," she said. Seeing the men stare at her expectantly, she continued, "You look like you think I should say something."

"Sorry, Beth," said Will. "It just seems there's a lot on your mind. We don't mean to pry. Sorry."

"Although, if you need any help, you've come to the right place," added Fitz.

"Why? Why would you want to help me?"

Fitz laughed. "Will here is always helping his friends. It's a weakness o' his." Darcy simply glared at his foreman, who wasn't cowed in the least.

Beth sighed. "I'm trying to understand… Oh! It seems everything I know is *wrong*."

"What do you mean?" asked Darcy.

Beth put down her glass and turned to him. "You've told me you've never owned any slaves. Yet, you fought for the Confederacy. I don't understand. Why did you fight for a cause you didn't believe in?"

Will shared a look with Fitz before speaking. "Beth, the war was about other things besides slavery." Will sat down next to Beth and collected his thoughts.

"The South's economy has always been based on agriculture. There weren't many factories down here before the war. We shipped out raw materials, be it cotton or tobacco or beef, to other places. The North, on the other hand, was becoming more industrial every day. They used our crops to make goods to sell overseas.

"The problem was, England and France wanted our crops, too. They wanted to trade directly with us, and sell us stuff, too, at prices less than what the factories up north charged.

"The big northern industrialists couldn't have that. They screamed for protection, and the Congress passed high tariffs on overseas goods. We couldn't sell our goods to anyone but those Yankee industrialists. We also paid top dollar for the goods they sold back to us. So, you see, the Yankees were taxing us to save their businesses. It was a tax on Northerners, too, but Southerners were the ones getting mad about it.

"This had gone on for a long time before the Congress started thinking about lowering those tariffs. For twenty years it got a little better, but right before the war, the industrialists got together with the Abolitionists in the Republican Party, and they said they were going to raise tariffs again. In other words, they would take money from the South and give it to the North. It was in the Republican Party platform in 1860, and the South had had enough.

"You see, every time we made a deal with those Yankees, be it bringing new states into the Union or respecting property rights, it always seemed the Yankees would eventually renege on the agreement. It got so that we thought we just couldn't trust them.

"We thought we had a lever to protect our rights. A lot of people figured that the Tenth Amendment gave the states the right to veto, or nullify, unfair federal laws. It was called States Rights. When the Republicans promised to raise tariffs again, the southern states said they had the right to declare their independence from the Union, since the Union didn't respect their rights."

"But what about slaves?"

Darcy grimaced. "It was part of it. Look, no matter what you think about slavery, it was legal. Most Southern folks never owned a slave, though I have to admit most supported it. We knew slavery wouldn't last forever. The papers were saying how expensive they were getting, and some rabble-rousers wanted to begin the re-importation of slaves. But that would've never gotten through Congress. To be honest, we expected slavery to die a slow death. People's hearts were changing.

"But the Abolitionists wanted it declared illegal—now—and without compensation to the slave owners. That would bankrupt thousands of farms. John Brown and his terrorist followers were willing to murder innocent people to free the slaves. With Mr. Lincoln's election, the fire eaters in the South screamed that the Abolitionists who had backed Brown and their northern industrialist friends were in control of the country and that we had no voice in how things would go."

"Slavery was still evil, Will," Beth said.

"My momma agreed with you. You know, most folks around here were against secession."

Beth was amazed.

Will went on. "We thought that the rabble-rousers were wrong, and that something could still be worked out with the Congress. After all, it was the government that put down Brown. But we were the minority, and Texas voted to throw in with the Confederacy. The Darcys' loyalty always was to Texas. Your family loved Ohio when y'all lived there, right? Same thing here.

"So, when the call went out to defend our new country against the foe, we thought we were living in 1776 or 1835 again. Victory for the cause. Freedom." Will looked out into the rain. "Well, you see how that turned out. And Congress did raise the tariffs, and they remain high today. And all the factories are still in the North. The whole damn thing was a waste." He tossed the remains of his cigar into the rain.

But the slaves are free, thought Beth, but she kept that observation to herself. She was digesting the view of the war from the Southern standpoint. Some northern newspapers had tried to make John Brown a hero, but Mr. Bennet called him a criminal who deserved what he got. She recalled something about the issue of tariffs from those times, but it had been submerged under the calls for preserving the Union and freeing the slaves. She could never understand why the Rebels fought with such ferocity at Shiloh and Gettysburg and Cold Mountain. It made no sense to die to keep men enslaved. But to fight for what you believed was your freedom—*that* she could understand.

Was the whole war one big mistake? Did Samuel and six hundred thousand others die because of greedy and stupid men on both sides?

"The winners write the history, Miss Beth," said Fitz as he blew a cloud of blue smoke. "I learned that at school."

Beth didn't respond, because Will suddenly stood up, peering into the rain. "Rider coming," he said evenly. Fitz's response was anything but calm. Jumping to his feet, he half-ran into the house, startling Beth by returning a moment later with a rifle in his hands. Staring out, he relaxed.

"It's Peter, Will," he said, lowering the weapon. Beth took a breath while Darcy moved forward as the rider jumped off his horse and came up the stairs.

Darcy looked at the man. "What's wrong?"

"There's trouble in town..." Peter looked first at Beth, then questioningly at Darcy.

"Go on," his employer commanded.

Water pooled about Peter's feet. "Something bad's happened at the new settlement." He glanced at Beth again. "Real bad."

"How bad?" Darcy demanded.

"That Washington family..." his voice trailed off as he shook his head in silent communication.

"Oh, no," Darcy breathed as terror gripped Beth's heart. "All of them?"

A pause and Peter nodded.

"*No!*" Beth gasped, hands over her mouth.

Sheriff Lucas stood in the downpour, rain dripping off his hat, as the half-dozen men stared at the tableau before them. The scene was lit by the glow of the tall, burning object planted in the yard of the homestead, the flames implausible in the rain.

"Must be tar on it," whispered Jones as the men remained frozen in horror. The dancing light and shadows made the figure hanging from the tree look almost alive. But that was not what held Lucas's attention, nor the *thing* lighting the place. It was the two bundles at the foot of the tree, one smaller than the other.

A cart arrived and a furious Reverend Tilney leapt from it. "Don't just stand there—cut him down! Cut that poor man down!" He seized the sheriff. "Come on, man! We can't leave him up there! And the rest of you!" He pointed at the burning cross. "Put that… that damnable thing out! It's an abomination!"

"With what?" Jones said stupidly.

"I don't know!" Tilney cried. "With your hands, if necessary!"

Sheriff Lucas roused himself to think. "Look around, boys. There must be a shovel or an ax about." He walked over to the tree with the preacher. A flash of his knife and the tree was empty of its burden. Lucas stared at the bodies huddled close to the roots, his blade held loosely in his hand. Tilney, kneeling down by the victims, ignored the rain falling in his face to look back up at the lawman.

"The boy," Lucas said. "They killed the little boy, too?" It wasn't really a question.

Tilney bent his head. "Go see if you can find some blankets in the house, Sheriff. They deserve at least that."

Lucas nodded and walked towards the front door of the little house, glad to be doing something. The loss of light and the hissing sound behind him as he opened the door told Lucas that the others had felled the *thing* outside. He welcomed the darkness as he began to search the place for whatever little comfort he could offer the Washingtons now.

Now that it was too late for anything else.

Chapter 13

IN HER FAMILY'S PEW in the Rosings Baptist Church, Beth kept her head as still as possible as Reverend Tilney read a passage from the New Testament while her eyes took in those assembled. To either side of her was her family. To her left were her father, looking grim, and her mother, dabbing her eyes with a handkerchief. To her right were Kathy and Lily, both unusually quiet. Next to them were Charles and Jane, little Susan resting quietly in her mother's arms.

Beth could not see behind her, but she had seen Sheriff Lucas and Charlotte before the beginning of the service and knew they were in attendance, as were George Whitehead and Billy Collins. Mary was at the church organ. Except for a few others, no one else was present.

It was embarrassing for a congregation that normally filled the church to stay away from the funeral for some of their own. Beth knew the reasons—some sensible, some appalling—and a bit of her old disgust for the South burned dimly in her breast. Beth was ashamed that the church was mostly empty.

Mostly, but not quite empty. Beth's eyes kept returning to the row of pews on the opposite side of the aisle. The seats that usually held the Burroughs family were instead occupied by William Darcy, his sister, Gaby, and two others. She did not know the short man in the black robe, but she assumed it was the Darcys' priest. It was shocking enough that a Catholic priest would attend a service in a Baptist Church, but even more amazing was that the Darcys' cook, Mrs. Reynolds, sat next to them. Beth also knew that two Darcy wranglers stood in the back near the front door of the church.

It would have been a wondrous occurrence were it not for the sorrowful nature of the gathering. She returned her attention to the wooden objects before the sanctuary—three coffins, two about six feet long flanking a much smaller one in the middle. Beth would have cried again over the fate of the Washingtons if she were not aware of one other jarring, frightening fact.

Every man in the church, except for the clergy and Collins, was armed—even Charles.

With a final blessing, the funeral service for the Washington family was complete. The women quietly filed out of the church into the noonday sun, Beth taking Gaby by the hand. They stood outside, close to a flatbed wagon with the back unlatched.

Within moments, the pallbearers began their grim duty. Apparently, an agreement had taken place inside the church. The first coffin that emerged was that of Mrs. Washington, borne by Mr. Bennet and the undertaker's helpers, assisted by Whitehead and Collins. William, Charles, and the Pemberley hands followed with Mr. Washington. They, too, carefully lifted their macabre burden onto the bed of the wagon, the undertaker directing the securing of the coffins. Finally, the last, small wooden box was carried out with infinite tenderness by Henry Tilney and Father Joseph. Both had tears in their eyes, as did most of the ladies assembled. A moment later, the wagon was ready.

The assemblage milled about, preparing to begin the procession. Gaby joined her brother and the Pemberley group. To Beth's displeasure, Whitehead and Collins approached the Bennets and Bingleys.

"It's a sad day, isn't it, Thomas?" Whitehead remarked.

Mr. Bennet was interrupted by Charles. "Tom, Fanny, I'm goin' to take Jane an' Susan back to the house. Y'all come by afterwards, all right?" With one sharp glare for Whitehead, the Bingleys walked toward their house, Beth still unnerved by the extraordinary sight of a pistol on Charles's hip.

Whitehead seemed to take no notice of the doctor. "Well, we've got to get back to work, eh, Billy? Tom, you going up to the burial?"

Told that the Bennet family would join the procession, Whitehead displayed an odd look that appeared to Beth as if he wished to dispose of a troublesome insect. The expression disappeared in an instant; Beth blinked, and Whitehead was his usually implacable self again. The chill that ran down Beth's spine was her only proof that she had not imagined the moment. With a smile, Whitehead took his leave of the Bennets, Collins trailing behind. Beth was relieved at Whitehead's departure, because she had disturbing thoughts about a person she once considered a friend and now feared and mistrusted.

With a word from Henry Tilney, the rest took their positions. The wagon driver flicked the reins, and the horses moved down the street, Henry sitting next to him. In the wagon with the coffins were the undertaker and his men. Following on foot were the remaining attendees. The Darcys were first, Gaby and Father Joseph next to William, while Mrs. Reynolds walked directly behind her employer. Mr. and Mrs. Bennet were next, their daughters trailing, Beth and Mary holding hands. The sheriff and Charlotte, along with the Pemberley hands, brought up the rear.

The streets of Rosings, usually bustling at midday, were practically deserted. A sense of fear was omnipresent. Beth glanced around her, catching a curtain move at Zimmerman's store. The blacksmith's shop was silent. The only sound was the tolling of the church bell and the creak of the wagon's wheels.

The story around town was that a roving band of the Ku Klux Klan had descended on the Washington homestead, and outsiders were to blame for the lynching. Beth was surprised and troubled at the rumors, for in the years she had lived in Rosings, there was not even the hint that the feared, masked terrorists were in the area. In fact, all the newspapers had said that the Klan was on its last legs, put down by the power of the army and the federal government. But if the Klan was riding the range killing former slaves, where had they come from? Why hadn't they heard about such outrages before? It didn't make sense to Beth.

Another thing that didn't make sense was the nonattendance of Richard Fitzwilliam. Beth was witness to the horror on the foreman's face when he learned the fate of the Washington family. With the Darcys present for the funeral, why was Fitz not? Was he needed at the ranch, or had Beth misjudged the man? She glanced behind her at Charlotte. Beth had known for several weeks of her friend's feelings for the Pemberley foreman, and she wondered how Charlotte felt about Fitz's absence.

The procession continued in silence to the major crossroads

of the town, passing Younge's Saloon before turning onto the North Road. Outside the barroom lounged two men, whispering to each other. Beth recognized one of them as Kid Denny, which set off another series of questions in her head. If Fitz was needed at Pemberley to keep things running, why was Denny absent from the B&R? She saw William look hard at the man, which drew a laugh from the gunfighter as he leaned back against the wall, a nasty smirk on his face.

The incident alarmed and angered Beth. Seeing Whitehead's cohort mock the funeral procession reinforced the nagging feeling she had that George knew more about the outrage than he was letting on. *I can forgive Will for having fought for the Confederacy,* she thought, *but I certainly won't pardon Denny! I can see why Denny is friends with Whitehead—two bad men found each other.*

Soon, the wagon reached the northern outskirts of town and began the ascent up the slight hill to the cemetery. The party had gone halfway up the narrow lane when four men on horseback appeared and blocked the way to the graveyard's gate. Beth recognized one of them as Wilkerson, the B&R hand who had driven her to the Burroughses' house back in July.

Henry called from his perch on the wagon, "Make way, gentlemen."

The man next to Wilkerson appeared to be the leader. "Not so fast, Preacher. You mean to plant them slaves in this here cemetery?"

Henry was enraged. "What business is it of yours, Nathan Thorpe? Stand aside!"

"You ain't puttin' no slaves in a white man's cemetery," the man identified as Thorpe repeated. He pointed out at the open range. "If you gotta stick 'em in the ground, there's plenty of room out there—not in here." His companions nodded, and one carried a rifle.

"Or maybe that Papist place across th' river," suggested Wilkerson with a sneer. "I heard they'd take anybody."

Beth thought that William would be angry at the insult from Wilkerson, but the tall rancher stood calmly in front of Gaby, shielding her, his face showing no expression.

It was Sheriff Lucas who responded. "That's enough of that!" he thundered. "You've got no right to stop these people, Thorpe."

Thorpe patted his holstered revolver. "Stay outta this if'n you know what's good for ya, Sheriff."

Beth's anger turned to fear. She grasped Mary's hand as Mr. Bennet jumped in front of her mother—

And then there was the unmistakable sound of numerous rifles being cocked.

"Stand easy, Thorpe. You're surrounded," drawled a familiar voice. Beth didn't need Charlotte's gasp of relief to know it was Richard Fitzwilliam.

Thorpe, Wilkerson, and the other gunmen looked around them in shock. Peeking out from behind trees and headstones were armed men, their rifles steady on their targets.

"Not too smart, Thorpe, scarin' off the gravediggers an' failing to reconnoiter the area properly," Fitz mocked the man. "Now, drop them gun belts!" A moment later, the four horse-men disarmed themselves.

William spoke for the first time. "Good work, Fitz."

Lucas turned to the rancher. "You knew this was gonna happen?"

William shrugged his shoulders. The implications of that

gesture astonished and delighted Beth—Will had foreseen what was going to happen and sent his best man to prevent any trouble.

"No violence!" cried Henry. "Thorpe, let us pass."

"Yeah," added Lucas, "you can pick up your guns at the jail later."

"Not so fast, Lucas," Fitz said, keeping his rifle armed at Thorpe. "You may want to ask these fellas about their whereabouts a few nights ago. Thorpe an' Wilkerson rode with Quantrill's outlaws, if I remember rightly."

"Outlaw? I was a soldier, same as you!" Thorpe insisted.

"I don't call what happened in Lawrence the work of a soldier, bushwhacker. Tell me—how many boys did you kill?"

Beth gasped; she had heard about William Quantrill's famous raid on Lawrence, Kansas, where up to two hundred men and boys had been slaughtered and the town burned to the ground in retaliation for Jayhawk attacks in Missouri. If these men had been members of Quantrill's Raiders, then Mrs. Burroughs had very dangerous people working for her.[6]

---

6 During the Civil War, partisans from Kansas and Missouri were engaged in violent guerrilla warfare between the "Jayhawkers" or "Redlegs" from Kansas and "bushwhackers" or "partisan rangers" from Missouri. The roots of the fighting came from the Border War ("Bleeding Kansas") between pro-slavery "Border Ruffians" and "Free-State" abolitionists that preceded the Civil War.

Both sides participated in atrocities. On the Jayhawk side, U.S. Senator James H. Lane sacked Osceola, Missouri, killing nine men, while Charles "Doc" Jennison was distinguished by his blatant plunder for personal gain. On the Missouri side, William Clarke Quantrill carried out the raid on Lawrence, Kansas, while William T. "Bloody Bill" Anderson and his men usually shot their prisoners and often mutilated and scalped the dead.

At first rejected by both the U.S. and Confederate governments, as the war dragged on, both sides made the guerrillas somewhat "respectable" by offering commissions in the volunteer forces. However, while Jayhawkers occasionally coordinated their activities with regular Union forces, bushwhackers almost

"I wasn't there," claimed Thorpe.

"Sure, you weren't. Like I'd trust your word."

Sheriff Lucas spoke up, "Thorpe, get your people outta here. Now—git!" The four riders took off down the hill, heading for town.

An annoyed Fitz walked up to the lawman. "Lucas, why did you let 'em go? I'm sure they had somethin' to do with—"

The sheriff cut him off. "Now's not the time, Fitz! We've got a funeral to finish. Let me do my job at my own pace."

"And when's that time gonna be?" Fitz shouted back. Beth could see that Charlotte was distressed over the argument.

William took Fitz by the arm. "That's enough," he told his foreman, staring him in the eye. Fitz grunted and William turned to Tilney. "Henry? Can we go on?"

Henry patted the driver on the shoulder, and the wagon rolled into the cemetery.

The last strains of "Shall We Gather at the River" had long since floated across the plains when the people left the cemetery to the sounds of the gravediggers completing their task. By the time Darcy helped Gaby into the carriage that had been brought up from town, the Bennets and the others were already halfway down the road. Darcy wished he could have taken his

---

always operated outside of the Confederate chain of command.

After the war, some bushwhackers became famous outlaws, such as Jesse and Frank James and the Younger brothers.

Important note: The term "bushwhacker" is also used for guerrillas—both Union and Confederate—in other theaters of the war.

leave of Beth, and disappointed, he took out his frustration with Fitzwilliam.

"What the hell do you think you were doing, challenging Sheriff Lucas like that? What did you hope to accomplish?"

Fitz was taken aback at his employer's anger. "I was just pointin' out to that old fool that he ain't doin' his job. You're not defending him, are you?"

Darcy took a moment to compose himself. "Look, I'm not saying that Lucas is the best sheriff we've ever had, but he's got an almost impossible job. It's one thing to suspect something, but it's a whole other thing to be able to prove something in court. Will you look around at what's going on?" He lowered his voice. "I suspect the same things as you, and I wouldn't be surprised if Lucas was of the same mind. But he's got to have evidence, and even then, he's got to convince a judge. Who is that judge, Fitz?"

"Phillips," Fitz said. "But can't he get another judge? Y'know—conflict of interest?"

Darcy nodded. "And he's got to be able to prove *that*, too. There's nothing easy about this—nothing at all. Lucas is in a trap."

"So, what do we do?"

"There's a town meeting called for tomorrow night. I aim to be there, and you can come along. Then we'll see." He half-turned and added, as if an afterthought, "Fitz, you might want to back off Lucas a little. It isn't doing your suit for Miss Charlotte any good."

Fitz's jaw dropped. "How… how do you know about that?"

Gaby smiled from her seat in the carriage. "Oh, Fitz, *everybody* knows about that." Darcy grinned as he took his seat next to his sister.

"See you back at the ranch, Fitz." With a quick twitch of the reins, the horses pulled away, leaving an astonished Richard Fitzwilliam in its wake.

The next night found Thomas Bennet sitting in a pew next to Dr. Bingley in the Rosings Baptist Church, attending an emergency town meeting. Oil lamps and candles lit the interior of the church, the pews filled with shopkeepers, cowboys, and others. Most of the men in town were there, all talking about the attack on the Washingtons.

Bennet noticed George Whitehead standing with Judge Phillips, Kid Denny, and Billy Collins in a corner, talking amongst themselves. The sight bothered him, for Bennet had been deeply troubled by the incident at the cemetery. He had not known that Denny's people had been bushwhackers in the war, and he was uneasy with George's connection with them. He remembered that he had told Beth that she should put the war behind her, but what Quantrill had done was nothing but murder in Bennet's eyes. He wasn't sure he could forgive a man for that, and he didn't like that George was friendly with one of those scoundrels.

To his surprise, he saw Will Darcy sitting with his foreman, Fitzwilliam, towards the back of the church. It was the first time Bennet could remember seeing Darcy attending any meeting concerning town business.

Mayor Zimmerman banged a gavel on the lectern and called the meeting to order. "As mayor of Rosings, I have called this town meeting to tell the people about what's being done to catch the men who caused the uhh… unfortunate incident."

"Unfortunate incident!" cried one man. "Cold-blooded murder is what I'd call it!" Others murmured their agreement.

"Uhh, yah, that's what it looks like—sure." Zimmerman, obviously nervous, wiped his forehead with a handkerchief. To Bennet the man seemed frightened. "I now call on Sheriff Lucas to give his report."

The lawman made his way to the lectern. "There ain't much to say right now, gentlemen," Lucas stated. "My men and I were called to investigate a fire at the new settlement, an' when we got there, we saw what had happened to the Washington family. The rain washed away most everything, but it was obvious from what hoof prints remained that there were at least a half-dozen men there. The McDaniels were the only witnesses. They told me afore they left town that they heard some gunshots, an' by the time they got outside, the cross was lit, and they saw a bunch o' riders headin' east."

"Heading east," a man near Bennet pointed out. "Heading away from town. So they *were* outsiders."

"I didn't say that," Lucas said. "There's a lot we don't understand. I'm asking for your help."

"Are you going to form a posse?" asked Dr. Bingley.

"I would if I knew where to look. It don't make any sense right now. I need more information."

"What else do ya need to know?" cried Wilkerson. "That was done by the Klan. Ain't nobody here in the Klan. The McDaniels said the riders were headed east. They done what they did, an' there ain't no reason for 'em to stay. I say that's the end to it."

"And I say you're wrong!" said the blacksmith. "There's killers running loose, an' they could come back. We gotta protect our families. Fellers that would do somethin' like that are likely to do just about anything." A general argument broke out amongst the men over Sheriff Lucas's call for calm. Bennet watched the brouhaha for a couple of minutes before one clear voice was heard over the din.

"That's enough, gentlemen."

The noise in the church died out as Will Darcy stood up. Even ten pews away Bennet could feel the authority flowing from him. Darcy slowly surveyed the room before speaking again.

"We've heard a lot of talk and a lot of conjecture but very few facts. Sheriff Lucas here has told you what he knows, so let's take a look at that. The Washington family was lynched in a fashion that has been used in the past by the Ku Klux Klan. They even had a burning cross in the yard. The only witnesses saw riders heading east. This is what we know.

"Now, there never has been Klan activity in Long Branch County or any county within a hundred miles. According to the newspaper, the army and the government in Austin put down the Klan in East Texas, where it had been strong, over two years ago. Yet, we're supposed to believe that a roving band of Klansmen just happened to be in the county four days ago. Now I ask you, have we heard about a group of robed riders terrorizing the area? No, we have not. So, where did these supposed Klansmen come from?"

Denny spoke up. "You don't believe it? Then what do *you* think happened, Darcy?"

Darcy glared at the gunman. "I think lots of things, Denny, and I dismiss nothing. When I know, then I'll act. Until then, I ask all of you to consider one thing." He paused as he looked about the church. "Who profits from this?" One could hear a pin drop in the silence that followed. "I ask again—who profits from the murder of the Washingtons?"

Darcy took his seat, which seemed to electrify a perspiring Billy Collins. "See here, what are you saying?"

Edmund Bertram, the manager of Darcy Bank, spoke up. "You foreclosed on the Washington property, didn't you, Collins?"

"Well, yes, but… but that was perfectly legal! There was no one left to pay the mortgage." He grew angry. "You would have done the same thing in my shoes, Bertram. Don't you deny it!"

"Eventually, but only after I exhausted all means of contacting any heirs or family," Bertram shot back. "Certainly not before the man was even buried. But maybe that's how things are done at Rosings Bank."

There was a troubled rumbling about the room, and Lucas finally acted to regain control. "Now, that's enough of that. Nobody's accusing anybody around here. Let's settle down and think of what's to be done." Even Bennet could see Fitzwilliam roll his eyes at that.

"I agree," said Judge Phillips as he rose from his seat and walked to the lectern. Sheriff Lucas was forced to surrender the podium to the judge, who smiled and announced, "The events of the last few days have been a trial upon us all. It's apparent to me that our families and livelihood are in some danger. It's also apparent that our very able sheriff is woefully undermanned and unable to meet the crisis.

"Therefore, I am happy to announce that effective immediately, I am deputizing a group of brave men to supplement our local law enforcement efforts. These special deputies of the court will assist Sheriff Lucas in bringing these perpetrators to justice while helping to keep Rosings quiet and peaceful."

To the astonishment of Bennet and many in the audience, Phillips said, "The head of this special detachment is here tonight. Mr. Denny, would you come right up?" There was a low rumbling as the gunfighter walked with a swagger to the front of the church.

"Thanks, Judge. I'm happy to accept this here assignment. Me an' my boys will see that everything 'round here will stay nice an' quiet."

"Hold on, Alton," cried Lucas. "I know nothing about this. How can you assign me deputies without my say-so?"

"They're not your deputies, Sheriff," Phillips said dryly. "They're officers of the court. They report to me."

Again the room grew quiet and Darcy stood up. "Your own private army, Alton?"

The judge turned to the rancher. "They won't cause any trouble except to troublemakers, Darcy."

Darcy nodded as if in thought before he spoke again. To Bennet's confusion, he didn't address Phillips or Denny; instead, he turned to the well-dressed man standing in the corner.

"I told you before, and I'll tell you again. Keep your people off Pemberley, or you'll regret it. If just one of your boys so much as spits on my property, I'm coming to see *you*."

"Threats, Darcy?" sneered George Whitehead.

"Promises, Whitehead." With that, the rancher walked out of the church, Fitzwilliam and Bertram trailing behind. Whitehead's only response was to raise a single eyebrow.

Judge Phillips rapped the gavel, closing the meeting. Immediately, the murmurings among the men returned in earnest. Bennet noted that both Mayor Zimmerman and Sheriff Lucas were stunned at the apparent transfer of power. Most of the others wore expressions ranging from confusion to fear. A few, Doc Bingley being one, were fuming.

"Well," he whispered in his father-in-law's car, "a line's been drawn in the sand. Every man's got to choose which side he'll stand on."

Bennet didn't doubt which side would be Charles's choice. As for himself, he was torn. Bennet could not but respect the quiet authority and courage of Will Darcy. His dealings with the young rancher had been forthright and profitable.

Bennet was troubled by Whitehead's association with Denny. He vowed that he would consider acts done during war in the heat of battle be left in the past. But whatever his sins—or Darcy's or Whitehead's—it was commonly believed that William Quantrill's actions during the war were criminal. Didn't Jesse and Frank James ride with him? The Younger brothers, too? "Bloody Bill" Anderson? All thieves and murderers. It wasn't too far a leap to lump Kid Denny into that group.

Yet, Whitehead had advised him on improvements to the farm. While the promised increase in yields had not yet been realized, Bennet could see the potential. Besides, Rosings Bank held the mortgage on the property, and Whitehead was close to both Collins and Cate Burroughs.

With a sinking feeling, Bennet realized that he was squarely in the middle of a potential range war with no way out, except to flee. As he would never do that, he could only have his family keep a low profile and hope they didn't get hit in the crossfire.

Darcy, Fitzwilliam, and Bertram walked out of the church into the warm night air, picking up two Pemberley riders who had stood guard outside the church.

"So, now do you believe me?" Fitz demanded.

"Do you believe me about Lucas being in a trap?" Darcy shot back before talking to his banker. "Is everything secure?"

Bertram nodded. "Everything's as ready as it can be. We've got the strongest safe this side of the Brazos. You sure you don't want me to sleep at the bank?"

"No. My people's lives are more important than money. I'll have two men keep an eye on the place at night. I don't think anything's going to happen, but I don't want to take any chances. Get yourself home to Mrs. Bertram, all right?" The banker agreed and strode off towards his house as Darcy turned to the others.

"From now on, no one rides alone," he demanded. "All details will be a minimum of two. Fitz, make sure your people are carrying a full load of ammo. Rosings is off limits until I say otherwise. Nobody goes to town for any reason unless personally directed by me. That goes double for Younge's Saloon. I want to give Denny no cause to start something."

"Boys are gonna be disappointed," pointed out José. "They gonna miss their Saturday nights."

"We'll have a bar set up at the ranch. They'll get their drinking in. As for the girls, well, we've all got to make sacrifices." His voice hardened. "This is serious. Whitehead's upping the ante, and I don't want to be caught shorthanded. We start nothing, understand? Anything happens, get back to me immediately. Remember, Whitehead can still call in the army, so we better have ourselves on the right side. Let's get home."

As they mounted, Fitz commented, "Well, Lucas can't be in the dark about Whitehead's intentions now."

Darcy looked at him. "I'm glad you have this all figured out, because I sure don't."

"Huh? What do you mean? You heard what Phillips said."

The party moved off at a slow pace, carefully working their way back to Pemberley in the dark. "Yes, and it doesn't make any sense. Phillips and Collins are Cate's creatures. They work for her, not Whitehead. Rosings Bank is calling in the loans on the new settlement homesteads, so the bank—and Cate by extension—has the bottomland. Why? What good does it do them? They lost money on the deal—they must have. So why work so hard to get it back?"

"Because they're planning to use it for something else? Is there gold there?"

"Not that I know of. But there's got to be a reason. And where does Whitehead fit into all this? He works for Cate, but all this feels like his idea. Why? What does he get out of this? How does it help him if Cate gets the bottomland back? There's something missing, and until we know what it is, Cate and Whitehead are going to be a step ahead of us."

"Why not ask her?"

Darcy snorted. "You think she'd tell me?"

Fitz paused, not wanting to ask the next question. "You think your cousin had something to do with the lynchings?"

Darcy was silent for a minute. "God, I hope not."

The lights were burning late in George Whitehead's office as an impromptu celebration took place. Joining Whitehead were Collins, Phillips, Denny, and Pyke.

"Congratulations, Denny," Phillips raised his glass. "Come by the office tomorrow for your swearing in. That was a pretty good idea of mine, wasn't it?"

Denny laughed. "Never thought I'd be wearin' a badge. Lookin' forward to it."

Whitehead sipped his drink thoughtfully. "Don't let it go to your head, my friend. Remember what I told you—we can't afford any more incidents."

"Look, I took care of them Washingtons, didn't I?" Denny sneered. Phillips looked away, and Whitehead narrowed his eyes.

"Yes, you did. You also failed to corral that hotheaded Thorpe. He almost caused a confrontation with Darcy, and we're not ready for that." Whitehead held up his hand as Denny tried to respond. "Look, everything is still going according to plan. The bank has the properties back. In a few months, this will all be over." Whitehead rose from his chair. "We're right where we need to be. We're *this* far from total success," he held two fingers about an inch apart, "but we must do *nothing* to put this deal off. No more violence. We'll handle Darcy later, once we're in complete control. Be patient, Denny, and get hold of your men."

Denny finished his drink and nodded. "All right. I'll go join the boys at Sally's. Make sure they don't cause another *incident*." He put on his hat and left the office.

"I'll be leaving, too," said Phillips. "I have a breakfast meeting with Cate. Will you be joining us?"

"Not tomorrow. I'll see her later. 'Night, Alton." The three watched the judge leave the building.

"Think he suspects anything?" asked Collins.

Whitehead smiled. "No. You heard what that fool said. He

took my suggestion for deputizing Denny and made it his own. Everything is proceeding as we planned. All of the land in the new settlement is back under our control. Everything is in place. Gentlemen, we've won."

"Not everything," Collins pointed out. "There's still one last piece."

"True, but that'll be no trouble. All I have to do is close my hand, and it'll fall to us."

Pyke was nervous. "What about Darcy? He just about called you out."

Whitehead chuckled. "Don't worry about Mr. Darcy, strutting around with his land and money. That half-breed doesn't even recognize when he's been outmaneuvered. He's powerless to stop us. If he causes any trouble, I can call for the weight of the government in Austin to fall upon him. Pemberley will just be ours sooner than anticipated."

Whitehead walked over to the window. "No, gentlemen, as long as we're patient, we've won. We now control the destiny of Long Branch County."

Chapter 14

September

THINGS CHANGED IN THE weeks following the lynchings, as a cloud of fear and suspicion descended upon the town of Rosings. Unnecessary gatherings were curtailed, and events like the Ladies' Musical Society meetings fell apart. Rather than the heat of battle, a cold mistrust pervaded the place as the people divided themselves into two camps: those who believed the tale of the roving band of Klansmen, and those who did not. The official explanation of the crime was championed by George Whitehead and Judge Phillips. Those who harbored doubts looked to William Darcy for leadership. Sheriff Lucas was caught in the middle.

Mr. Bennet kept his opinions to himself, refusing to discuss the doings in town with his family except to strictly enforce new rules around the farm. None of the women, including Mrs. Bennet, could go anywhere out of the house alone; they had to be accompanied by at least one other. Trips to town for any reason except supplies and church were forbidden. And he and Hill worked the barn and fields armed.

It was frustrating to Beth because the father she adored, a

man who had always been open with her, was now silent and unbending. Nothing she did could convince him to talk about what was worrying him, but she knew he was worried; it was plain to see in his eyes. He worked from sunup to sundown, taking his meals in the fields and retiring to his study after supper. Beth could see that her mother, too, was at a loss to ease her father's cares. So the family continued on as they had always done: they did their chores—only now they were done in silence. Only Lily seemed insensible to the strained atmosphere.

Try as he might, Bennet could not make his farm completely self-sufficient. Supplies were still needed from town. Most of the time he himself would take the wagon in, but one day the harvest was in full swing and none of the male hands could be excused. As the supplies were desperately needed, it was reluctantly agreed that Beth would journey to town that day with Lily keeping her company, the family shotgun in a box beneath the seat.

Instructed to go directly to Zimmerman's and back, the girls passed the Bingley place without stopping. Lily kept up an endless stream of inane conversation to which Beth paid little mind. She was struck, instead, at how empty the streets of Rosings were. Usually at that time of day, people would be everywhere—working, shopping, or just visiting. Now the place resembled a ghost town.

The wagon team secured, Beth and Lily entered the general store. The place was empty; the small bell on the door alerted Mr. and Mrs. Zimmerman that customers had arrived. Obviously happy to have patrons, Zimmerman took the list of supplies Beth handed him and left to fill the order, leaving his wife to keep the girls company.

"Oh, we're so happy to see you!" Mrs. Zimmerman said after

exchanging the usual pleasantries. "Everything in town has been very… quiet. No one comes around anymore. We can see the smithy across the street, and it's the same there. Business is bad." She shook her head. "With that last family leaving the new settlement after that Washington family got killed, we see nobody. Everyone is so scared."

She lowered her voice. "Some people say that the reason that black man was killed was that he took advantage of a white woman back east. That's why those Klansmen came here."

Beth blanched and turned, assuring herself that Lily was still looking at fabric samples on the other side of the store and was out of earshot. Beth did not want her sister to hear of such a story, for Lily was a bigger gossip even than their mother. She returned to the storekeeper's wife.

"Mrs. Zimmerman, I never heard any such thing. Who said that about Mr. Washington?"

"Umm, I overheard one of Mr. Denny's men—Thorpe, I think it was—say that," the woman admitted.

Beth grew angry as she recalled the confrontation at the cemetery. Thorpe was the leader of the men who tried to stop the funeral. "I wouldn't put too much stock in what Mr. Thorpe has to say. The Washingtons were members of our church, remember, and no one had a bad word to say about them."

"True." The woman was abashed. "They always paid cash— never asked for credit. And they were always respectful to me. Maybe Washington was confused with someone else? Yes, that must be what happened. Slaves all look the same to me and, I guess, to most folks. Oh, it's awful, just awful! Those poor people. I can't stop thinking about that poor little boy."

Beth was both touched and frustrated with Mrs. Zimmerman.

It seemed the woman was casting about for any explanation of the tragedy that would prove it was done by outsiders. The alternative was apparently too frightening for her to contemplate.

The alternative had occupied Beth's mind since the funeral. The actions of the B&R hands like Denny, Thorpe, and Wilkerson—all members of Denny's gang—seemed to point to a very frightening conclusion. Denny and his people seemed capable of perpetrating the outrage; they had been members of Quantrill's infamous Raiders after all. The last few weeks had challenged Beth's deeply held beliefs about the war, but her opinion of bushwhackers had been justified by unimpeachable sources: Confederate veterans like William and Fitz were disgusted by bushwhackers and disavowed their actions. She felt safe to mistrust Denny.

This led her thoughts to George Whitehead. Beth could not shake the nagging feeling that it wasn't a matter of *whether* George was involved in the killings of the Washingtons, but *how much*. Casting her eyes on Mrs. Zimmerman, she assumed the same thoughts had occurred to her.

Just then, the front door bell rang, the woman before her blanched, and Beth's conjectures were proven correct.

"George!" cried Lily.

Beth turned to see George Whitehead close the door. With unclouded eyes, Beth could now see things in him that she had missed before. George was undeniably a good-looking man, but there was a hardness in his eyes that his smile could never completely hide. His confident walk was more like an arrogant swagger. He had nothing good to say about anyone who was not of use to him, and he demanded deference from others through fear.

Will Darcy didn't do that, Beth realized. William earned the admiration of others by his deeds.

"Good afternoon, ladies," Whitehead said, tipping his hat. "Doing some shopping, I see?"

Lily answered him. "Yes, Father sent us to pick up some supplies. It's been so boring lately! Father won't let us go anywhere. Maybe you could talk to him?"

"Lily," Beth calmly admonished her. "I'm sure George is far too busy for such a silly request. With things being as they are in town," she turned to Whitehead as she spoke, "Father is only being properly cautious in seeing we're *fully* protected."

"Very wise of him," Whitehead drawled.

Beth continued. "It's uncomfortable to work a field with a gun belt on, but such are the days we're living in now." For some reason, Beth felt she had to give Whitehead the gentle warning. The slight narrowing of his eyes showed that the message was received.

Lily then called Whitehead's attention to a piece of lace she had been admiring. This gave Beth the opportunity to watch Mrs. Zimmerman again. She quickly learned that her initial estimation of the woman was wrong. By the mixture of fear and suspicion in her eye, it was apparent that Mrs. Zimmerman was not ignorant of the possibility that the Washingtons were attacked by one of their own. The shopkeeper's wife was terrified. When Mr. Zimmerman joined them a moment later, his pale, nervous expression showed that he was in full agreement with his spouse's fears.

"Good… good afternoon, Mr. Whitehead," Zimmerman was able to manage. "Umm… what can I do for you?"

"Nothing, Zimmerman, just stopped on by to see how things were." Whitehead seemed amused by the shakiness in the proprietor's voice. Beth noticed his enjoyment of the Zimmermans' fear with a sinking feeling. Now, with complete certainty, she knew George Whitehead was an evil man. She wanted nothing more than to be out of his presence.

"Do you have our order, sir?" Beth asked Zimmerman. Beth settled the bill and called Lily over to help. Despite Beth's protests, Whitehead insisted on carrying the packages to their wagon. Back up on the seat, the two Bennet girls took their leave of Whitehead.

"Won't you come over for dinner soon, George?" Lily begged.

"Well, I've been pretty busy lately," George begged off, "but who knows? I might find the time to come by the place when you least expect me." He grinned in that lopsided way of his, his eyes still cold, and Beth felt a shot of fear course through her. Whitehead tipped his hat and reentered the store.

As Beth took a moment to settle her emotions, Lily took the opportunity to gaze about the town. "Beth, look!" she hissed.

At Younge's Saloon, three young women, dressed in the usual style of dancehall girls, were on the balcony waving at a couple of cowboys riding away. Their raucous laughter could easily be heard.

"What pretty dresses!" Lily cried. "Wouldn't you love to have one of those?"

"Lily! Be quiet!" Beth turned the team away from the barroom and urged them along the road home. "Don't be a simpleton! You know what those sinful girls do for a living. They're fallen women!"

"I know that! I know they're whores," Lily lightly responded.

"Lily—your language!"

"Sorry. I know those... women are going to the nether

region. I do listen in church, you know." At Beth's questioning look, she added, "Well, most of the time. I only like the dresses. I'd love to own pretty dresses, one for each day, and do nothing but sit around telling other people what to do. Like Miss Gaby or Miss Anne." Lily waved her hands. "'Smith, fetch me some tea!'"

Beth laughed. "Yes, I can just see you. You were made to be a lady of leisure."

Lily tossed her head. "Don't laugh! I'm sure I am. It would be just the thing. Oh, what a life! Better than what we have now."

"Father's worked very hard to provide for us, you ungrateful creature!"

"Oh, I know, but he's not the only one who works! Chores, chores, chores. I hate it! We work all day until we're too tired to do anything else at night but go to bed. Day after day. Feed the chickens. Milk the cow. Churn the butter. I hate churning butter!"

"And you're so uncommonly good at it." Beth couldn't resist. Lily did have the most adorable pout on her face, after all.

"You always say that! Pooh!"

Beth reached over and took Lily's hand. "Maybe I do. Still, you have to admit our life isn't so bad. We have food on the table and a warm bed to sleep in every night." Beth lowered her voice. "Many can't say the same."

Lily nodded. "You're right." She thought for a moment. "Do you want to ride once we get home? We can practice jumping rails with Buster and Turner again. That's so much fun!"

"I'd love to, but you know what Father said. It's too dangerous."

"Maybe just around the farm? If you ask Father, I'm sure he'd let us."

Beth thought. "All right, I'll ask." She held up a hand at Lily's squeal of joy, trying not to smile at her sister's youthful exuberance. "I'll ask, but it's up to Father. We'll be good and accept his decision, all right, sister dear?"

Lily sighed in agreement and then grinned, as she changed the subject back to their original conversation. "Tell me the truth. Wouldn't you like to live like Miss Darcy? You've seen her house. I'll bet it's grand, and she has servants everywhere." Lily bounced on the wagon seat. "Wouldn't you just love to live in a place like Pemberley?"

Beth nearly choked as she blushed. *Lily, you have no idea!*

Lily continued. "If I ever get the chance to live like that, I would—oh!"

Beth was surprised at Lily's outburst, and turned to see what had caused it. Standing outside the Rosings Bank was Kid Denny and a member of his gang—new, shiny badges of authority from Judge Phillips hanging on their shirts. That was disconcerting enough; what made it worse was that Denny was staring at them, an unreadable expression on his face.

No—he wasn't staring at them. His eyes were locked on Lily. Beth shivered and moved slightly closer to her youngest sister, trying to shield her from his gaze.

"Beth?" asked Lily in a low, frightened voice, one that had lost all good humor. "Can we go home now?"

Beth turned to see that Lily was just as affected by Denny as she. Beth nodded. "Don't be afraid. We'll be home soon."

"I'm not afraid," Lily protested. "I… I just want to go riding with you, that's all."

Beth was not fooled by Lily's statement, but chose not to challenge her. "Of course, love. Hang on." Determined to protect her beloved sister, Beth's lips drew into a firm line as she prodded the horses to move faster.

As the days of September passed, the only sign that fall was approaching was that the days were growing shorter. It was still hot, and the dry season was upon them. That meant dove hunting in Texas, and Pemberley was always a dependable roosting area.

Early on this particular day, a hunting party of Will Darcy, Richard Fitzwilliam, and Charles Bingley worked a field near a wooded area about three miles from the main house. All three carried double-barreled shotguns, but had neither beaters nor dogs. Will did not own any hunting dogs, and he would not use his employees to scare up game. Still the sport had been productive and each man had bagged his share.

"You're a fair shot, for a doctor," Fitz observed as the three took their ease, sharing a flask with their lunches.

"Not as good as you," Charles said. "Did you miss any? I would swear you didn't."

"If you think that was good, you should see Fitz with a rifle," Will grinned. "I'll bet if we made him use a Winchester instead of a shotgun, he'd still bag as many birds."

"Naw, you don't want to do that," Fitz drawled. "Wouldn't leave much o' the bird left to eat, an' then Miz Reynolds would have my hide."

"You scared of Will's cook?"

"Nope. Scared she'd quit him, and then the other hands will get sore and come after me!"

Will laughed. "You're right about that. Mrs. Reynolds has a lot of friends in the bunkhouse."

The men continued talking until Fitz suddenly stood up. "Hear that?"

"What?" Darcy started, before he did hear, faintly.

"*Mr. Darcy! Mr. Darcy!*" came from a distance away.

"Sounds like Peter," Fitz judged.

Will nodded, got to his feet while pulling his Colt, and fired three rounds in the air. Alerted by the sound, the Pemberley rider found them in short order. Darcy was surprised at Peter's companion—a very distraught Beth.

"Mr. Darcy," Peter called as they came to a halt. "Miss Bennet here needs to talk to Doc Bingley."

"Good God, what's the matter?" Darcy exclaimed as he half-ran to Turner. Beth's face was dirty, as dust clung to the tears she had undoubtedly shed earlier. He took the paint's reins and held up a hand to help Beth dismount. Charles was right on Darcy's heels.

Beth allowed Will to help her down before saying, "Charles, you have to come home, please—"

Bingley turned white. "Jane? Susan? My God, has anything happened?"

"No, no!" Beth cried in a mixture of grief and frustration. "They're fine! It's Lily! She's gone—missing! We think she's run away!"

Will had not released Beth's hand and his grip tightened. "Are you sure?"

"Yes—no—we don't know! She's just gone! She went to bed last night, but she wasn't there this morning! We've been looking all over for her!"

"Come sit down, Beth. Do you need anything? Some water? We've got water. Or maybe something stronger?"

"No, nothing please. Just let me catch my breath."

"You know anything?" Fitz asked Peter.

"No. Miss Bennet come ridin' up to Pemberley, wantin' to

talk to the doc. She said there was a family emergency. Miss Gaby told me to find y'all, an' Miss Bennet insisted on comin' along. Don't know about any missing girl."

Will sat down next to Beth and took her hands in his. "What's been done to find Lily?"

Beth stared into Will's caring eyes. "Father and I rode to town to get Charles. Jane said he was here, so I went on to get him. Father's gone to Sheriff Lucas."

"Has there been any sign of her?"

"No. No note. Just that one of our horses is missing. It was Lily's horse."

"Has Lily said anything about meeting somebody? Was she sweet on some fellow?"

"No. There's been no one."

"All right. Do you need anything right now?"

She shook her head. "No. I have to get back to Charles's place—Father will be waiting for me there."

"Then, I won't detain you." Will stood up and began barking orders. "All right. Fitz, I want you to ride back to Pemberley and begin assembling a search team. Saddle up anyone we can spare. Make sure they're armed. We don't know what's happened to Lily, if she's been kidnapped or not."

"Will, she took her own horse," Fitz pointed out.

"I heard that, and maybe she did ride out to meet somebody, and maybe she changed her mind. It's happened before," Will shot back. "We're not taking any chances, all right?"

Fitz got the allusion to Gaby and nodded.

"Peter, ride out and tell the wranglers to keep an eye out for a girl on a... what kind of horse was that, Beth?"

"Buster is brown, with a white flash on the chest."

"Got that description? Good. Fitz, when you get your team assembled, meet me at the Bingleys."

Beth stared at him. "You're coming with us?"

"Yep. Fitz, you better take my birds with you to the house. Everyone clear on what to do? Good. Let's ride."

Directly upon reaching the Bingleys', Darcy set up a command post. He commandeered the Bingley dining room table, spreading a map of the county upon it. When Fitz arrived with a dozen men from Pemberley, Darcy assembled them into two-man teams and assigned them various locations to search. Beth was impressed by his quick command of the situation, and she was pleased with the easy respect his men held for their employer.

She was not the only witness—besides the Bingleys, Mr. Bennet was in attendance, having come to his son-in-law's house after talking to both the sheriff and Judge Phillips. Bennet wanted to join in the search, but Darcy talked him out of it, pointing out that he could most help the effort by reflecting on his daughter and trying to divine where she might have gone.

Fitz and the Pemberley riders spread out all over the north bank of the Long Branch. Denny and his men, called in by Phillips, preferred to look for the wayward girl *en masse*. Thirty men rode all over the B&R until sundown without success.

As the disappointed and worried Bennets prepared to go home for the night, William approached them. "Sir, I'll have my men out at first light. We won't rest 'til we find her." Will was talking to Mr. Bennet, but Beth thought his words were for her, too.

"I thank you kindly," said an exhausted Mr. Bennet.

"Whatever you can do, however long you can help, well… you've got my thanks."

"No thanks necessary." He paused, and Beth thought he was going to say more, but besides a quick glance at her, he fell silent. He nodded as the father and daughter mounted their horses for the ride back to the farm. Beth wasn't surprised that they were escorted by two Pemberley wranglers, but her father was. Bennet first greeted his waiting family and gave them the disappointing news of their failure. After Mrs. Bennet, Mary, and Kathy returned to the house and the escort left, the farmer questioned Beth as they attended to their animals in the barn.

"I'm very thankful that Mr. Darcy is showing a great deal of interest in our family, Beth," he said as he unsaddled his horse, "but, it's surprising, given his lack of dealings between us. Or maybe not so much of a lack of dealings as I believe?" He turned to his daughter. "Beth, is there something you want to tell me?"

Beth hoped the darkness hid the blush she was certain was covering her face. "Will Darcy's a good man, Father—better than we've been given reason to think. But I wouldn't read too much into it. I'm sure he'd do the same for anybody. Look what he did for the Washingtons—he bought their burial plots, you know."

"Yes," Bennet said. To Beth he sounded strangely disappointed. "Well, let's pray for better news tomorrow."

Unfortunately, the news was not what they had hoped. Lily's horse was found grazing on B&R land between town and the Bennet farm. There was no sign of its rider.

Chapter 15

October

Before, Beth had always thought of the period following Samuel's death as the worst of her life. With Lily's disappearance, she realized that things could be worse. It was horrible to know that a beloved son and brother had died far away from home, but at least that fateful telegram had given the family the finality of closure. With Lily, the uncertainty made the experience almost unbearable. Hope battled despair in the hearts of the Bennets. Without knowing what had become of Lily, there was no way of not thinking about her.

Rumors swirled around the town. All sorts of theories were put forth, but the one that seemed to be believed by most was that the band of Klansmen had returned and Lily Bennet had either been kidnapped or convinced to run off with them. A cowpoke from the B&R claimed he awoke from his bedroll on the range to the sound of horses in the distance the night Lily disappeared. Nothing was confirmed, but that was enough for those who needed something to believe.

Judge Phillips called off the search after a few days. The rest of the town was nearly insensible with fear. They could convince themselves that the attack on the Washingtons was an isolated incident, but now that a neighbor's daughter was missing and presumed stolen away, the people could no longer ignore what was happening. Evil was riding the range, and everyone was terrified that they or their family could be next.

Doors were locked tight, guns were kept loaded, and social-izing stopped. The storekeepers were concerned over their liveli-hoods, as shopping for anything save the barest of necessities had ceased. Church attendance was cut in half. The streets in town belonged to the tumbleweeds, dogs, and Judge Phillips's deputies.

As September turned into October, the Bennets lived in a sort of half-life. No matter the fears and anxieties, fields needed to be tended, animals needed to be fed, and chores needed to be done. The family went about their duties listlessly, one ear cocked to hear the approach of news that never came. There was no escape from the gloom. Mr. Bennet made it clear that none of the women were to leave the farm, and that included church. The once-a-week trips for supplies would be done by either Mr. Bennet or the farmhand, Hill, and neither would be absent from the farm at the same time.

Those trips were the only relief Beth received during this time, because there would always be a note from Charlotte brought from town to her. Not all of the family's friends abandoned them. The Bingleys would come by as often as they could, and Reverend Tilney's occasional visits were appreciated, especially by Mary, but they were cold comfort to Beth. She yearned for the company of a man she had once hated—a person she realized was the best man she had ever known.

For it was there in Charlotte's letters—while the rest of

town had given up on the search for Lily, even the sheriff—that Beth learned that the story from Pemberley was different. Will Darcy's men, when they could be excused from their duties, spent their time searching every nook and cranny in the county, looking for a sign of the girl. Charlotte never said who supplied her information, but Beth had an idea who it was. No one who had witnessed the attentions paid to the girl by Richard Fitzwilliam at the Burroughses' party back in July could fail to see the signs of a blooming romance.

Beth was thrilled at William's constancy. He had promised he wouldn't give up, and he hadn't. Her heart whispered it was for her, but her better sense tamped down her hopes. Will Darcy was a great man—kind and generous—and she thought he would do the same for anyone. Could he still love her?

Beth now knew she was in love with Will Darcy. She could not pinpoint the time or place when it had happened; the feeling had come to her so gradually. Certainly, by the time she visited Pemberley she was well on her way. Perhaps watching firsthand how well he handled the twin disasters that had befallen Rosings—the lynchings and Lily's disappearance—had proven to her that Will was not a proud and willful martinet. Rather, he was a quick-thinking and forceful leader, ready to step forward when the time called for action. Perhaps as the last of the numerous misunderstandings of his character fell away, she could do nothing but admire and love him.

Her joy was tempered with anguish. Letters from others extolling his goodness were not enough. Even though she knew he was busy and the times were dangerous, she still longed to see him again—to talk with him again, to dance in his arms again. Why did he not come to visit? Was he embarrassed to associate himself with her family? She was being nonsensical, she knew. Darcy had never been invited to their house in the past. In fact, he had been on Bennet land only once to the best of her knowledge—during the cattle drive in the spring. Why would he ever think he would be welcomed?

But a woman's heart was never completely rational. Beth desired only two things—Lily returned home and for herself to be in Darcy's arms—and she was afraid she would see neither ever again.

Summer had finally broken, and the residents enjoyed the moderation of temperatures that passed for fall in Central Texas. On such a bright and sunny day, Charlotte descended from her cart and was in the act of securing the horse when the bells of Santa Maria began to mark the hour. As the twelfth and final peal faded, Charlotte walked not into the mission chapel but the graveyard beyond. There, in the shadows afford by a group of oak trees, stood a tall cowboy wearing a black hat with a silver band.

A moment later, Charlotte was in Fitz's arms, their lips hungrily searching for the other's. Arms about Fitz's neck, Charlotte delighted in the feelings their kisses inflamed in her body and soul. The breath seemed to be squeezed out of her lungs, so tight was her beloved's embrace. A warm dizziness enveloped her, and she could not support herself on her now trembling legs. Her companion seemed to understand, for they were soon on their knees, and then prone on the soft grass between the headstones, lost in lovemaking.

Fitz's mouth drew away long enough to gasp, "You're wearin' your rose water." Charlotte smiled widely, her eyes alive with love and passion, lighting up her plain features, before drawing Fitz back for another kiss.

It had begun in late June, soon after Fitzwilliam returned from Kansas. He appeared at the Lucases' back door one evening while the sheriff was working at the jail. He was dressed in his Sunday best, a small wrapped gift in his hand. Tenderly, Charlotte unwrapped the package to discover a small bottle of perfume. Shyly glancing at the man, she lifted the stopper to the smell of roses.

"They had some o' that made of gardenias," Fitz had said, looking at the bottle, "but I was thinkin' that stuff was too showy for you. Roses seemed a better choice. I hope you like it."

"I… I love it." She was confused, yet hopeful.

He finally raised his eyes to hers. "I hope you don't think I'm too forward."

She nervously licked her lips. "Not at all."

"Sorry I came to the back door an' all—you deserve better than that—but I didn't want to cause any fuss with your kin."

"I understand."

He paused, as if to gather his courage—a strange thing to do, Charlotte thought at the time, as she had nothing but admiration for the ranch foreman.

"You goin' to the Burroughses' party?" he asked. Told that she was, he gulped.

"Will you spare a dance for me?"

From that moment, Charlotte knew she had a sweetheart. She agreed to dance with Fitz, thanking him for the gift and the invitation with a light peck on his cheek. The look of wonder on his lined face was priceless. She almost wept with joy. He left a minute later, the slightly goofy expression still there.

Charlotte carefully hid her gift in her room, not wanting to answer uncomfortable questions from her father. She used it only for special occasions, and those times were reserved for Richard Fitzwilliam. She wore it to the dance, delighting the man. She offered no resistance when, late in the afternoon, they were able to steal away from the crowd, finding a quiet, private place to share their first kiss. It was everything Charlotte had dreamed it would be.

Their courtship, however, was not. Sheriff Lucas had questioned his daughter severely upon returning home. He had seen her dance with Fitz, and he made his displeasure plain. So firm was his admonition of her behavior—to him, dancing with Fitz was turning her back on his authority as her father—that Charlotte realized discussion or argument was useless. Nothing she could say would soften her father's heart. Fitz was unworthy of her, and that was it. She would not be able to meet with Fitzwilliam openly, and as she had no intention of giving him up, they would have to meet secretly.

The solution was easily found. Gaby had expressed a desire to practice music with Charlotte on a weekly basis. Rather than making Miss Lucas go all the way to Pemberley, they would meet at the Catholic mission. Charlotte understood the concern over Whitehead; she had noticed his interest in both the Pemberley and B&R heiresses. The mission was close to town, so Gaby would still be safe on Pemberley land, and the church had a piano. One in the afternoon was the agreed time.

However, when securing her father's permission for the scheme, Charlotte told one little lie—she said they would meet at noon and have a shared lunch before practice. Sheriff Lucas consented, happy that Miss Darcy was his daughter's friend. But it wasn't Gaby who Charlotte arranged to meet at noon, but Fitzwilliam. They would share a basket lunch weekly and have an hour of each other's company in the shade of the trees near the mission's cemetery.

Charlotte was certain that Gaby had no idea their musical meetings were a cover for her assignations with Fitzwilliam. She felt a bit guilty over using her friend, but she convinced herself that she had no other choice. As for Father Joseph, if he was aware of the goings-on in his cemetery, he made no comment.

As July stretched into August, the couple spent less time eating and more time enjoying each other's company in more demonstrative ways. By September, Charlotte was certainly compromised, but not irreversibly so. They had not consummated their love and passion, but each week it grew more difficult to restrain their mutual desire—as it had today.

The troubles in town might have ended the meetings of the Ladies Musical Society, but Charlotte's weekly visits with Gaby continued. The plain sheriff's daughter was thought to be immune from whatever was going on. She could travel in town openly and without escort as long as it was during the day. Besides, the queer girl was known to be armed and an excellent shot, as she had proved during rodeos past. So, Charlotte was able to keep her rendezvous with her lover while most women were shut at home.

Whether it was the cool weather, the tension in town, or simply because it had been a week since she had been in Fitz's arms, Charlotte was more passionate than ever. The air seemed to rush past her ears as she lost herself to her emotions. Fitz's lips traced a trail down her neck as his hand lightly teased the cloth that covered her breasts. The girl was on fire, a low moan escaping her lips. In the back of her desire-intoxicated mind, she knew if Fitz lowered his hand and raised her skirts, she would willingly part her legs and allow him to take her. Therefore, it took her a moment to realize the cowboy was no longer half-lying on top of her but had instead rolled over onto his side.

"Oh, God, sweetheart, I love you," he panted.

For an instant, Charlotte was aggrieved and disappointed before her modesty and common sense caught up with her emotions. Once again, Fitz had shown more restraint than she had, and though she flushed with shame at her behavior, her love for and pride in him increased. She tenderly stroked his face.

"It feels like a wonderful dream, every time I'm in your arms. I keep waiting to wake up and find out that you don't really care for me—that this has never happened." He kissed her fingers to reassure her. She smiled, the heat infusing her body starting to fade. "I'd best get the lunch. Gaby will be here soon."

Fitz turned his eyes to her. "No hurry. Gaby's not coming."

"What?" Charlotte sat right up, pulling her hand away from his. "Why not? Is anything wrong?"

Fitz was on his side, his head propped up by one arm. "Naw. She's fine. It's just that Will's gone to Fort Worth, an' he don't want Gaby to leave the house 'til he gets back."

Charlotte was initially relieved, until another thought struck her. "How long have you known this?"

"Since Monday."

"And you didn't get word to me? Oh!" The girl stood up, wrapped her arms around herself, and paced furiously. Fitz scrambled to his feet.

"Honey, what's the matter?"

"Nothing. Everything. Oh!" Fitz tried to console her without success. How could Charlotte explain her feelings? It was one thing to fib to her father and come early for her meetings with Gaby so that she could spend time with Fitz. It was another thing entirely if Gaby wasn't there at all. The sensible part of her mind whispered that deceit was deceit, and there was little difference between the two. But a woman in a forbidden romance was hardly sensible, and it would take some minutes before the girl could manage her guilty emotions.

"I'm all right, Fitz," she said into his dusty shirt as he held her to his chest. "I'd best get the luncheon from the cart."

Soon the two were nibbling on cheese, bread, and apples, sharing water from Fitz's canteen. The romantic spell had been broken for now, so they discussed the doings around town.

"Denny's men are still crawling all over the place," Charlotte told Fitz. "They walk around as if they own the town, demanding favors from the shopkeepers. Mrs. Zimmerman's told me she can't keep sweets in stock." She noticed the concern and anger on Fitz's face. "Oh, they leave me alone, don't worry."

"Like hell I won't! What makes you so sure you're safe walkin' the streets?"

"Besides being the sheriff's daughter? They'll have to notice me, first. Being plain has its advantages."

"You ain't plain," Fitz said with conviction and not for the first time.

Charlotte smiled. "I'm glad *you* think that."

Fitz grimaced. "Humph. I reckon I ought to be grateful them bushwhackers must be blind as well as greedy," he said without a smidgen of counterfeit praise. Charlotte was amused, gratified, and just a little mystified at this continued evidence of her boyfriend's admiration. "You sure you're safe?"

"Absolutely."

Fitz sighed. "I still don't like this. What's your paw doin' about it?"

"He's had words with Judge Phillips, and he's been told that they'll be reined in. Besides, there's not much he can do if the folks won't swear out an official complaint. They're scared of Denny, and they won't, so all Paw and his deputies can do is try to keep an eye on things."

Fitz tossed an apple core into the woods. "He ought to do more," he grumbled.

"With what? Fitz, there's only the three of them. How can he go up against Denny? He's outnumbered four-to-one."

Fitz paused. "I suppose they ain't spendin' a whole lot o' time lookin' for Miss Lily."

"No. Ever since they found her horse, they've given up on the search, no matter how much they claim otherwise. Paw's busy watching Denny, and…" She looked away. "Fitz, do you really think Lily can be found?"

"I don't know, but Will says we gotta keep an eye open for her. He promised the Bennets he wouldn't quit, an' he won't until she's found, alive or… well, until she's found."

Charlotte sighed. "Mr. Darcy must really love Beth."

"I reckon so. Why he don't just ask th' girl to marry him is just plumb loco."

Charlotte looked at her sweetheart through her eyelashes. "So, you think a man in love ought to propose to his intended?"

Fitz's sardonic grin faded. "I do if'n he thinks th' girl in question will give him the answer he wants." His eyes bore into hers. "For example, would she marry without her father's approval?"

Charlotte felt her tears rising. "Fitz, I… I…"

"Shush, sweetie," he said as he gathered her into his arms. "We'll just give him a little more time to accept us." He grinned without humor. "A *little* more time."

"But what if he never comes around?"

"Then we got us a decision to make."

Charlotte wasn't fooled by Fitz's use of the word "us"—it was *she* who would have to decide between father and lover. The unfairness of it all threatened to cause her unshed tears to fall.

"I'd best be getting back home," she said to cover up her distress. Fitz refused to release her hand.

"Can you come next week? As long as it's safe, I mean."

Charlotte knew she shouldn't. "Of course."

The man behind the desk rose from his chair upon Darcy's entrance into the office. "Good evening, Mr. Darcy," said the middle-aged, well-dressed man as he walked around the desk, hand held out in greeting. "I hope I can answer any questions you may still have after the presentation this afternoon."

"I'm sure you can, Mr. Knightly," answered Darcy as they shook hands. Knightly suggested they take a seat around a small table in one corner of the office. As Darcy made himself comfortable, he surveyed both the office and the man who occupied it. The room was ten feet square, not overly large for such a place in Fort Worth. The furnishings were in good condition but showed a bit of age. A bookcase with glass doors was against one wall, and next to it was a large safe. The room was neat, but not overly so. The small pile of papers on the desk and the stack of maps in one corner were proof it was the working office of an organized mind and not a set on a stage.

Knightly, too, he judged. He had heard of the Knightly brothers, John and Gabriel. They had worked as assistants on several railroad projects, but this was their first time setting up their own syndicate. The man who sat opposite him was open and calm. John Knightly had answered all questions at the presentation with confidence and honesty. What he knew, he shared; and if he or his brother didn't know the answer, he said so. Darcy felt he could trust them.

The project was interesting: a proposed new railroad between Fort Worth and Abilene, Texas. Darcy had been one of a number of potential investors invited to the meeting. The large amount requested was not daunting; he had made such investments before, and the brothers owned an excellent reputation. Normally, he would have just made a decision in the quiet of his hotel room after reading the prospectus, but this project had electrified him—and for more reasons than being just another in a line of promising investments.

"Now, sir, how can I be of service?" John Knightly smiled, his hands clasped on the tabletop.

"Thank you for agreeing to meet with me on such short notice. Your presentation was intriguing, to say the least." That was an understatement; Darcy was shocked silent when the plans were revealed. It was as if a great fog had lifted from his eyes only to reveal a horrible suspicion.

Knightly laughed lightly. "I imagine so, as we'll be running the rail line right through your property. But we want more than to purchase the right-of-way. We need visionary investors to carry this new company forward. I hope you will join us."

"Before I can make up my mind, I must ask to see the maps of the proposed railroad, particularly those of Long Branch County."

"Of course. Excuse me." Knightly walked over to the safe and worked the combination. He opened the door and extracted a stack of documents, which he carried back to the table.

"We'll spread the right map out here," he said. "As you can see, we take no chances. Security is very important."

Darcy understood that. Should speculators learn of the proposed route, they could buy up the land in advance and charge excessive amounts for the rights. The correct map was found and Knightly opened it up. Just then, there was a knock on the door.

"Sir?" A thin, short man stuck his head in. His nose was more prominent than his chin and he spoke with a nervous stammer. "Would you want me to make some coffee for you and the gentleman?" His large eyes seemed to be fixed on the table instead of his employer.

Knightly looked silently at Darcy, who shook his head. "No, that's all right, Elton," said Knightly, "you can go home now. Gabriel and I will be working late. We'll lock up. See you in the morning." After the clerk shut the door, the gentlemen's attention returned to the map.

"See?" Knightly ran a finger along a line drawn on it. "My advance team chose this route about a year ago. We looked at it several more times. As you can see, it runs along the north bank of the Long Branch River through the town before crossing here and onto your land."

Darcy's stomach turned as his blood ran cold. "I have to ask you—are you certain no one has seen this?"

Knightly was affronted but tried to hide it. "Absolutely. We have shown these, the only maps of the project, to no one before tonight. These are the only copies, and they are kept in that safe. Only my brother and I have the combination."

"I beg your pardon, Mr. Knightly, but I had to ask."

"Is something wrong?"

Darcy struggled with how to answer. He had only suspicions, not proof. "I don't know. Is it possible that your advance team was questioned?"

"No. You see, Mr. Darcy, my surveyors are instructed most carefully on what to say if approached. I have worked with them on other projects, and they have never violated our trust. To what do these questions pertain?"

Darcy sighed. "There've been some… incidents over this area." He pointed to the new settlements.

"Hmm. That's problematic. If we run into any difficulties, we can always go a bit farther north. I'd hate to put an unnecessary curve in the line, but that's better than extortion."

"That won't help. All the land north of the river is owned by the same landowner now."

Knightly looked up. "Really? I understand your questions, then. Perhaps the team was observed and a lucky guess was made. It's never happened before, but there's always the first time. I suppose you know the owner."

Darcy wanted to be sick. "Yes, I do."

"Do you think there will be a problem securing the right-of-way?"

"I'm not sure." Darcy ran other possible motivations for seeking control of the bottomland through his head and came up with only one reason. *To sell.* "Probably not."

Knightly sat back. "Well, if there gets to be a problem—if the price is driven up too high—we can always go to our alternative route. Actually, that's better for you, as we'd be buying more rights from your Pemberley."

"Perhaps. But no stop on that route, correct?"

"True. We'll only put in a station if we go through the Town of Rosings."

Darcy's stomach clenched again. "The station would be of greater overall value to me and everyone else. I have to ask you to try to use the original route."

"That's our opinion as well. If you decide to invest in this project, can we count on you to help calm any rough waters?"

Darcy swallowed thickly. "You have my assurances. I'm in. I'll be happy to invest in your company."

"Wonderful!" Knightly cried, taking the rancher by the hand. "We've just about raised all the capital we'll need to get started."

"I'll be by tomorrow to finalize the papers and arrange for delivery of the funds." The two chatted for a few more minutes before Darcy took his leave. As he walked out of the office building, José Estrada, who had accompanied his employer to Fort Worth, fell in step beside him.

"So, we get the dinner now, boss?" José asked as the two walked the sidewalks of the city towards their hotel.

Darcy couldn't answer—he just nodded his head. He was too busy reevaluating his cousin, Catherine Burroughs. He always knew she was a hard-nosed businesswoman, but he never dreamed she was capable of murder.

Until now.

TO G WHITEHEAD—stop—HARVEST IS
IN—stop—SILO IS FULL—stop—READY TO
START ON NEW BARN—stop—SUGGEST
YOU PREPARE BACK FORTY—stop—MOTHER
MISSES YOU—stop—E—end

"What the hell does that mean?" cried Denny.

Whitehead laughed. "It's a coded message from Elton, my man inside the Knightly syndicate. Allow me to enlighten you. 'Harvest is in'—that means that the investor meetings are completed. 'Silo is full' and 'ready to start on the new barn' means that the Knightlys have all the funds they need to move forward with the railroad and that construction will start soon. The words 'back forty' means that we better have all our affairs in order, because the syndicate will start acquiring rights-of-way." He tossed the telegram on the desk. "See? I told you all we had to do was wait and the riches would come to us!"

"Yeah? When?"

"Soon."

"What's that about your mother? I thought you said you was an orphan."

"That means Elton's available for a meeting."

"So, you goin'?"

Whitehead nodded, his face studying Denny's countenance. A sudden idea came to him. "Why don't you come with me? That way you can talk to Elton yourself—see how things are going. What about it?"

Collins perked up. "All of us?"

"No, you need to stay here to help keep Burroughs and Phillips happy. It'll just be Denny and me with a couple of riders."

"What about… her?" Pyke asked, pointing a finger upstairs.

"That's your job," Whitehead said easily, betraying the tension he felt when talking about the girl. "Keep her out of sight. You can do that, can't you?"

"Yeah," sneered Denny, "keep my property well looked after. Just don't look *too* close, partner," he added, patting his holstered gun.

Collins started to open his mouth, but whatever he was going to say, he thought better of it. Whitehead didn't need to hear it, anyway, for the banker was only going to voice what had been running through his own mind. The girl had become a distraction and a threat. Things were too important; the money and the power that would come with it were too damn close to chance that she would be discovered.

Denny walked to the window. "When do you wanna leave? Been raining hard for two days. Roads will be muddy for sure."

"As soon as it stops. We'll go on horseback rather than the carriage. Be faster."

Yes, Whitehead thought, *the faster I get to Fort Worth to get my update from Elton, the faster I can get back here and tie up all loose ends. And that includes the girl. Denny will just have to find another toy. Lily Bennet needs to disappear for good.*

It didn't stop raining until after Darcy returned to Pemberley. The next evening he learned from his spies in town that Whitehead, Denny, and a couple of riders had left that morning for Fort Worth.

Ironic, he thought. *Another day and we might have met on the road. I wonder what would have happened. Would Whitehead and his party have just passed by, or would we have settled this thing out there in the wilderness once and for all?* Darcy knew he wouldn't have started anything, but he also knew he was prepared to end it.

He forced himself to stop thinking of Whitehead; he had more pressing issues on his mind. The storms had scattered his cattle all over the range. Every hand was needed for the roundup. He knew he had days in the saddle before him.

It would only delay the confrontation with Cate Burroughs.

The rains may have stopped, but the river kept rising as the storm waters flowed into Rosings Creek and the Long Branch. Higher and higher the river rose, turning Thompson Crossing into a raging torrent. Downriver, the townspeople watched the single bridge across the river with concern, hoping it wouldn't fail. It survived, but just barely.

The same couldn't be said for the abandoned homesteads in the new settlement. The long-timers' predictions rang true when the Long Branch overflowed its banks, inundating the bottomland and the houses that stood like lonely sentinels. They were flooded one by one, and a few, like the Washingtons' place, could not stand the deluge and were swept away.

One old wag opined that God Himself was cleaning the foul stench of the crime that had been committed there. Publicly, most scoffed at the idea, but it was telling that, for generations, folks in Long Branch County would consider the site haunted.

Chapter 16

October 31

THE DAYS WERE GROWING shorter as October ended, but the air still held a hint of summer's warmth. Therefore, Charlotte was not chilled as she carefully walked home from the jail, the streets still damp and slightly muddy from the rains that had fallen for the past week, and she was able to lose herself in thoughts of Fitz. Her progress was halted by a loud noise, and she turned to observe some of Denny's men entering Younge's Saloon, singing and cursing. Charlotte frowned, wondering again why Rosings tolerated such an establishment. She looked up and down the muddy street at the storefronts and shops, at the banks and the church, at the new schoolhouse going up. All signs that the town was leaving its frontier roots. Even Whitehead's building, next to Younge's, spoke of the future—

Charlotte froze.

Looking from a second-floor window in Whitehead's building was a young, blonde woman. Her face was painted and her clothes could only be described as indecent, but Charlotte recognized the girl beneath the harlot. A moment later, the woman turned from the window, responding to a voice within the room. Then a man's arm drew the curtains closed.

Charlotte blinked. A less self-assured person might have thought the sighting had never happened, but Miss Lucas was nothing if not confident. She looked about to see if her response was of note to anyone on the street. Assured of her safety, she quickly returned to her father's office.

"Charlotte, are you *certain* of this?" cried Sheriff Lucas.

Charlotte rubbed her forehead, weary of the interrogation. "Yes, Paw. It was Lily Bennet. I know it! It was her!"

"Maybe we oughta go and take a peek," Deputy Smith offered helpfully. He blanched at the look his boss threw at him.

"I'm still not convinced it was the Bennet girl," Sheriff Lucas insisted. "Perhaps it was a trick of the light—"

"Paw!" Charlotte cried. "I know what I saw! It was Lily Bennet looking out a window in George Whitehead's building not thirty minutes ago. I know it as sure as I'm sitting here. Why do you insist I didn't see what I saw? Are you afraid?"

"*Yes!*" Lucas shouted as he leapt to his feet. "Yes, I am, and so should you be! Do you understand what'll happen if I go stormin' in there? Do you want Denny and his gang shootin' up the town? Three lawmen against a dozen trained killers? There are more things to think about than one foolish girl!"

Charlotte stared at the two men in shock. Her father was flushed while Smith would not meet her eye. "Paw—"

Lucas cut her off. "No more, Charlotte. Not another word. I've said my piece. Now, get yourself back to the house. Smith, go walk her home."

"No, Paw. It's not necessary. I can find my own way home. To be honest, I'd rather not suffer your company, or Smith's, any more than I have to tonight." Charlotte did not wait to hear her father's response, as she was out the door the next instant. But she did not head towards their house at the edge of town. Instead, she made her way to the livery stable.

As usual at Pemberley, the Darcys had their supper early and had their top hands join them. They were half-finished with their meal, and José was in the middle of an amusing story about a priest and a rabbi in a saloon, when Reynaldo approached the table.

"*Señor* Darcy, there is a young woman here to see *Señor* Fitz."

Both men exchanged confused glances before Darcy told his butler to escort the lady in. The confusion was doubled as Charlotte was introduced.

"Miss Lucas," Darcy greeted her, "you are very welcome, but may I ask why you're here—alone, I take it? Has something happened to your father?"

The agitated girl shook her head. "No, no, he's fine. Please excuse me, Miss Gaby, but I have to talk to Fitz right now!" She glanced at Darcy. "And, perhaps, you too, Mr. Will."

Darcy looked at Fitz. "Very well, shall we adjourn to my study?"

"Charlotte, are you *certain* of this?" cried Fitz.

"Of course, I am!" she returned with some heat. "Do you think I rode all this way in the evening to tell you tales?"

William turned from staring out the window. "Miss Lucas, please calm yourself. We believe you. It's just... so...

fantastic." He turned back to gaze outside. "All this time we've been looking for her and she's been right under our noses." He sighed.

"This changes things, Will," said Fitz. "What're we going to do?"

"What do you mean?" Charlotte cried. "Aren't you going to help her? Are you scared of Whitehead, too?"

Fitz tried to soothe her. "Charlotte, please, if Miss Lily went there of her own free will… well… what *can* we do?"

"Tell her family," said Darcy quietly. "They deserve to know. But," he turned to face the room, "I want to make certain that Miss Lily did go there and wishes to stay there voluntarily. Miss Charlotte, you said she looked… how?"

The girl thought. "Sad… frightened. She was scared of the man in the room."

Darcy nodded. "That's good enough for me. I'm going into town. Fitz?"

Fitz jumped to his feet, still holding Charlotte's hand. "Of course I'm comin'! But I think we're goin' to need some help."

Darcy was already moving to his gun case. "Four men—no more. We leave in five minutes." He belted on his Colt. "Whitehead and Denny are out of town. We ride light."

Darkness had fully fallen by the time the riders from Pemberley reached Rosings. Over the protests of Fitz, they made their way to the sheriff's office rather than storming the Whitehead building. Dismounting, Darcy, Fitz, and Charlotte went inside.

"Evening, Sheriff," Darcy said, while Fitz only glared at his girl's father.

"Darcy," Lucas returned before he spoke to Charlotte. "I thought I told you to go home—"

Fitz interrupted him. "She was doin' *your* job, Lucas!"

The sheriff got to his feet while Deputy Smith watched uncomfortably. "You can't speak to me like that in front of my daughter, Fitzwilliam! She ain't your wife—yet—and never will be, if I have my say about it!"

"Stop it, both of you!" cried Charlotte.

"Miss Charlotte is right," Darcy agreed. "We've got more important things to discuss than courtship." The other two men were properly embarrassed. "I understand that Lily Bennet's been seen in Whitehead's place. My men and I are going over there to talk to her. What I want to know is if you're going to join us."

Lucas looked Darcy dead in the eye. "You know what this means?"

"I do."

"You gonna see this all the way through? You and all your men?"

Darcy glanced at the floor. "I wasn't ready before, but I am now." He returned Lucas's stare. "All the way. You either help or get out of the way. This is war."

Lucas sat back, considering. "Aw, hell." He shook his head. "I guess I ain't gonna live forever. Smith!"

The deputy jumped. "Yessir!"

"Go to the hotel and get Jones. Tell 'em I need him here. We're payin' a call on Mr. Whitehead."

Fifteen minutes later, Sheriff Lucas and Darcy approached the front door of the Whitehead building along with one of the Pemberley riders. Oil lamps on either side of the door lit the entrance. Lucas moved to knock on the door and said, "Last chance to back out, Darcy." Darcy gestured at the door and Lucas pounded on the doorframe. "Hello in there! This is Sheriff Lucas! Open up!"

There was some noise and voices. Lucas banged again, and a moment later, Sally Younge opened the door. "What can I do for you, Sheriff... Mr. Darcy!? What are *you* doing here?"

"Sally, fancy seeing you here," drawled Lucas. "Who's minding the saloon?"

Darcy was grim. "Younge, we're here to see Miss Lily Bennet. Don't bother lying; we know she's here. Bring her to us immediately."

Her face losing all color, Younge barred the way. "I... I don't know what you mean. Look, Mr. Whitehead ain't here. You can't come in—"

Darcy brushed the woman aside and moved into the front hall, the others close behind. Younge was still squawking her protests when there was a loud crash from the rear of the building. Without hesitation, the three men ran towards the back door. In the alleyway between Whitehead's and the saloon, they beheld a young blond woman in a dressing gown between Deputy Smith and Fitz, while two Pemberley riders had their guns drawn on one of Denny's gang.

Darcy's face was thunderous. "Pyke—still doing Whitehead's dirty work."

Pyke held his hands up. "I wasn't doin' nothin'! This here girl just wanted some air, is all. I didn't know she was that missing girl—I swear!"

"Strange, I don't recall mentioning anything about a missing girl or Miss Lily," Fitz snarled. "Should I just shoot him, boss?"

Darcy shook his head as he approached Lily. As gently as he could, he asked, "Did this man harm you, Miss Lily?" Lily stared at him for a moment before shaking her head. "You're safe now," he continued. "I won't let anyone harm you, all right?" Satisfied he had calmed Beth's sister as best he could, he turned to Whitehead's henchman. "Pyke, you've been a thorn in my side for far too long. I'll give you this one final warning: Get out of Rosings. Trouble me or mine again and I'll kill you myself. Do you hear me?"

Pyke's bravado faded as he could see only death in Darcy's eyes. "All right, all right—I'm goin'. Let me inside just to get my things—"

"You've lost that opportunity, Pyke." Darcy was relentless. "Leave. Town. Now." Pyke, realizing he was living on borrowed time, scampered from the alley. Darcy turned to Lily again, only to be intercepted by the sheriff.

"Darcy—" he began.

"No, Sheriff," Darcy barked, "don't start. Like I said—this is war. Don't argue with me."

Lucas shrugged. "Just ask me next time, all right?"

Darcy nodded. "Let's get Miss Lily out of this night air." He took her by the arm and brought her back inside. "Miss Lily, I mean to take you home. Let's go and get your things," he suggested, moving towards the stairs.

She stopped cold, resisting going upstairs.

"We can leave now, if you want," Darcy offered.

Lily looked into his eyes again. "You really mean to get me out of here?"

"Yes."

"You're George's enemy?"

Darcy nodded slowly. "Does that make a difference?"

Lily bit her lip, deciding. She abruptly took Darcy by the hand and began pulling him down a hallway. "You better come with me. I've got something to show you."

Darcy and the sheriff sat in Whitehead's office, the safe open and a pile of papers spread before them. At that moment, he felt he could have kissed Lily.

"Unbelievable," Lucas muttered again as he perused the stack.

Darcy read one sheet after another. "The missing piece. I *knew* there was more to this. Now it all makes sense."

Fitz walked in the door. "The girl's finally gettin' decent. What are you so happy about, Will?"

Darcy grinned. "I finally know what Whitehead's been up to," and he explained what he and Lucas had found—money, papers, telegrams, letters, bank books, and most importantly, the deeds from the foreclosed homesteads. Fitz had to sit down, shaking his head.

"Where did Whitehead get the money to pull this off?"

Lucas passed him a sheet. "Can't say for sure, but there's this train schedule for a Federal payroll back in '64."

Fitz took the paper. "You think Whitehead *robbed a train?*"

Darcy shrugged. "Where else could he get over twenty thousand dollars? It doesn't matter, anyway. Everything's tied up in these deeds." He waved at the table.

Lucas thought. "When Mrs. Burroughs finds out about this, it could ruin Rosings Bank. Collins *has* been a slick bastard."

"It would serve her right," Darcy said darkly. "She's been in on this for months, thinking she'd sell to the railroad. She just didn't know that Whitehead and Collins have been double dealing." He tossed the papers on the desk. "This is partly my fault. If I had been minding business and watching what was going on in Rosings, none of this would've happened. Those poor settlers, the Washingtons… none of it. Damn!"

Fitz changed the subject. "Was Whitehead stupid enough to leave his safe open?"

Darcy smiled again. "Miss Lily's smarter than you think. She watched Whitehead and learned the combination. She thought it might come in handy."

"Well, it surely did. So, now what?"

Darcy looked at Lucas. "Whitehead and Denny are due back from Fort Worth tomorrow?"

"That or the next day's what I heard."

Fitz whistled. "When Whitehead sees all this, all hell's gonna break loose."

"That's what I'm thinking." Darcy spoke quietly to the other two. "First thing he's going to do is go after Miss Lily. She knows too much. Then, he's coming after me. So, this is what we do. I'll take Miss Lily to the Bennet place and convince the women to hole up at Pemberley until this is over. Meanwhile, I'll set a little ambush for Whitehead and Denny at the farm. They won't be expecting anything like that from Bennet."

Fitz grinned. "I think I'm gonna like that."

Darcy shook his head. "No, you won't, Fitz. Whitehead might do the unexpected, so I want you in charge of Pemberley's defenses, just in case. You send a wagon with supplies and a few extra men to the Bennet place. We'll use that to transport the women back to Pemberley. Send José. We'll arrange the ambush."

"Can't say that I like that idea, boss."

"I understand, but I'll rest easy knowing that Gaby and the Bennet women are under your protection."

Lucas gestured at the papers. "I'll take all this evidence over to the jail for safekeeping, telegraph for them soldier boys at Fort Richardson, and hole up 'til this blows over."

Fitz chuckled. "Never thought I'd be pleased to see the Yankee Cavalry."

Darcy looked the sheriff in the eye. "Will you be able to hold out, Lucas?"

"Nobody knows I've got this stuff, and Whitehead don't think much of me, so it won't even cross his mind. Besides, the jail's the strongest building in town. Me and my deputies will be okay."

Fitz grew troubled. "You can hole up at Pemberley."

Lucas waved him off. "No. I ain't abandoning my town. I know I've made a lot o' mistakes, but I ain't no coward, dammit." He glanced at Fitz. "No matter what some folks say."

Darcy and Fitz shared a look. "If you're set about it, Lucas…"

"I am."

Darcy slammed his hand down. "Then, that's the plan. Let's get moving. Fitz, you and the others help the sheriff. Haul all this paperwork over to the jail while I collect Miss Lily."

Darcy quietly made his way into the bedroom. He could see that Lily had changed her clothes but was still dressed in something more suited for a dancehall than a homecoming, sitting stone-faced on the bed, her hands clenched tightly in her lap.

"Pardon me, Miss Lily." Darcy removed his hat. "I hope you're ready to go home."

The girl looked away. "I thank you kindly for rescuing me, Mr. Darcy, but I can't be going home. I'm... I'm—" She broke off.

Gingerly, he sat in a chair near the bed, taking care not to come too close. Keeping his voice in a gentle tone, he said, "Now, Miss Lily, let's have none of that. Your momma and poppa are worried sick over you."

"I can't go back!" she cried, leaping to her feet, her face red and wild. "Don't you see? I'm ruined! I'm dirty and unfit for decent people!" When Darcy tried to persuade her away from such thoughts, she rounded on him. "Should I tell you what happened to me? Do you want to know? I came here—by my own desire. I tricked my family and came here to offer all I had to George!"

Her story spilled out, as if a dam broke. "I... I loved him, and I thought that if he knew it, he'd love me, too. He was so surprised! I thought, at first, he was going to send me away. But I made him think better of it. I begged him to make me a woman. And he did. It was glorious!" She threw her head back, her expression soft and glowing.

"I was so happy. I had done what none of my sisters, save Jane, had done, and with such a man! So handsome! So dashing—or so I thought." She changed again, her face becoming dark and foreboding. Her hands clutched her skirt so tightly that Darcy thought she might tear the fabric.

"A week after I came here, just as I began to think that George and I should marry and surprise my family, my bedroom door opened. But it wasn't George. It was Denny." She panted loudly. "He had this cruel gleam in his eye. I asked him his business, and he laughed! 'You're my business, girl. You're mine now!'

"'You'd better not let George hear you say that,' I told him, 'or he'll shoot you dead!' He just laughed again and grabbed my arm. 'You silly slut! I said you're mine. He gave you to me. Your precious George gave you to me!'"

Lily closed her eyes, pain etched on every corner of her face. "And then he took me. Threw me on the bed, ripped off my chemise, and took me! I fought and I fought and I yelled and I screamed, but no one came; nobody helped. George didn't come; Sally didn't come—nobody! In the end, Denny had his way with me." She walked over to the window, hands clutched together, leaving Darcy to struggle to restrain his anger and horror in the silence. When she resumed talking, her back to her rescuer, it was with a voice that had lost all emotion.

"When he had spent his filth in me, he stood up and did up his pants. 'Not bad, lovey,' he told me, 'but you best be better next time, or you'll be sorry. Remember this, my girl—you've no home left, except here. If I ever tire of you, you'll be working for Sally, livin' off your back, pleasurin' cowhands and salesmen and such for four bits a toss. You're dead to your family.'"

Darcy thought he was going to be sick.

"The next morning, I came down for breakfast, and there was George. He wouldn't even look at me! I cried, 'Why, George? Why did you throw me over? Why did you give me to Denny? I love you.' Do you know what he said? He said, 'You were a ripe toss, girl, but you're in more proper hands, now. When I marry, it will be a lady with land like Miss Darcy or Miss Burroughs. Not some fluff from the farm.'"

Darcy knew if Whitehead had been in the room at that moment, he would have strangled the bastard with his bare hands.

"So I stayed and made the best of it. I knew when Denny would visit me—Sally always seemed to know—and so I made sure I had plenty of whiskey close by. It… it helped. Most of the time, I just wanted to die.

"When he would finish with me, Denny would brag about what he'd done. He killed that Washington family, you know. He said, 'Yeah, me and my boys killed them like the dogs they were, an' they won't be the last ones. There's plenty o' folks that need killin' around here.'"

Her story done, she turned back to him, a single tear running down her face, her hands turning white as they clutched together. "Now do you understand, Mr. Darcy?"

Darcy submerged his rage, walked over to Lily, sat her on the bed, slowly pulled her hands apart, and held them in his. She tried to resist, but he was persistent. He knelt before her, his head and hers at the same level.

"Miss Lily—and you are still a 'Miss' to me—I must tell you I don't hold with the idea that if a woman's attacked and taken advantage of, that somehow it's her fault, and she's damaged goods." She would not look at him; instead, she stared at the floor. "You're a victim, Miss Lily, of two evil men, and I swear to you on my mother's grave these two things.

"One—your family will take you back with open arms."

She looked up at that. "You… you sure?"

"Yes."

She looked down again, more tears running down her face. "And the other promise?"

In as flat a voice as Darcy could manage, he said, "Whitehead and Denny will pay for what they've done."

Lily studied Darcy's cold blue eyes. Apparently, she saw

what she was looking for, because she was on her feet the next instant. "I guess we should be going now, Mr. Darcy. I sure can't stay here anymore."

She walked out the door without a backward look. Darcy stood, picked up her carpetbag, and followed her down the stairs.

Sheriff Lucas escorted Sally Younge over to the jail for her "protection," while Fitz and the deputy followed with the stacks of papers. What no one saw was the face of Pyke, peering out of the livery stable barn and watching every move.

Chapter 17

November 1

IT WAS PAST MIDNIGHT when six riders approached the entrance into the Bennet farm, the full moon lighting the lane between two low hills. Darcy looked to either side as they moved along the lane, spotting proper sites to stage his ambush before turning his thoughts to the task ahead. What he had to tell Mr. Bennet was beyond painful, and he hoped the man would believe him. He refused to allow himself to speculate how Beth would take the news. To hurt *her* was unthinkable, and he needed all his courage and resolution for the hours ahead.

He glanced at the young woman riding next to him. Thankfully, Lily's impassioned outburst seemed to drain the girl of any more words—that and the natural discomfort she must have felt over her impending reunion with her family. Darcy's words to her held more hope than conviction, and for her sake, he prayed that Thomas Bennet was a Christian man in more than name only.

The riders finally reached their destination. They passed

a series of low structures—chicken coops and hog pens by the smell—and entered a large, open area before the pitch-dark farmhouse. It was a low-slung building, a porch spanning the whole of the front exposure, with two sets of windows framing the center door. The house faced due east, better to catch the morning light in what was sure to be the living area of the place while protecting it from the hot afternoon sun. There were no trees to fall on the house in case of a storm, and a large barn was off to the left. They could see no well or outhouse, and he assumed those were in the rear.

Darcy waved his hand, and the Pemberley riders formed a semicircle before the house, Darcy and Lily in the middle. Darcy stood up in his saddle and called out.

"Hello, the house! Bennet! Tom Bennet! It's Will Darcy! I come in peace! I've found something that belongs to you! Hello, Tom Bennet, it's Will Darcy!"

Darcy waited for a minute, wondering if he would have to shout again, when he saw a light moving from inside the house. Motioning to his companions to be still, he watched the front door open.

"Who's there? I... I see you! Who are you?" A disheveled man, still in his nightclothes, peeked out, brandishing a shotgun.

Darcy called back, "Are you deaf, Tom Bennet? It's Will Darcy, come to visit!"

"Will Darcy?" Bennet stepped out onto the porch. "What the hell are you about, man, coming around here at this time of night?" He started as his eyes adjusted to the darkness and could see the others in the moonlight. He raised his gun to his shoulder, aiming at Darcy. "Why are you all here? I know how to use this! Speak smartly now!"

"Put those guns away!" Darcy barked at his men, some of whom had drawn their pistols at the threat from Bennet. He dismounted and began to walk towards the irate farmer, holding his hands out wide. "Now just hold on, Bennet! I mean no harm! I've got something here that belongs to you, and I figured you'd want it back right away." Looking closely, Darcy could see faces peeking from behind the window curtains. Knowing them to be the Bennet women, he wondered which one was Beth.

Bennet lowered his gun, his face a mass of uncertainty. "Something of mine? What're you talking about?"

"You'll see." Darcy slowly turned and gestured. A moment later, Lily, still in her dancehall outfit, dismounted and walked slowly towards the house.

"Who... who's that?" croaked Bennet.

As gently as he could, Darcy said, "It's your daughter, Lily, come home."

Bennet gasped. "L-Lily!?"

"Daddy?" Lily managed as the light of the lantern lit her face.

Bennet made a strange sound in his throat, dropped the shotgun, and ran towards the girl, arms outstretched. "Lily? My God, Lily!"

Tears running down her face, Lily met him halfway. As they embraced, a screech came from the house, and a white blur ran out the door. Fanny Bennet threw herself upon her husband and daughter, screaming and crying. Darcy tore his eyes from the spectacle to the porch. There, three Bennet girls stood, two in unbelieving confusion, the third staring directly at him. Darcy's heart jumped at the sight of Beth Bennet, holding a robe closed at her throat, her curly hair half obscuring an unreadable expression on her face. He wondered if she knew that he was doing all this for her and her alone.

Bennet's voice broke him out of his ruminations. "I must thank you, Mr. Darcy, for returning my daughter." His voice grew harder. "I don't wish to seem ungrateful, but I must ask— how is it that Lily came to be in your company?"

"Father!" cried Beth, capturing Darcy's attention again. "You shouldn't be questioning Mr. Darcy. We owe him a debt we can never repay!" By then, Mrs. Bennet and Lily had reached the porch, and the wayward girl was greeted with great emotion by her sisters.

Bennet turned to the door. "Quiet, girl, and get yourself inside! All of you! You aren't decent!"

"Men, dismount and take your ease," Darcy called and moved next to the farmer. "Bennet, I've much to tell you, and we've little time. This isn't the place for our talk. May we go inside?"

Darcy stared out into the moonlight outside the window in Bennet's small study, trying to give the weeping Tom Bennet a smidgeon of privacy. After offering such a disturbing report, Darcy had needed to settle his own emotions. To convince Bennet of the gravity of the threat his family faced, Darcy had no recourse but to tell the man all the horrible indignities suffered by Lily. It was one of the most painful episodes in Darcy's life.

Finally, a sniffing Bennet addressed him again from behind his desk. "I… I thank you, sir, from the bottom of my heart, for all that you have done for my family."

"I am sincerely sorry for what has happened."

"Thank you, Darcy. We… we hoped she was still alive, but

in truth, we began to lose faith. I can't tell you how we felt!" His red eyes grew angry. "But what she has suffered! Ruined at the hands of a man I trusted! Whose opinion I relied on! Who ate in my house!" A string of curses followed. "I'll kill him!"

Darcy turned. "I've no right to ask, I know, but what's to be done with Miss Lily?"

Bennet caught himself. "I... I don't know. But she's my daughter. I won't abandon her."

Darcy nodded in satisfaction. "Bennet, this is your house and your family. But may I say how much I respect you for your words? I'll stand by you, and you and yours will always be welcomed in my home." Darcy waited until his words had sunk in. "But we've got other matters before us—serious matters." Darcy leaned on the desk. "I don't say this lightly. You and your family are in grave danger. Whitehead will not sit idly by—no sir. He'll come, and he'll bring Denny and his hired killers with him. You must get your women out of here."

"Come here? Why?" Bennet's confusion gave way to understanding. "Is it because of Lily—of what she knows?"

Darcy nodded. "Yes, sir, that's part of the answer. Whitehead has ambitions—of marrying well and political office. His treatment of your daughter will seriously damage those plans, should her story become widely known—if not ruin them altogether. He can't allow her to run loose in the county; the risk is too great. But there is more to this. All of Whitehead's plans hinge on one thing, and you, Bennet, are it. You're the linchpin."

"How can that be? Whitehead has advised me on things— that's so—but I'm not involved in any business with him."

"You've something he wants."

Bennet grew angry. "Lily? That bastard wants my Lily back?"

"He wants Thompson Crossing."

Bennet blinked. "He wants the ford across the Long Branch? Whatever for?"

A soft voice came from behind the men. "Does it have to do with the railroad?"

The men whirled about to behold Beth Bennet at the door of the study. Her hair was up, and she was dressed in her usual work clothes of dungarees and an oversized gingham shirt, but to Darcy, she looked like an angel. Before Bennet could object to her presence, Darcy cut in.

"What do you know about the railroad, Miss Beth?"

"Something Lily said about George and railroads."

"What railroad?" Bennet demanded of Darcy. "Is the railroad coming here?"

"It is," Darcy replied grimly. "Do you own a map of the county, sir?"

The map was found and soon spread over the expanse of Bennet's desk. The three gathered about it as Darcy traced the course of the Long Branch River. "See how the river cuts the county in twain? It comes down from the north before turning eastward right by your farm, Bennet. It then runs generally southeast to eventually join with the Brazos. Most of the land to the north belongs to the B&R, while all south is Pemberley.

"Last week, I attended a meeting of potential investors in a proposed railroad from Fort Worth to Abilene, Texas. The company revealed its plans, and it's something that'll put the town on the map. The preferred route's along the Long Branch River, crossing it near here before continuing westward." He ran his finger slowly across the map. "This is the route, and here's where they wish to build the bridge—right on your land,

Bennet." His finger rested on Thompson Crossing, a half-mile south of the Bennet farmhouse. "They'll be paying top dollar for land. Would you be willing to sell the right-of-way?"

Bennet nodded. "It's far enough away from the house as not to be a bother, and it would get me out from under the mortgage. If the price is fair, I'll sell. But what does this have to do with Whitehead?"

"Do you see something else about the route?" Darcy asked.

Beth gasped. "It goes across the new settlement!"

Darcy nodded. "You're catching on, Beth."

Bennet shook his head. "I don't understand!"

Darcy straightened to his full height. "After we freed Miss Lily from Whitehead's place, we discovered his private papers. Apparently, Whitehead has an accomplice inside the railroad company. Letters and telegrams indicate that he's known about these plans for almost a year. I said Whitehead was ambitious. To achieve everything he wants, he needs money—lots of it. So he plans to get it from the railroad when they start buying up land for the route. He now owns all this," he swept his hand over the homesteaders' bottomland.

"But I thought the bank foreclosed on all those places. Doesn't all that land belong to Rosings Bank and Mrs. Burroughs?" Bennet asked.

Darcy grimaced. "She thinks so, but she's been cheated. The deeds were all transferred to a land company for pennies on the dollar, and Cate believes she owns it. Apparently, she knows about the railroad. She thought she was smart, stealing from her own bank. But she's wrong—Whitehead actually controls the company. Billy Collins, the bank manager, is in on it. He's played Cate false. And since Whitehead is the recorder of deeds, he simply made them out in his name. Whitehead owns all the bottomland."

Beth looked out of the window into the darkness. "All those homesteaders run off. That poor Washington family." She turned back in anger. "All because of George's greed! And Mrs. Burroughs's, too! I suppose they had something to do with the lynching?"

Darcy reported what Lily had said.

Bennet sat in his chair. "So much evil in a small town! But, still, what does this have to do with me?"

"Thompson Crossing isn't the only place the railroad has considered crossing the Long Branch. There's another ford several miles downriver. If they build the bridge there, they would bypass the town and cross Pemberley land several miles south of my house. The company would prefer Thompson Crossing, as they planned to build a station in Rosings. Should they choose to cross at the other place, there wouldn't be a stop for another twenty miles." Darcy moved closer to the other man. "Knowing what you do now, would you still sell?"

Bennet rubbed his face. "I… I don't rightly know. I hate the idea of putting money in the pocket of the man who has caused so much pain to my family." He glanced at Darcy. "I suppose you would prefer I didn't."

Darcy shook his head. "You're wrong, Mr. Bennet. Rosings needs that train stop. It means a stockyard for all the cattlemen. No more drives to Kansas City. New people, new goods, stores, schools—the town needs the railroad, sir."

"That's generous of you, Darcy, as the other route would mean the railroad would be paying you."

"The company would still be buying Pemberley land on the other side of Thompson Crossing," Darcy admitted, "and I'm an investor, so I'll make money no matter what. This way, we get a station. Everyone benefits."

"So, if I agree to sell, where's the danger?"

"Whitehead doesn't have your goodness. All he sees is that you could be a barrier to his plans. How much are you in for to Rosings Bank?"

Bennet held his head in his hands and told him, a figure that drew a gasp from his daughter. "Father! That's more than half the value of the farm. How can we repay that?"

The man moaned. "I've been a damn fool, Beth, listening to Whitehead's silver tongue. He said the improvements would increase the farm's yields by fivefold. And now, I know it's all been a lie!" He looked at her. "I did it all for you and your sisters, child. I wanted you all to have a better life."

Darcy leaned on the desk, thinking. "I take it Whitehead's 'advice' began around the New Year?"

"It did. So, I suppose he wants this place?"

"Perhaps. Perhaps he just wanted to be able to apply pressure on you to make sure you sold when the time came. Or maybe he's just greedy and wants it all. It doesn't matter now." Darcy leaned in. "What I want to know, Bennet, is what are you going to do about it?"

Bennet was anguished. "What can I do? Whitehead and Rosings Bank hold the mortgage! They have all the cards!"

Darcy grinned. "Perhaps not. May I have pen and paper?" He was quickly supplied, and the others watched in speculation as Darcy wrote furiously. A few minutes later, he presented the paper to Mr. Bennet. It didn't take long for him to cry out in surprise.

He lowered the paper, a look of wonder on his face. "Are you in earnest?"

"Absolutely."

Beth could stand no more. "Father, what did Will write?" He handed her the paper.

"Darcy is offering to assume all my debts."

Beth's eyes flew to a composed Darcy. She then turned her attention to the document in her hands. Sure enough, William Darcy proposed to assume all debts held by Thomas Bennet immediately in exchange for a minority ownership portion of Bennet Farm.

"Rosings Bank won't be able to foreclose on the farm if I'm a partner," Will said as she read, "as I can pay the whole off in an instant. Whitehead, Catherine, and Collins will have no financial power over you if you sign that paper, Bennet."

"But how can I repay you?" Bennet asked.

"That we can talk about later. Perhaps we can use the proceeds from the land sale to the railroad, or we can join our herds together. We'll work out something to our mutual satisfaction."

"Join our herds? You've a hundred head to my one!"

"Bennet, I won't cheat you."

Bennet frowned. "I didn't think you would, but I'm afraid that this is not a fair deal for you! Why should you be so generous to me, a man who hasn't been very neighborly to you? This is surely a gift, for you know I can never pay it back."

Beth knew instantly Darcy's motivation, and her heart danced as her eyes sought his, but he refused even to glance her way.

"Then let our grandchildren argue about it! Bennet, will you not accept my help?"

Bennet tried to stare Darcy down but soon capitulated. "I've no choice, have I? Where do I sign?" In a moment, the two men affixed their signatures. Darcy folded the paper and put it in the inside pocket of his vest.

"Excellent," he said. "Now we must plan our next step."

Bennet sat back. "Yes, Darcy, you said that Whitehead and his men would be heading here. With all due respect and gratitude for your help, I don't think that piece of paper is going to stop them."

Darcy grinned. "First, as we are now partners, I insist you call me Will." He extended his hand, which Bennet readily took.

"Very well, Will," Bennet chuckled. "So, what the hell do we do now?"

"I think you must agree that the women should leave here as soon as possible. I offer Pemberley as sanctuary." Bennet nodded. "The next matter to resolve is you. What are your plans?" Darcy looked hard at him. "Do you mean to defend your home against Whitehead and his men? Do you mean to fight?"

Bennet looked at his desk. "This farm is all I have. No one is going to take it from me."

"Father!" Beth cried.

Darcy was grim. "You know what they'll do when they get here, don't you? They'll try to burn you out, whether you're here or not, just for spite."

"Are you advising me to run?" Bennet cried angrily.

"No. I'm just trying to gauge your level of determination. Whitehead and his men have been running wild for far too long. It's time they received justice. My men and I intend to administer that justice directly upon their arrival at your place."

Bennet cocked an eyebrow. "Ambush?"

"Do you object?"

Bennet grinned. "No, in fact, I admire your way of thinking.

I believe I would dearly like to help you give a warm welcome to my former business advisor and defiler of young girls!"

Beth realized their intentions and cried out, "Stop it, both of you! This is not a game. You're talking about life and death. Why not have Sheriff Lucas arrest them?"

"Beth," her father said, "these are desperate men with no love for the law. They would just as soon shoot the sheriff down as not. No," he turned to Darcy, "Will here has the right of it. This is war, and there is no law in war. Do you have enough men?"

"I've a wagon coming from Pemberley for the women," he answered, "carrying more men and ammunition. They'll be here before long."

"On the way—now?" Bennet observed with amusement. "Sent for before you got here?" At Darcy's nod, he laughed. "Very sure of yourself, aren't you?"

"I placed my faith in your sensibleness," Darcy said dryly, which earned another laugh from Bennet.

"I'd best go talk to Mrs. Bennet and prepare for their departure," he said as he rose from his desk chair. "Make yourself at home, Will. Beth, as you're dressed, please see to his men's comfort." With that, he left the room.

Darcy and Beth eyed each other, both afraid to speak what was in their hearts.

Chapter 18

AN UNCOMFORTABLE SILENCE DESCENDED upon the couple. For his part, Darcy was desperately trying to think of something else to talk about besides his all-encompassing feelings when Beth spoke.

"Will, I want to thank you so much for what you've done and have pledged to do for my family. We don't deserve your goodness, I most especially." Will made to interrupt, but Beth would have none of it. "It's true! You're risking your life for us, and after all the hateful, unjust things I said to you last July—"

This time, Darcy did cut her off. "You've nothing to apologize for! I'm sorry for your brother, and I can see how that could make you feel bitter. But, let's be honest—I did nothing to improve your opinion of me in our earliest days. All you could rely on was Whitehead's lies." He looked away. "My... proposal to you was beyond insulting, and your reproofs... well, how can I deny the truths you threw in my face?"

"Will," she cried, "I didn't know what I was saying!"

Darcy went on, disregarding her words. "I hid at Pemberley and wished the world to hell. I turned my back on all the people of the town when they needed me the most. My father must have been spinning in his grave. All that has happened is my fault."

"Will, stop it! You didn't do any of this! Denny and Whitehead did!"

"I could've stopped it."

Without conscious thought, she moved to him and took his hands, looking at them intently. "You're stopping him now. Father's right—this is a war. Don't let my cruel words torture you. I spoke to you in ignorance and prejudice." She lifted her face and in a determined voice, continued. "But now my eyes are open and I see you as the best man I've ever known. You saved my sister and you've pledged to protect my family. I can never repay you for your courage and generosity. I'm proud to call you my friend!" She so wanted to say more, but couldn't.

Darcy's eyes watered and his thumbs caressed the back of Beth's hands. "Friend, Beth? Yeah, I'm glad to be your friend. But..." He looked away, his thoughts in turmoil. He drew a deep breath and blurted out, "You're not one to lead a man on. If you've changed your mind about me since the summer, tell me straight up. My wishes haven't changed; my love's been as constant as the North Star. I'd be honored if you would even think about accepting me." He flinched at the amazed look on her face. "Beth, I'm sorry to be putting you in this situation—it's only been a few months since July—but I've just got to know! I'm keeping my word to your father about helping out, whatever you say. Just... just tell me true. If you can't..." He gulped. "If you can't, I'll understand. I'll be content being friends, and I'll never bother you again for as long as I live."

The anguish on his face loosened her tongue. "Oh, Will! I... I... my feelings!" She paused to gather her disconnected thoughts. "I'm heartily ashamed of my words at the Burroughses', and I want to take back every cruel thing I've ever said! As for my feelings, they're about as opposite from what they were as they can be!" To punctuate her declaration, she gripped William's hands firmly.

Will stared at their intertwined hands and then searched her face. "Beth Bennet, I want things to be clear between us. I love you."

"And I love you, Will Darcy."

Beth was almost ashamed of how Darcy's face lit up in incandescent happiness, knowing how she had hurt him months before. Another moment and her painful recollections vanished, for she was swept up in Darcy's strong arms. She buried her face in his vest as he kissed the top of her head, murmuring sweet nothings.

But just as swiftly as it had begun, the joyful interlude ended. Darcy took her gently by the shoulders and held her at arm's length. Beth was confused at the anguished expression marring Darcy's masculine beauty. He looked deeply into her eyes, his mouth in a hard line.

Darcy's voice trembled. "This is not out of gratitude for what I did for Lily, is it?"

Beth blinked. "What do you mean? Of course, I'm grateful for what you did! Why are you unhappy?" To her astonishment, William's face nearly crumbled.

"Oh, Beth, if you're accepting me out of gratitude, well... well, I just couldn't stand it!"

Beth was incredulous at William's stubborn inability to grasp what was so clear. Couldn't the fool see that she loved him body and soul? Only one way to clarify things came to mind. With a look of determination, she reached up and lightly kissed him on the cheek. As she drew back slightly, she said to his amazed face, "That's for Lily!" and in a softer tone, she added, "And this is for me." This time her lips firmly met his with a scalding kiss.

Beth was starting to become concerned over William's lack of response, but then she felt his strong hands on her shoulders gently pull her closer as he deepened their kiss. Beth was relieved and thrilled, and it was pleasant to learn that Will's lips felt very soft against her mouth. Her arms moved by their own volition to twine around his neck as her body arched against his. They seemed to become one. Her moans of delight were a counterpoint to his. An intoxicating dizziness overtook her senses. She felt she could remain thus occupied for the rest of her days.

"What the devil is this!?"

The two were startled by Mr. Bennet's cry and jumped apart as if the other were on fire. Beth could feel the heat of mortification replace the warmth of desire on her face. Mr. Bennet glowered from the doorway of the study, his mouth working soundlessly in his righteous anger. Darcy was the first to break out of his shocked stupor and begin a rambling apology. This seemed to accomplish nothing but to unlock Bennet's tongue.

"Keep your mealymouthed assurances to yourself. I've no time for your perfidy," he growled in a low tone, his desire not to alert the entire household evident. "You return my youngest from that bastard Whitehead, I turn my back on you, and you reward me by treating her elder sister in exactly the same manner!"

"No, Father, please. Don't blame Will. This is my fault," Beth claimed.

"*Your* fault!" Bennet laughed incredulously. "I suppose you threw yourself at him!"

Before Beth could assure her father that that was *exactly* what she had done, Darcy cut in. "Mr. Bennet, sir, this is my fault. I pledge to you that my intentions are honorable. I respect you and Miss Beth, but… I'm ashamed to give you reason to doubt me. I beg to explain myself."

Bennet thought it over for a moment. "Beth, leave us."

Beth looked between her father and her lover and clenched her teeth. She would *not* let these two men—whom she loved most in the world—decide her fate without her attendance. Instead of obeying her dismissal, she defiantly moved closer to Will and took one of his hands in both of hers. "No, Father, as this concerns me, I'll remain."

Darcy turned, his face registering his concern. "Beth, are you certain—"

Beth returned his look with a glint of steel. "I'll stay by your side. There's nowhere else I want to be."

A relieved grin stole across Darcy's face. He nodded and faced their inquisitor. "Mr. Bennet, I'll tell you straight up that I've admired Miss Beth for some time—since our first meeting, I'd say. The plain truth is that I love her. Tonight, I've learned that she returns those sentiments, and well… I let things get out of hand in expressing my happiness."

Bennet eyed the young man closely. "You say you love my daughter?" At Darcy's confirmation, he asked, "And would I be wrong to think that she is your motivation for your involvement in my family's concerns?"

Darcy sensed dangerous ground, but answered truthfully. "You wouldn't be wrong, sir."

"No," Bennet declared. "No. No, sir! You ask far more than I can pay."

"What?"

"Elizabeth will *not* be the price of your benevolence!"

Darcy was dismayed. "But... but she isn't!"

"Father," Beth injected, "you wrong him—and me!"

"How?" he shot back. "Don't you feel gratitude for his actions?"

"Of course, I do! But my feelings for Will have roots before tonight!"

"Indeed, sir," Darcy agreed. "I asked her that very question before I asked her to marry me."

Bennet turned to Beth. "And have you accepted him?"

Beth wasn't sure that she understood that there was an actual *second* proposal in William's earlier words, but apparently he thought so, and she was willing to concede to his thinking. Besides, it would give her enormous ammunition to tease him for the next twenty years.

"Father, Will has proposed to me, and I've accepted," she stated with a small smile at Darcy.

Bennet was unhappy with Beth's declaration and took it out on Darcy. "I have to question your sense of timing, Darcy, if you think that the situation in which we find ourselves is one that compels you to propose to Beth *tonight*."

Darcy's expression showed he agreed with Bennet's observation, at least to some extent. "I can't argue with that, sir."

Bennet's anger cooled a bit, but he had one last shot for his soon-to-be son-in-law. "And I don't take too kindly to a young man making love to my daughter in my own house."

Darcy hung his head. "I plead nothing but my undying love for her as my excuse." He was very unhappy, but Beth was not. She knew her father well enough to know that he was well on the way to forgiving them, if he had not already. The gleam in Bennet's eye, missed by Darcy, proved that Beth was not far wrong.

Bennet sighed. "Darcy, I want to talk to Beth alone."

Darcy nodded and smiled a farewell to Beth. She, on the other hand, wanted to prove something to both of them, and kissed her fiancé on the cheek. Bennet's look darkened as Darcy's lightened, and he had a relatively light step out the house.

"Well, Father?" Beth crossed her arms, her look a clear challenge.

Bennet sighed again. "Perhaps you did throw yourself at him." Beth said not a word, but her upraised eyebrows told the tale. Bennet groaned. "Are you witless, girl? Didn't you tell me you couldn't stand the man?"

Beth bit her lip. "I did, but I changed my mind."

"Changed your mind? You're going to spend a lifetime with him based on changing your mind?"

"Have you no objection but that?"

Bennet crossed to his chair and sat down. "Beth, you know I didn't hold the same poor opinion of the boy that you did. I always thought you were too hard on him. It now seems he may be an even better man than I thought."

"He's the *best* man I've ever known. I'm sorry if that hurts you, but that's the truth."

Bennet flinched at Beth's words but recovered quickly. "If I was to lose your company, I always hoped it'd be to a better man than me. But are you sure about this? He's a very serious sort of fellow. I like him, but will you be happy with a man like that?"

"Father, if you knew what I know..." She paused and realized she would have to tell him everything. She gave her father a brief history of her acquaintance with Darcy and their unorthodox courtship. She left out most of the details of their late-night clearing of the air in the Burroughses' library and the shocking discovery of Darcy's old injuries, but enough was said to amuse the older man.

"My, my, you've had quite the time of it, haven't you, my girl," he laughed. "Turned him down! I'd have paid money to see that!" He sobered. "And yet, he didn't throw you over."

Beth bit her lip again. "No, he didn't. I don't deserve that kind of devotion."

"You're wrong, dear," Bennet said softy. "Everyone deserves that kind of devotion." He rose and crossed over to take her hands in his. "If you truly love him, then I've nothing to say but that you have my blessings—both of you." They hugged each other, Beth drowning in her happiness, until she could feel strange movement from her father.

She pulled away from his embrace. "Father, are you laughing?"

Bennet rubbed an eye and said sheepishly, "I was just reminiscing about when I was courting your mother." At her expectant look, he continued. "I used to go to dinner at your grandpa's house after church, and one Sunday your mother and I were walking about, and she was showing me her father's place, and there was the barn, and one thing led to another…"

Beth was horrified. *"Father! You didn't!"*

"Oh, no, no! Nothing *seriously* wrong!" he claimed. "Although it looked bad enough to your grandpa! Helped settle our courtship in a more rapid manner, I can tell you that."

Beth was still scandalized. "No wonder Grandpa didn't like you."

Bennet chuckled. "Nope, he didn't. I hope to get along with your young man better—as long as he minds his manners and behaves himself in my house!" Beth nodded happily and received a kiss on the forehead. "Now," Bennet grew more serious, "go and help your mother and sisters pack. That wagon from Pemberley'll be here any time now. Go on with yourself." Beth left for the back of the house, and Bennet steeled himself for his talk with Darcy.

He walked out onto the front porch. There was Darcy, talking in low tones to one of his men, pointing towards the low hills at the entrance to the farm. The movement from the doorway caught his eye, and he dismissed his hireling to await Beth's father. Bennet walked beside him and looked out into the moonlit darkness. They stood together for a time, not sharing a look or a word.

Finally, Bennet broke the silence. "You'll take care of her?"

Darcy didn't have to ask whom the older man referred to. "Yes, sir."

Bennet sighed. "A man's not supposed to favor one of his children over the others. It's a sin. But, Lord help me, Elizabeth's the child of my heart. When you're a father, Will, you'll understand."

Will faced the man beside him and saw that Bennet seemed to have aged before his eyes. "Rest easy, sir—Beth will want for nothing. She'll be comfortable, cared for, and safe. I pledge my life on it."

"*Well...* I hope it doesn't come to *that*," Bennet teased half-heartedly. They shook hands in the darkness and Bennet turned the conversation to Darcy's plans for Whitehead. It was a few minutes later when a lookout reported that a wagon was spotted approaching the turnout. Another few minutes saw the arrival of a flatbed open wagon, with three men in it and a rider as escort. The wagon stopped before the house, and Darcy ordered it unloaded. Two long boxes and one smaller one were carried into the house. Bennet was surprised as to the contents.

"Henry rifles?"

Darcy shook his head, grinning. "No, sir. These are Winchesters—Model 1866 lever action repeating rifles. Fires the same .44 caliber cartridge as the Henry, but it's more reliable. All my riders carry Winchesters."

Bennet looked at the two cases, each with six rifles. "And you've brought along a dozen more?"

"Even at fifteen rounds, a man can run out of ammunition. Having two loaded rifles can make the difference in a gunfight. That last box is a case of ammo."

Bennet shook his head. At almost fifty dollars a rifle and knowing that Darcy had two dozen men working for him, he was looking at more money than some farmhands would see in their lifetimes. "You're a generous man, Will Darcy."

Darcy shrugged. "If you want a man to do his job, you give him the tools he needs. Bennet, I don't mean to rush anything, but the sooner the women are on their way to Pemberley, the better I'll feel."

Bennet called for his wife and daughters to prepare to leave. Turning to Darcy, he asked, "You're sure about Pemberley?"

"Yes, sir. It was built to withstand Indian raids. I've sent Fitzwilliam to organize the defense of the house. It's the safest place in fifty miles."

The ladies made their appearance, Lily now in her own clothing. All were taken aback at the sight of the firearms, but none said a word as they were escorted outside. Darcy had Beth on his arm, and he was just reaching to lift her up into the wagon when a rider came in hot.

"Ethan," greeted Darcy, "what news? Why did you leave your post in town?"

The young cowhand pulled up in front of his employer. "Whitehead, Mr. Darcy," he panted. "Whitehead's done come back early from Fort Worth. He an' Denny an' his riders were at Whitehead's place in town when I left, and they didn't sound too happy from what I heard."

Darcy stared at his man, while José cursed something in Spanish. "They'll be coming 'ere, boss," he told Darcy. "What'll we do with the women?"

"We can't go through town," said Ethan. "They'll see us for sure."

"Can we cross at the ford?" suggested a voice from the darkness.

"No," said Bennet. "The water's still too high from the rains. We'd be washed away."

Darcy's eye was caught by a glint of light from the hilltop, as the lookout used a mirror to flash a warning in the moonlight.

Riders.

Darcy's insides turned to ice. They were trapped and out of time.

Chapter 19

RIDING IN THE MOONLIGHT at the head of his army towards the Bennet place, a very angry George Whitehead wondered how everything could have gone so wrong so fast.

Whitehead had taken Collins and Denny to Fort Worth for a sort of victory celebration. The railroad was about ready to start buying up the useless bottomland he had stolen from Mrs. Burroughs. Everything had been in place. The riches from the railroad would allow him to turn his twenty-five thousand into his own political kingdom. Soon, either Miss Gaby or Miss Anne would be Mrs. Whitehead, and with them came half the county. With land and army, he would conquer the rest. After that—who knew? The governor's house in Austin? A senator's seat in Washington, D.C.? All things were possible.

Whitehead's first clue that things might not be going exactly to plan was when his spy, Elton, told him that Darcy was one of the investors in the railroad. Elton assured him that the rancher was unaware that anyone else in Rosings knew of the project, but Whitehead was uneasy with this turn of circumstance. He chewed over this intelligence during the ride back to Rosings, wondering if adjustments to the plan might be necessary. However, upon his arrival in town he discovered that Darcy knowing of the railroad was the least of his worries.

All of George Whitehead's dreams were threatened by a whore named Lily.

Whitehead cursed under his breath. *I knew I should have sent that slut back to her father's place when she showed up at the back door. I knew it! But she was so young, so ripe, so eager. Dammit!*

Whitehead stole a glance at Denny riding beside him. The damned fool was infatuated with Lily and demanded her in lieu of the hundreds Whitehead had promised. A bigger fool, Whitehead had agreed to the trade. He should have known better. Had his own bitter and unforgiving mother not shown him that there was no fury like a scorned woman? He should have had the girl killed.

Now everything Whitehead had built—everything that he had planned, dreamed, and killed for—teetered on the edge of the abyss. There was only one thing to do. What he could not win by guile he would take by the gun.

Two by two the riders moved along the trail leading from the main road to the house. Soon the party had formed a semicircle before the dark building, Denny in the middle and Whitehead over to his right. At the end was Billy Collins. Whitehead had insisted his pet bank manager accompany him on this bloody mission. He could not afford to lose any allies now, and after a few minutes' work, Collins would be tied to him once and for all, being as guilty of murder as the rest.

Kid Denny rose in his saddle. "Bennet! Tom Bennet! This is Denny! Come out, Bennet! I've got an order of foreclosure, an' I means to enforce it! Come out, Bennet, or we'll come in after you!"

The gang sat in the moonlight before the house, fingering their guns. They saw no light. The only sign of life was a light smoke rising from the chimney.

Then the front door opened a crack. "Well, hello there, Denny! A bit early for visiting, ain't it?" Mr. Bennet's sardonic voice came from inside the darkened doorway.

"Come out, Bennet, an' nobody gets hurt!"

Bennet's voice was mocking. "Now, why would I believe that, Denny? Why would I leave my house?"

Denny held up a sheet of paper. "I've got me a proper order of foreclosure! That ain't your house no more, Bennet! You're trespassing, and I've got the right to throw you outta there!"

"Is that so? By whose authority, may I ask?"

"Judge Phillips!"

"Well, it's debatable if that sycophant has enough brains to *be* an authority on anything, but I'll leave that argument to my friend, Whitehead. By the way, you wouldn't happen to know where he is, would you?"

Denny and Whitehead shared a look before George answered. "I'm right here, Tom! You'd better come on out!"

"George! I'm mightily glad to see that *you're* here! What's all this about a foreclosure? I'm paid up until the fifteenth."

"I'm sorry, Tom, but Rosings Bank has called the loan! There's nothing I can do about it tonight! You'd better come on out, or there might be trouble! We'll try to straighten it out in the morning!"

Bennet's voice was as teasing as ever. "I've a better idea, George. Why don't you come on inside? I'm sure we can resolve *all issues* that way."

Whitehead glanced at Denny. "I can't do that, Tom!"

"I see." Bennet's false cheer had disappeared. "But you can take advantage of a mere child, is that it? Brave war hero that you are."

Whitehead was not surprised by Bennet's words; in fact, he was pleased. It told him that Lily had returned home. Denny, however, was not so sanguine.

"She was a ripe jolly piece, Bennet, an' I might be willin' to take her back, if'n she gets her ass out here in the next two minutes—her an' all of you!"

"Go to hell, you son-of-a-bitch!" Bennet cried. "You want her?! Come and get her!"

Before Whitehead could say anything, Denny whipped out his six-shooter and unloaded it at the farmhouse. The rest of the gang joined in, and the house was struck by scores of rounds. For almost a minute the air was filled with gunshots and smoke. No fire was returned from inside the house. As suddenly as the violence started, it stopped, and an unholy quiet descended upon the farm.

Whitehead dismounted, saying to Denny, "All right, go in there and—" when the night was torn with the bark of rifles as the house erupted in light and smoke. Whitehead and his men dove for cover. A couple of horses fell and the rest ran off in terror. Whitehead, prone on the damp ground, pulled out his Colt and returned fire while Collins whimpered in fear. The others were desperately trying to reload.

The firing from the house ceased, and Denny crawled over to Whitehead and Collins, who had taken shelter behind an overturned wheelbarrow. "What the hell's goin' on here?" his henchman demanded.

"Hell if I know," Whitehead shot back. "How are we?"

Pyke joined them. "Wilkerson's dead! And a couple o' horses, besides!"

"Shit!" Whitehead peeked out. "Got some company, Tom?!"

"Sure do, George!" the farmer returned. "Why don't you come on in and meet 'em?!"

"Fuck!" Denny pounded the soft ground with a fist. "Darcy sent some of his men!"

Whitehead nodded, an idea coming to him. "Hello, the house! Look, boys, you've surprised us proper, I'll give you that! But let me tell you, Darcy did you wrong! We're the law here, and you're on the wrong side! You're aiding and abetting and we've got the right to kill anyone that stands in the way of enforcing a court order! Come on out now, and we'll let you go!"

A Spanish-flavored voice responded. "Sorry, *señor*, but we are comfortable 'ere! If you *hombres* want to continue living, maybe you should be the ones leaving, I think!"

"That's that fuckin' Estrada—Fitzwilliam's Number Two," Denny advised.

"Right." At the house, Whitehead shouted, "Dying's not a great way of making a living, boys, no matter how much Darcy's paying you! Just remember, you're trapped here! We've got you outnumbered, and he's safe back at the ranch! That don't sound too fair, does it?!"

"We 'ere, you 'ere, everyone gots to be somewhere! I think we stay!"

A trembling Collins gripped Whitehead by the shoulder. "Now what? If this gets out, we're finished!"

"Shut up, Collins! I have to think!"

Darcy enjoyed the taunting of Whitehead and Denny while he reloaded, but he wasn't fool enough not to know the situation he was in. With no time to set up a proper ambush, they had no choice but to fall back into the Bennet farmhouse. Darcy had six men with him and Bennet. Two others had gone to hide the wagon in the barn and were holed up there with the farmhand, Hill. José Estrada covered the rear, while the rest were positioned at the windows in the front and sides of the house. Tom Bennet had the front door, while Darcy took the window to the left.

Darcy counted the advantages to his position. One, everyone was armed with Winchesters, and all had plenty of ammo. Two, the full moon helped the defenders more than the attackers. Three, Darcy could count on the skill, dedication, and loyalty of his men. Four, Whitehead had no clear idea who he was dealing with, since Darcy let José do the talking.

In the deficit column, however, was the fact that Whitehead was in control of the fight. He had more men and room to maneuver. He could choose when, how, and where to attack. His people were ruthless and wouldn't hesitate to kill. And Whitehead was desperate. Meanwhile, Darcy was handicapped by the women and the old man he was sworn to protect, and he had no idea if Hill would hold up. If they became trapped and needed to escape, they would have to shoot their way out.

Darcy would not kid himself—his position was precarious.

His musings were interrupted by a jostling of his boot. Glancing behind him, he was startled to see two large, dark eyes framed by a mass of curly hair.

"Beth! By God, woman, what are you doing out of the root cellar?" Darcy hissed. When the party retreated into the house, the women had been herded into the cellar for their protection.

Her eyes flashed in annoyance as she crawled closer. "We're trying to help!" she said in a strong whisper as she shoved a rifle into his hands.

"What the—" Darcy looked beyond his beloved. In the dim light of the smoldering fire in the hearth he could make out two more figures crawling from the entrance of the cellar and one other person half-raised, handling a gun.

"Fanny!" Bennet tried to keep his voice down. "What are you doing?"

Mrs. Bennet had no qualms about staying quiet. "Thomas Bennet, I may not know how to shoot a gun, but I certainly can load one! You men keep an eye on those scoundrels out there, and me and my girls will pass you fresh weapons."

"But... but, dear, you might get shot."

"Not if we stay low to the floor. Now, hush up, or those evil men will hear you!"

Bennet shrugged and in a mock-serious tone to Darcy claimed, "Get the whip hand over them at once, Will! At once! You see what happens if you don't?"

Beth grinned and began to crawl back. "Wait!" said Darcy. "Instead of reloading the extra rifles in one spot, split up the ammo—Kathy and Mary to that side, and you and Miz Bennet here. It'll go faster."

"Will," complained Bennet, "don't encourage them!"

"Sorry, Bennet, but it's a good idea." He turned back to Beth. "Just stay down!"

Beth retrieved another rifle. Just as she moved to Ethan by the north window, Whitehead's people started shooting up the house again. Darcy returned fire, trying to hit the shadows. "Fire at the gun flashes!" he cried.

He noted that the fire seemed heaviest at his side of the house, and he could feel the hair on the back of his neck rise in warning. *Denny was a bushwhacker*, he remembered. *He knows all kinds of tricks.*

It was then he heard a cry to his left. Everything seemed to move in slow motion as he turned towards the noise. There was Ethan writhing on the floor, Beth kneeling beside him, and there was a strange orange glow outside the side window.

Fire! his tired mind screamed. *They're trying to burn us out!*

Darcy tried to get moving towards the window, but he couldn't seem to get his legs to move right. As he yelled a warning, Beth reached down and picked up Ethan's rifle. To Darcy's horror, she stood up and took aim out the window. Darcy got his feet under him, and a moment later, he slammed into the wall beside Beth just as she fired the Winchester.

"Get down!" he screamed as he took aim. He saw a figure twenty yards away, reaching back to throw a lighted torch at the roof. The gunshot that knocked the man off his feet sounded unnaturally loud, and it was then Darcy realized Beth had fired at the same time as he did.

Beth, her eyes wide, expertly worked the lever, chambering another round. "Did we get them?"

"Don't know—keep firing!" The two kept a steady rhythm of suppression fire going until the enemy withdrew. As they took cover, Darcy noted that there were two dying torches on the ground—one twenty yards away, another ten yards beyond, each with a dark, still figure nearby.

"Are… are they dead?" asked Beth softly.

"Yeah." He turned to Beth. "How is Ethan?"

She dropped down to look the man over until her mother

arrived a moment later. "I... I think it's his shoulder. I'm not sure."

"Get him by the fire!" Mrs. Bennet barked. The three of them dragged the groaning man to the hearth where Mary was waiting. "We'll take care of this! Get back to the window!"

They returned to their guns, and Darcy turned on Beth. "Just what the hell did you think you were doing?"

"What do you think?" she spat back. "Ethan was shot, and those men were coming. I had to do something!"

Darcy breathed hard, but try as he might, he couldn't overcome her logic. "Where'd you learn to shoot like that?"

To his surprise, it was Bennet that answered. "I taught all my girls to shoot, Will. You never know what you'll find in the woods. Beth here is almost as good as her brother was."

"Better!" she claimed with a smile.

"Boss," said José from the back, "we're a man short. You'd better let *señorita* keep that rifle, I think."

Darcy didn't like it, but he had no choice. "All right! But will you do as I say?"

Beth nodded, and Darcy positioned her at the far left window. José took over Ethan's place, another man took the rear of the house, and Darcy exchanged places with Bennet. If Beth was going to fight, he reasoned, at least she would be surrounded by people who were very good with a gun. Now at the door, Darcy peeked out into the night. The moon was behind the house, and the shadows grew long. Dawn would not be far away.

Darcy grew grim. He knew Whitehead was still out there somewhere. This gambit of his had failed, but there would be others. Whitehead would have to move in soon; with the sunrise, he would lose all cover.

Maybe not, Darcy realized. The house faced due east. With the dawn, the defenders would be staring directly into the sun. For a few minutes they would be blind.

If I know that, Whitehead can figure it out. Denny certainly will.

"Everyone get an extra rifle. The next attack will be better coordinated than the last one. Peter!"

"Yo, boss," came a voice from Bennet's study.

"Keep a sharp eye on the barn. They haven't tried taking it yet. Make sure you cover our people." Darcy then turned his attention to his casualties. "Miz Bennet, how's Ethan?"

Fanny's determined voice had disappeared. "I've stopped the bleeding, but he's lost a lot of blood. We need a doctor!"

"I think we know that, dear," Bennet wearily stated. He turned to Darcy. "When will they come, son?"

Darcy swallowed. He couldn't quite make it out, but he thought he saw Beth smile in reaction to her father's choice of words. "Soon. Probably with the sunrise." He paused. "You're a good man with a rifle, sir."

"Call me Tom, Will. Yeah, I do all right." He paused and continued in a whisper. "It's not good, is it?"

Will had to tell the truth. "No, it isn't."

"You'll take care of my family?"

"Tom…"

"Son, don't pee on my boot and tell me it's raining. Anything happens to me, you'll watch over them?"

"Like they were my own."

"All right, then." Bennet didn't say another word but stared out into the darkness.

Pyke was reporting to Whitehead. "We lost three men, including Thorpe." Collins groaned and held his head in his hands.

"Well, let me tell ya what we oughta do, GW!" Denny then lowered his voice. "We oughta figure out a way of gittin' this here job done without losin' any more of my boys. The rest are gittin' antsy, an' that ain't a good thing."

Collins picked up his head. "I thought you could keep your gang in line!"

"Looky here, ya jackass! Why don't *you* carry the next torch up to the house, huh?" Denny pulled his gun. "In fact, why don't you do it right now, *Collins?*"

Collins recoiled in terror, and Whitehead held out his hand. "Put that away, Denny, and take it easy."

Instead of doing as he was told, Denny turned on his employer. "And you can keep your orders to yourself, GW! You better remember who those boys listen to, and it ain't you!" Eyes wide and breathing hard, Denny waved his pistol between his three companions. "Big words, big promises. You spun me a fancy tale, Whitehead; I was gonna be rich, but so far I ain't seen nothin'! My boys are lookin' for gold, and all they're gittin' tonight is lead. They're 'bout ready to break, an' I'm 'bout ready to join 'em. Ya better come up with a good idea quick, or you'll find yourself by yourself!"

Whitehead could feel the eyes of Pyke and Collins on him, waiting for him to take control of the situation. The problem was Whitehead was out of ideas. His talent was in strategic planning; the tactics he left to people like Collins and Denny. All he had left was his powers of persuasion. Whitehead had to be careful now with Denny. One wrong word and he could end up dead.

"Denny, I know how you feel. I want what's coming to me,

too. But it's those people that stand between us and our riches! Railroad money, Denny! Cash on the barrelhead! You heard my friend in Fort Worth. This is for real. But without this farm, the railroad won't be coming here. I'll lose everything!

"You're lucky. This thing falls apart, you're no worse off than before. Hell, you've had it pretty good, haven't you? Two meals a day, a dry bed at night, liquor, women. Sure, you had to ride some cattle, but it's better than how it was in Missouri, right?

"But me—I've got my whole life riding on this. This blows up, I'm done, and so is Collins here. But we can still win! We can still get everything we've ever wanted! But we got to finish the job tonight!"

Whitehead held his breath, wondering if Denny believed him. The gunfighter stared a hole through him and then holstered his gun. "All right—how?"

Whitehead exhaled, knowing he had placated Denny for now. "Look, I got you the railroad. You tell me what to do now. This is *your* province, bushwhacker."

Denny rocked back on his heels and thought. "Only way to git them people out is to burn 'em out."

Pyke groaned. "We tried that!"

"No!" Denny snapped. "Not the right way! What we need here is a wagon, filled with hay. Set that sucker on fire, an' push it against the side o' the house. That'll git 'em! The wagon'll shield us from their guns, so they can't stop us. Once that place is burnin' we just wait 'til they start runnin' like rabbits. Shoot 'em as they come out the door."

"But," Pyke complained, "we ain't got a wagon."

Denny pointed towards the barn. "I'll betcha there's one in there! We just gotta go git it!"

Whitehead frowned. "There's got to be people in there. No way they would've left it undefended."

"Right. That's th' problem."

Whitehead sat back for a moment, considering. He glanced around the wheelbarrow at the house again. "What time is it, Collins?"

The banker pulled out his pocket watch. "It's hard to read… about four."

"Fuck!" cried Denny. "We'll be sittin' ducks after th' sun comes up."

"Sunrise in little over an hour…" Whitehead said half to himself. "Denny, would you say that house faced due east?"

Denny looked around. "Sure looks that way. So?"

Whitehead turned to him. "So, the sun will be in their eyes, right?"

Denny thought about it and grinned. "Yeah. They won't see nothin'."

"That's when we make our move—right at sunrise. Half of us will take the barn while the rest will lay down covering fire. Once you secure the wagon, we'll finish 'em off."

"That might work," Denny allowed.

Whitehead laughed. "Of course, it's going to work! So, let's get ready. Denny, pick the men you trust to take that barn. Pyke, take a couple of fellows and try to round up what horses you can. I thought I saw mine wandering around over by the chicken coop. Collins, go help him."

Collins started. "But I don't like horses!"

"Damn momma's boy," grumbled Pyke. "Get your ass up and help me."

Whitehead watched as the others left to fulfill their duties.

As he reloaded his Colt, he began to think again about the finale of his grand scheme, and what he was going to do about an increasingly unstable Kid Denny. He had hired the gunslinger to enforce his will, but Denny's usefulness was quickly coming to an end. Denny would have to die, he knew, but not just yet. Once this job was done and the Bennet Farm was firmly in hand, there was still the matter of Will Darcy, Richard Fitzwilliam, and Pemberley Ranch.

Whitehead grinned. All that was needed to take care of those two was one little ambush, and that was something at which Denny excelled. Then, nothing would stop George Whitehead. He would get both Pemberley and the B&R. He would be King of Long Branch County.

He glanced at the eastern sky as it slowly began to lighten.

Mrs. Bennet was able to brew a little coffee for the defenders of the homestead, and Beth volunteered to share a mug with William. Bennet just chuckled and kept watch outside as the two lovers enjoyed a moment to themselves.

Darcy sipped the coffee as he sat on the floor with Beth curled up against him, her curly hair soft on his cheek. He handed her the mug, which she accepted thankfully. She returned the cup after having her fill and said in a hesitant voice, "Will… I…"

He quieted her with soothing sounds and stroking of her tresses. "Hush, darlin'—there's nothing to say."

"Yes, there is. I love you, Will."

He kissed the top of her head. "And I love you too, Beth. My one wish is that you, your mother, and your sisters were safely out of here."

She hugged him tight. "And I wouldn't want to be any-where else."

He grinned slightly. "Now, that's a damn fool thing to say, Miss Bennet."

She looked him in the eye. "Will Darcy, shut up and kiss me." Knowing the place and time to be about as inappropriate as it could be, Will and Beth shared a chaste, quick peck on the lips. It still drew a glance of disapproval from Mary.

Bennet didn't want to steal whatever time the two had left, but there were things Darcy needed to know. "Umm... sun's starting to come up, Will."

Instantly, the lovesick Will was replaced by the stern Master of Pemberley. Darcy kissed Beth's forehead and retrieved his rifle. He crouched low as he stole a peek out the window. "It sure is. Any movement?"

"I haven't seen anything," Bennet replied. By now, Beth had returned to her post, Winchester in hand.

José cut in. "I think I saw some *hombres* moving near the barn, boss."

"Right." Darcy had learned over the years to trust his people. If José said he thought he saw something, then Darcy could count on it. "Peter, look alive over there," he called out softly to his right. "There's some activity towards the barn."

"Yes, sir... yeah, people are movin', Mr. Darcy." There was the sound of a cocking rifle. "Looks like we're gonna get busy again."

Darcy took command. "All right, I figure they're going to try to take the barn. We'll probably take some fire as they try to distract us. Look alive. Our boys in the barn are going to need our help. Don't waste shots—try to make every one count."

"Boss!" cried José. "Look! Riders comin' in!"

Darcy looked out, his heart sinking. Sure enough, in the half-light of the dawn, dust was rising from the east. Men on horseback were coming from the main road.

"Any chance those are your people, Will?" asked Bennet.

"No, I'm afraid not," he admitted. They couldn't be Pemberley riders. He had been firm with Fitz about that. Fitzwilliam was to command the defense of the ranch, and nobody was to leave until Darcy returned. Those riders could only be reinforcements from the B&R. The odds against those trapped in the farmhouse just got longer.

Bennet sighed. "Didn't think so."

Darcy gritted his teeth, for he knew the possibility of them holding out now were practically nil. It had been a long road from Vicksburg, and he didn't want it to end this way, now that he had found Beth. But there was nothing for it. No retreat, no surrender—he would have to kill or be killed. If this was to be his last stand, it would be a memorable one. He would make those bastards pay.

Darcy sang out, "Look sharp, boys! They're on the move! You see somebody or something, shoot it! Let's send those sons-of-bitches to hell!"

A Rebel Yell arose from all those assembled—even the Bennets joined in. Darcy and his people bore down to face the final act of what folks in future times would call the Battle of Thompson Crossing.

Chapter 20

PYKE AND COLLINS HAD recovered several horses and had placed them in a small corral near the chicken coop. Once the pair returned, Denny judged that it was time to begin getting the men into place, as the sunrise was almost upon them. Pyke was sent to tell the others to prepare to move in; Denny would arrive soon to begin the assault. Whitehead would be in charge of the distraction.

As Whitehead and Denny finalized their plans, Collins half rose from his hiding place, using one hand to block the morning light. "Mr. Whitehead, I think… yes! Someone's coming! Look!" He pointed into the rising sun with his free hand.

"What?" Whitehead looked up but could see nothing. "Denny?"

The gunfighter had a better angle. "Four… no, five riders comin' in hard."

"About time," Whitehead grumbled. "I told those fools to get over here once they got the papers back from Lucas."

Denny frowned. "I thought ya sent two men."

"I did—they must've gone back to the B&R for more."

Denny watched as the men were almost upon them, trying to see who had come, and if they should join in the attack on the barn. All he could see were outlines. He flinched as his eyes caught a glint of light that flashed from the lead rider's silver hatband…

A black hat with a silver hatband.

Instantly, Denny was scrambling to his feet, pulling at his Colt. Kid Denny was a quick dead shot—one of the few men who could confidently hit someone on horseback ten yards away with a handgun. And he was greased lightning on the draw.

Unfortunately for the gunfighter, the man before him was Richard Fitzwilliam on Jeb Stuart with a Winchester in his hand.

Faster than it took to describe it, Fitz pulled hard on the reins, yanking his faithful steed to his right, dropped his rifle on his upraised left arm, and snapped off a shot. Denny was knocked clear off his feet by the impact of the .44 caliber slug slamming into his chest, exploding his heart, causing his pistol shot to go wide. By the time the body hit the ground, Joshua "Kid" Denny was no more.

Whitehead was stunned at the rapid change of fortune. One moment he was on the verge of victory; now all his plans were as dead as Denny. He cowered in the shadow afforded by the wheelbarrow. Fitz was turning his head every which way, looking for foes. Whitehead was a decent shot, and he stood a chance of hitting Fitzwilliam should he try. But even if he was able to fell the Pemberley foreman, his companions were sure to enact their instant and deadly revenge upon him, and Whitehead had no desire to quit the world anytime soon.

The sound of gunfire caught Fitzwilliam's attention. He pointed at the barn, yelling for his men to follow. The riders took off, firing upon the remnants of Denny's gang. This was Whitehead's chance; he reached over and seized a terrified Collins by the shirt.

"Come on, Billy, my lad. It's time we made ourselves scarce." Before Collins could utter a word, Whitehead was running hunched over towards the chicken coop, half-dragging the banker behind.

Will Darcy tried to disregard the growing despair in his belly as he raised his rifle. Sighting down the barrel, squinting in the sun, he noticed something familiar about the horse galloping over the ridge. He slowly tightened his finger on the trigger as he tried to recall. It seemed important.

At the instant, a man stood up from behind an overturned wheelbarrow. Darcy was so surprised he forgot about the horse; his attention instantly shifted to the moving figure, trying to determine if it was Whitehead. It was then that he recognized the rider out of the corner of his eye.

"*Fitzwilliam?!* My God, it's Fitzwilliam!" He turned to his men. "Boys, boys, don't shoot the riders—they're from Pemberley! They're ours! Fitzwilliam's brought reinforcements!"

The household cheered at the news of deliverance, a sound redoubled as Denny fell. Peter's voice was heard over the din.

"Boss, the barn is under attack!!" Gunshot punctuated his cry. The defenders instantly turned to help their fellows, and soon the outlaws were under fire from three directions. B&R ranch hands and gang members were falling one after another.

Beth, by the far window, had no angle to assist, so she leaned against the wall, stunned in wonder by the miracle. Tears of thanksgiving ran down her face as she tried to catch Darcy's eye. He wasn't shooting; instead he surveyed the land before the house in quiet satisfaction.

Suddenly, he stiffened. Before Beth could inquire, he stood up and shouted to no one in particular, "Cover me!" To Beth's horror he ran out the door.

Stumbling, the pair made it around the chicken coop before Collins lost his footing for good next to the pigsty. With a suppressed snarl, Whitehead reached down to pull his companion to his feet.

"What are we going to do?" Collins panted. "George, what are we going to do? They'll kill us!"

Whitehead gritted his teeth. "Calm yourself, Billy! All will be well—we just have to relocate, that's all."

"But… but how? Where?"

Whitehead was fighting to restrain his anger. His carefully laid strategy was dust, and he knew he no longer had prospects in Rosings—or anywhere in Texas, for that matter. His future plans were still a work in progress—head west into New Mexico or north into the Indian Territories—but he knew he needed money. And Billy Collins was the key to that. The first thing to do was to stop by the Rosings Bank and make an unscheduled withdrawal. And perhaps one last visit to the B&R and that bitch, Catherine Burroughs… Perhaps Anne Burroughs might be of a mind to escape her overbearing mother's attentions and seek a bit of adventure; she certainly would help keep his bedroll warm.

Whitehead had not considered how long he would suffer to have Collins in his company. The half-baked plan was that he would accompany him out of town. But now Whitehead was beginning to reconsider, and wondered if it wouldn't be better to just shoot the idiot after he unlocked the safe in the bank. But regardless as to the ultimate fate of Collins, he needed him alive until they got to the bank.

Whitehead shook Collins by his lapels. "Settle down, you fool. Listen, we're partners, right? We're getting out of town, together, after we make a couple of stops first…"

"*Hold it, Whitehead!*"

Whitehead was stunned not only by the threat but also by the particular voice making it. Ignoring his terrified cohort, he slowly turned his head right to behold the inconceivable. It *couldn't* be… it was *impossible*… he *knew* Will Darcy was back at Pemberley, protecting his precious sister. Yet—*there he was*—hatless in a white shirt and black vest, a rifle at his waist pointed unwaveringly in his direction. The totality of his failure struck him; once again he had underestimated Darcy. This was no mirage—if Whitehead wasn't extremely careful, this was his death.

Darcy's look was as black as night. "Now… move real slow… raise your hands."

Whitehead froze, thinking furiously. *A second! A second is all I need to think!*

"Don't shoot me, Mr. Darcy!" Collins cried, throwing his hands in the air. "Please, don't shoot me!"

Collins's fear gave Whitehead the distraction he needed. *No one expects a left-handed man.*

"Shut up, Collins!" Darcy demanded. "Whitehead…"

"You see what I have to put up with?" Whitehead grinned as he shrugged. "Well, I give up, Darcy; you've got the drop on me…"

As the words left his lips, Whitehead shoved Collins slightly; the man was now off-balance. Whitehead ground his left leg firmly into the ground while shifting his weight to his right, dropping his left hand to his holster. At the same time, he yanked as hard as he could with his right hand, pulling the banker across his body as he raised his Colt with his left, lining it up with the surprised rancher…

As soon as Darcy dashed out the door, Beth moved to follow him, but her progress was stopped by her father.

"Beth, what are you doing, girl?" Bennet held on to her arm.

"Father, *let me be!*" She threw off his hands and followed her lover out of the house, rifle in hand. She stopped after she descended the porch stairs, for Darcy seemed to have disappeared. The shooting had stopped, and Beth turned to her right. She saw Pemberley hands on horseback milling about near the barn, pointing rifles at men with their hands in the air. The battle was won; Beth decided to see if Will had run off to join his men.

Before she took three steps, two gunshots, quick upon the other, rang out behind her.

She spun about, dread in her heart. *Will!* She knew, somehow, that Darcy was involved. Her father called for her to return to safety, but she heeded him not, and moved with quicker and quicker steps towards the chicken coop. By the time she rounded the corner, she was at a full run, and the sight before her brought her to a dead stop.

There, in the long shadows of the early morning sun, lay a hatless figure face down.

Frozen, Beth inched towards it; her unbelieving eyes refused to take in any details save the man's black hair. Lips moving, she finally managed, "W... Will?"

"Beth."

She jerked her head to the right—*and there he was*—half leaning against the back of the coop, his bright blue eyes seeking hers, his left arm extended in welcome.

The Winchester slid from her nerveless fingers; it hit the ground as she threw her arms about his neck, crying tears of relief. She buried her face into his vest, sobbing incoherently, feeling his strong arm embrace her, taking in that sweet aroma of cologne and leather and sweat and masculinity that would be forever the smell of her William. His attempt to console her only drove Beth to tighten her grasp.

"Shush... shush..." he murmured, "everything's going to be fine, Beth... everything's going to—*freeze, you son-of-a-bitch, or I'll blow your goddamned head off!*"

Beth's head jerked up from her comfortable position. A glance at Will's stony face told her his words were meant for another. It was then she realized that Will's right arm had not embraced her; it, in fact, was pointed straight out. Beth's eyes ran down the length of his arm and the barrel of his Winchester to see over her shoulder that there was not one body on the ground by the pigsty but *two*—and one was weeping.

"Please, please don't shoot me, Mr. Darcy!" sobbed Billy Collins.

"I won't, if you lie still!" Will half-turned Beth away from any line of fire.

Collins ran his hands through his hair, which caused him to scream. "Please! You have to let me up! Please! *He's all over me!*"

Darcy was relentless. "Stay still, damn it!"

Beth narrowed her eyes in concentration. Collins didn't seem to be injured, but there was something strange on the back of his head and jacket. Something pinkish-gray... Her eyes slammed wide open in recognition—she knew what was all over the protesting man. Holding back the bile that rose in her throat, she turned her face back into Darcy's vest. But as tightly as she closed her eyes, she could not shut her ears.

"I'm... I'm going to be sick—" Collins's words were cut off by retching. Darcy's concerns were only for his beloved.

"Are you all right, Beth?" She nodded into his chest, not trusting herself to speak. The sound of footsteps heralded the arrival of others.

"Will! Are you... oh, for crying out loud!" Fitzwilliam's sarcastic voice was balm on Beth's frayed nerves, as was her father's cry of relief.

"I... I'm fine, Father," Beth managed, remaining deep in Darcy's one-handed embrace.

"Everything secure?" Darcy asked.

"Yeah," Fitzwilliam answered, "Our arrival really took the fight outta 'em; we only had to shoot a couple. What about here?"

"Help me, Fitzwilliam," moaned Collins. "Whitehead tried to use me as a shield and... and Darcy shot him and... and his *brains* are all over me!"

"Oh, shut your piehole, Collins, or it'll be *your* brains all over Whitehead! How d'you wanna handle this, Will?"

"This rifle's getting heavy," Darcy said. "Cover him, will you?" Beth heard Fitzwilliam command Collins to move slowly off Whitehead—there was the sound of metal on wood—and now two arms held her close.

There was the sound of more arrivals as Fitzwilliam whistled. "Ooo-wee! You plugged this sum-bitch square in the right eye, Will! Blew the back of his cotton-pickin' head clean out! No wonder Collins is cryin' like a baby. Damn good shootin'."

Darcy's voice was ice-cold. "Right eye? Then I missed, Fitz. I was aiming for the bridge of the bastard's nose. Sorry to make such a mess, Collins."

Beth whimpered and drove her face deeper into his vest.

"Darcy..." Bennet's voice carried a warning.

"Sorry." To Beth, Darcy repeated, "I'm sorry, darlin'."

"It's okay," she shakily returned. "Just hold me."

In a lighter tone, Darcy asked, "Far be it that I look a gift horse in the mouth, but what the hell are y'all doing here, Fitz? I thought I told you to guard Pemberley."

Fitz laughed, "You did, an' that's just what I was doin', 'cept we got real worried about the wagon not showin' up last night. About an hour before dawn, Gaby had enough an' ordered me to take some boys an' see what the delay was."

"Ordered you? *Gaby?*"

"Damn right, she did! Said, 'With my brother gone, I'm in charge of Pemberley, and you'd best do as you're told!' Sounded just like you, boss!"

Darcy laughed, and Beth couldn't help joining him. She chanced a glimpse at Fitzwilliam, keeping her eyes away from the wreckage that was once George Whitehead.

"Well," said Darcy, "I'm mighty glad to see you, Fitz. When I saw y'all charging across that rise, I never been so happy to see an order of mine disobeyed in my life!"

"Me too," Bennet added. "You saved us all, Fitzwilliam."

The crowd moved closer to get a better look—Beth estimated

it was about a half-dozen—when there was a disruption. The men parted before a short, female figure.

"Lily!" cried her father. He tried to pull her away from the scene, but she would have none of it; she fought him off and approached the body, whimpering.

"George? George? Are you dead, George? Are you dead?"

Bennet tried again. "Lily, please—come away from there."

"No!" she screamed. The glare in her eyes, tinged with a hint of madness, held everyone at bay. She drew closer to Whitehead. The girl had changed into plain dress, and the makeup was washed from her face. She looked like the Lily of before, but there was something that told Beth that *that* girl was gone forever.

"George? Why, George? Why did you do it? Why did you throw me away—why did you give me to... to *Denny?* How could you betray me? I loved you, George. I gave you everything. Do you understand? *Everything!*"

Beth could no longer watch and turned again into Will's strong chest.

"No—don't touch me, Father! Did you know what that did to me, George? Did you know what *he* did to me? Did you? Damn you, did you?" She punctuated her screams with kicks to Whitehead's limp body. She kicked him again and again, crying, "Damn you to hell! Damn you to hell!" in time with her kicks. The sound of foot striking body pounded into Beth's head, again and again.

Beth's nightmare only ended when Bennet was finally able to control her hysterical sister and carry her back to the house. Everyone stood silent—the only sound was Lily's anguished howls.

A lone rider dashed hell bent for leather in the early morning light.

Normally, Pyke would be scared stiff riding on uneven terrain on a strange horse, but he was too terrified to worry about what he was doing. Unlike everyone else, he had recognized the Pemberley riders as soon as they made the top of the ridge. At Denny's fall, he instantly knew the game was up, no matter what happened to Whitehead, and Pyke's only thought now was escape. In the chaos of the battle, he had been able to secure a horse and slip away unnoticed. He took no chances; he rode like a demon, crouched down low in the saddle, expecting a bullet in the back at any time. He would not look back and see if he was followed, for he was afraid he'd see a whole posse giving chase.

Pyke rode hard towards the B&R. He had to get out of the county, and he wasn't going empty-handed.

Darcy sat on the porch steps, drinking a cup of coffee and listening to the reports, while Beth was glued firmly to his side, holding one of his hands.

"All my boys are okay," Fitzwilliam was saying. "I figure we shot about four of 'em, not includin' Whitehead."

"And we got at least three more," claimed José. "How many bodies we got?"

"Nine," said Peter, "and five prisoners. Our only casualty is Ethan."

"How is he?" Darcy demanded.

A worried Mrs. Bennet spoke from the door. "Will, he's in bad shape. We need Charles."

"All right; I'll go get Doc Bingley right away," Fitz said. At that Darcy stood.

"You'll be coming with me, Fitz. We've got to check on Sheriff Lucas, too. Bring two men. This ain't over with yet." Fitz made to object—Darcy's exhaustion was plain to see—but a glare from his boss silenced him. Instead, he ordered Darcy's horse brought around.

Bennet crossed over to Darcy. "I know the sheriff is important, but get Charles first, all right?" Darcy nodded and Bennet patted his shoulder. "Son, it *is* over. All that's left is rounding up the stragglers. So, take care, eh?"

Darcy turned to take his leave of Beth, only to find her gone. Puzzled, and not a little disappointed, he climbed aboard Caesar, only to see her coming from the house with his hat. Wordlessly, she handed it to him, not responding to his small smile. As he put it on, Beth frowned and placed her fists on her hips.

"You come back to me, Will Darcy! You hear me?"

A grin spread over Darcy's features. He tipped his hat and spurred his horse. Beth watched the four riders head out towards town.

Chapter 21

THE STOP AT THE Bingley place on the outskirts of Rosings was short. Charles had just sat down for breakfast when Darcy and his party arrived. With their assistance, Jane and Charles, along with his medicine bag and their infant daughter, were soon aboard their buggy heading to the Bennet Farm.

The four riders then split up—Darcy and Fitz would approach the sheriff's office from the street, while the other two covered them from the rear. Darcy waited five minutes to allow his men to get into position, then he and Fitz slowly made their way along the main street. It was early, and the shadows were still long as the pair passed the Whitehead Building. They were cautious, in case Denny left a rear guard. Because their attention was on Whitehead's place, they didn't notice the lone figure on the porch of the sheriff's office until they were almost upon him. Startled, Fitz halfway drew his revolver.

Darcy was the first to speak. "Mornin', Sheriff."

Sheriff Lucas was seated, leaning his chair back on the rear legs while resting his boots on a post, hat low over his eyes, whittling at a piece of wood. He glanced up at the greeting before returning his attention to his task, replying, "Mornin', Mr. Darcy, Fitzwilliam. You boys are up early." A sliver of wood floated to the porch.

Fitz holstered his weapon, an incredulous expression on his face. Darcy, for his part, was amused as he leaned over the saddle horn. "You too, I see. Had a good night?"

Lucas kept whittling. "Can't complain."

Fitz couldn't restrain himself. "But we heard Denny set some of his men after you."

Lucas didn't raise his head. "Yep, he surely did."

"Then, what happened?" Fitz cried.

Lucas glanced up, a smirk on his face. "He'd best send better boys next time. The two he did are coolin' their heels in a jail cell, keepin' Miz Sally company," he said as he pointed the piece of wood over his shoulder. "Huh! The day I can't handle two goat ropers like that with my deputies backin' me up is the day I retire."

Darcy's voice was flat. "There won't be a next time, Sheriff."

That got Lucas's attention. "That so?"

"Yes. Gunfight at the Bennet place all night. Just ended. George Whitehead and Kid Denny are dead, along with seven of Denny's gang. Took the rest prisoner, including Billy Collins. He's singing like a bird."

"Damn!" With a bang, Lucas straightened up his chair and stood up. "And how did your people make out?"

"One wounded—Doc Bingley's seeing to him now."

Lucas shook his head. "I'll be damned. Whitehead's dead? Then it's all over."

"No, it ain't." Darcy's face was hard. "One loose thread left."

Lucas eyed him. "Yeah, I reckon so. You thinkin' o' payin' a visit to Cate?"

Darcy nodded. "This ends today."

Lucas sighed. "I reckon I'll best be goin' with you. You boys had any breakfast? Coffee's hot, an' Charlotte's come in and whipped up some bacon 'n' eggs." He turned his head to Fitzwilliam. "She made biscuits."

Fitz grinned. "That's mighty neighborly of you, Sheriff. Will?"

Darcy shrugged. "A half-hour won't make any difference. We'll be pleased to enjoy your hospitality." He had noted with satisfaction Fitz's use of Lucas's title. *Perhaps there's hope for the two of them, after all. I sure hope so, for Miss Charlotte's peace of mind.*

As the two dismounted, Lucas opened the front door of the office. "I'll send Smith over to the Bennets' place to take the prisoners into official custody." He stopped and turned. "Oh, by the by, you'd best tell whatever riders you sent to come up the back way to make themselves known. I can't speak for Deputy Jones's nerves, an' I don't want somebody to get hisself shot by accident."

Fitz's jaw dropped. "How'd you know about that?"

Lucas snorted. "'Cause that's what I would've done in your place, Fitz, an' I reckon you ain't no fool."

After eating breakfast and enduring Fitz's flirting with the cook, Darcy climbed aboard his black stallion and rode with the others towards the B&R ranch house. Sheriff Lucas insisted Deputy Jones come with them, and deputized one of Darcy's men to guard the prisoners in the jail.

The small group rode north out of town along the road

beside Rose Creek. At a rise a half-mile from their objective, Darcy signaled for the men to halt.

"All right. This is what we do. Fitz, you and Peter go around and sneak into the ranch house from the kitchen, if you can. Get Anne out of there. You see *any* trouble, you get out pronto. Got it?"

"Yes, sir."

"Sheriff—you, Deputy Jones, and I will go in from the other side."

"What side's that, Mr. Darcy?"

"The front door, Sheriff." He turned to Fitz. "We'll give you a couple minutes' head start. Y'all best be going."

The two men galloped off to the west. Darcy watched them until they disappeared behind a ridge, then signaled to his companions to continue to the house. They took their time, holding their mounts to a trot, carefully taking in their surroundings.

"Notice anything?" asked Darcy in a low voice.

"Yeah," the lawman answered, "where the hell is everybody?"

The B&R Ranch should have been a hub of noise and effort; instead, it was completely deserted. If it wasn't for the lowing of the cattle, one could easily believe the place had been abandoned.

"Ah," breathed Darcy. "Look to the northwest." There, past the low hills, was a faint cloud of dust.

"Sheriff, it looks like everybody done rode off," said Deputy Jones.

"Rats abandoning a sinking ship," observed Lucas. "Think they heard about the gunfight?"

Darcy watched the distant disturbance. "Hmm, maybe. I thought we got everybody, but maybe one of Denny's gang got away. Hell, it doesn't matter. Keep a sharp eye out, in case somebody stayed behind."

The three rode in, stopping before the main house. Tied to a hitching post was Judge Phillips's buggy. "Well, lookie here," drawled Lucas as he dismounted. "Seems Cate's pet judge has come for breakfast. We get two birds with one stone."

The men dismounted and tied their horses to the hitching post. It was then their good cheer ended—the front door was ajar. Without a word, Darcy, Lucas, and Jones drew their revolvers and slowly made their way up the porch stairs to the door. They moved to either side of the opening, looking at each other.

"I'll go in..." Lucas began when Darcy cut him off in a low voice.

"No—I'll go first. I know this house better than either of you. Stay close."

Taking a deep breath, Darcy moved the door open with the toe of his boot, keeping as much of the rest of his body hidden from sight as he could. When the opening was wide enough, he moved like lightning into the ranch house, crouching low, Colt before him. Darcy stopped some ten feet in, hard against the left wall of the hallway while his companions followed, moving over to the right. Without a word, Darcy signaled for them to move deeper down the hallway slowly.

The three crept along the carpeted hallway, peeking into first the parlor, then the sitting room. It wasn't until Jones got to the dining room that any sound was made.

"Oh, my God!"

The sheriff and Darcy looked into a scene of horror. The sun shone through the curtains, moving in the morning breeze, the light glowing off the yellow paint of the walls and gleaming hardwood of the table. Unfinished breakfast plates and one overturned coffee cup were on the table. And there was a man slumped over a plate, a dark red substance staining the table-cloth, while the chair at the head of the table had fallen over, partially hiding a woman's body.

"Cate!" Darcy gasped. Disregarding any danger, he ran to his cousin's side, knowing all the while he was too late. And he was—Catherine Burroughs had been shot in the torso, her body still warm to the touch.

The sheriff was by the side of the male victim while Jones remained at the doorway. "It's Judge Phillips," Lucas said. "He's dead—shot in the chest." He looked over. "Miz Burroughs, too?"

"Yes," Darcy croaked, his emotions a whirl. He had had his disagreements with Catherine, and he couldn't say he actually liked her, but to see his cousin's murdered body was a shock. He glanced at her face. Now, only in death, had her dour face relaxed into something other than the hard woman he had known all his life.

Anne! His mind screamed. Darcy stood with a jerk. "They've been murdered, and my cousin, Anne, may be next. Come on."

The three dashed out of the room, heedless of the noise, heading for the stairs. Before Darcy reached the first step, he heard shouting—several voices, Fitz's among them. A second later, there was the explosion of gunfire. Darcy tried to run as fast as he could, fear almost overwhelming him. *Am I too late again?*

He turned at the landing to see three men crouched at the head of the stairs. *Fitzwilliam!* They glanced down at them, guns pointed, before lowering them. Just as Darcy and the others reached them, they stood. Darcy didn't wait—he pushed through the group and down the upstairs hallway.

He got only two steps before coming to a dead halt. A man lay prone on the floor before what he knew to be Anne's room. Darcy turned to his foreman, the obvious question on his face.

"Not me," said Fitz. "The shot came from inside the bedroom. He fell as if someone shot him in the back."

"Who's there?" came an uneven female voice from the bedroom.

"Annie! It's Will! I'm here with help!"

"*Will!*" the woman screamed. Darcy and the others ran forward, stepping over the body and into the bedroom. There, against the far wall, was a terrified Anne Burroughs. There was another person in the room, or rather, in her closet, a smoking double-barreled shotgun in his trembling hands.

"Bartholomew!" Darcy cried, hands up in the air. "Don't shoot! It's me!"

"Mr. Darcy. Oh, thank God! Thank God you've come." The aged butler lowered his weapon as Anne dashed over to support him.

Anne spoke as the two made their way to a chair, Darcy helping them. "He... he was trying to get in... We heard gun shots... We hid. Mother? What happened to Mother? Is Mother all right?"

Darcy struggled to speak, but it wasn't necessary—his face told all. Anne went white, and Darcy had to hold up his distraught cousin as Bartholomew half-fell into a chair. It would be some moments before Darcy could leave the room. He found the others looking at the dead man, his body showing the results of taking a load of buckshot at close range.

Sheriff Lucas looked around. "You think this is the only intruder?"

"Why don't you go find out, you old fool?" Fitzwilliam spat.

Darcy sighed. *Well, that good feeling didn't last long.* "Why don't you and the others check out the house, Sheriff? Fitz, you go with him. I'll stay here with… who is it, Fitz?"

Fitz turned the dead man's face to the side. "Pyke. It's Pyke." Fitz stood and, sharing a relatively friendly look with Lucas, set off down the hallway.

Fifteen minutes later, the group assembled in the study, Darcy taking care that Anne did not look into the dining room. There were signs that the room had been ransacked, but Catherine's safe was still locked.

"If I had to venture a guess," Lucas said, "it seems Pyke ki… er, did away with the others before he came in here, lookin' for money. He must've been panicked, seeing how he, umm… did *that*," he gestured toward the dining room, "afore he come in here. He didn't get the combination first. Stupid."

Darcy grimaced. He knew the oaf was trying not to upset Anne, yet he kept talking anyway.

Anne stopped sobbing into a handkerchief. "We… we heard arguing before two gunshots. That's what gave Bartholomew time to get a gun and get me in my room. That man… came up after a few minutes, shouting for money, saying I'd be all right if I did as he said. But I didn't believe him. He broke in the door—Bartholomew was in the closet—I thought that man was going to kill me."

"I wasn't hiding," the butler said in his usual unperturbed manner, now that he had time to compose himself. "I was trying to 'get the drop on him,' I think it's called. Mr. Fitzwilliam's distraction was most timely."

Darcy walked over to shake Bartholomew's hand. "I don't know how to thank you. You saved Anne's life for sure."

A flicker of emotion passed in the butler's eyes. "Seeing to Miss Anne has always been more than my duty, Mr. Darcy. She's been, well, like the daughter I'll never have. I only ask to go with her wherever she lives."

"I can assure you of that," Darcy promised him. He then ordered Fitz and the others to prepare a wagon for Anne and Bartholomew. He knew he needed to get them out of the house as soon as possible—and inform the undertaker he had more business ahead.

"My God," breathed Tom Bennet as he and Darcy shared a drink in the study at the Bennet farm. "What will happen to Miss Anne now?"

Darcy sat in an armchair across from the farmer, Beth seated next to him, holding one of his hands in hers. "I don't know. We've sent her to Pemberley, she and Bartholomew both, and Charles is seeing to her. She's got a home with me as long as she wants. I don't know what's to become of her, except I can't figure she'd ever want to go back to the B&R."

"Will Charles be able to do anything for her?" asked Beth.

"I don't know, sweetheart. I guess he'll give her something to help her sleep. That'll help tonight, but tomorrow and afterwards? At least Charles has been able to report that Ethan was out of danger."

Bennet glanced at Samuel's photograph, a bullet hole next to it. "Death of a loved one is never easy. If we can help in any way, just call on us." He took a sip of his whiskey. "I heard there was a run on Rosings Bank."

Darcy nodded. "Everybody heard about the shootout here and that Collins was involved. The bank's cash couldn't make good on the claims and Rosings failed. Sheriff Lucas had to close the place by one in the afternoon, which didn't make the folks still in line too happy." He looked at Bennet. "Don't you worry, Tom. I'll make good on any money you had in there."

Bennet put down his glass. "Son, you don't have to do that. You've done so much already."

Darcy grunted. "Forgive me, but my promise isn't just for you. I'm going to make good for everybody. You see, Anne was Cate's only heir, and like I said, she's got no use for either the B&R or Rosings. We'll work out a deal—sell land or cattle, pledge future income, something—and use that to settle with everyone."

"But won't Miss Anne lose everything?"

Darcy sighed. "She might, but she's got family back east. We'll see. As for the landowners that were forced into foreclosure, we'll try to give them their land back."

Beth thought about that. "Most of those folks have moved on. How are you going to let them know about their property?"

"We'll send letters after them, or to their next of kin. If we get no reply after several years, we'll sell the land and put the money in trust for them or keep the land untouched—a park for the people."

Bennet eyed his future son-in-law. "You've done a bit of thinking about this."

Darcy shrugged. "Yes, well, I had to do something waiting for the undertaker to show up at the B&R."

Beth shuddered. "That's pretty cold, son," Bennet observed.

"Well, you didn't hear what I did. Annie's been talking. A quiet one, that Anne. Apparently she overheard a great deal sneakin' around the house like she did. Didn't tell anybody 'til now, 'cause she was afraid she'd lose whatever affection Cate had for her. She was scared Cate would throw her out of the house. Now, I ask you, what kind of mother would instill that much fear in her only child?

"Cate had been up to her eyeballs in Whitehead's plans. Knew all about the railroad and stealing the land from the homesteaders. 'Course, Cate didn't have any idea that Whitehead and Collins were double-crossing her. And while she didn't know what Denny planned for the Washingtons beforehand, Cate wasn't all that upset over the murders. Know what she said when she heard about the lynching? According to Anne, Cate said, 'Serves them right—they should have stayed in Louisiana where their kind belongs.' God forgive me, but it's kind of hard to grieve over a woman like that."

Mrs. Bennet walked through the open study door and spoke to the subdued group. "Will, dear, I've got some food on. You're welcome to stay."

Darcy got to his feet, shaking his head, and Beth got up with him, still holding his hand. "Thank you kindly, Miz Fanny, but I've got to get back to Pemberley. I'm sure Gaby's ready to pitch a fit about now. Besides, I've got to see how Anne's making out." Darcy received a kiss on the cheek from his future mother-in-law, took his leave of Bennet, and allowed Beth to walk him out of the house to his horse. Before he climbed on his steed, he held Beth close in his arms and the two shared a long, slow kiss.

Will pulled back with a dazed look on his face. "Now, Beth, you keep that up, and I'm not likely to leave."

Beth smirked. "Is that so, cowboy? Maybe we should do that again."

Darcy ran his thumbs along her jaw line, sending chills through his fiancée. "Soon, darlin'. Soon we'll be married, and I won't have to say goodbye ever again. You *will* marry me soon, won't you?"

Beth nodded. "As soon as I learn all that Catholic stuff—all that kneeling and bowing and prayer beads."

One of Darcy's eyebrows rose up to his hair line. "Kneeling and bowing and prayer beads? If I didn't know better, I swear you've been talking to Fitz."

Beth just smiled and kissed him. A moment later, she watched Darcy and Caesar make their way down the lane towards the main road and Pemberley.

Chapter 22

TWO DAYS LATER, A company of cavalry from Fort Richardson under the command of Captain Buford arrived in response to Sheriff Lucas's telegram. Buford immediately held a court of inquiry, and after a couple of hours of testimony, took Sally Younge, Billy Collins, and the surviving members of Denny's gang into federal custody. As there was no longer a magistrate in Long Branch County, the prisoners were transferred to Fort Richardson to await trial by a traveling circuit judge. The evidence being irrefutable and the victims notable, the verdicts were never in doubt. All were convicted on conspiracy to commit fraud. Collins and the other men were also found guilty of conspiracy to commit murder. The only thing that saved the malefactors from the noose was that it could not be proven beyond a reasonable doubt that any had participated in the deaths of Mrs. Burroughs, Judge Phillips, or the Washingtons. Twenty years in prison for all was the sentence handed down.

As it turned out, neither Collins nor Younge would serve a full year in jail. Collins had managed to offend so many of his fellow inmates with his disdainful and aggravating ways that it was impossible to know which one had the strongest motivation to stick a handmade knife into his ribs one evening after dinner. He was buried in the prison cemetery next to so many others who had sought the easy way to riches by stealing from their fellow man.

Sally Younge was like a cat, always landing on her feet. Using her best talents—seduction and manipulation—she was able to corrupt an official of the women's prison into allowing her escape. She fled into the expanses of the west and all trace of her was lost. A legend arose that she made her way to the mining towns of the Rocky Mountains, and under an assumed name captured the attentions of a newly rich mine owner. It was said that the couple moved to Denver where she became one of the matrons of society. It was a nice story, fit for penny novels, but no one knew if it was true.

In the tragic circumstances that Catherine Burroughs had helped create, the B&R was finally reunited with Pemberley, but not in the way she had imagined. Anne wanted nothing to do with the legacy left to her and signed away her rights to the vast ranch to Darcy as soon as she could. Texas held too many painful memories for the girl, and in the spring of 1872 at the train station in Fort Worth, her family and friends waved good-bye as Anne Burroughs began her journey to a new life with her Matlock relations in New York City, her elderly faithful servant Bartholomew right behind, carrying her satchel. He would care for the heiress for years until he grew too old to serve her, when they changed positions and Anne would see to his comfort for the rest of his life.

Anne's was not the only departure from Rosings. Lily was welcomed back into the Bennet family, but there was no way she could remain with them. Everyone in town knew what had happened to her, so it was an intolerable situation. Tearfully, her parents sent her to live with the Gardiners in St. Louis, where no one would ever know her history. Letters from Missouri would report that she had been established as a salesgirl in the family store, a task for which she proved very well suited. In the years to come, she would catch the eye of a young bank clerk, and it was hoped by her family in Texas that Lily would find her happiness someday.

Mary Bennet would find her happiness in the aftermath of the assault. Three days after the attack on the Bennet farm, Tom Bennet found a nervous Henry Tilney in his study, stuttering his request for Mary's hand in marriage. The request was not unexpected, and it was in Bennet's character to use such a moment as an excuse to tease, but given all the horror they had experienced, his heart was not in it. Instead, he surprised the young preacher by embracing him, welcoming Henry into the family. As the courtship had been of some duration, a wedding date two weeks hence was settled on. Mrs. Bennet could not be happy with it, for there was no time for a new dress to be ordered or made, but she bowed to her daughter's desire. Mary gave not a fig for finery—she only wanted to be Mrs. Henry Tilney and to be so as soon as practical.

Darcy would manage the B&R Ranch for the benefit of the victims of Whitehead and Cate Burroughs, using the profits to pay back the landowners and holders of claims against the now-defunct Rosings Bank. To run the place, renamed Rosings Ranch, Darcy appointed Richard Fitzwilliam as executive manager. José Estrada was promoted to take Fitz's place as Pemberley foreman.

Fitz may have been in charge of the ranch, but no one was going to be living in the house. One night soon after the battle, someone—a disgruntled Rosings Bank customer, it was thought—set the abandoned mansion ablaze. It would be over an hour before the people from town would arrive, and there was nothing they could do once they got there, the firefighting equipment being inadequate, except watch the place burn to the ground.

This chain of events would have an interesting effect on the lives of Fitz and his beloved Charlotte. A few nights after the appointment, the couple, hand in hand, confronted Sheriff Lucas, announcing their intention to marry. Instead of the expected explosion, a grim Lucas asked a simple question.

"Fitzwilliam, will my girl ever go hungry?"

Stunned by the question, it took a moment before Fitz could answer.

"No, never. I stake my life on it."

Lucas's bleak expression gave way to one of resignation and grief. "Then you have my permission. Take care of my baby girl."

The couple shared an incredulous look. Charlotte said gently, "Paw, I think you ought to know we were thinking of living here, in the house, with you, if that's all right."

The tears that had formed in the older man's eyes flowed freely as he responded, "That… that would be fine. I'd be glad for the company. Mighty glad indeed…" He broke down as the couple rushed to embrace him.

As improvements needed to be made on the house, the wedding would not take place until mid-January. The event would not be as bittersweet as many feared, as it seemed that Fitz and Lucas had settled most of their differences. But if anyone thought that there would be smooth sailing in the Fitzwilliam/ Lucas household, they would be wrong. Two stubborn men were bound to butt heads from time to time, and if Lucas and Fitz were good at anything, it was arguing with each other.

Still, they were united in their love for Charlotte and fear of her displeasure. In the crisis, Charlotte had found her own strength, and she was no longer afraid to express it. It was surprising indeed for the town to learn that Sheriff Lucas could be henpecked, but there was soon no question that Mrs. Fitzwilliam was the person who ruled that household. Fitz would have no complaints—*he* knew best how to please his wife—and within a few years the yard about the house was filled with their children.

With one wedding in November and another in January, it was easy for Beth and William to settle on mid-December. Mrs. Bennet was happy that at least one of her daughters would not be married in her Sunday best, but she was confused by Beth's intention of becoming Catholic. Wasn't her brother-in-law's church good enough, she had asked.

Beth smiled and kindly, yet firmly, said, "Mother, when I marry Will, I will have to promise to God that I will raise my children in the Catholic faith. I will *not* be a different religion from my children. I hope you can see that."

So on a bright December Sunday morning, Elizabeth Bennet, dressed in a new white dress, received First Communion and was confirmed into the Roman Catholic Church. Five days later, wearing the same dress, she again walked down the aisle of the Santa Maria Catholic Mission chapel, this time to become Mrs. William Darcy. Her intended stood tall and still, his white shirt gleaming against his black suit. His face was impassive, as was his wont when he was emotional, his fiancée now knew.

She had only to gaze into his intense blue eyes to see the fireworks of happiness that his demeanor masked. To help set aside the terrors of the months past, the various families had decided to make the three weddings a town event, so it was standing room only as Father Joseph proclaimed the couple man and wife, in the name of the Father and of the Son and of the Holy Ghost, and prayed that God's peace would descend upon the people of Rosings.

Epilogue

May, 1873

Two men on horseback stood in the shade of a single oak tree atop a ridge on Pemberley. A tall man in a black vest was astride a black Arabian, the man's tan ten-gallon hat nodding as his companion spoke. He was of a slightly shorter stature, sitting on a brown horse, and wearing a black hat with a silver hatband. As they talked they gazed over the sea of prairie before them, dotted with hundreds of cattle, lowing and grazing. They were not alone; a handful of wranglers carefully moved their cowponies around the vast herd, keeping an eye out for trouble.

There was an unfamiliar sound on the breeze—that of construction from across the river. The taller of the two men gestured in that direction.

"Soon, Fitz," said William Darcy, owner of Pemberley Ranch, "soon the railroad will be through the town, the stockyard will be built, and we won't have to drive our cattle to Kansas ever again. I reckon you're looking forward to that."

"That's for certain, Will," answered Richard Fitzwilliam,

manager of Rosings Ranch. "Ten more days and it's the last roundup. I just hope I can get back afore Charlotte has the baby."

"Hoping for a boy?"

Fitz smiled. "Don't get me wrong. I'd be pleased with a son, but I think I'd rather a pretty little girl that takes after her momma." He wasn't giving his wife false praise, either. Marriage had done wonders for Charlotte Fitzwilliam, Darcy thought. Maybe it was because she was always smiling, but the lady had never looked so pretty in her life.

Fitz pointed towards the main house. "Speaking of little mammas, here comes one. Howdy, Miz Beth!"

Will turned, a smile lighting his face to watch Beth ride up on her paint, Turner. She was dressed in the Spanish style: a white blouse with a black vest over flowing black trousers, the better to ride a horse astride. She had her curly hair pulled back and a wide-rimmed flat hat. For an instant, Darcy was reminded of his mother. Beth answered her husband's smile with one of her own.

"Howdy yourself, Fitz. How's Charlotte?"

"Ready to birth that baby."

Beth pulled Turner to a halt next to Will. "But she's only seven months along."

Fitz grinned. "She's missin' her feet, she says." The comment earned a laugh from the lady. "Speakin' o' Charlotte, I'd best be gettin' home. I'll be by to take my leave of y'all afore I head out to Kansas." He waved as he spurred Jeb Stuart towards town.

Beth turned to Darcy. "What were you talking about? The drive?"

"That and the future. Things are changing, sweetheart. The railroad, Gaby…"

Beth eyed her husband closely. "Are you having second thoughts?"

Will sighed. "Not really. Gaby needs to get out and meet new people. Miss Dashwood's School for Young Ladies in Austin is a fine place. Gaby wants to go, and if I win in November—"

Beth interrupted him. "*When* you win in November."

Will smiled, amused by his wife's confidence in him being elected to a seat in the Texas Legislature. "Right—then we can get us a place at the capital and spend some time with her, in-between all the hearings and meetings and such."

"Well, if you don't have time, I certainly will." The word was the Democrats felt they had the votes to take control of the state government away from the Reconstruction Republicans. The federal government under Grant had lost all taste for the fight, and the opportunity was there to reestablish local control. There was talk of a new Texas State Constitution. With such changes before them, Darcy knew he had to be a part of it.

"You still planning on coming with me to Austin?"

"Someone's got to host your soirées. José will have everything handled here. So there's no reason for us to stay behind. Besides," she smiled, "I don't want those society women getting their claws into you."

Will grinned. "Are you jealous, Mrs. Darcy?"

"Just putting my brand on my own, Mr. Darcy." Beth tried to look serious and failed. "I rode out to tell you Father's here." Tom Bennet, the new chairman of the Long Branch County Democratic Party, was manager of Darcy's campaign.

"I hope you left him in good spirits."

"He's always in good spirits, as long as Samuel's there."

Will rolled his eyes. "Wonderful. I'd better get back, before my son's grandfather spoils him rotten."

Beth lowered her eyes. "Will, I've been thinking."

"About what?"

"Do you think it's time we thought about a brother or sister for Sam?"

Will reached out for her hand. "Are you sure? It's only been eight months."

She blushed. "I only asked if we want to think about it."

"All right. Let's go talk to Tom, and then let's go for a swim in the lake and… talk about it."

Beth raised an eyebrow. "Humph. There won't be much talking, then. You and swimming—you love to get me in the water. Why?"

Will turned bright red. "Umm… maybe one day I'll tell you. Meanwhile…" He reached over and caught her lips with his. Satisfied—for the moment—the two rode back to the house.

The only addition to the Pemberley Ranch was a flagpole. Flying from it was a single flag of red, white, and blue. It was the visible sign of the compromises made between the former-Yankee farm girl and one-time-Confederate rancher. It was the flag of their home, and their children's home, and their children's children's home.

The Lone Star flag of the State of Texas.

In the beauty of the lilies Christ was born across the sea,
With a glory in his bosom that transfigures you and me;
As he died to make men holy, let us die to make men free,
While God is marching on.
Glory! Glory! Hallelujah!

Glory! Glory! Hallelujah!
Glory! Glory! Hallelujah!
While God is marching on.

"The Battle Hymn of the Republic"
by Julia Ward Howe, 1861

THE END

In Appreciation

My thanks go to Debbie Styne, Mary Anne Mushatt, and Ellen Pickels, who worked endless hours editing this work.

To Abigail Reynolds, for all her advice and support.

To all the members of the JA Internet Community, who encouraged me to try to get this published.

I could not have done it without all of you.

ABOUT THE AUTHOR

Jack Caldwell, a native of Louisiana living in Wisconsin, is an economic developer by trade. Mr. Caldwell has been an amateur history buff and a fan of Miss Austen for many years. *Pemberley Ranch* is his first published work. He is married with three sons.

A Darcy Christmas

Amanda Grange, Sharon Lathan, & Carolyn Eberhart

A Holiday Tribute to Jane Austen

Mr. and Mrs. Darcy wish you a very Merry Christmas and a Happy New Year!

Share in the magic of the season in these three warm and wonderful holiday novellas from bestselling authors.

Christmas Present
By Amanda Grange

A Darcy Christmas
By Sharon Lathan

Mr. Darcy's Christmas Carol
By Carolyn Eberhart

978-1-4022-4339-4
$14.99 US/$17.99 CAN/£9.99 UK

Mr. Fitzwilliam Darcy:
THE LAST MAN IN THE WORLD
A *Pride and Prejudice* Variation
ABIGAIL REYNOLDS

What if Elizabeth had accepted Mr. Darcy the first time he asked?

In Jane Austen's *Pride and Prejudice*, Elizabeth Bennet tells the proud Mr. Fitzwilliam Darcy that she wouldn't marry him if he were the last man in the world. But what if circumstances conspired to make her accept Darcy the first time he proposes? In this installment of Abigail Reynolds' acclaimed *Pride and Prejudice* Variations, Elizabeth agrees to marry Darcy against her better judgment, setting off a chain of events that nearly brings disaster to them both. Ultimately, Darcy and Elizabeth will have to work together on their tumultuous and passionate journey to make a success of their ill-timed marriage.

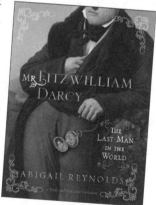

What readers are saying:

"A highly original story, immensely satisfying."

"Anyone who loves the story of Darcy and Elizabeth will love this variation."

"I was hooked from page one."

"A refreshing new look at what might have happened if…"

"Another good book to curl up with… I never wanted to put it down…"

978-1-4022-2947-3
$14.99 US/$18.99 CAN/£7.99 UK

In the Arms of Mr. Darcy
SHARON LATHAN

If only everyone could be as happy as they are...

Darcy and Elizabeth are as much in love as ever—even more so as their relationship matures. Their passion inspires everyone around them, and as winter turns to spring, romance blossoms around them.

Confirmed bachelor Richard Fitzwilliam sets his sights on a seemingly unattainable, beautiful widow; Georgiana Darcy learns to flirt outrageously; the very flighty Kitty Bennet develops her first crush, and Caroline Bingley meets her match.

But the path of true love never does run smooth, and Elizabeth and Darcy are kept busy navigating their friends and loved ones through the inevitable separations, misunderstandings, misgivings, and lovers' quarrels to reach their own happily ever afters...

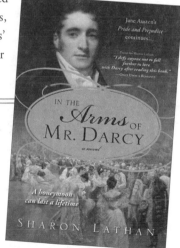

"If you love *Pride and Prejudice* sequels then this series should be on the top of your list!" —*Royal Reviews*

"Sharon really knows how to make Regency come alive." —*Love Romance Passion*

978-1-4022-3699-0
$14.99 US/$17.99 CAN/£9.99 UK

WICKHAM'S DIARY

AMANDA GRANGE

Jane Austen's quintessential bad boy has his say…

Enter the clandestine world of the cold-hearted Wickham…

… in the pages of his private diary. Always aware of the inferiority of his social status compared to his friend Fitzwilliam Darcy, Wickham chases wealth and women in an attempt to attain the power he lusts for. But as Wickham gambles and cavorts his way through his funds, Darcy still comes out on top.

But now Wickham has found his chance to seduce the young Georgiana Darcy, which will finally secure the fortune—and the revenge—he's always dreamed of…

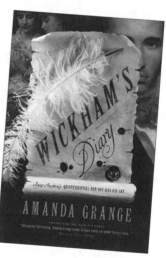

Praise for Amanda Grange:

"Amanda Grange has taken on the challenge of reworking a much loved romance and succeeds brilliantly." —*Historical Novels Review*

"Amanda Grange is a writer who tells an engaging, thoroughly enjoyable story!" —*Romance Reader at Heart*

Available April 2011
978-1-4022-5186-3
$12.99 US

WILLOUGHBY'S RETURN

JANE AUSTEN'S *SENSE AND SENSIBILITY* CONTINUES

JANE ODIWE

"A tale of almost irresistible temptation."

A lost love returns, rekindling forgotten passions…

When Marianne Dashwood marries Colonel Brandon, she puts her heartbreak over dashing scoundrel John Willoughby behind her. Three years later, Willoughby's return throws Marianne into a tizzy of painful memories and exquisite feelings of uncertainty. Willoughby is as charming, as roguish, and as much in love with her as ever. And the timing couldn't be worse—with Colonel Brandon away and Willoughby determined to win her back…

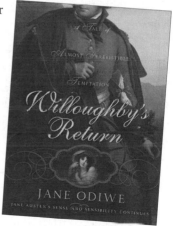

Praise for *Lydia Bennet's Story*:

"A breathtaking Regency romp!" —Diana Birchall, author of *Mrs. Darcy's Dilemma*

"An absolute delight." —*Historical Novels Review*

"Odiwe emulates Austen's famous wit, and manages to give Lydia a happily-ever-after ending worthy of any Regency romance heroine." —*Booklist*

"Odiwe pays nice homage to Austen's stylings and endears the reader to the formerly secondary character, spoiled and impulsive Lydia Bennet." —*Publishers Weekly*

978-1-4022-2267-2
$14.99 US/$18.99 CAN/£7.99 UK

THE OTHER MR. DARCY

PRIDE AND PREJUDICE CONTINUES…

MONICA FAIRVIEW

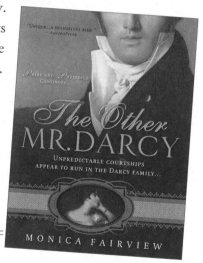

"A lovely story… a joy to read."
—*Bookishly Attentive*

Unpredictable courtships appear to run in the Darcy family…

When Caroline Bingley collapses to the floor and sobs at Mr. Darcy's wedding, imagine her humiliation when she discovers that a stranger has witnessed her emotional display. Miss Bingley, understandably, resents this gentleman very much, even if he is Mr. Darcy's American cousin. Mr. Robert Darcy is as charming as Mr. Fitzwilliam Darcy is proud, and he is stunned to find a beautiful young woman weeping broken-heartedly at his cousin's wedding. Such depth of love, he thinks, is rare and precious. For him, it's love at first sight…

"An intriguing concept…
a delightful ride in the park."
—*AustenProse*

978-1-4022-2513-0
$14.99 US/$18.99 CAN/£7.99 UK